ENEMY'S ENEMY

ENEMY'S ENEMY

A Novel by

Jan Guillou

Translated from
the Swedish by
Thomas Keeland

Alfred A. Knopf

New York

1992

GUILLOU,

Library of Congress Cataloging-in-Publication Data

Guillou, Jan, [date]

[Fiendens fiende.   English]

APR 1 4 1992   Enemy's enemy / Jan Guillou.

p.   cm.

Translation of: Fiendens fiende.

ISBN 0-394-58989-0

I. Title.

PT9876.17.U38F513   1992

839.7'374—dc20   91-52803   CIP

Contents

ENEMY'S ENEMY

Prologue

Every time he had tried to strangle a woman he had failed. But that was his old self; he had been sick, confused, depressed, or drunk, and he hadn't had serious intentions. This time everything was different.

She misunderstood him when he turned off the light in the bunk, and she even giggled when he turned her over on her stomach and sat straddled across her back.

Then he started strangling her, almost tenderly, as if it were an act of love, as if she were his wife.

He pressed the weight of his knees on her upper arms and searched carefully with his thumbs along the back of her neck until he found the point where the skull and the cervical vertebrae meet, and then he extended his grip with his fingers down around her throat.

It took a few seconds before she seemed to understand what was happening. She struggled a little, kicking her legs up and down the way a landed fish flaps its tail. But the soft bedclothes absorbed the sound, and after fifteen very long seconds she began to lose consciousness as the blood flow to her brain was cut off, and she stopped moving.

He held the grip as long as he could. Then he got up heavily and stood for a while in the darkness, massaging his stiff fingers.

He unscrewed the brass knobs of the cabin porthole and opened it, pulled up a stool, and stuck out his head. Cold wind and hard rain whipped his face. He looked up and from side to side, but the wind and freezing rain made it impossible to see anything.

It was two in the morning during the darkest part of the year, and the ferry was out in the Baltic on the open sea. The risk that a fellow passenger might be standing on deck admiring the sea view was negligible.

He pulled his head back inside and stepped down to the floor, wiping his face on the curtain. Then he took a few deep breaths, collected himself, and walked over to the bunk in the dark and pulled off her nightgown. It was made of soft, silky fabric, something synthetic that would be airtight. You could have made air bubbles inside it.

Then he took off her rings and wristwatch and threw them out into the black emptiness. He slung her right arm over his shoulder and wrestled her up toward the round opening; he had some trouble before he got her upper body and both arms outside. He grabbed her around the knees and lifted them upward so that her center of gravity slipped over the edge of the porthole, and suddenly and silently she was gone.

He screwed the porthole shut and stood leaning with his forehead against the cold, wet glass.

Their cabin was approximately amidships. The drop was about thirty feet. The probability that the water turbulence would drag her twenty or thirty feet under or into the propeller wash was fairly good; the probability that she would ever be found was slight; and the probability that she would drift ashore on Swedish territory in one identifiable piece was all but nonexistent.

Anyway, it didn't matter. By that time he would already have won or lost; it would all be decided by then.

He went over to the door and turned on the light. Then he took a handkerchief and wiped off the rainwater around the porthole and on the floor below.

He packed her belongings into the little travel bag, her toiletries neatly in the overnight bag, with the silky white nightgown on top. Then he got dressed, smoothed out the bedclothes in the lower bunk, and lay down with his hands folded behind his head.

Three days ago he had turned fifty, and for this family occasion, in accordance with some Paragraph 82, he received forty-eight hours' leave from prison; when the leave ran out he would already be on the other side. They wouldn't put out a bulletin on him before then; his colleagues sitting in a car outside the suburban apartment where she lived—where she had lived, he corrected himself—his colleagues would simply relieve each other and then sit for eight more hours guarding an empty flat and a rental car that would never be used, parked illegally outside the front door.

If they did manage to put out a bulletin on him, the Finnish police at the dock at Naantali would be looking for a middle-aged couple in a rental car they didn't have the license number of, and they wouldn't be concerned with a Swedish man traveling alone. Anyway, they wouldn't have received the alarm yet, wouldn't even be there waiting.

Then he had eight hours after that to worry about, four to drive to Helsinki and then four before the Helsinki ferry left for Tallinn.

Without her it never would have worked. She had rented the three cars and bought the ferry tickets and served as the reason for his "accompanied"—that is, unsupervised—leave. It was one of the many humane features of the Swedish penal system that husband and wife, as much as possible, should be undisturbed when they were together. No doubt they hadn't even bugged her apartment. Sweden was a sloppy country, naïve and stupid.

Anyway, she couldn't have lived in Moscow. He had promised her that her children and grandchildren could visit her there after a few years, and she had been Swedish enough to believe him. He had told her that, as a major in the GRU, he was entitled to an apartment in the city and a dacha by the Black Sea, and she had believed that, too, that they would live happy and all to themselves, forever. She would have believed anything.

She was surely better off now than she would have been at the end of the trip. He would have had to explain that she had just been a cover to make his escape possible (and he would never have said more than that), and then they might have simply taken her away and sent her to Siberia; more likely they would have shot and buried her.

Possibly, they would invite *him* to take that trip. After all, the Russians might well find it unimaginable that someone convicted of spying for the Soviet Union in a hostile country had been allowed to waltz off on leave—and a reasonable conclusion would be that Western intelligence had turned him and was trying to do what they had never succeeded in doing before: to put a double agent into the GRU's headquarters in Moscow. If the Russians did draw this conclusion, only one outcome was likely, and it was painful.

On the other hand, his escape would certainly create so much publicity and trouble in Stockholm that they'd probably realize there *was* one country on earth where a low-ranking Soviet spy could obtain leave, a pension, escape money, a new name, and a genuine passport.

Besides, he had gotten rid of her. Obviously, Swedish authorities wouldn't have gone along with that as part of an operation to create a cover for him. And if the Russians doubted him on that point, the only alternative interpretation was that the authorities in Sweden had made her go up in smoke. A mother and grandmother? Impossible to pull off in a country where every citizen was assigned a number at birth, all the telephones could be tapped, and everything got into the newspapers.

So he had killed her as part of his life insurance policy. And she was better off now than she would ever have been in Moscow or Siberia. Maybe she had even been happy for a while.

It had been the best solution for both of them.

Anyway, at certain times he had despised her. She was almost ten years older than he and looked it, and she had seriously believed that he loved her and wanted to live the rest of his life with her. They had met one summer ages ago, when he was in the military for a month-long refresher course. She had started writing letters to him a couple of years after his conviction, when he had been so depressed in jail.

Now he was fifty, true, but he was in better shape than he had ever been since he did his time in the commandos. For seven years he had lived a sober, healthy life, which was the good thing about prison, and he had worked out every day; he weighed twenty kilos less than when he was sentenced, and he could manage seventy-five situps and bench-press ninety kilos. The time of humiliations was long gone.

He could feel hate and adrenaline bubbling up inside him, so that his pulse started pounding.

The Israelis had almost broken him, there was no denying that. He had been in bad shape, drinking a lot and careless, and they had caught him after a few days. Then they had filled him with whiskey before they threatened him with extrajudiciary execution if he didn't cooperate. And then he had gambled that they didn't know everything they said they knew, and he told them that he was indeed a GRU officer, though not a captain as they believed but a major, and that his mission was directed against Sweden and not against Israel. And then he had rattled off a number of real and made-up operations inside Sweden to win his release.

Finally they filled him with whiskey again and put him on an El Al plane to Copenhagen, and in his groggy condition he thought for a while he had actually escaped. But in Copenhagen the Swedish Security Police (Säpo), waiting for him, had already received the telexed reports and transcripts of the interrogation.

These colleagues of his believed everything he had told the Israelis and accused him of working as an agent against Swedish interests, which called for a life sentence. In addition, they gave him a Jewish lawyer who didn't want to hear about any irregularities in Israel. Instead, the lawyer confessed on his behalf to everything that the cops presented to him to sign. And when, after six months or so, he had pulled himself together and understood on what grounds he could appeal the conviction, the lawyer had gone rushing to the Security Police and then drummed it into him that appealing would only result in an even harsher sentence, and besides, his wife would get a few years in prison if he persisted. And so he had given up, shrunk back into his prison cell, and even tried to commit suicide. The society of laws they all said they were defending seemed like their own libelous pictures of the Soviet Union. He owed nothing to them or to Sweden. Now instead they could pay their debt to him.

He was an officer in the GRU, that was all, an officer and a professional, and his only homeland was his work. Without intelligence services the world would be more unstable, and in that equation it didn't really matter what side the spies were working on. It evened out in the end.

He had at least fifteen professional years left, and starting today he would be a very good professional. No alcohol, no women, at least not like before. Two of them had once gone to Säk and informed on him. Fortunately the people there were then working on the theory that first, the Soviet Union was no longer operating with conventional spies (which was how they explained that no Soviet spies were ever arrested in Sweden: they simply didn't exist); second, that Stig Sandström couldn't be a spy since he was in Säpo, after all; and third, that international terrorism—for all practical purposes this meant left-wing demonstrators and swarthy foreign workers—was the primary danger.

So. A new life with order and discipline, less booze and fewer women. The Russians would set such conditions for continued cooperation anyway.

As the ship approached Naantali he went up and shaved and packed his toiletries in his pilot bag, where he kept his belongings. He checked that nothing was left behind and wiped all the surfaces he or she might have touched. He took the two bags and went down the stairs to the automobile deck, putting her bag in the trunk and his own on the back seat. He felt surprisingly calm, though his trip was now nearing its most critical point.

It was still dark when the cars starting rolling out, but there was nothing resembling policemen looking for someone, and no customs. The whole thing was almost alarmingly easy.

He was careful to obey the speed limits on the way to Helsinki, and he stopped once to drink coffee and try to see if he was being followed.

As he approached Helsinki he was sure everything would go smoothly. There was only one critical moment left.

He drove off the expressway in a suburb, parked somewhere, and took his bag from the back seat; he was just about to leave when he remembered about fingerprints. No, he hadn't sat in the car without gloves, neither now nor on the road between Stockholm and Norr-tälje. It wasn't that important. The car wouldn't be found for a week or two, and by that time the connection would be obvious.

He opened the left front door and took the glove off his right hand; then he carefully stamped a clear fingerprint with his right middle finger on the dashboard.

He laughed to himself and stuck up his middle finger in one last parting gesture to his colleagues. Then he slammed the door, locked it, and headed over toward something that looked like a shopping center, where he could surely find a bus to the center of town.

There was only one thing left. About an hour before the ferry sailed for Tallinn, he would have to get hold of the first mate; not the captain or the second mate—it had to be the first mate. No matter which first mate was on watch, he would be the GRU's officer on duty, and three words in private were all that was needed. Then he would disappear forever from the view of Swedish intelligence. And then they would start paying him back.

He imagined the long train trip from Tallinn via Leningrad to Moscow.

He was wrong. After being locked up for a day in Tallinn, he was flown in a military plane directly to the old airport in Moscow. When the plane taxied toward a tall building at the far end of the airport, he knew where they were taking him. That building was not only one of the world's most heavily guarded structures, but one of the most legendary. It was Zentral, where approximately five thousand people worked: the heart of the GRU's world-encompassing network.

· · ·

Twenty-eight hours after the Soviet spy Stig Sandström escaped—or, to use the official terminology, "abused his leave" (he wasn't entered in the escape statistics until three months later)—a nationwide alert was put out for him in Sweden. By that time he had been locked in a messy room with a broken teakettle in the harbor of Tallinn for about six hours.

From the Soviet point of view, or more precisely from the GRU's point of view, the main question now was to determine whether Sandström's incredible escape story was true. Everything depended on the answer. If his escape had been arranged by Swedish or other Western authorities with the intention of palming off an infiltrator on the GRU, the consequence would be simple and logical. Stig Sandström would disappear forever, preferably after confessing. If, on the other hand, they could definitively confirm that the impossible was in fact possible, that a spy sentenced to life imprisonment had obtained leave without supervision, the question was whether and to what extent they could continue to make use of their former information sources.

The risk was considerable that they would wind up with uncertain conclusions. And for Yuri Chivartshev, the ranking military attaché at the Soviet embassy in Stockholm and in reality agent in place for the GRU in Scandinavia and a major general, the issue was that sooner or later he would sign a report, and if it turned out to be wrong, no matter how long afterward, it would cost him his continued career—at best. It was thus enormously important to give Zentral a precise report with a correct analysis of the situation. The fellows back in Moscow would be hard to convince.

Chivartshev's spontaneous and intuitive conclusion was this: there was only one country, regardless of its political system, where an occurrence like this was possible, and that was Sweden. Not in some Central American banana republic. Of course not in any of the hard Western countries. Nowhere in the third world either, or any socialist country, or even any of the other soft Western countries like Austria or Finland—nowhere would a Soviet spy sentenced to life imprisonment be able to walk away on unsupervised furlough and leave the country with a new passport, a new appearance, and money in his pocket that he got from the authorities for his pension and sick pay.

Not in any country on earth except Sweden. So it was theoretically possible that they were dealing with a real escape.

Chivartshev sighed. He got up from his desk and took one of his routine thinking promenades around his spacious office. He stopped by the window and cast a thoughtful glance at the blue neon sign far up on the brick façade across the street, which announced that in this building was located the most fanatically anti-Soviet publication in Scandinavia. Still, *Svenska Dagbladet*, in its continuous zeal to needle the Social Democratic government by publishing top-secret military information, was an important and reliable open source for the GRU: a very helpful enemy, in other words. And this relationship applied to the present story too. The background analysis on Sandström's apparently inexplicable escape was based almost wholly on openly published sources.

As yet he had not signed the report, other than with his initials on a couple of attachments. The summary itself lay in a white folder on top of his otherwise bare desk.

He went back and read through it again.

All logical conclusions had to be drawn from the chronology of the events themselves. That was the primary way to establish the sequence of verifiable facts.

On September 26, Stig Sandström's petition for parole had been turned down by the Swedish government: the Prison Commission and the civil security service accepted it, but the military authorities did not.

One week before his forty-eight-hour leave, scheduled for November 6–7, Sandström was advised of his furlough, and of the fact that it would be virtually unsupervised. An official from the Prison Commission was to escort him to his wife's apartment, leave him there, and pick him up one and a half days later for return transport to the prison.

The Security Police assigned two men to watch the apartment building, but only from the front. Since the escape must then have taken place from the back, the chief of Sweden's police actually explained—in all seriousness, on the official news program on state television—that they had only been watching the front "because normally no visitors would go in the back way." And since the Security Police terminated their surveillance at midnight, clearly because of union contracts and rules for overtime, this same police chief explained in the same official manner that "normally no visitors would come after midnight."

The new Säpo guards took up their watch at eight o'clock the following morning, approximately eight hours after the presumed time of the escape itself; they did not verify that the object of their surveillance was present, but were content to sit and stare at the front door and the illegally parked rented car for more than four hours. At noon, when the official escort from the Prison Commission arrived to pick up the furloughed prisoner, they broke off their surveillance and departed, still without ascertaining whether the object of their surveillance was in the apartment.

When the Prison Commission officer found the apartment empty, he telephoned the prison in Norrköping, the Norrköping police station, and the Security Police.

At Säpo headquarters, they thought it extraordinary that Sandström had disappeared, "since his car was right outside the door." They therefore decided to pay a visit to the Stockholm central train station along with officials from the Prison Commission "to see whether Sandström would turn up."

He didn't.

The police in Norrköping assumed that Säpo had put out a nationwide alert. Säpo did not regard a nationwide alert as a measure within its scope. So no one put out an alert. By this time Sandström was already in Helsinki.

A full twenty-four hours after the escape an alert was put out, at which point the police sent out the wrong pictures of Sandström and his wife.

Several more days later, it was discovered that Mrs. Annalisa Sandström had rented three cars, not one. This was termed by the newly appointed investigation authorities as "a breakthrough in the investigation."

After that they devoted several days' effort to watching one of the three rental cars, which was rediscovered—with obvious traces of theft—in a Stockholm suburb.

Then they watched the PLO's villa in Djursholm for eight hours, but without results. About a week after the escape, "the borders were sealed."

That was roughly how the purely factual, external chronology looked. Chivartshev sighed. If you were content to analyze the outward course of events, there could only be one conclusion. No security police in the world, not even Sweden's, could act so incompetently. Therefore, they had turned their spy and sent him on a suicide mission to Moscow with the object of infiltrating Zentral.

But there was also an internal side to the events, and it changed the whole picture.

The Swedish authorities and government had gotten themselves involved in a complicated game over responsibility in which everyone tried to get away without being left holding the bag. The Prison Commission maintained they were only in charge of the spy while he was in prison. When he was outside prison, he was the responsibility of the Security Police. Säpo adamantly denied this and declared that an individual agency could not override the decision of another agency; only the elected government could do that.

Then the Prison Commission claimed that the government had been told about the conditions of Sandström's leave. The Ministry of Justice at first categorically denied this but it turned out that it *had* received a letter from the Prison Commission (entered in a daybook, according to good bureaucratic procedure), which stated that Sandström was to have either an unsupervised or a supervised furlough before his fiftieth birthday. The official who received it stuffed it in a drawer without reading it and then went on vacation, but he left a memo behind for his boss in which he said he hadn't read the letter. His boss didn't read it either, and thus could not account for its contents to *his* boss, the minister of justice.

Eventually this led to the forced resignation of not only the two officials but the minister of justice as well.

This was of crucial importance to Chivartshev. If the whole thing was an operation by Swedish intelligence—the Security Police were not an option, given their incompetence—then it was so complicated that the resignation of many politically responsible people was required in order to cover it up. This would mean that about ten bureaucrats and politicians would have known what was going on from the beginning.

And that was ten too many. It could never have worked, and at worst, the truth would have been published quickly in *Svenska Dagbladet*, a paper that was willing to condemn its countrymen to death in its eagerness to criticize the Social Democrats in power. Way too risky all around. Not even the Old Man, or his younger colleagues in the Joint Chiefs' military-security covert section, could have or would have wanted to take such risks.

On top of that, the prime minister would not have asked his own minister of justice to resign because of nonexistent incompetence, and that meant that the prime minister would have known about the operation and authorized it. Impossible—the Swedes didn't work that way.

Furthermore, how could the thing have been carried out behind the backs of the Security Police without anyone suspecting anything? No one in his right mind, especially not the Old Man, would draw up a plan like that; not even he could assume Säpo's *total* incompetence. The most important presumption would have been that Sweden's own Security Police—spontaneously, voluntarily, and entirely on their own initiative—happened to guard only one of two doors, and then only for half the time the spy was behind them. Not even hardened defense authorities would count on such unconventional behavior.

There was one crucial question left. Did Säpo know about this putative operation to deceive Sweden's public and government as well as Soviet intelligence?

Chivartshev could answer that question with a definite no. In no other security police in the West was the GRU so well represented as in Sweden's. If there had been a cover-up in Säpo—and this one would have involved personnel from at least three different operational and decision-making levels—the GRU would have received reports on it from all three levels.

But all the reports they were getting told quite a different story: Soviet agents inside Swedish security reported panic and confusion.

Chivartshev picked up his thick French fountain pen and slowly unscrewed the cap. He looked at the gold nib for a moment and then decisively turned to the last page of the comprehensive report summary and signed his name, slowly and clearly.

He let the ink dry, put the cap back on the pen, and pressed the button on the intercom to his personal code technician.

A pale and rather pimply second lieutenant from one of the Baltic republics came in and received instructions to encode the main text and send it at once to Zentral, copy the original and put the copy in the archives, and then send the original in the next diplomatic pouch to Moscow.

"So there, my good comrade Sandström," Chivartshev muttered to himself when he was alone again. "Now you've saved your neck and maybe gotten a new job you didn't have in mind."

Sandström had been only one Soviet agent of many in the Swedish Security Police. Chivartshev remembered the details of his case well, even though the file had gone to Moscow several weeks ago. What distinguished Sandström from the others was primarily that he had been recruited so long after he had become not only a member but an officer in Säpo. That was rather unconventional. The usual pattern was based on the simple assumption that Säpo itself always recruited from among regular policemen; the GRU recruited students and persuaded them to give up the academic life and instead apply to the police school in Solna. The next step was almost always the same. They didn't have to apply to Säpo themselves after a few years' police service; they would be recruited into it—sometimes even reluctantly. For twenty-five years this had been the natural entryway.

But Sandström had been an ordinary good-for-nothing, a womanizer, alcoholic, adventurer, and in addition, foolishly, a convinced anti-Semite. They had recruited him during his UN military service in the Middle East and induced him to work for the cause of peace and justice by gathering information on the Israelis—for good pay, of course.

The question was whether that kind of person was suitable for the work assignments now under discussion. Soviet agents in Sweden were busy with passive intelligence gathering, and the GRU, for its part, was conscientious enough not to put them into situations where they would harm, or in any case not realize they were harming, their colleagues.

But the work assignments in the Scandinavian department at Zentral were more aggressive. So now they were investigating the possibilities of transforming this drunkard into a more offensive instrument against his own people.

As far as Chivartshev was concerned, there wasn't much to speculate about. If the reeducation went well in Moscow or wherever they took Sandström, he'd sooner or later get the hint of what objective was coming up in Sweden.

Chivartshev wanted to wipe away the thought of what that was, but it occurred often enough whenever he happened to fasten his eyes on the oil portrait that hung on the long wall right across from his desk, next to the maps of Sweden and Stockholm.

FYODOR MATREYEVICH APRAKSIN it said on a little gold nameplate under the portrait. No one else in the embassy knew why the oil portrait of one of tsarist Russia's naval heroes hung there. And no one dared breathe a word of criticism of it or even ask about it; whoever is GRU agent in place can get away with almost anything without being questioned.

Apraksin was the name of one of three Soviet underwater installations in Stockholm's archipelago, equipped with the most advanced and sophisticated instruments that the Soviet Union's armed forces could deploy, and they would have had a very interesting role to play in a theoretical—well yes, highly theoretical—war.

But personnel from Swedish intelligence had blown up all three installations thirteen months earlier. They had even gone behind the back of their own government to ensure success.

As a military man and colleague, Chivartshev had to admit that the Swedish officers had carried out a brilliant operation. They certainly hadn't been dealing with "the madhouse on Kungsholmen," as they themselves called the civilian Security Police. Or was it "the monkey house on Kungsholmen"? Well, it didn't make any difference.

But for Soviet citizen Yuri Chivartshev it was a tragic event. Two hundred forty-eight of his countrymen had perished, drowned like rats.

And Chivartshev had a good idea who was responsible for the Swedish operation and who had carried it out: a young commander who by now must be one of Sweden's most decorated officers, and who was now quite bothered by the surveillance to which the KGB was subjecting him.

It was quite clear: if one were to ask Chivartshev what objective in Sweden was vital for the Soviet Union's tactical operative intelligence service—which is what the initials GRU stood for—then Swedish intelligence officers in general, and that young commander in particular, would be high on his list of candidates.

The time would come. Chivartshev called his morning meeting, and his respectful subordinates gathered in the room.

I

Stockholm

One

For once it looked like it was going to be a clear, genuinely sunny
Midsummer holiday, just as he remembered in his childhood, and on
the way in from Berga he drove slightly over the speed limit with both
windows rolled halfway down and Glenn Gould's recording of Bach's
Goldberg Variations full blast on the car stereo.

The sound quality could have been better, but it was the Defense
Ministry's car, not his own. For the last year and a half he had avoided
using his own car because the KGB's field operators in Stockholm had
begun to take an interest in him that was both stubborn and hard to
explain. Whatever the reason, it was unpleasant and it made him
irritable.

That's probably why he flashed his brights at the Volvo up ahead
in the left lane as soon as he got close enough.

The Volvo didn't move over, but demonstratively slowed down. A
young woman was driving and the passenger next to her in the front
seat was also a woman. They looked to be between twenty-five and
thirty. He flashed again without having any effect, leaning on the
horn at the same time as he shifted down, and when the Volvo reluctantly slid over, he furiously accelerated past them.

But when he saw that the Volvo took up the chase, he grew
thoughtful. He knew most of the Chekists' field operators in this
region by sight, and these two definitely looked like normal Swedish
girls. But they were closing on him steadily. He slowed down, reached
over to the glove compartment and took out his revolver, sliding it

under his suede jacket on the right front seat, and then he pulled into the right lane.

The Volvo accelerated past and slipped in tight in front of him, and a few seconds later the girl on the right rolled down her window and stuck out a round, spadelike sign in red and white with clear black letters which said POLICE. At the same time the Volvo began to decrease its speed and signal to the right. He followed it over to the side of the road and stopped.

When he saw the two blond women get out and resolutely head toward him, he broke out laughing, turned on his emergency blinkers, and rolled down the window. He was still laughing when they reached him; the one who came first was holding out her police ID and the other had a pen and notepad in her right hand. They were wearing jeans and American blazers.

"Okay, Mr. Macho, go ahead and laugh—this is going to be expensive," said the first one as she stuffed her ID back into her pocket.

"Oh, I don't know about that," he replied as he gathered up his suede jacket with his revolver inside it and placed the bundle on the floor in the back; he turned off the stereo and unlocked the doors so they could get in and start the paperwork.

"What's so damned funny?" asked the second one as she got into the front seat and opened her notepad. "Do you have a driver's license?"

"Yes, here you are," he replied as he handed it over. "You know, I was just thinking, God sometimes doles out instant retribution. You think 'damned broads' and step a little harder on the gas and land with your hand right in the cookie jar, right?"

"Carl Gustaf Gilbert Hamilton," she read. "Place of employment?"

"Defense Ministry."

"What section?"

"Defense Ministry is enough."

"An officer and a gentleman who's out speeding today," snickered the first officer, who was now sitting in the back seat.

"An officer, maybe, but my gentlemanly behavior hasn't been perfect lately. God must have become a feminist. What speed are you thinking of putting down?"

"One forty-five—we clocked you at one forty-five for at least several hundred meters," answered the officer in the front seat.

"Oh, put down one thirty-five instead so we can get this over with—or else I'll have to contest it and then you'll have to go to court, and they'll knock it down to one thirty-five anyway, and then we'll be wasting a lot of time for nothing. Besides, it only takes a couple of seconds to drive quote several hundred meters unquote at one forty-five—you know that as well as I do." Carl's good humor was increasing, and it seemed to rub off on the two women. No doubt they'd encountered speeding suckers a lot less pleasant than he.

"Okay," said the police officer in the front seat, "what's your occupation and home address?"

"Commander. Drakens Lane in Gamla Stan."

"What the hell exactly do you mean by commander?" she interrupted.

"Like a major, except in the navy, that's what it's called now," said the one in the back seat as she settled herself more comfortably. Carl glanced quickly back at her, for her right foot was now only a few inches away from his hidden revolver.

"Shouldn't you be out driving a torpedo boat, so you could have a legal outlet for your urges?" muttered the woman with the form as she copied from a business card that Carl handed her.

"Torpedo boats are obsolete," sighed Carl, suddenly gloomy, "and so are destroyers and cruisers and half the guided missile boats."

"So you're not out chasing those Russian submarines?" asked the officer in the back seat. "They *are* Russian, aren't they?"

"Yes, they're Russian. No, I mostly sit and fill out papers, just like you when you're not lurking after innocent, normally law-abiding male drivers."

"All right, if I can just have your signature right at the bottom, then you'll be out a thousand kronor," said the police officer in the front seat as she handed him the filled-out form.

They joked a little about the week's most docile sucker and were getting out of the car when Carl had an idea that was just as unexpected as it was sudden.

"When do you get off your shift?" he asked the one in the back as she slammed the car door.

"What? What did you say?" She bent toward him, feigning surprise as she pushed her sunglasses up on her forehead. Her eyes were dark blue, and her sunglasses were the same aviator kind that American feminists had worn like a kind of uniform for years, with lenses that gradually changed from almost impenetrable dark brown on top to clear on the bottom.

"I asked when you got off your shift tonight," repeated Carl. He was embarrassed, already regretting it.

"Five o'clock—why?"

"Because I thought we could celebrate my getting caught speeding for the first time, and being nabbed by female personnel at that—I mean, I'd like to invite you to dinner."

"If you're trying to bribe us, you're sure pushing it," she chuckled, shoving down her sunglasses and calling to her colleague walking back to the Volvo. "Did you hear that? The sucker wants to invite us to dinner!" she reported cheerfully.

Her colleague froze, then made a show of turning around slowly, and walking back slowly until she was leaning both elbows on the window rolled halfway down on the passenger side.

"Hey, Casanova," she hissed, "the ticket is written up, and I'm married to a damn jealous, damn big, damn strong policeman."

"Fine," answered Carl coldly, "then I suggest you bring him along so we can arm-wrestle over coffee—police versus the navy."

"Shove it, Casanova," she drawled, turning the gum over in her mouth, and headed back to the Volvo.

"What do you say," sighed Carl in resignation, "seven o'clock at Reisen on Skeppsbron? Can you find it? I'll reserve a table."

"Do you think you're irresistible or do you think you can talk your way out of a ticket?" laughed the officer with the feminist glasses.

"Right now I feel quite resistible. The fine was only a thousand kronor, and the food will be much more expensive, so I'm obviously a sucker, both as a con man and as a shrewd businessman." Carl reached for the ignition key.

"Okay, I'll be there," she replied quickly. "Seven o'clock at Reisen. Your name is Hamilton and mine is—"

"Jönsson. Eva-Britt Jönsson, unless you're driving around with a fake ID."

"You have a cop's gift for observation. But if you don't show up, I'll raise the fine or change the speed to one forty-five. You'll be the loser, not me—keep that in mind." She laughed and shook her head as she walked back to her car, started it up, and disappeared with a roar in a cloud of blue exhaust.

Carl sat there feeling stupid and duped. He was sure she wouldn't show up. But what's done is done.

On the way in to town he kept to the speed limit, and when he passed Enskede, he took the plastic cover off the car phone and made a reservation for two for seven o'clock at Reisen.

. . .

At five minutes to seven he was sitting at his usual window table in Reisen and looking out toward Skeppsholmen across the surface of water still glittering in the sun. For appearance' sake he decided to wait at least a quarter of an hour. And for the first time that he could remember, he said yes when the waiter asked if he wanted a drink before dinner. He vaguely recalled something made of tequila and something sweet with a circle of salt around the rim of the glass. Yes, a margarita. He ordered one, and then fell into thought again with his gaze on the glittering water.

It was eighteen months now since Operation Big Red. But the surface of the Baltic Sea looked as it had always looked, no matter where his eyes fell. And the Swedish people still believed that the Defense Ministry continued to fail in its attempts to counteract foreign submarine activity, if there really was such a thing.

For the past several months he had been having trouble sleeping. He told himself it was because of the nights becoming lighter, even though that had never bothered him before. And when he finally did fall asleep, sometimes after several hours of tossing around in sheets that got twisted up like rope, he would have nightmares. One recurrent nightmare had him trapped deep below the surface of the water in something that might be a submarine, when suddenly a jet of white water, hard as metal, gushed in and filled up the space as he floated up into a corner in the last pocket of air, which grew smaller and smaller until he woke up.

Clear enough what that was about. An unknown number of Soviet seamen and officers had died this way a year and a half ago less than thirty kilometers from the window table at Reisen.

He wondered whether Steelglove and Lundwall had similar dreams. Soon they'd both be back from California to start their real work in the operations department.

Samuel Ulfsson, head of Operations Section 5, had always dismissed the idea that the KGB's irritating interest in Carl had anything to do with Big Red. According to Sam, it was more than doubtful whether the KGB's Stockholm station had known about the Soviet installations in watery Swedish territory, and even less likely that they would know who had carried out the operation against them.

But their investigative efforts had the annoying consequence that Carl had to keep busy up at the Defense Ministry with Sam while the reorganization of "Hamilton Computer Systems" was going on. The new office was finished—a consulting department in a multinational company up in Gärdet, with its own offices on the top floor. Carl hadn't been there more than a few times, in spite of the fact that it was his actual place of work.

She arrived, breathless, ten minutes late, wearing a flowery summer dress with a pink jacket slung over her shoulders. Her legs were bare, strong and supple, and around her shoulders there seemed to be signs of weightlifting—if it hadn't been for that, she would have looked like any other office girl. A strawberry-blond Swedish office girl with straight, shoulder-length hair and aviator glasses to correct a certain nearsightedness.

Carl stood up at once and went around to pull out the chair for her, taking note that she covered up a little surprise at this natural gesture.

"As an officer and a gentleman, you'll forgive me for being a little late, I hope," she laughed, embarrassed.

As she put down her handbag, Carl observed that it was clearly heavy and something in it rattled slightly. Resuming his seat he repressed an impulse to ask her whether it was customary for her to meet men with her service revolver and handcuffs in her pocketbook.

"I can assure Senior Police Constable Jönsson that I will at least do my utmost to be more gentlemanly than the last time we met." He smiled at her.

"Police *Inspector*, at least acting police inspector," she quickly corrected him.

"That's not bad for a twenty-nine-year-old."

"How do you know I'm twenty-nine?"

"Also according to your—we must assume—genuine police ID. Your birthday is May sixteenth, so you were born under the sign of Taurus."

"You should have been a cop or a detective or a criminal investigator. Why did you ask me out?"

"Because I felt like it, because I thought you were nice, because I live alone and only associate with colleagues and only think and talk about work all the time. Why did you come?"

"Because I thought you were an interesting type, not as aggressive as other guys who get caught like that, because I live alone and only associate with colleagues and only think and talk about work all the time."

"What would you like to eat and drink?"

"Damned if I know. This is a fancy place, isn't it? It's a little out of my league, I have to admit."

"Fish or meat?"

"Fish."

"You talk as if you were from the working class and came from Söder in Stockholm, but do you have relatives in Skåne?"

"Yes, why?"

"Because your name is Jönsson—just a guess. I have relatives in Skåne too."

"Not exactly sugar-beet pickers, are they?"

"No, why?"

"Because your name is Hamilton."

"Let me order the food and the wine—I promise it will be good."

"It's best to leave these difficult things to the upper class. Are you trying to impress me?"

"No. More than anything I don't want to look as if I were trying to impress you. But the upper class is better than the lower class at ordering in restaurants. That's all I was trying to imply." He smiled.

He closed the menu and wine list, waved over the waiter, and quickly ordered eel and gravlax pâté with a Gewürztraminer, and broiled turbot with a white burgundy, Château Meursault 1984, for the main course. Later on, she commented that the Alsatian wine was "a little odd, but definitely okay," and the burgundy "damned good, as a matter of fact." These were the best comments about wine he had heard for years in ever more crass and egotistical Sweden, where wine snobbery assumed ridiculous proportions.

After a while, they were more relaxed, and he began to ask her about her police work, partly out of personal curiosity and partly as a professional reflex.

She alternated between investigative assignments and a desk job at VD1, she told him, Stockholm's most obscure police station. She had always wanted to be a police officer, ever since she was in grammar school. Maybe her religious upbringing—she was still a member of the Missionary Society—encouraged her to consider police work as primarily social work. She wanted to retain that point of view, but it wasn't so easy at VD1, where the main thing was dragging in drunks for the night, breaking up street fights, bringing in petty crooks and small-time pushers who all too often were set free before she and her colleagues could fill out the paperwork. She lived alone in a house out in Spånga, near a little lake, with a German shepherd named Roy. She painted watercolors in her free time, mostly landscapes. She talked with a rich mixture of male police slang and social worker jargon, or maybe it was some kind of Christian jargon filled with completely genuine sympathy for society's underprivileged—she used that phrase once. He asked her whether she didn't think it was problematic to be a believing Christian and have a job that involved so much violence. For example, would she be able to shoot one of those punks if she found herself in a situation where service regulations prescribed it?

"It's never happened to me," she said. "If it did, I suppose I wouldn't shoot, but it's hard to say. Isn't that a strange question from a military man—what about you in the same situation?"

He looked her in the eye, then turned his gaze to the water between Skeppsbron and Skeppsholmen, still glittering in the evening sun, and answered slowly that he had never been faced with that kind of decision and had never had occasion to speculate about the matter, while he silently tallied up how many people he had killed—how many he had killed that he had actually seen and known about.

When she asked him about his job, he told her he was busy with computer programs for analyzing the deviations in sonar systems in relation to different layers of salinity in the Baltic, acoustical effects at different distances and depths, things like that. These were not direct lies, but dull enough mathematically so that by the second bottle of wine he could lead the conversation back to her and get more personal. He asked her why she wasn't married, and the gist of her answer was that two relationships with colleagues had broken up because of "different philosophies of life," which he assumed had something to do with her religion, but after a while it turned out to have more to do with violence. She had been engaged to one of the ten or fifteen policemen who are reported most for assault. "*Actually*," she said carefully, "he was a nice person," but the word "actually" made it sound as if he were a sadist.

Then it was, of course, her turn. Why at the age of thirty-four was Carl still not married? He tried as truthfully as possible to describe how he had clung for far too long to a hopeless love for a girl named Tessie O'Connor, whom he had met during his student days in California when he was studying computers. She had many merits, but at the same time she lived in another country in a completely different culture and was trained in a field that wasn't useful in Sweden. Besides, she was married to a rich businessman in Santa Barbara and they had a child.

She chuckled when he mentioned these last obstacles, and her seeing the situation from a humorous perspective was contagious. He told her, with somewhat forced merriment, how he had made a fool of himself a year or two before when he pushed his way into Tessie's house and was driven out by her husband, who threatened to sic the dogs on him. But he didn't hint at how, in that case, he would have killed the dogs or how, afterward, he stood shaking with hatred and rage, throwing gravel into the gray and greenish-blue water, trying to stifle his fantasies about what would have happened if the man had raised his hand against him.

As far as he knew, he was still in love with Tessie, he said, no matter how hopeless it seemed. So his relationships with women for the past few years had been rather peculiar: he really only met women by chance and for one night—never to sit and talk like this.

As he was telling her about Tessie, Carl considered the notion that the police Volvo out on Nynäsvägen might have been waiting for him. It was odd that a police officer would take her service revolver along to dinner when she was off duty. But he decided to ignore this possibility. Instead, he asked her when she would be working for the next few days. Perhaps he would call her at work on some pretext, to see if she was actually there.

"And why did you join the armed forces?" she asked as she drank the last drop of wine in her glass.

"Shall we order more wine?" he asked with a glance at her glass.

"No, thanks. It's true I don't have to be at work until late tomorrow, but just the same . . . And don't try to change the subject—why did you join?"

Again he gazed out the window across the water. Could he even answer that question for himself? One thing had led to another. The Old Man had fished him out during basic training and offered him five years of training in the United States at the armed services' expense, and five years later everything had somehow seemed obvious.

"That's not so easy to answer," he said with his eyes still fixed on the surface of the water in the evening light. "But in the beginning I and a lot of my comrades—I belonged to Clarté and other radical groups—applied for specialized training of one kind or another when we had to do our time in the service. A lot of them were accepted in Säpo, of course, and were purged at an early stage, but some of us became paratroopers and commandos and things like that . . . Well, later I thought about continuing on in the reserves, so I did, and then I stayed."

"Were you a Communist?"

"Yes, I suppose I have to admit it."

"And what are you today?"

"An officer."

"I mean politically."

"I don't know. Not a Communist. Not a Social Democrat, not a right-winger—above all, not that. What are you?"

"A Social Democrat. But you didn't answer the question. I wasn't asking *how* you became an officer, but why."

"The interrogation continues?"

"Yes."

"I think it was something like this. I got a damned complicated education that I felt I had to use in some respectable way. At the same time the Social Democrats were busy disarming Sweden under some kind of illusion that they could knock out the Russians with talk instead of being strong enough to . . . The little Swedish hedgehog, you know. I thought it was the only decent thing I could do—it was in line with my convictions."

"Freedom is always worth defending and that kind of thing?"

"Yes, but it's no joke for me."

"Me neither. I'm sorry. I didn't mean it that way, even if it sounded thoughtless. But don't officers get lousy pay?"

"Yes, about the same as a cop's."

"Then we'd better split the bill."

"No, absolutely not. I invited you."

"An old-fashioned officer and gentleman shouldn't tell a liberated modern police officer how she should behave in matters of principle."

"It's not a matter of principle in that sense," he replied as he called for the bill. "It's a practical matter of equality and justice."

"I've already cost you a thousand kronor in fines."

They both laughed.

But when the bill arrived and he was signing the credit-card slip, she was quicker. She picked up the bill and studied the arithmetic as she put out her other hand for her handbag. But she stopped herself when she saw the total.

"It's the wine," he said gently. "I have a better idea. This time me, next time it's on you."

"You wanted to impress me after all, damn it. What's the point of all this?"

"I can afford it and you can't."

"Is this some kind of business expense?"

"With a police officer who just ticketed me? Hardly! No, I'm rich, so you can look on it as a private, socialist method of redistributing wealth, and then we'll have stuffed cabbage and light beer at your place next time."

He reached for the bill, which she was clutching tightly to her breast, grabbed it and tore it up, tossing the pieces into the ashtray.

"Exactly how rich are you?" Her voice had suddenly acquired a certain sharpness; for the first time that evening she looked like a police officer.

"I don't know," he replied in a low voice.

"Bullshit. You're a millionaire?"

"Yes."

"How many million?"

"I don't know—it's a matter of bookkeeping, or if you will, a philosophical or political question."

"And you pay taxes on it?"

"Yes, of course—do you mean on my wages?"

"Yes, for example."

"A hundred and twenty percent, I think. Are you satisfied?"

"So you're not one of those damned zero-taxpayers?"

"No, and I wouldn't have anything against paying more taxes—it's more complicated than you think. It's the property tax that's the thing. I pay a lot of property tax . . . Oh, can't we talk about something else?"

"Does this topic bother you?"

"Yes. And I wouldn't mind if Police Inspector Jönsson would be kind enough to offer me a coffee."

"At my place?"

"No, not the first night—let's go out somewhere."

She gave him a long look with a completely neutral expression. Then she smiled, even laughed. "You're a pretty terrific fellow, for an upper-class bore. Okay, I'll treat you to coffee somewhere in Djurgården."

They walked arm in arm along Strandvägen. She had her left hand on his right, and in her right hand she carried her rather too heavy handbag. She waved to some colleagues in a passing blue and white

Dodge van, and since she had to wave with her handbag, he could clearly see the weight of it.

Sig-sauer, he thought. She has the new service weapon. Nine millimeters and fifteen rounds in the clip, the same as a Beretta.

At his suggestion they stopped a little past Djurgårdsbron and went into the open-air café at Ulla Winblad. She kept looking around alertly, but he didn't feel like asking her why. It could be just automatic police behavior.

They couldn't have coffee by itself—that was against the rules there—and neither of them wanted a schnapps, so they had beer instead.

She asked him if he'd like to go sailing. She and about ten of her colleagues were co-owners of two little sailboats, and they took turns according to a complicated schedule. On the Midsummer holiday weekend almost all of them were going, seven of them. But as a single girl, she had the right to invite a guy along provided he knew how to sail fairly well and wasn't in Säpo.

"Why not in Säpo?" he asked, surprised.

"Because they're not real cops, I guess. Real smart-ass types, and there'd be trouble."

"But naval officers are okay?"

"Sure—do you know how to navigate, by the way?"

"Very funny. Next question."

"Day after tomorrow, three p.m. at Stavsnäs wharf—will you come?"

He spontaneously said yes before he remembered that for the first time in several years he had promised to visit his mother and her relatives. Oh well, he would call and cancel, blaming his work.

He escorted her home in a cab to Spånga, to her house by the lake. When he got out and held open the car door for her, she invited him in for coffee, but he said no, thanks.

He sat up half the night and listened to music.

For six months, Carl had worked in an office on the top floor of the east wing in the Joint Chiefs' red brick building on Lidingövägen. According to his own ironic evaluation, he functioned as something between an executive secretary and a jack-of-all-trades in the intelligence service bureaucracy. He reported directly to Samuel Ulfsson, head of military intelligence, and they both knew it was a temporary arrangement while the covert part of it was reorganized, cleverly stuffed away as Hamilton Computer Systems, a small company in the computer consulting and accounting business that was officially owned by Carl and also related to an appropriately unprofitable enterprise. The important thing was the business in the inner regions, where only military personnel were allowed and the big IBM mainframes reigned.

It was a new idea in Swedish intelligence to combine an operations department with an analysis and processing entity, but there were practical reasons for it. Carl and those who would come after him had all had their training in California divided equally between computer technology and "operations fieldwork," as it was carefully called. In the daytime, they were regular officers working on analysis and computer programs and at night, hired assassins, Sam liked to joke.

But it was also part of the overall idea that "operations fieldwork" was an unassuming plant in the Swedish garden of security and intelligence. There hadn't been many nighttime assassinations—none at all on Swedish territory—and Carl was responsible, virtually single-handedly, for the violent intermezzos of recent years that had "engaged personnel within the Swedish intelligence service," as the military-memo jargon had it.

Samuel Ulfsson had had a hard time making up his mind about Commander Hamilton. It was hard not to worry about the contrast between, on the one hand, the young man as polite and well trained as a flag cadet, calm and systematic, with all his weird computer lists in the right place at the right time—and, on the other, the extraordinary specially trained saboteur and assassin, who—through a play of circumstances and undoubtedly his own initiative—had knocked off a professional Israeli assassination commando, exterminated a West German terrorist organization, averted a hijacking, and led Operation Big Red to something which, expressed in old-fashioned terms, might be called the biggest Swedish military victory against Russia since the Battle of Narva in 1700.

How the hell did the man do it? Sam wondered to himself, moments before Carl was to appear. Did he dash into a telephone booth to don his Superman clothes? Or was it simply a matter of five years' hellish American training? How many Hamiltons did the Americans have? Not to mention the Russians.

On the dot, there was a knock on the door. The precision in timing was no surprise.

"Come in, Carl," he called, reaching for one of his eternal, extra-mild Ultima Blend cigarettes which he smoked at his wife's insistence instead of the dark unfiltered ones he preferred.

"Good morning, Commodore." Carl stood at attention without being too ostentatious or superficial about it.

"Sit down, Carl, and by the way, call me Sam when it's just the two of us. Do you have any suggestions?"

"Thanks, Sam. Yes, I've put together three lists: of possible reports for publication, reports that should be published because they've already come out, and reports I feel we ought to mark Classified. That is, by 'we' I mean—"

"In general, the two of us here in this room, along with the Chief—is that what you mean?"

"Yes, that's correct." Carl opened his briefcase and took out three reports with copies which he divided into six piles, and then he started his presentation.

There were several sensitive issues. The Defense Chief's semi-annual report on foreign underwater activities had already been delayed, but several conflicting interests made it difficult to produce a text acceptable to everyone for publication.

If the politicians and certain segments of the defense establishment had their way, no foreign—that is, Soviet—underwater activities would be publicized. On the other hand, certain factions of the military, especially in the navy, wanted almost everything known, including the fact that, at this point, they even had the names and numbers of several Soviet and two Polish submarines; they could identify them conclusively as soon as they input into their computers more than five seconds of propeller sounds—just like fingerprints.

But this was the kind of information that military intelligence wanted to keep secret. Sweden might not have very many technological advantages over the Russians, but they shouldn't brag about the few they had.

On top of these well-known antagonisms, already sufficient to keep the taxpayers in the dark, there were special circumstances that Ulfsson soon hinted at.

Since "personnel from the operations divisions of Swedish intelligence had engaged in a covert operation of unknown scope," as the action eighteen months earlier had been succinctly described in the Defense Chief's annual report to the government, it was especially interesting to study signs of underwater activity in the vicinity of a former station Bodisko, a station Chichagov, and a station Apraksin. Were the Russians making efforts to transport matériel and the dead back home, for example, or were they attempting to rebuild somewhere else?

Carl's list of reports to be stamped Classified included some on this matter; the shorter list concerned events—such as this winter's usual unsuccessful search for underwater craft in the vicinity of Vaxholm—that should be made public since they had already been publicized.

It was all quite clear and simple, and Carl had perfectly prepared the computer printout. Ulfsson knew that all he had to do was sign it and pass it on to the Chief. He hadn't made it through more than four Ultima Blends before they were finished.

"How are things going, Carl? Are you happy here with us?" he asked as Carl put away his file copies.

Carl looked up, surprised, and as he did his eyes fell on a strange painting hanging on the opposite wall. It depicted the forced conscription of a boy sometime during the nineteenth century. The boy was wearing wooden clogs and looked scared, apparently with good reason. The army sergeant major had a saber and wore a tricorne—he looked authoritative and had every reason to.

"Well, not *exactly* like that," replied Carl with a nod to the painting when he saw that Ulfsson had followed his glance.

"But almost?" persisted Ulfsson.

"No, no, but what we're sitting and doing now doesn't feel right. You want me to answer honestly, not just be polite?"

"Yes, we're family now. What do you mean?"

"We sit here in Stockholm and this is the capital, and we're hired to protect our country and we're hired to keep an eye on what the Russians are up to, but the citizens aren't told anything. Out there most people think we're fiddling around with budget submarines, and we have to classify anything that moves, so the taxpayers never realize why it is that they should be putting more into the defense budget. That just doesn't seem right."

"Do you know any reliable journalists?"

"Yes, I think so—one, at least."

"Would you consider . . . well, you know."

"At a certain time I think everyone should consider it. I haven't reached that point. The Commodore probably hasn't reached that point either."

"Sam. Call me Sam when we're alone. No, I haven't. But are you restless? Do you want to go back to the operations department?"

"I don't know . . . This has been educational, but I'm not here to push papers."

"What are you here for, Carl?" Ulfsson stated his question so gently that it sounded loaded. It hung in the air for a moment while he lit another cigarette. "Well?" He exhaled a cloud of smoke—surprisingly thick, coming from a nicotine-free tobacco-free cigarette, according to the ads.

He must have inhaled half the cigarette in one breath, thought Carl as he considered how to avoid the question. "I'm here to track down the Russians, head them off, and if necessary confront them," he replied hesitantly.

Ulfsson burst into hearty laughter. "Confront! Wonderful, Carl! You mean, I suppose, cut their throats?"

"If I have instructions to do so, yes!" answered Carl, feigning mirth. The situation didn't seem the least bit funny.

"Seriously, Carl, are you worried about the KGB tail?"

"Well, there's the problem that I couldn't fly anywhere, even under an assumed name, all last year. Ever since that hijacking they've known who I am. And they ferreted out our operations office. The question is, will they find out the new address by following me? I assume I'll be going back, won't I?"

"Yes, of course, and we can certainly deploy some countermeasures. What's important isn't whether they know where we work, it's that they don't know what we're up to or what we think. Take some time off now while the weather's nice."

"It's nice weather for the Russians out there, too."

"Well, we can always call you in. I'll see you at the Monday meeting, and thanks for your paperwork. I didn't tell you, by the way, that you're very good at paperwork."

"Thanks, Com— Thanks, Sam."

"Have a nice holiday."

"Same to you, Sam."

In his temporary office farther down the hall, Carl gathered up the notes on his desk, swept them into a plastic bag and sealed it, and on his way out placed it in a basket marked for material to be shredded.

In the evening he devoted himself to a furious workout inside the locked room behind a steel door with an electronic combination lock. He had discovered that he now weighed ninety-four kilos, and that was three kilos more than he had ever weighed, so it was a matter of getting rid of the spare tire around his waist. He was thirty-four, and starting to feel old and a little stiff, and with incomprehensible fury he went at his heavy, sand-filled leather punching bag with the almost eradicated human features on it for more than an hour.

When he was done with the physical workout, he fired ten series with a small-bore pistol down the room's homemade firing range. He thought he should shoot as much as possible when he was sweaty and tired and angry, since he was getting too good at shooting in peace and quiet at stationary targets. Shooting in real life took place only under agitated circumstances.

He seemed able to suppress all feeling with the help of a weapon. As soon as he snapped the clip into the pistol butt a kind of peace came over him, and all his concentration and will gathered at one point— the line between the bead and the sight melded into one clear point, with the target blurred, always blurred, in the background.

He fired three series for fifty points, four series for forty-nine points, and two series for forty-eight. Shooting was now the only sport where he could hold his own. By that he meant "win."

After he had locked up his workout room and taken a shower, he drank a liter of orange juice, made some tea, and sat for several hours with tea and California honey and Bach's *Goldberg Variations*. By then he had stopped sweating. In spite of the summer heat, he closed the tall, deepset windows, went into the bedroom, pulled out the Beretta from underneath his pillow and placed it on the night table. For the first time in a long time, he fell asleep almost immediately.

When he woke he couldn't tell why or how long he had been sleeping. He only knew that suddenly he was alert and wide awake. He reached for the pistol, pulled it under the bedclothes, and took off the safety catch, all in a single automatic movement.

Then he sat up cautiously and paused to think.

He hadn't been having a nightmare. He looked at the clock. It was a little past three.

The sheets felt soft and cool—he hadn't been sweating. And yet he was now sitting there wide awake with a pistol in his hand.

In the silence he could hear the ticking of the wall clock in the hall. But he could feel the presence of something else, and he was certain he wasn't imagining it.

Then he heard the first clear sounds.

Someone was walking softly down the corridor; his view was blocked because the bedroom door was half closed.

He silently rolled out of bed, leaving the blanket and pillow crumpled up so that in a pinch it would look like someone was lying there, and moved quickly across the floor in his bare feet. He stood near the high doorway with its eighteenth-century moldings, his weapon raised in front of his face.

Then he concentrated on listening again. The other person had gone into the library.

He took a quick look down the hallway and caught a glimpse of a flashlight from the library at the end. Someone had let himself in with a skeleton key and was searching for something, but there was nothing in the library except books and classical music and some liquor. And that same person had not even bothered to make sure the apartment was empty before starting to work. That went against all the rules.

He cautiously pulled on a pair of pants, made sure that nothing sharp was sticking out of the pockets, buckled his belt properly, and then carefully pushed the bedroom door all the way open with his left hand. It swung back without a sound; Carl abhorred creaking doors.

He crept cautiously down the corridor, the darkest part of the apartment. Outside the windows thrushes were singing; it was starting to get light, and a flashlight in the library was actually unnecessary.

He passed the dining room door, closed, and noticed that the key was in its usual place, so the door was locked.

Now only a few feet from the library, he cocked his pistol, then took a deep breath and stepped quickly and silently into the room with his weapon in front of him.

Four yards away a man was trying to open the locked drawer of his antique desk. The flashlight lay on the desk. The man had long blond hair, a tattered leather jacket, frayed jeans, and running shoes with three stripes; one of his shoes was carelessly tied so the lace lay loosely around his foot; he was standing with his back to Carl.

An amateur, thought Carl, a damned amateur is trying to break into my desk drawer in the middle of the night! I can't shoot an amateur.

He took a cautious step back through the door and into the hall and tried to think. He used two hands to put the safety catch back on the pistol without causing any earsplitting clicks and then decided on two things in turn. First he tiptoed over to the front door, locked the deadbolt, and put the key in his pocket. As he went back he discovered that the remote control for the TV for some reason was lying on the newspaper table in the entryway. He picked it up and returned to the corridor that opened onto the library.

The man was still trying to jimmy the lock on the desk drawer. Near the flashlight lay a big camera.

Carl aimed the remote control at the television set, which immediately began to roar. The man gave a start, looked around at the television set, and started to go over to it. At the same moment, Carl flipped the switch to light the chandelier, raised his pistol, and waited quietly to be noticed. The situation was completely under control.

The man now turned around and looked in terror at Carl. He seemed to be somewhere between thirty and forty years old, and his eyes, with enlarged pupils, were bulging. He must be on something, Carl thought. When he caught sight of the big black pistol, and possibly when he saw or felt Carl's gaze, the man slowly raised his hands and tried to pull himself together to say something. "Don't shoot! Don't shoot, damn it!" His voice was cracking, hoarse.

Carl regarded him in silence.

"On the floor, face down on the floor, and spread your arms and legs," he commanded at last.

The man obeyed in a flash, and Carl went over to him and pulled out of his pockets two syringes and a heavy key ring, which he tossed onto the desk alongside the big screwdriver the man had left there. "Lie still, don't move, or I'll blow your head off," he commanded and moved quickly over to the door to the workout room. He opened the old carved oak door, then entered the code on the lock to the inner steel door behind it, and went in. He opened one of his weapons cupboards and took out a pair of American handcuffs. When he returned, to his surprise the man was still lying in the same position; Carl had been expecting to run out in the hall and pull him down as he scrambled at the apartment door to escape.

He snapped the handcuffs around the man's wrists and then lifted the whole bundle over to the sofa, where he dumped his victim.

He turned on a table lamp and sat down in an armchair across from him.

"Are you a cop?" asked the intruder with an optimism in his voice as sudden as it was incomprehensible.

"No, you've gotten yourself mixed up in something much worse than that. Now you and I are going to have a little chat, and if I find out what I want to know, I won't go to the cops."

"I'd rather go to hell. Go ahead and call the cops," said the man stubbornly.

Carl leaned forward and found a wallet in the thief's jacket pocket. He pulled out a bus pass and a prescription for methadone issued under the same name.

"What's your name?" he asked. "And what's your birth number?"

"Go fuck yourself, you son-of-a-bitch. Go ahead and call the cops," answered the man. He sounded quite self-confident.

Carl sighed and stood up. Then he took two rapid steps forward and struck him across the face with the back of his hand, intending more to shock than to injure him.

"What's your name and birth number?" he shouted.

"I'll report you for police brutality, you bastard . . ."

Carl hit him again—this time a good deal harder. The man finally answered, "640117-1279 Kenneth Henrik Carlsson, Carlsson with a C. So call the cops, you bastard."

Carl stuck the pistol into its usual place in the waistband of his pants at the small of his back. Why was the thief so eager to be picked up?

"Okay, I'll call the police," he said, walking to his desk. He lifted the receiver and was about to dial the number when he realized he only knew the telephone number for Säpo—he had never called the regular police. "Do you know the number?" he asked with a smile.

He got the number from information and asked for the officer on duty at VD1, and she answered herself.

"Hi, this is Carl. I need help with something."

"You're coming tomorrow, aren't you?"

"Yes, I'm coming, but can you look up a thief for me in the arrest records?"

"It's not accessible to the public."

"I know, but I have the thief in my apartment and I want to verify his identity."

"Shall I send a car to bring him in?"

"Well, he actually does seem surprisingly eager—probably because you'll let him go right away. But I want to know something about him before I throw him out."

"He's not threatening you in any way? Do you have the situation under control?"

"Yes, the situation is completely under control."

"Okay, what's his name?"

"640117-1279 Kenneth Henrik Carlsson," read Carl from the methadone prescription.

She was gone for a few minutes. Carl placed the receiver on its side and opened the curtains in front of the library's big French windows. He observed the surroundings for a moment but nothing seemed suspicious. Down there on the cobblestones Saint George and the dragon were alone in their eternal stony struggle. Beyond the rooftops there was an unobstructed view, toward Skeppsholmen, of the three masts of the *af Chapman*. He opened the window. The only audible sounds were of blackbirds and an occasional car down on Skeppsbron.

"Well, it's a long story, this one," sighed Eva-Britt Jönsson when she returned to the telephone. "Do you want all the details or a general picture or what?"

"If I can just find out what kind of guy he is, that'll be fine," replied Carl with a glance at his sulking prisoner.

"Let's see . . . a little more than thirty items in his record: theft, drug misdemeanor, grand larceny, shoplifting, intimidation, drug misdemeanor, robbery, petty and grand larceny, shoplifting, resisting arrest, et cetera. Known as Kenta. No assault charges. A thief and a junkie, gets a legal prescription for methadone . . . is that enough? Nice visitor you've got."

"Identifying marks?"

"Let's see . . . yes, jailbird-type tattoos on his forearms; the one on his left arm is some kind of black cross with a compass, and it says 'Kicki' around his wrist."

"That's enough. See you tomorrow."

"Are you sure you don't want us to pick him up?"

"No, there's no sense in that—he didn't manage to swipe anything. See you tomorrow."

Carl didn't wait for an answer before he put down the receiver. Then he took out the little key for the handcuffs, went over to the thief, and unlocked the left cuff. He pushed up the prisoner's sleeve and ascertained that the tattoos were there. He snapped the free handcuff around the sofa leg so that his prisoner was forced to sit bent over with his right arm stretched toward the floor. Then he went back to the desk and studied the objects there for a moment. On the key ring from the thief's pocket he found his own door key marked with a "3." That was interesting.

He went into the bedroom and pulled on his shirt, socks, and shoes, then returned to the library and stopped in the middle of the room. The thief now looked more angry than frightened.

"It's like this, Kenta. You and I are going to have a nice long talk," Carl began, but he was immediately interrupted.

"I'd rather go to hell. You can just go ahead and call the cops, or else this is unlawful imprisonment. That's an offense that society takes seriously. I'm just a thief, so I won't get anything, but you'll be locked up if you don't let me go."

Carl couldn't help laughing. In principle the thief was right.

"Well . . ." he said slowly, "I guess you don't understand what a hell of a mess you're in. Do you know who I am?"

"I don't give a shit. Just call the cops. You have no right to interrogate me."

"Do you want something to drink? Whiskey, wine, beer?"

"A shot of whiskey would be nice, but you have to take off these damn handcuffs," answered the thief with a glint of optimism in his eyes.

Carl threw a glance at the open window. He didn't want to be involved in chasing a thief across the rooftops of Gamla Stan. So first he closed the window, then pulled out a bottle of Jack Daniel's and two glasses, filled one of them halfway, and poured a few drops in the bottom of the other for himself. He set both glasses on the table in front of the sofa. He put on some music, unlocked the man's handcuffs, and pulled up an armchair, so that they were sitting quite close to each other.

"Skål, Kenta," he said and raised his glass as he regarded the thief. Kenta lifted his glass hesitantly to his lips, took a gulp, put it down, and began to massage his wrists while he waited.

There was no doubt that he was a real thief. He looked watchful, scared, and haggard; he had bad skin and gave off an unpleasant odor.

Carl tried to start off as gently as he could. "It's like this, Kenta. You won't get out of here unless—"

"Damn it all. I'm no fink—I'm a pro, get it? So I'm not talking either to you or to any damn cop."

"Oh sure. Stop interrupting and I'll tell you what'll happen." Carl paused. "If you're an ordinary thief trying to commit an ordinary burglary, then what you say is true—there won't be any penalty for burglary number two thousand or whatever it is in your case. Now listen to me! All right. I'm an officer in the Joint Chiefs' operations section, and my job has had a lot to do with defense secrets. You come here with keys and head straight for a certain desk drawer and you're not here to steal—or you would have taken your screwdriver and broken into the drawer. This is no ordinary little burglary, Kenta. Whether you know it or not, you're working for foreign powers. That's not called burglary or robbery, that's called espionage. You're not looking at a three-month sentence lumped together with some other jobs—you're looking at ten years. Do you understand what I'm talking about?"

"No," the man said, "I don't get it." He sounded terrified.

"Oh yes, Kenta, you get it all right. This means that it's not ordinary cops you may end up with. First I'm going to beat the shit out of you, and you can forget about reporting me for police brutality or anything like that: it doesn't apply when it's a matter of national security. Then I'm going to take you to a secret little place where you can sit for a few months under interrogation until we know everything. And then you'll go in for a very long sentence. No, don't interrupt me! That's the unpleasant option for you. Now I'll tell you about the pleasant one. You're a thief, right? Someone hired you. You didn't understand what this someone was getting you into. So we won't prosecute you, because you're just a thief; we want to catch the ones who hired you."

"I'm no fink . . ." There was a great deal of doubt in his voice.

Carl picked up his glass, nodded a *skål* at the thief, who took a big gulp.

He gestured at the big camera on his desk, a Polaroid that any amateur could handle. "You were going to photograph something here, Kenta. Then you were supposed to put everything back in place. I know where the key came from that you used to get in. Well, Kenta, what were you supposed to photograph? Secret documents?"

"No, nothing like that. It seemed a little nuts, but I never thought it was espionage or anything like that; it doesn't have anything to do with submarines or that kind of thing, goddammit."

Carl watched Kenta while he wrestled with his thief's honor and his terror. At last the fear won out.

"It was just some goddamned medals. How the hell could that be espionage?"

"Medals?"

"Yes, they were supposed to be in that drawer."

Carl got up and walked thoughtfully over to the desk. That was true. In the drawer were quite a few private papers, but at the very bottom lay several blue boxes with Carl's collected honors. He had almost forgotten they were there. Now he took out the boxes and opened one with the initials "RF" on it. He dangled the Legion of Honor and Knight Commander's Cross from his finger and gestured at Kenta.

"Is this what you were supposed to photograph?"

"Yes, and it's nothing worth bitching about. It had something to do with a bet."

"What was the bet about?"

"It was about those little round yellow ones—about whether you had one or two."

Carl picked out the Royal Swedish medal for bravery in the field. He held it between his thumb and forefinger by the little blue and yellow ribbon and swung it back and forth.

"So this is the one it was all about?"

"Yes, it was supposed to say something about bravery or whatever the hell."

"And what was the important thing?"

"Whether there was one or two. That's what they had bet on."

"*Who* had bet on it?"

"How the hell do I know?"

Carl came across the room and tossed the medal onto the coffee table in front of the sofa. He poured some more whiskey for his prisoner. Then he sat in silence for a while, thinking, and seemed to be listening to the music. It was still the *Goldberg Variations*. He had forgotten to take off the disc.

Kenta the thief cautiously drank his whiskey.

Finally Carl seemed to reach a decision. "Here's the deal," he began firmly. "The people who said they had made a bet are Soviet spies. They want to get certain information from me that may be more important than you think. I can't tell you what it's about, because what the Russians want to find out is something that concerns national secrets. So the question is, what should you and I do now? How much were you going to get paid, by the way?"

"Three thousand. Fifteen hundred in advance and fifteen hundred when I delivered the pictures."

"What did you do with the fifteen hundred?"

"Spent most of it. I had a few debts and so on."

"Hm. I assume you don't have anything against cashing in the other fifteen hundred."

"Obviously. But I'm no damned spy. I'm an honest thief, but no damned spy."

"I'm glad you're a patriot. Here's my proposal. We take a picture for them. You deliver it and get your money, but you don't say a word about getting caught. But I have to know who gave you the assignment, and you have to say it on tape."

"Do you think I'm crazy? Do you think I'm going to sit here and admit to being a spy or something like that and get caught later? Not on your life."

"No, on the contrary. If you work for me, you'll be a Swedish agent, pronto. Then you'll only get punished if you break your pledge of secrecy, because that would mean you'd be cooperating with the enemy. But as long as you're a Swedish agent, you won't be breaking any laws. This will be in effect just for this one operation."

"Can I get that in writing?"

"No, of course not, nobody does. On the other hand, you do have to fill out a military form. Wait a minute."

Carl stood up and went into his inner sanctum and opened the other large weapons cupboard. On one of the top shelves lay a thin stack of forms marked "JCS #107" in the lower left-hand corner and headed "Proof of Reminder Received Concerning Secrecy Pledge." It was hardly applicable to run-of-the-mill thieves in the Stockholm region, which even the introductory text indicated:

> I have on this day . . . received a reminder that I shall not divulge to unauthorized personnel any information of a secret nature, either during my employment or at the conclusion thereof. Regarding procedures and security at my place of employment, the administration of documents with secret contents, together with other security measures, I have received special instructions. . . .

Carl had a hard time not laughing when he sat down at his desk and filled in his own and the thief Kenta's names. You could well ask what "during my employment or at the conclusion thereof" meant in Kenta's case. But in principle he was drawing up a genuine document.

"All right," he said as he put the form on the coffee table in front of Kenta. "Read it carefully and then sign at the bottom. And note the last lines, right above your signature: 'I am aware that a breach of this secrecy pledge may result in punishment, even if the breach should occur through carelessness without criminal intent.' Sign there and you're a Swedish agent—just for this special operation, that is—and the only crime you could commit would be to squeal on me. Beyond that you're free and clear. What do you think?"

The thief leaned forward tensely and slowly read through the text twice. Then he solemnly took the pen out of Carl's hand and hesitantly signed his name on the dotted line.

Carl took the form and pen from him and wrote his own name on the line for the officer receiving the document.

"All right," he said, "now we can get to work. Welcome to His Majesty's secret service."

Whistling to himself, he went back into the inner sanctum and got a little cassette player that he tested on his way back into the library. Then he turned off the music, set up the tape recorder on the coffee table, and began:

"It is now 3:26 a.m. on Friday, June 17. We are at home in my apartment, Commander Carl Hamilton, and with me is . . . 640117-1279 Kenneth Henrik Carlsson . . . who let himself into my apartment with the intention of taking some photographs for another employer. Is that right, Kenneth?"

"Is that damned tape recorder on?"

"Yes, and I'm asking you whether that's right."

"Sure it's right."

"Who gave you the photo assignment, Kenta?"

"A guy named Lelle."

"Was that the same person who gave you the key to my apartment?"

"Yes. He said you'd be gone for the Midsummer holiday."

"We're talking about a man who's about thirty years old, five foot eight, stocky, with black, curly hair?"

"Yes, that's a good description."

"What were you supposed to photograph?"

"Your medals . . . the ones in the desk drawer over there."

"What was the important thing that you were supposed to determine by photographing them?"

"Whether there was one or two of those round yellow ones. I was supposed to take out all the medals and take a picture of them all together. Then I was supposed to put everything back—I wasn't supposed to swipe anything."

"No. And what were you going to get paid for it?"

"Three thousand kronor, half up front and half on delivery."

"What do you know about this Lelle's employers?"

"Nothing. He said that someone had made a bet, someone who was jealous or something, and that it wasn't dangerous and not even burglary."

"Thanks, that's enough, Kenta."

Carl turned off the tape recorder and went over to the desk and unpacked the Commander's medal, the Bundesverdienstkreuz, the Commander's Cross of the Legion of Honor, and one of his two royal medals for bravery; he put the other one discreetly away in its box. Then he took a picture of the now slightly diminished medal collection and waited until the picture appeared out of the negative. The honors, as well as part of the library, were clearly visible.

"This will do nicely," he said. "This is the picture you will deliver. But now I want a picture of you too. Come and stand here next to the medals."

Kenta Carlsson obeyed reluctantly. Carl took one picture and then had another idea; he went out and grabbed a *Dagens Nyheter* from underneath the letter slot in the hallway, put the newspaper in the hand of the reluctantly posing Kenta, and took another picture.

"All right, Kenta, now we can get to work. The only thing you have to do is deliver this picture, precisely as your employer expects. And then you can cash in your other fifteen hundred kronor and try to forget the whole thing. But if they want you to break in here again, you have to let me know—it's your duty as a Swedish agent, remember that. And not a word—you've signed a pledge of secrecy."

"Is that all—am I through now?"

"Yes. Keep your mouth shut about this, deliver the picture and say that everything went the way it was supposed to—then you're through. But if you blab, we'll bring you in. No squealing, no hustling, no bragging around town about being a secret agent. Agreed?"

"All right, goddammit, it's a deal. Could I have another shot of whiskey?"

Carl was in his temporary but increasingly permanent office at OP5 well before eight o'clock. He was still sweating from his morning workout in the inner sanctum—there'd be no shirking from the exercises until the three kilos of excess weight were gone.

One of his first actions was to fill out the application to gain access to the Säpo records office and take out any reports on the superintendent in his apartment building, Lars-Erik Sundberg, who evidently called himself Lelle under certain circumstances.

He had forgotten to tell Sundberg that he wouldn't be gone over the holiday weekend and so wouldn't need him to water the flowers. Carl abhorred withered, dead plants—ever since the time when he came home from an unexpectedly long and unpleasant trip in West Germany and found all of his newly purchased plants dead in the library.

Sundberg had had an ordinary leftist record at the beginning of his career—FLN groups and the like. Later he spent time in Stockholm's extremely small division of Norrbotten's Communist party, which was loyal to Moscow, and then he seemed to have lost contact with the left and made his living as some kind of artist and as the custodian of Carl's condominium.

Most likely he was a direct link to the Russians.

Carl prepared as complete a report as possible, in three copies—for the head of military intelligence (Sam himself), the head of the internal security division (JCS/MS), and the head of his department, Captain Lallerstedt.

He had all three reports on Samuel Ulfsson's desk at ten o'clock, and this led to a four-hour-long discussion between himself, Ulfsson, and Lieutenant Colonel Borgström, the head of JCS/MS.

Borgström felt that the matter should be turned over immediately to the Security Police so they could bring in that custodian or at least instigate surveillance of him. It wasn't every day that they had a definite tip on a Soviet spy.

Carl adamantly disagreed. The agent was already exposed, and they could take him whenever they wanted to, when the time was right. But at the moment he had been given some information that the Russians had requested, and this information had been falsified in one important aspect by Carl himself. It would be better to wait and let the Russians receive their disinformation. If they took Lelle now, everything would crack wide open.

Borgström made a few sarcastic comments about the balancing act between, on the one hand, a young commander and his personal whims, and on the other hand the importance of tracking down and neutralizing enemy agents.

Carl could not openly argue, but he requested a private meeting with Samuel Ulfsson, which was granted.

The room was already filled with the smoke of Ulfsson's perpetual Ultima Blend when they were finally alone.

"Okay, Carl, out with it," said the commodore after he had lit another cigarette from the butt he was holding. "What are they after?"

"They wanted to know whether I have one or two medals for bravery in the field."

"Yes, and you have two, you devil. Wonder if von Döbeln even had two. So?"

"And that stupid Borgström doesn't know—"

"The commander should use more respectful language about his superiors."

"Yes, excuse me. Our genius in security fails to realize the point."

"Which is?"

"I received the second medal for Operation Big Red. The Russians want to know whether I was part of the operation. Their tailing me has to do with this. They want to know who blew them straight to hell. Now they've been given the wrong information."

"What does it matter to them exactly who carried out the operation?"

"Damned if I know. It doesn't seem very Russian to want to take revenge against individual agents. I can't understand it."

"And what do you want me to do?"

"You're the boss. Give the orders, damn it."

"What orders?"

"Tell Borgström of the sweaty upper lip that the matter is closed and classified and not to be sent to the monkey house at Kungsholmen until further notice."

"And when will that be?"

"Damned if I know."

"But we can't just let Russian agents run around loose. *Lieutenant Colonel* Borgström has a point there."

"Yes, but my custodian is small potatoes. He's running the errands; we can take him in, get him sentenced for who knows what, and then we can have his controls deported—nothing more. But if the Russians are digging into Operation Big Red, there are bigger people involved."

"Are you worried about your safety?"

"They've got photographic evidence that I only have one medal for bravery, so therefore that I wasn't in on Big Red. If they get contradictory proof, then we'll have them on our backs—or rather I'll have them on my back—forever. Damn it, Sam, I want to go back to operations. I want to get into the field. I can't sit here and push papers until I retire."

"What would you do in the field?"

"When Steelglove and Lundwall come back from California, we

have some interesting diving projects we could take up. We've got better capabilities and equipment than our regular personnel, after all . . . Damn it, Sam, we could get more evidence!"

"Strange to hear that from you, of all people."

"Why's that?"

"You're one of the few people in Sweden who doesn't need more evidence; you know more about what it looks like down there than anyone else."

"Yes, but that will be secret forever. But they're still at it, Sam; damned if they aren't out there every day. They're up to some new deviltry and we've got to stop them, Sam."

"The mouse is roaring. I've never heard you swear so much."

"Look, if we mowed them down once, we can do it again. But there's a certain significance in the fact that they don't know who did it the first time. Lundwall and Steelglove and I are valuable, Sam. Just think what an expensive education we got in California."

"You're right, of course. Your training cost a lot. And it would be unpleasant if the Russians directed actions against our personnel in peacetime. Damned unpleasant . . . not just for you, I have to add. Okay, we'll let the matter rest. The spy goes free for now."

"He's presumably not a spy, just a shitty little agent."

"Yes, he'll have to wait. Shall we say six months?"

"That depends on how you want him. If you turn him over to the monkey house, they'll never figure out how to take him."

"All right, we'll address that question later. What are you doing for the holiday?"

"Going sailing."

"A private expedition, I hope. But is that a good idea?"

"I'll have seven police officers keeping me company, including three female ones. Speaking of which, I have a couple of speeding tickets that I'd like you to sign off for me."

Acting Inspector Eva-Britt Jönsson had a hard time figuring out Carl Hamilton.

There was no doubt that he was an authentic naval officer. Among the police officers everybody was an amateur sailor, and even though two of them had their skipper's licenses, Carl was the one who solved all the navigational problems quickly and easily. And besides, he understood a lot of markers that were explained only on military charts.

He seemed calm and relaxed and didn't say much behind his sunglasses. When the men tried to test him in various ways, as men try to do, he evaded them without any apparent concern about the male pecking order, which she'd seen a lot of in her almost ten years' association with policemen—with the emphasis on *men*.

They sailed out toward Sandhamn and continued beyond, to Hästholmarna, before they dropped anchor for the night. They tied up the boats in the shelter of a steep cliff where the water was unfortunately quite deep—unfortunately, because one of the women somehow managed to lose a steel and gold Rolex wristwatch while tying up the anchor line. The policewoman started to cry in a most unpolicelike way. Her girlfriend, who was a flight attendant, had bought it cheap at the airport in Amsterdam or somewhere, she explained, snuffling.

The men started diving, though it was terribly cold in the water, but they quickly gave up and said it was impossible—they couldn't even see the bottom when they tried.

She glanced at Carl, sitting motionless, wearing his sunglasses though it was already dusk. Finally, after the others had given up, he hesitated for a long time before asking to borrow a skindiver's mask. Then when he took off his T-shirt—he had been so careful about keeping it on the whole time—she saw that his entire chest had been slashed; she had seen a lot of knife marks in her job, but nothing like this. And it seemed as though he was trying to hide it, because as soon as he took off his shirt, he jumped into the water, holding on to the railing with one hand while he tightened the strap on the mask and spit into it and rubbed the saliva around. He swept his head backward into the water so that his dark blond hair was slicked back on his head, and put on the face mask with one hand as if it were the easiest thing in the world. Then he took a deep breath and disappeared without so much as a splash.

To their astonishment, almost horror, he seemed to have vanished. He must have been gone for two or three minutes. Then there was a glimpse of his white body at the edge of the boat and he popped up with the watch in one hand. He caught hold of the railing, tossed the watch onto the deck, and swung himself up out of the water and onto the deck with no apparent effort. He walked rapidly over to the cabin to put on his clothes. She just managed to catch sight of what she was unconsciously looking for.

Above the knife scars on his chest she had noticed something that looked like a bullet scar, just under his collarbone on the right. Now, when he bent down to go into the cabin, she could see the exit hole. The bullet had passed straight through his right shoulder blade; the exit hole was as big as an old-fashioned five-öre coin.

When he came back on deck he was wearing jeans and a blue military sweater, and when they threw themselves at him and asked him how the hell he could dive so well and how deep he thought it was, he answered briefly that it was thirty or thirty-five feet deep, with a sandy bottom, very easy to find a shiny object, and that he had done his basic training in underwater demolition—diving was quite simply what he was good at.

He seemed very relaxed and happy and quickly changed the subject. In his place any one of the other men would have spent a long time talking about his exploit.

After they had eaten—new potatoes from a can and pickled herring with sour cream and chives—someone took a beer can and filled it a third full of water and set it on the stern.

They were all alone at Hästholmarna and could play their usual game. They had two .22-caliber target pistols, and they took turns shooting at the can; according to the rules of the game, whoever came in last had to do the dishes. The first couple of years it had been taken for granted that it would be one of the female officers who would come in last.

She watched Carl as he attentively followed the shooting, and she was certain that he would take a turn too; now and then he had almost imperceptibly chuckled at the others' less successful shots. But when one of her colleagues handed him the pistol, he merely said he wasn't much for shooting but would gladly wash the dishes nevertheless, and then he actually did.

Later that night, when some of the men were starting to get a little rowdy from too many beers, Carl took his sleeping bag—it seemed to be a rather high-tech type of sleeping bag—and left, with the explanation that he would rather sleep in the open, that it would be too stuffy in the cabin.

She woke up early, before the others, and so she crept out and went to the island, going in the direction where he had disappeared in the night. When she reached the other side of the island, she first found his sleeping bag, and then saw that he was diving and swimming—as if it were the middle of summer and sixty-eight degrees instead of fifty-three!

She sat down where he couldn't see her and watched. He was doing a kind of exercise that he repeated over and over. First he swam fifteen or twenty yards at top speed, then dove and was gone for a long time, until he came up and repeated the exercise all over again.

Later he slowly swam out quite far, took a deep breath, and disappeared. She timed him. It took two minutes and forty seconds before he came up again.

Then he swam toward shore, almost straight toward her, dove, and disappeared again.

This time her watch showed almost four minutes, and she began to think that something had gone wrong. Uneasily she leaned over the side of the cliff to see more of the shoreline.

"Hi," Carl said cheerfully. He was standing six feet behind her. "Is it customary for the police inspector to spy on naked men? You know how embarrassingly tiny it gets in cold water."

He had already pulled on his jeans.

"You're not afraid of cold water, obviously," she gasped.

"No, I've dived a lot in California. The water is colder there than people think—just a matter of getting used to it."

His chest was bare, and he noticed her inquiring eyes. He got his blue sweater out of the sleeping bag and pulled it on.

She followed and sat down close by. "What happened to your chest?" she asked.

"You mean the scars?"

"Yes."

"Went diving in some sharp coral without a wetsuit one summer, and it got too narrow when I tried to get through an opening to a grotto."

He looked away when he spoke, so you couldn't tell that he was lying. She decided not to persist, and not to ask about the entry or exit hole either, which couldn't be explained away with chitchat about coral.

"When we get back to town it's your turn to ask me to dinner," he said after a while.

"Gladly," she replied. "At a posh restaurant or at my place?"

"Preferably your place."

She was more attracted to him than she would admit to herself. Most men who land in the company of four big, strong police officers—extraordinarily big and strong—get defensive and flustered. Once one of the other girls had dragged along an architect, and the holiday sailing trip had ended in arguments, unhappiness, and a virtual fist-fight. But Carl had a natural way of evading the usual male measuring of rooster combs without seeming insecure. There was something odd about him, something he wouldn't talk about or even hint at. On his left cheek he had a scar from something that in police jargon would be described as powerful, external, blunt force. On his chest were the scars from a knifing that had probably exceeded anything even the most experienced of her colleagues had encountered. And she had discovered one more bullet-hole scar: he had been shot in his right thigh. The entry hole looked like a little white spot, but the exit scar in the back was oblong and had been sewn up with three stitches. The injuries were only a few years old, as far as she could tell.

Usually anyone who had these kinds of scars and was not a police officer was a criminal. But there was no doubt that he was a real naval officer. He was able to entertain the party on their way back to town by tying an endless number of seaman's knots on a scrap of anchor line. And when someone saw a submarine conning tower in the distance, which created as much of a sensation among the police party as among other Swedish parties now out on the water, it took only a quick look through Carl's rubber-coated military binoculars for him to conclude that it was HMS *Västergötland*, Sweden's most modern submarine, and anyone who doubted him could have a look at the three gold crowns on a blue background and a limp, wet Swedish flag as soon as the tower came closer. And, by the way, Swedish submarines often ran with the whole tower surfaced when near inhabited areas in order to decrease the number of submarine alarms.

Yes, of course he was a real naval officer. How had he gotten those wounds?

Carl was in a resolutely good mood. He liked the police officers. He felt distantly related to them, and they seemed without exception totally decent. Oh, sure, they admitted that sometimes in handling thugs they might squeeze some stubborn devil a little too hard; but that kind of thing happened most often when you were inexperienced, and in the police world people divided themselves up roughly according to violence levels—they sought out work partners like themselves—and this group was an unusually friendly, nice bunch within the large and motley crowd at VD1. At least that's what they said.

Carl didn't doubt it. They were nice people about his own age or slightly younger, and he thought he'd enjoy keeping in contact with them. Solitude was starting to bother him, and police officers would understand if he had to refrain from answering questions.

His diving exhibition had been inescapable, but on the other hand, there was nothing strange about a former underwater demolition expert being able to dive better than a policeman. And he hadn't even needed to try to get out of the shooting contest. He had laughingly said no, thanks, to a wrestling match. Only a few years ago he would have grabbed one of the pistols and put a whole clip into the beer can, maybe even have rapid-fired a series into it, and then he would have felt childishly clever. Later he would have tied up the two biggest guys like pretzels, almost playfully. He would have caused amazement and made a fool of himself.

It had been wonderful diving in the Baltic again. He remembered from his childhood that half-sweet taste of the dark water. And it had been surprisingly clear out there with good visibility below the thirty-foot level. He had been almost happy as he moved forward through the brown seaweed and the pale green sea grass on the border between sunlight and darkness. As far as he could tell, he could free-dive just as well as he had several years ago; his lung capacity had not deteriorated even though aging was aging. He might be feeling a little fat and be worrying about losing his hair, but he had dived away his worries.

Had she come to spy on him that morning? When he discovered her doing it and dived evasively so as to come up outside her field of vision, go around her, study her from the back, she had merely seemed uneasy.

She was a wonderful girl. She had gone into police work because she believed in it, and she was probably very good at it. She was pretty in spite of a slightly marred complexion, and he was charmed by her mixture of tough police slang, something else that sounded almost churchy and a little countrified, and her working-class city dialect.

It was certainly odd that she went out to a restaurant dinner armed with a service weapon and handcuffs. But maybe that was part of her routine; she did a lot of investigative work.

What would happen when they were alone after dinner at her place and sat on the sofa looking at watercolors or whatever? He was afraid she would try to seduce him or that he would try to seduce her; it was a peculiar uneasiness, but he had a hard time with women he liked. He wanted to be either with Tessie or else with some woman he didn't care about—then it was easy. A Christian police officer seemed to him very difficult.

It was late in the afternoon and the sun was no longer in their eyes. He took off his shades and laughed a little to himself at the thought that his only worry in life right now was whether he was going to sleep with a police officer.

At that very moment all hell was about to break loose.

Two

Sir Geoffrey Hunt, assistant director of MI6, was in a good mood as he parted with his friend and colleague at Stockholm's Arlanda Airport. He would be back in London in plenty of time for his whist game at the club, and he'd had a good visit to Stockholm in spite of the rather sinister nature of his mission. On the one hand, he'd been able to help the Swedes out, in accordance with the cooperative agreement between the two intelligence services from three years ago, and on the other hand, the *opposition* (he never thought of the Russians in any other term) would suffer some kind of defeat as a consequence of the Tristan papers.

One couldn't be too certain about that, of course. The Swedish spy hunters hadn't exactly made themselves an international reputation for efficiency. But that wasn't his problem. Satiated and content after gravlax—an excellent Swedish salmon specialty, he had to admit—and cool white wine, he was on his way home.

His companion seemed gloomy and depressed, but that was the nature of the business, and besides, Commodore Ulfsson was no more cheerful than the average Swede; a softer kind of German, that's what they really were.

Sir Geoffrey climbed on board his British Airways plane, and from then on thought more about the evening whist game than about the consequences of the Tristan report. For British intelligence, the operation was now completed, relegated to the archives. Whatever happened now no longer concerned them; it was only a matter of the

Crown's prosecuting attorney sweeping up the remains and bringing an indictment against three Soviet agents who had already confessed. Later the Foreign Office might demand that one or another of Tristan's controls be deported. Maybe MI6 would get some supplemental information from the Swedes, but that wasn't likely, considering their inefficiency, and considering that it was irrelevant.

But for Commodore Ulfsson, who was at the same moment on his way back to downtown Stockholm in a staff car, the situation could only be described as a profound crisis.

No, worse, a catastrophe. Samuel Ulfsson had not even hinted to his very English colleague what conclusions he was drawing from the Tristan report. But if its information turned out to be correct, then the gist was that for almost a decade, the Soviet Union had had access to every piece of information of any importance from the so-called Russian Bureau of Sweden's Security Police, everything from the supreme commander's own orders concerning tactical deployments against Soviet underwater activities in Swedish territory, to . . . He couldn't make himself finish.

He went straight back to his office, called in the duty officer, and asked him to locate the supreme commander—the Defense Chief; then the head of JCS/MS's covert operations department, or Special Missions—the Old Man; the acting (and soon to be) head of operations; and the head of security at the Ministry of Defense. He gave instructions to have a conference call put through to all these men on a clean line as soon as contacts had been established, and then he went over to his safe and took out the Tristan report again and placed it in front of him on his bare, dark brown desk.

As he reached for his pack of cigarettes and the ashtray, he was suddenly struck by a fit of rage that was both spontaneous and hard to explain. Fiercely, he crushed the cigarette pack, his knuckles white, and flung it, along with the ashtray, into the empty wastebasket under his desk.

It was a strange time to decide to stop smoking. The workdays ahead would be long and hard.

He started reading through the report again.

MI6 had succeeded in recruiting a defector from the GRU, and it was naturally of great significance that the initiative had come from the British themselves, not from Tristan.

Tristan—God only knew what the code name stood for—had been a clerk in Aeroflot's London office. He had been having an affair with a woman with connections to MI6 (what these connections were was not stated), and so, of course, the whole business had landed there instead of with the competition at MI5, which was usually responsible for operations of this kind. But the boundaries between the security service and the intelligence agency were traditionally more fluid in Great Britain than in other Western countries.

The operation was a success. They had picked him up at Heathrow, driven him to a safe house somewhere outside London, and promised him the whole schmeer; after various difficulties with the Foreign Office and the Soviet embassy, screaming about kidnapping, they had been able to proceed.

The results for the British were not shabby. Tristan not only revealed the identity of the other GRU officers in Aeroflot—of which at least two were unknown to the English, even though they were on the list of suspected or possible GRU officers—but also exposed his own little spy ring, and this is what later led to the arrest of three Englishmen with evidence and everything in their own apartments. They confessed when they were confronted with the results of the search, and they were now awaiting sentencing, which would be prison terms of not less than twenty years. This was on its way to becoming the next big spy scandal in Great Britain, and the prime minister was going to make it public in Parliament at a politically advantageous moment, whenever that might be.

In terms of the British activities, Tristan's own field of operation, everything was crystal clear and nothing was left in question. A classic and apparently completely successful operation.

The problems were with the Swedish connection.

Tristan had apparently worked some years ago at Zentral in Moscow, and his office had been right next to Directorate Seven, which dealt with Scandinavia. His neighbor had handled certain routine payments to agents in Scandinavia, and had once told him some amusing stories about difficulties with some of them.

One incident concerned an officer in the Swedish security service who had a taste for such conspicuous clothes (especially loud, checked jackets) that, in a crowd of a hundred people, he was the only one that everyone would be sure to remember. His controls in GRU as well as his Swedish superiors tried to persuade him to dress more discreetly, but not even these combined efforts had been able to change his manner of dress. And that was the funny part.

Regarding an officer who, according to Tristan's informant, practically worked in the lap of the Swedish supreme commander, it was said that he had a funny habit of flipping up his extra pair of clip-on sunglasses, which he wore fastened over his regular sunglasses, so they stood out like wings from his eyebrows, which is why he had the code name Osprey. But he himself had never understood the humor behind the name. For Ulfsson, who realized at once who Osprey was, the description didn't seem amusing.

The funny thing about the third agent came in two parts. First, he had participated in a hijacking in which the opponents had been unknowingly supplied with blanks, and even so he had almost blown it. And second, he had been recruited during his training in the United States, and that was the first time a Swedish agent had been recruited in California, of all places. That was supposed to be amusing.

The Defense Chief telephoned. Over the electronic howl of the clean line Ulfsson briefly reported that they were in for the biggest crisis they had ever experienced and asked permission to call two meetings the next morning—one with the military personnel involved and one with security representatives in the Joint Chiefs of Staff. The request was immediately granted, and the first meeting was set for 6:30 a.m.

Right afterward the Old Man was put through on the line, calling from his apple orchard in Kivik.

"I have some very disturbing news, O.M., and I'll try to keep it brief," began Ulfsson, fumbling for his cigarette pack and remembering at the same moment that he had just quit smoking. "Can you be here early tomorrow morning, at six-thirty?"

"It'll have to be later," muttered O.M. on the other end. "The first plane from Sturup doesn't go until six-twenty."

"Come up by car from Skåne tonight. We'll requisition transportation from South Base if nothing else, or you could go over to some air force wing and we could fly you up. Yes, it's that serious."

"It's that serious?"

"Yes."

"Does this damned howling debugging device do anything except make it hard for us to hear each other?"

"Yes, we hope so."

"Can you tell me what it's all about?"

"No. Be here at headquarters tomorrow at the designated time. Shall we get you car transportation from the base or a plane?"

"Car."

"Fine. I'll take care of it. You'll be picked up around eleven o'clock tonight. See you tomorrow."

Ulfsson went out in the empty hallway and stretched. He continued toward the toilet at the far end of the corridor instead of using his own—he didn't know why—and splashed his face with cold water and looked at himself in the mirror for a moment. A rather thin-haired, slightly graying, former naval officer who had been wearing out a desk for many years and who was now facing his biggest professional crisis ever.

He went back to his office and called home to say he'd be late. He almost had a fit of hysterical laughter when his wife reminded him of the imminent arrival of dinner guests and declared that nothing could be so important as to detain him. He promised curtly to hurry as fast as he could and slammed down the receiver. It was the first time he had ever talked to his wife this way.

Then he took out what was available in the department's big safe about Commander Carl Gustaf Gilbert Hamilton.

If Hamilton was a Soviet agent, the consequences were completely incalculable. And if he had been recruited in California, it meant that that training option would be closed to Swedish military personnel in the future, and in addition there would be a hell of a lot of unpleasantness with the Americans.

Hamilton had been a personal recruit of the Old Man, who had handpicked him from a whole year's crop of draftees. O.M. himself thought he had been extremely careful in his selection since it was, in fact, a prototype position—a position for which he was virtually the only backer among the military brass at that time.

After some difficulty in placing Hamilton when he returned home, he had wound up as a kind of temporary employee in Säpo. That had resulted in a massacre of Israeli agents in Stockholm; and on the instigation and decision of the previous prime minister (the murdered one), it led to Hamilton's receiving the first medal for bravery in the field awarded to a Swedish officer since 1905.

He was supposed to have been a Soviet agent even then? Well, true, the operation had not conflicted in any way with Soviet interests.

The following year he had been loaned out to the West German Verfassungsschutz for an operation under deep cover that ended in yet another massacre, this time of terrorists in West Germany. This operation could not be said to have conflicted with Soviet interests either.

Last year, however, Hamilton had rescued a Soviet defector and brought him to Sweden under rather spectacular circumstances, to put it mildly. This is where things began to get tangled. As far as they knew, the defector was a Soviet vice admiral with a known identity and a known position as commander of the military base at Kaliningrad, etc., etc. If the identity was genuine, Hamilton's operation was blatantly in conflict with Soviet interests, but what if he was a phony? Then Hamilton's diverse heroic efforts had the effect of falsely verifying his authenticity. Yet the Russians had subsequently located the admiral and murdered him on Swedish territory. Why would they do that?

Or was that what it was really all about? All of this had led to Sweden's best-kept military secret: Operation Big Red, when Hamilton and his two colleagues in California had blown up three Soviet underwater bases in Swedish territory.

Or had they?

Working this out further greatly depended on ascertaining what the two other California recruits had experienced. Assuming that Hamilton hadn't turned them too. In which case, Sweden's military commanders and certain sections of its government were going through their greatest crisis since World War II in one long drama arranged and directed by the Soviet Union. In certain terms, the course of events could be described as a kind of limited and prolonged military coup d'état. With the Soviet Union at the helm?

She dropped him off on Skeppsbron right across from Reisen. He bent down and kissed her gently and shyly on the cheek. She looked pretty in her police uniform—in fact, more attractive than in jeans and a sweater.

He gazed after her Volvo for a moment with its dog cage in the back as it disappeared toward the city. Then he walked over to the edge of the quay and looked at the water and *af Chapman*'s three masts on the other side.

He felt contrite and worthless as a man; it had gone exactly as he had feared, and now when he forced himself to think back, his palms grew sweaty. He couldn't do it—he couldn't make love to someone he liked too much or loved too little.

Naturally she had said not to worry, that it happened to all men, and so on. She had been totally—damnably—understanding, and that made it worse.

The water was crystal clear by the edge of the quay, and he caught a glimpse of a bicycle and a wastebasket a little ways out, where the water began to get murky.

He slung his jacket over his shoulder with the green military bag on top of it, and walked home, quite slowly and with his head down.

He had a sudden memory of the day before, when he was sitting on the boat with one hand trailing in the cold water, just before someone caught sight of HMS *Västergötland* in the distance. At that moment he had felt more at peace, possibly even happier than he had been in a long time. Now he was ashamed and depressed, and he vacillated desperately between the thought of never seeing her and her police friends again and the idea of trying to mobilize himself to sexual revenge in some unfathomable way.

No one had been in his apartment, he ascertained quickly. The green light on his answering machine was blinking, and he turned it on, still with his bag and jacket over his shoulder.

It was Sam's secretary, Ulrika. She told him to report to headquarters as soon as possible, and that he was also supposed to call in as soon as he got the message. It was only 8:10 in the morning, and he thought he was on vacation, so he decided it could wait another hour and a half; he wanted to avoid interruptions in his workout.

Contrary to the normal routine, he decided to start with shooting practice. He wanted to see how his present low mood would affect his precision—when you were depressed or angry, just as when you were afraid or upset, your precision should decrease dramatically.

He chose a revolver and fired a series of six rounds at the proportionately reduced targets, but the results were not at all what he had expected—he shot almost seven perfect series out of the eight the box held.

He was transformed by the weapon, that's what it was. At the very instant that his hand closed around the butt of the revolver, everything else vanished. It was as though everything else in the world were obliterated except for the signals between his right index finger, his brain, and his eye, as if precisely this were his real identity, the only thing that did not waver in a universe of illusion and the uncertainty of the imagination.

He sprayed the revolver with gun oil and cleaned it before he put it back in its place and locked the weapons cupboard. Then he changed and went through his exercise and martial-arts program with a mixture of fury and despair.

After he had showered and shaved he called Sam's secretary and said that he was on his way in half an hour. No, she didn't know what it was about, but it was obviously something big because there had been nonstop meetings since six o'clock that morning, or at least long before she got there. Everybody seemed upset.

He debated whether to take a taxi, but decided it was just as well to arrive after the meetings had produced some results in the form of decisions. After all, he was only an agent, and whether the strategies went one way or another, he was seldom in a position to give more than marginal suggestions for tactical improvements. He decided to walk over to headquarters, for it was a beautiful summer morning.

At 9:13 a.m. the representatives of the Security Police returned to Kungsholmen to open the gates of hell for the head of the Russian Bureau, Police Superintendent Stig Larsson, well known for his peculiar jackets.

The part of the Tristan report that concerned their own man had been presented to the Säpo men—but to them nothing was said about Carl or the head of the Defense Ministry's special strategic naval unit who, according to Tristan, had the code name Osprey.

The order of business was obvious. Since the so-called Osprey was on vacation at his summer house on Furusund, the only measures that could be taken against him right now were to bug his telephone and establish visual surveillance. However, an interrogation and house search could be initiated against Police Superintendent Larsson, and that was up to Säpo to do. As for Hamilton, the meeting that started an hour and a half before Säpo's representatives arrived principally concerned him; the military men had been far from agreeing whether they should keep the section of the Tristan report regarding Hamilton secret from their civilian Säpo colleagues.

From a legal standpoint it was problematic. It was Säpo's official function to investigate suspicions of espionage among military as well as civilian personnel, but in the practical and political senses, the matter was different. What the Defense Chief knew about Carl and Operation Big Red, what Ulfsson and the Old Man knew, and what Captain Lallerstedt knew was totally unknown to the head of military security, Lieutenant Colonel Borgström. And consequently he was firmly insisting that the Tristan report be presented in its entirety to Säpo. At the same time Borgström was the one who had to take responsibility for interrogating and investigating Commander Hamilton.

After the meeting with the Säpo men, the Defense Chief called a new meeting in which Borgström did not participate but the minister of defense did. Borgström was given instructions to prepare for interrogating Hamilton right after lunch.

Before they called in Hamilton, they had to decide whether he would be allowed to see his own section of the Tristan report. Since the unavoidable interrogation would quickly reveal its contents, since Hamilton was a highly professional intelligence officer, and since the impending internal investigation required total cooperation even from the ones under suspicion—it was not precisely a matter of questioning someone with an attorney present, according to the law—they decided to divulge the contents to him immediately, but not to say whether it was all or only a sampling of the Tristan information and assertions.

Carl sat alone for about an hour in Samuel Ulfsson's office with the extraordinary instruction not to leave the room until he was called. He regarded this as a manifestation of excessive nervous resolve, and when he finally was sent down the corridor to the other end of the building, where the Chief had his office, he was sure something very big was going on. It must have to do with the Russians. He enjoyed a certain sense of eager anticipation.

He felt the atmosphere the moment he entered the Defense Chief's conference room and saw the staring eyes directed at him. The men greeted him with great reserve, and when he looked at the Old Man inquiringly, O.M. turned away. He sat down at the head of the rectangular table; there was a gap of several yards between him and the five other men.

"Go ahead and read the report in front of you," said the Chief curtly, and then the others sat motionless as Carl began to read, and they let him feel their eyes boring into him.

He glanced quickly through the introduction of the Tristan report. Where was the Swedish connection? After the introduction there was only one short page of ten lines under the heading "Agent III."

After two lines Carl lost his concentration and had to start over. Then, summoning all his will power, he read through the text, slowly but only once. Then he pushed it away gently to signal that he was done and looked up at the Chief, who sat directly across from him, eyes nailed on him. Carl thought for a moment they might burst out laughing at their terrible joke. The next minute he felt as if he would faint.

"Well?" asked the Chief finally.

Carl's mind was blank. Should he start to defend himself, or what?

"What's your spontaneous reaction?" The Chief was remorseless.

"I don't really know what to say," Carl began at last, and the words seemed to stick in his dry mouth. "Do you mean we should take this seriously? What am I supposed to say?"

"So your position is that the information is false?"

"Yes, of course."

"Entirely groundless?"

"That is correct."

"There's nothing in it, no misunderstandings that you can explain or clarify?"

"No, the information is fabricated. All of it."

"Convince us!"

Carl had to suppress a nervous impulse to break out laughing. It was as if there were an echo in the room, as if he were hearing in a dream everything being said. "I can't do that, of course," he said as he desperately tried to gain control over his mind. "None of the gentlemen in this room could defend himself against a cleverly prepared report like this. I can only say that I'm innocent and that, naturally, I'm at the Chief's disposal as far as any kind of . . . well, investigations in order to find an explanation for this."

"Present some arguments, at least," interrupted the minister of defense. "Take up each of the claims one at a time and start analyzing them."

Carl pulled the report toward him and read through it again while the others waited, motionless, in complete silence.

"The report has been bowdlerized, of course?" asked Carl when he looked up again.

"Bowdler— What did you say?" asked the Chief, annoyed.

"Reworked or rewritten so that you can't get an impression of the appearance or formulations of the original document. *Bowdlerized*, an English technical term," explained Ulfsson self-consciously. "Yes, of course it is—that's possibly because it's been translated into Swedish," he continued, immediately regretting his sarcasm. He was suffering along with Carl but couldn't show it.

Carl's thought processes were finally starting to function. "If we take it point by point," he said, "I was supposedly recruited in California. . . . I assume I can speak freely in here, without worrying about classified information?"

"Of course. It's undeniably part of the very nature of this conference," snapped the Chief, his glasses flashing. "Commander Hamilton naturally has complete freedom to touch on anything of importance. Continue!"

"Last year, a little over a year ago," Carl began, and took a deep breath, "Ensigns Steelglove and Lundwall and I attacked three Soviet underwater installations in Swedish territory. The targets were destroyed and the Soviet casualties are certainly unknown to us, but based on Vice Admiral Koskov's information they were no fewer than fifty and no more than three hundred men. This seems to me rather unconventional behavior for a Soviet agent."

"But just imagine if that operation had not occurred in reality, but only in Commander Hamilton's report," objected the Chief, emphasizing each syllable. All five at the other end of the table were staring intently at Carl.

"But we . . ." Carl hesitated as he tried to contemplate the unreasonable, "had contact with the opposition. We could hear them, and at the last base they tried to escape in an underwater vehicle. Ensign Steelglove risked his life when he . . . when he destroyed the target. Lallerstedt here met us when the helicopter landed on Lidingö. We had certain symptoms of the bends, I had a burst eardrum . . . Basically, this Tristan line of reasoning would have to presume that all three of us were working for the Soviet Union. Precisely! But please note the Russians don't say a word here about Operation Big Red. That's because they don't know who or what carried it out. That's why they've been after me, that's why they've been trying to find out whether possibly I got a second medal for bravery. They don't even dare guess, so they don't mention it. They don't know anything about Lundwall or Steelglove. That's where their reasoning falls apart, in my opinion. They haven't got total control over who they name and what logical consequences might result if they singled me out. They are fishing."

"That's a conclusion worth considering, but it may not be totally without objections, Commander Hamilton. We have made a note of it. But try to give it some more thought. I think it's of a certain significance what we come up with during this first, spontaneous interro—conversation," replied the Chief, his jaw clenched.

"Is our 'conversation' being taped?" asked Carl, who had just realized that no one else was making any comments.

"Of course. Now please be kind enough to continue, Commander."

"I was the one who brought Vice Admiral Koskov in," continued Carl, recovering now from his paralysis, "and it was by the skin of our teeth, and it cost three people their lives, including two terrorist hijackers who were after us. The French grabbed another one, who survived, and as far as I know, he's still in prison in France. I confiscated one of their bullets and turned it in, and included that confiscation in my final report. The French, by the way, must have seized both the weapons and the ammunition they found on the hijackers. And the hijackers killed someone else, thinking it was me, with that ammunition. It wasn't a completely harmless operation, and we have the technical evidence. On top of that, the KGB, or more likely the GRU, later tracked down Vice Admiral Koskov and liquidated him here in Sweden. I had no idea where he was, but it must be possible to ascertain who did. I wasn't one of them. By the way, I've had the impression that Koskov's information was invaluable to us and always proved to be accurate."

He paused for a moment, but the other men were implacable. "If we look at the whole of Operation Big Red and imagine it as a Russian plant, then the Russians first sent over a genuine vice admiral, or at least someone who played the role perfectly, then let him supply us with a whole pile of accurate but worthless information, and later, as thanks for his help (which he had probably not agreed to), liquidated him despite our best efforts to protect him. And they had to accept very heavy losses . . ."

The silence continued. "Actually," said Carl, lucidly and very very quietly, "there *is* one sure way to call this bluff."

"How?" the Chief managed to exclaim before several of the others.

"Bring up one of the installations. Examine the wreckage. Send down deep-sea divers and cranes and drag up the whole mess for public examination. There's a slight risk that the Russians have taken the stuff away, but I don't think so, and anyway they can't have removed every trace. If Big Red happened as I reported that it did, you'll find what I told you I found and it's reasonable to assume I'm innocent. It seems to me a simple enough conclusion."

"We will note your opinion. Does Commander Hamilton have any other spontaneous thoughts to convey?" asked the Chief, more gently this time. It seemed as if Carl's last argument had made an impression.

"Yes, it's of lesser importance, but in any case . . . the thief. I had a break-in at my apartment several nights ago, and as I understand it, the fellow had been hired to find out for someone whether I had received a second royal medal. The answer to that question is also the answer to the question whether I participated in Operation Big Red—whose existence the Russians, at any rate, do not doubt." Carl tried to restrain his impatience. "In that respect, our enemy believes me more than my own defense leadership does."

"We'll thank you not to make that type of remark, Commander!" snapped the defense minister.

"I've risked my life for Sweden. I nearly died for Sweden any number of times."

"Yes, yes, we're aware of that. Continue, Hamilton, and let's try to stick to the point," said the Chief with what at least resembled an appeal in his voice.

"All right, forgive me. So . . . the thief. I taped his confession. I photographed him in my apartment with a verification of the date, with a newspaper in his hand, the day's paper—it's classic. He has been positively identified. If you bring him in for interrogation, and if you bring in the man who hired him, who happens to be a custodian in my building, then we'll have definite proof that the Russians want to know whether I was involved in Big Red."

"Anything else?" asked the Chief carefully.

Carl felt once again inwardly desperate, overwhelmed by the dreamlike absurdity of the whole situation. "No," he said at last. "At the moment I can't come up with anything else of crucial importance."

"That's fine, Commander Hamilton. Would you wait outside for a minute while we confer?"

Carl got up, stood at attention, bowed stiffly as if in a courtroom, and went into the secretary's office. An armed guard sat there.

Carl sank down into one of the visitor's chairs with his head in his hands. An armed guard! A single armed guard, and a Swedish one at that, with a safety catch on his weapon according to regulations. This was more a hindrance than a security precaution. If Carl really were a Soviet agent, first the guard would die before he even had a chance to touch his damned safety catch, and then several members of the Swedish defense leadership would follow suit; and it wasn't unlikely that Carl could still make his way out of the building and out of Sweden.

If he were a Soviet agent.

If he were a Soviet agent.

IF HE WERE A SOVIET AGENT!

They must have gone crazy. Ever since his rebellious student days in Clarté he had regarded the Soviet Union as an enemy, not only to socialism all over the world but first and foremost to Sweden. That's why he had joined an elite group when he was called up. That's why the Old Man had been able to recruit him. That's why he had worked like a dog for five years in California with double training. That's why he had risked his life for Sweden.

He had no idea how long he had been waiting when they called him in again. He walked forward to his place and sat down with a brief, inquisitive glance at the defense chief.

The men at the other end of the table sat in ominous silence as the Chief considered how he should begin. Finally he cleared his throat. The others looked down at the blond wood of the tabletop.

"We have now reached certain conclusions, Commander Hamilton," began the Chief with an obvious effort. "Let me say this first. It's our impression that the information must be false. But it's also our impression that we have to get to the bottom of it . . ." This was a rather unfortunate metaphor under the circumstances, and he paused before continuing.

"First, we have an additional question. I'll tell you what it is. According to this Tristan report, you were supposedly recruited by foreign powers while studying in California. Whether the information is false or true, it still means that foreign powers have knowledge of the type of training you underwent in California. How can you explain this?"

Carl thought for a moment. During his five years in California he hadn't even told Tessie what he was doing when he regularly left the University of California in San Diego to go to the Sunset Farm and the secret military part of his work. That's why it had gone the way it did between them.

"I have no explanation for that," he said at last. "It's a problem, I admit. It must come either from the U.S. Navy or from here at headquarters. So far as I know, it can't have any other source. It didn't come from me—that much I know."

"You may have let it slip at some time," Ulfsson appealed. "You were young and inexperienced and you were there for five years, after all."

"No, I'm positive I never did. The love of my life went to hell because I didn't, and I've regretted that ever since. I'm absolutely positive. The information about California—whatever it consists of, because there must be more than what you've shown me—didn't come from me. That's all I can say."

The group fell into a worried silence. Finally the Chief took the floor again. "Then I must advise you of our decision. We have to instigate some form of inquiry, and we have to keep it in-house. You will be interrogated by Lennart Borgström, and the interrogation will begin right after lunch. There is one restriction. You will not—I repeat—will not under any circumstances mention the so-called Operation Big Red while under interrogation. Is that understood?"

"Yes, that's understood."

"What measures would you suggest yourself?"

"What did you say?"

"You're a professional. What measures would you suggest yourself?"

Carl felt the urge to laugh, but he tried to compose himself. "First of all," he began with some effort, "I would suggest an in-depth analysis of the information that came from Vice Admiral Koskov. Second, an examination of the remains of the destroyed Soviet installations at the three known locations in the archipelago. Third, questioning of Ensigns Steelglove and Lundwall. Fourth, a technical examination of the bullet I brought with me from the Air France plane, possibly with supplementary evidence from the French, who must have made their own inquiries and at least have the material on hand. Fifth, interrogation of the thief, with a possible follow-up operation against my custodian. But I would wait with that unless it's absolutely necessary. And sixth—and here I have to admit I am more hesitant—I would suggest a search of my own apartment."

"Well, that's pretty much in line with what we ourselves had proposed," muttered the Chief. "But may I ask why we should wait to follow up the thief's trail and why we shouldn't conduct a search of your home immediately?"

Carl sighed. He had tried to answer logically and professionally, but it obviously sounded like he was evading something.

"Well," he said, "as far as Lars-Erik Sundberg is concerned—that's the custodian—if I understand it correctly, he will have just relayed the message to his Soviet employer that I was *not* involved in Big Red. If you take him, you'll confuse that message, which I think would be a shame. As for the house search, well, good Lord, if I'm a Soviet spy, then in certain respects I differ from other spies. I'm a pro. You'd be looking for the classic things: a radio transmitter hidden in something that looks like a transistor radio, but most importantly codebooks. We know—or we think we know—that Soviet agents use one-time code keys that look like little notepads that you tear off, key after key, no bigger than a postage stamp. In an eighteenth-century apartment with four large rooms and a kitchen, a professional spy could find more than a thousand good hiding places. You would have to destroy my home to be sure you'd checked everything, and even then you wouldn't know for certain, since as you know I also have access to about ten other houses in the Stockholm area with attics and basements and all that. I could hide that kind of equipment anywhere. I wouldn't even need my own shortwave radio—I have access to our own equipment."

"But in *principle* you're not opposed to such a search of your home. In that case, we'll have to bring in the police," muttered the Chief. He didn't seem to have much faith in the project.

"No, of course not. But it will take three or four days and leave the place in terrible shape. If you like I can give you all the combinations to my safes and codes to my locks."

"Can you stay somewhere else meanwhile?" asked the Old Man. It was the first question he had asked during the whole meeting.

"Yes, that's no problem. I assume that I'm free to stay at a hotel, and that I can buy new clothes and some toiletries at the Joint Chiefs' expense. What else can I help with?"

The Chief sighed. "As far as you're concerned, the following: You report to Borgström at once and then the interrogation will begin. It will be up to Borgström to continue until he feels he's done. You are not to return home until given the all-clear. You leave your keys and codes and whatever is needed with Borgström. Is that understood?"

"Yes, it's understood."

When Carl had left, a long silence fell over the Defense Chief's office. The five men sat as if paralyzed, and everyone seemed to be waiting for someone else to speak first. Ulfsson was desperately in need of a cigarette but remembered that he had quit smoking and that this was no moment for weakness, as if the very small issue were connected to the very big one.

Finally the Chief cleared his throat—it was obvious that all the others were waiting for him. "The question is, when should I inform the government? By the way, do the rest of you gentlemen share my impression that this, quite simply, can't be true? Or is that just wishful thinking, which, under the circumstances, is quite understandable?"

His questions hung in the air for a moment.

"We can hardly avoid informing the government." The defense minister was thinking out loud. "The question is just how we ought to present it. We have received information from a friendly power which we have to take seriously, and we have started an investigation and will keep them informed, and so forth."

"Can't we do as Hamilton suggested—send down some divers and examine the Soviet bases? That would be the clincher to the problem as far as Hamilton is concerned. If he's telling the truth, which I'm inclined to believe—and I want to stress that this suggestion was actually his own first spontaneous idea—then the matter is closed." It was the Old Man speaking, and he made an effort to be mild and controlled, though he was raging inside.

"No," said the Chief, "that idea is unfortunately not an option. You will remember that last year the government—well, at least the prime minister—decided that under no circumstances were we to touch the wreckage, since inevitably then the incident would become public: dead Soviet sailors, et cetera, et cetera. He wanted to avoid that at all costs."

Silence fell again over the gathering, but then they all seemed to force themselves to take the initiative at the same time, and during the next quarter of an hour a series of concrete decisions was made.

Samuel Ulfsson would be personally responsible for instigating a new evaluation and analysis of the information from the murdered Vice Admiral Koskov. He would also ask Forensics to conduct a technical examination of the ammunition sample that Carl had brought back from the hijacked Air France plane. They dropped the option of bringing in the American authorities—that would have to wait until other investigations gave results, positive or negative. They also decided to wait on bringing in the thief who had been in Carl's apartment, and on following up with the custodian.

One small practical problem remained, and that was the question of what personnel would be needed to search Hamilton's apartment. Experts were to be found in Säpo, but the idea of bringing them in so early was unpleasant: gossip was rampant at the monkey house on Kungsholmen, and it would be like going directly to *Expressen*. Besides, everyone in the room was convinced that Säpo had far too many direct connections to Moscow, and nobody doubted the information regarding the head of the Russian Bureau, Police Superintendent what's-his-name.

They resolved the problem by requisitioning personnel from the security division and putting them under a pledge of secrecy in relation to their civilian employers.

The meeting was over. The Chief already had a whole stack of urgent things to do, and subordinates were stomping around out in his waiting room.

When Ulfsson got back to his office he found a telephone message that was more than ominous. He was supposed to call a familiar direct line at the American embassy.

Of course, he thought. Even if we're allied secretly only with Britain, the United States is their big brother. They've already received the Tristan report.

He fumbled for his cigarette pack until he remembered, and then he stretched out his hand for the receiver to make his second smoke-free phone call in more than twenty years.

Carl sat in a bare room at a table with microphones in the center, with the head of the security division of the Joint Chiefs and a subordinate sitting across from him, and he was boiling. He hadn't had that much to do with Lennart Borgström, but he definitely did not like the man. Possibly this had something to do with the fact that Borgström had long opposed his being hired in the first place. According to Borgström, Carl was a security risk because of his political past, the same political past that had been an important factor in the Old Man's selecting him. According to Carl, Borgström was invariably stupid. Now he was trying to forget all this and not let himself be provoked or reveal his furious humiliation.

"Well . . ." began C JCS/MS, as he was called in the report, "we have a big job ahead of us, and to start with I shall assume that your position is that you are willing to cooperate?"

Carl nodded, scowling.

"You will have to answer in words, otherwise it won't go on the tape," continued Borgström in the tone one uses when speaking to a recalcitrant child.

"Yes, that is correct," mumbled Carl. "I am prepared to assist with this investigation to the best of my ability."

"And your position is that you are innocent of the charges?" Borgström smiled politely.

Carl had to make an effort to reply. "Yes, that is also correct."

"Then we'll take it from the beginning," continued Borgström, now more businesslike. "And we'll be stopping to change the tape and record the time and date each time. As we begin the questioning of Commander Carl Hamilton, it is June twentieth, the time is twelve-fifteen p.m., and we are in the offices of OP5. Leading the interrogation is Lieutenant Colonel Lennart Borgström. Shall we begin?"

Carl nodded sullenly before he remembered. "Yes, let's start," he muttered, looking down at the little black microphone on the green table.

"Would the Commander first of all explain how he came in contact with Communist teachings? How he, shall we say, was convinced, and then how he attached himself to extremist groups or organizations hostile to the state?"

The interrogator shot out the questions the way you jab a heavy billiard ball across a completely smooth surface, the way you set a hidden force in motion. He looked quite pleased, as if he was enjoying it. His glasses gleamed, there was a drop of sweat on his upper lip, and his face was shiny.

Carl tried to look straight into Borgström's eyes, but the man looked away.

"So . . . may we get started?" asked the interrogator lightly, looking out the window. His assistant watched Carl, mesmerized, as if he couldn't believe what was going on.

"Is the question meant seriously?" asked Carl in a steady but rather high-pitched voice.

"Yes, of course."

The situation was totally grotesque. "Look here, Borgström," Carl began cautiously, "regardless of your own opinions about me and my political background, I am a pro. I have more than six years' military experience, including five years of highly specialized training with emphasis on strategic and tactical intelligence work, and I have six years behind me in the secret service of Sweden." He couldn't make himself continue.

"Yes, we are aware of that, but if the Commander wouldn't mind getting to the point." The interrogator smiled too politely.

Carl had to give it another try. "The point is," he said slowly, then picked up speed, "the point is simply that if there's going to be any meaning to this kind of an interrogation, then it shouldn't be sloppy. You're not interrogating a suspected flower-seller, but a colleague in the business. I explained my political background in my application papers, and there was also an account of it, for the most part correct, in Säk archives long before that. I refuse to waste our precious time on stupid things like this."

"Is the Commander intimating, then, that he no longer embraces Communist teachings?" asked the interrogator in a tone of voice that made Carl think the whole thing was a sadistic game.

"I don't think I'm going to put up with this foolishness. It's an insult not only to me but to the entire organization to start an inter-rogation regarding a serious matter as if we were in a cellar of the secret police in the 1940s. I would remind the Lieutenant Colonel that we are nearing the year 2000 and that we are in the headquarters of the Joint Chiefs of Staff of the Swedish Armed Forces." Carl wiped his mouth and tried again to control his adrenaline.

"Am I to understand by this that the Commander will not coop-erate?" continued Borgström in the same tone of voice.

Carl sighed. Then very quickly he stood up and left. He did not slam the door, but he almost ran down the hallway, taking the stairs instead of the elevator to the ground floor, turning right and then out the front entrance. He was almost to Lidingövägen before he stopped to collect his thoughts.

The oak trees already had thick, light-green foliage, and the sun-shine coming through reminded him of the French Impressionists, that painting about a picnic in the woods. Slowly he shoved his hands deep inside his jacket pockets. His right hand closed around some-thing that felt and looked like a Swiss Army knife but was actually a cross between a burglar's tool and what is called a "concealed weapon" in American police jargon. His left hand closed tightly around a key ring. He remembered that he couldn't go home.

Damn, he thought. Damn it to hell, and they need the keys.

He started to walk back toward the main entrance, but soon he increased his speed and finally ran the whole way up the stairs to Samuel Ulfsson's office on the fifth floor. He dashed right in without knocking and stopped irresolutely in the middle of the room, out of breath.

Ulfsson and the Old Man looked up in surprise.

No one said a word. Carl turned around and closed the door and took a deep breath to control his breathlessness.

"Sit down," said Ulfsson curtly.

Carl pulled up a chair so that all three of them were sitting quite close to each other under the picture of the sergeant and the forced conscription of the farm boy.

"Well?" asked the Old Man.

"Well what?" muttered Carl. "That Borgström is an idiot, and I'll go crazy if I have to sit there with him and go through my whole life. Do you know how he started off? 'Would the Commander please explain how you first came into contact with Communist teachings, how you came to embrace them, and then how you decided to become a traitor to your country?' Something like that. Do I really have to sit there and take shit like that from a blockhead? Is that what you want?"

"We know how you feel," said Ulfsson softly. "But it would be better if you didn't make this any more difficult than it already is."

"Know how I feel?! I wonder. Just imagine if you went in to the Chief and he accused you to your face of being a traitor. Please."

"What do you think we should do? You must have something specific in mind since you burst in like this," said O.M. with a harshness in his voice that in no way matched his feelings.

"Get that baboon off my back. I'm willing to be interrogated, but—"

"But not by him," concluded Ulfsson. "Listen, Hamilton, pull yourself together. O.M. and I are on your side. The accusation could just as well have been directed at us, and in a way it is. We're sitting here dividing up certain projects between us; we have no damned intention of sitting on our rear ends until this matter is over. But you've got to help us—I hope you can realize that."

"What are you planning to do, and how can I help?"

"It's probably not appropriate for me to tell the accused, if you'll pardon the expression, what we're planning to do." Ulfsson gave a crooked smile, uncertain whether it was wise to joke with Hamilton just then. He had never seen him in this state before. "The only thing we ask of you," he continued as he unconsciously looked around for his nonexistent pack of cigarettes, "is to play out the farce with Borgström to the end. Yes, I understand your objections to such a, shall we say, conventional interrogation, but speaking objectively, it's of no real importance. His reports will just collect dust and take up archive space."

"Why can't I go through a real interrogation? And one where I can touch on the most important thing, which would allow me to prove my innocence? How the hell am I supposed to make any sense out of this?"

"The Chief has decided to keep the business within the family," said Ulfsson firmly. "He thinks that the head of the security division is the most suitable person to conduct this questioning. One can question that decision, but it's pointless. Don't take it more seriously than you have to—just get it over with . . ."

They were interrupted by the ringing of a telephone, and Ulfsson got up heavily, something almost like desperation in his eyes. It probably had more to do with being interrupted and being smoke-free than with the gravity of the moment.

"Yes, Ulfsson!" he shouted into the telephone, and then he listened for a while.

"No, Hamilton is here with me. He'll be back in five minutes, and try to understand his distress . . . no, nothing more than that. He'll be there in five minutes."

He slammed down the receiver, annoyed. "Well, you heard for yourself," he said.

"So, it's back to the baboon," concluded Carl, resigned.

"I find the term unfortunate, but speaking objectively, yes!"

Carl nodded, stood up, and left without another word.

The two men in the room exchanged a long look.

"You've got to understand how he feels," said the Old Man.

"Yes, and we'd better get started now, both of us. When do you leave?"

"Sometime tomorrow."

"If you're lucky, you'll be back before the holiday is over."

"Well, probably not until after the holiday. Children and grand-children and all that, and the last apple blossoms. Yes, I have quite a few late varieties that are still in bloom. But it has to be done."

"Yes, this really does have to be done. When are you retiring?"

"In three months. Assuming we can clear up this matter before then."

"Good hunting, O.M."

"Same to you."

Carl stood for ten seconds outside the door before he knocked. He counted on three days of this ordeal, since he assumed that the inter-rogators wouldn't want to spoil their whole Midsummer holiday with something they merely thought was fun rather than really believed in. His calculations were not entirely correct.

He began by turning in his keys and writing down the combination code for the steel door to his inner sanctum and the number combination for the two big weapons cupboards. Then he took off his jacket, hung it on the back of the chair, and sat down again in front of the microphones. Not until then did Borgström say a word.

"All right," he said, "the interrogation begins again at 12:58 p.m., same day and place as before. Would Commander Hamilton please describe how he first came into contact with Communist teachings, how he came to embrace this ideology, and how this led to association with diverse organizations with views hostile to the Swedish state?"

Carl sighed. For the first time since reentering the building he felt relatively under control.

"It started with the Vietnam war," he said. And then he talked without interruption for twenty minutes as the lieutenant colonel followed along in the archive files in front of him, where practically everything was already recorded.

Three

The Old Man was riding in a car with tinted windows that belonged to the U.S. Navy, and he still had an hour to go, through the desert. His mood swung between depression and fury, or at least furious determination.

There were two options.

Either the opposition had succeeded in recruiting Carl here, in California, of all places, in which case they had succeeded with an operation against Sweden that defied all logic. In which case Operation Big Red need never have taken place, and the Soviet Union could do whatever they liked in Sweden, pitting the government and the defense leadership against each other any way they chose. An unimaginable thought.

Or else the Russians had once again succeeded with *maskirovka*— Tristan was a phony defector with correct information as bait and a lot of false information to create confusion later, making for suspicion among the various security and intelligence agencies, an endless hunt for traitors who were not traitors. The real traitors were likely to be among the interrogators and harassers of the innocent.

The Old Man had been an intelligence operative for most of his career, and head of the most secret section of Swedish intelligence for almost thirty years. He belonged to the generation that spoke better German than English, and most of his technical literature was in German. He didn't know much at first hand about the painful British experience of Soviet defectors armed with disinformation. But on the other hand, the Tristan report had led to the conviction of several actual Russian agents in England.

Had the Russians sacrificed a spy ring in England in order to foist off a provocation in Sweden with Hamilton? What would they gain by that? What was important enough for them to pay this price?

Maybe the answer to the mystery could be found out here in the California desert, at the U.S. Naval Weapons Center, which Carl used to refer to as Sunset Farm, surely one of the world's—at least the Western world's—most unusual training centers. Here men like Carl Gustaf Gilbert Hamilton were created, and two more Swedes were here in the final phase of a five-year cycle.

It all depended on these two. Either they were Soviet agents too, or else the GRU didn't even know about them.

The car stopped at a central guardhouse, and O.M. got a very polite American reception from young officers who had him marked down as a colonel and "assistant director of Swedish military intelligence."

He was taken to a guest room where he showered and changed before a young lieutenant escorted him to the man who had had the main responsibility for Carl's training, as well as that of the new ensigns.

Lieutenant Colonel Skip Harrier's office was small and messy, with a roaring air conditioner, empty beer cans flung around, and a desk in chaotic disarray, in spite of the fact that he was expecting a visitor.

O.M. judged Harrier, a gray-haired man with a crew cut, to be just under fifty years old. The left breast of his uniform boasted of what must have been a long, fierce battle career: he had five rows of military honors, and O.M. was secretly relieved that he himself was dressed in civilian clothes.

Harrier greeted him with a bone-crunching American handshake. "Well, Colonel," he began as soon as O.M. had sat down and, astonished, accepted a can of beer. "It's a hell of a situation those motherfucking Russkies have gotten us into, if you don't mind my saying so."

"What do you mean, Colonel?" O.M. was as disturbed by Harrier's choice of words as by the uncanny accuracy of the statement.

"Well, because," continued Harrier, pausing to take a gulp of beer, "well, because if those motherfuckers recruited Carl, then I'm Mickey Mouse. And I might as well say it straight out: *I love that boy.* Do you follow me, Colonel?"

"Yes, I have to admit that I have similar feelings for Commander

Hamilton. But how do you know about it? I'm asking because I wasn't briefed on that."

"Well, we had a couple of knuckleheads from Naval Intelligence and the DIA here yesterday, and they pulled out all this shit from the Brits' Tristan report, and I just told them to go fuck themselves, although I probably expressed it in more diplomatic terms. Plus I gave them my opinion about the likelihood of a Soviet recruiting operation here at Sunset Farm, which is that in that case I would be the recruiter myself. Then I finally told them to go fuck themselves anyway, without the diplomatic terminology."

"I see," said O.M., rather faintly. "And did they? I mean, were they satisfied with that message, or what?"

"Damned if I know. They're probably going to turn San Diego upside down over this, but that's not your problem, and it's not my problem. But damn it, we don't have Russian recruits running around here."

"That's an optimistic outlook."

"Optimistic? Do you know how hard it is to get accepted for this training? Do you have any idea what security checks we run beforehand? Besides, everybody who comes here has to be born for it, and I'll be damned if there are very many who are. Try to imagine smuggling in an infiltrator under those conditions."

"Yes, I see your point. But foreign recruits? I assume there are others besides Swedes here?"

"Only a few. Most of our allies do their own training. And you Swedes selected these boys—I assume that you're going to squeeze the shit out of whoever recruited Carl in Sweden?"

"Well, I don't think we'll do that. I picked him myself."

"Colonel! Congratulations! Then you yourself are a damned KGB-ite or whatever for getting him in here. Congratulations on your discovery! Out of a population of eight million, you found the one Swede who was both a Soviet agent and a genius in our field. A simple matter of probability, dear colleague, as the Englishman said."

"Yes, this is a concern—all those assertions by the English."

"Those damned queers have an intelligence service that has been practically run from Moscow since the 1940s. How the hell can you take their shit seriously?"

"We are skeptical, but the matter has to be investigated. Do the other two Swedes here know what my visit is about?"

"Ix-nay. Carl was the only one the English spilled the beans on. But can't you see that this is a KGB provocation, a typical *maskirovka?*

They obviously want to retaliate for the time Carl wiped them out, don't you think?"

"Carl did what?" asked O.M. He felt himself go cold.

"I don't know a hell of a lot, not as much as I'd like to know. But Carl was here last year and took the boys home for some kind of operation. He didn't tell me anything, but some damned bureaucrat gave me a list to sign, and do you know what was on that list?"

"No."

"Explosive devices, bombs with directional charges for underwater use, our most advanced diving unit—a Mark 15 or whatever they're called—certain types of timers, and a few other items. It's true that I'm just a simple strangler of Communists, but I'm not totally stupid. One look at an atlas is enough. Over there in little Sweden you have a neighbor known for certain underwater activities in your territory, and Carl comes here and borrows two boys who are specialists in his field, and several months later the boys are back and have that faraway look in their eyes—I don't know how to describe it, but they'd been out on their first real job, you could tell that. So damned if the Russians don't have a right to sulk a little and try to do some mischief. Am I right, Colonel?"

"Your thought process shows a great deal of logic, Colonel. Did the boys hint at what they supposedly took part in?"

"No, not a word. And I didn't squeeze anything out of Carl except for a semiadmission that it was something big, but I already knew that from the list of matériel."

"When can I see them?"

"As soon as you like, Colonel. They're sitting locked up in their barracks, waiting for you. I assumed you wanted to see them separately. Don't tell me they're Russian agents too, or I'll laugh myself silly."

"Do you like them too?"

"Yes, they're fine boys, fine boys, Colonel. You seem to have a nice little crop there in Sweden. I guess Swedes aren't numbskulls after all, when it comes down to it."

"How were they? I mean, can you tell me anything else about the boys when they came back?"

"A little out of sorts, nothing serious. I thought it had something to do with deep diving and the compression time or something like that, but that's not my bag. We let them take it easy for a few weeks, a few medical tests, shit like that."

"Any symptoms?"

"Don't ask me, ask the doctors or their medical reports."

"Do they have medical reports?"

"Everyone does here—even I do, damned shriveled-up liver, ha ha."

"May I have a copy of the reports?"

"Certainly, Colonel, of course. I'll fix it while you're interrogating them."

"Is the interrogation room bugged?"

"Not by us. I take care of our internal security, and those moth- erfuckers from Naval intelligence and the other agencies don't run around up here with us. We're secure."

"So I don't need to take the boys out and interrogate them on the prairie?"

"The *desert*, Colonel, we're not on the prairie here. No, you have my word." He paused. "Truly I *love* that boy. If you harm one hair on Carl's head, I'll kick your balls off—do I make myself clear, Colo- nel?"

"Yes, quite. I appreciate your frankness. It's just that I'm not ac- customed to it. If you'll take care of the copies of the medical reports, then we'll meet again after I've talked to the boys, all right?"

"Certainly. How much time do you need, Colonel?"

"Hard to say. At least a day, two at the most."

The Old Man smiled to himself, excessively pleased, when the orderly took him away toward the barracks where Sweden's two new Carl Hamiltons were waiting for him. That's how he pictured them. The alternative would be two Soviet agents.

Joar Lundwall had been sitting alone for two hours in a stuffy room in a vacant barracks, and the only thing he knew was that the head of the covert division of Swedish intelligence was coming for a control discussion. He assumed it was about signing up or not signing up, and he had decided a long time ago. He was going to sign up.

He had devoted practically all his time and interest to his training for the past year, and he was in better condition than he had ever been in his life—strong and optimistic.

The hours of waiting had so little effect on him that he didn't even think about it. He was trained to withstand interrogation for weeks or months or years. He had lived in Alaska with a knife and magnesium fire-starters as his only equipment. He had learned to decipher mes- sages in the middle of hellish noise and under a deadline. He had jumped with a black parachute in the dark at high speeds and from low altitudes over the sea, and he had parachuted from an altitude of thirty thousand feet toward a specific ocean target. And he had learned to maneuver laterally for tens of miles through the atmosphere to the right place. He had mastered more than a hundred weapons and almost as many methods of killing a fellow human being with his bare hands. He was almost twenty-six years old, soon to be a lieutenant in the Swedish coastal artillery, and full of boundless self-confidence. He was looking forward to this meeting with the boss, about whom he knew only that he was an old man with prominent eyebrows that made him look like a horned owl.

That was true. The man who was suddenly standing in the doorway looked like a horned owl.

Joar Lundwall leapt to attention the way the American drills had taught him. He looked straight ahead without speaking and without trying to catch the owl's eye.

The owl walked all the way around him, muttering something inaudible, and then pulled up a chair, which he turned around backward before sitting down. He took out a small cassette recorder from his jacket pocket and wiped the sweat off his forehead. Only then did he speak.

"At ease, Ensign. Pull up a chair and sit down in front of me."

Lundwall obeyed like lightning.

"Hello, Ensign," continued the Old Man.

"Hello, Lieutenant Colonel!" shouted Joar Lundwall.

"All right, maybe we'd better assume a more Swedish manner of talking. Do you speak Swedish or English with your colleague?"

"English, Lieutenant Colonel, sir!" shouted Lundwall with an expressionless face as he stared straight ahead without meeting the Old Man's eyes.

O.M. sighed and straightened his clothes. "I have two questions for you, Joar, and try to relax a little. We're not in the United States now, we're in Sweden, just you and me. Is that understood?"

"Yes, sir! I mean, yes, that's understood," added Lundwall. He felt he might be blushing.

"The first question is whether you intend to seek a position in my department after you've completed your training."

"Affirmative."

"Are you quite certain about that?"

"I was in doubt for a while, sir—pardon me. I was in doubt for a long time, but since last year, I've made up my mind."

"Since Operation Big Red?"

Lundwall hesitated. "Can we talk about that here, sir?"

"Yes. You and I have the same clearance for it, as you know. Since Big Red you've made up your mind, you mean?"

"Yes."

"Why is that?"

"I don't know, I just did." Lundwall hesitated again. "But I think that—"

"Yes? You think . . ?"

"That whoever has been involved in something like that and—how do you say it?—*pulled it off*, managed it successfully, I mean, he's in it for good."

O.M. sat in silence, thoughtfully regarding one of the Defense Ministry's most secret, and truthfully one of its most effective, weapons. At least that had been his own notion when he initiated the experiment, despite opposition from certain segments in the defense leadership, years ago.

A young and obviously well-trained man who looked rather like an athlete—you might have guessed a pole-vaulter, for instance; a young man who might be a Central European or a Russian or a Swede or an American or just about anything, dressed in camouflage fatigues without any kind of identification except for a pair of gold wings with a little symbol in the middle pinned to the right breast of his uniform.

"What kind of thing is that?" asked the Old Man, pointing.

"The gold wings of the Seals, sir—excuse me, I mean Lieutenant Colonel."

"I see. And what's it for?"

"If you pass certain tests in Seal training, then you get one of these. It's eighteen-karat gold."

"What kind of tests?"

"Mostly physical—diving, airborne landing at night, survival exercises, a little of everything. About ten percent of those who go through get the wings."

"I see. Does your colleague have them?"

"Steelglove? Yes, he didn't have any trouble, and then of course Commander Hamilton. But—"

"Yes?"

"It's not part of the uniform—it's an honor. You have the right to wear it on your uniform like other honors."

"Something like the King's medal for bravery?"

"Correct."

O.M. smiled. The boy was twenty-six years old and not even an ensign yet, but he still had more gold on his uniform, and much finer gold, than any living Swedish general. "Do you always go around with those on?"

"No. But . . . well, you might say that I dressed up a little for this meeting."

"So those wings will be decorating the ensign's coast artillery uniform back home in Sweden?"

"Yes, if I wear a uniform."

"Hm. Well, now we've got to move on to something more sinister. Congratulations on the royal medal for bravery, by the way. It was well deserved."

"Thank you, sir!"

"And stop calling me sir."

"Yes, Lieutenant Colonel!"

The Old Man sighed again. "Tell me how you carried out Operation Big Red."

In the beginning, Lundwall thought this was just a matter of a curious digression, and he gave a rather brief report. But the man who looked like an owl assiduously continued, demanding more and more details: about diving depth, compression conditions, and other matters he apparently didn't quite grasp, along with time factors, how the transport from one target to another was managed, the preparations, the exercises, the differences between Swedish and American equipment, the effect of directional charges under water, what signs there were that the targets were manned, and what happened at the last target when Steelglove attacked and destroyed an underwater craft.

It went on for an hour and a half. Now and then the old owl would calmly change the cassette in his tape recorder, and what at first began as unease in Lundwall finally grew into certainty. This was an interrogation, nothing else. The big shots doubted whether the operation had actually occurred, they seemed to suspect that the targets still existed and nothing had been destroyed, or something like that.

After a while Lundwall could restrain himself no longer. "Permission to speak, sir! Excuse me, I mean, may I ask you something?"

"Of course." O.M. gazed searchingly into Lundwall's face. "Of course, go ahead, go ahead and ask."

Lundwall sat in silence for a moment. He needed to collect himself. "Excuse me for being blunt, Lieutenant Colonel. But this is absolute bullshit, what you're doing. We heard them, we killed them, and above all, we very nearly died ourselves. And the intention of this questioning is . . . if you have doubts, isn't it just a matter of examining the remains?"

"How did you almost die? Was it because of the overextended compression time?" asked O.M. coldly, ignoring the question.

"No, not just because of that. By the time we got to the last target the Russians knew that something was going on—it might have been the longwave radio from Kaliningrad or something—and they had automatic emergency buoys that went up with transmitters when they were blown up . . . well, anyway. They were in the middle of trying to escape, and Commander Hamilton set the timer for such a short period that we didn't know how we could get away before it blew up. And then he ordered Steelglove to go after the minisub on its way out—and cut him loose. So we circled around on the surface with the helicopter behind us, and we thought we'd never see Steelglove again."

"Ordered? How did he do that under water?"

"He cut the signal line between us, took Steelglove by the hand, and gave him an RSV and a timer and pointed. That's how orders are given under water; we're trained to understand each other and we practiced a lot beforehand."

O.M. stopped the tape recorder and stood up heavily. He felt old and a little tired, and he had heard enough.

Lundwall leapt to attention as soon as O.M. stood, and O.M. smiled at him as he put out his hand. "Unfortunately, I will have retired by the time Ensign Lundwall enters service in Swedish intelligence," he said. "But if it would give you any pleasure, I can tell you that your immediate superior will be Commander Hamilton."

"Thank you, sir!" shouted Lundwall. He looked incredibly relieved.

O.M. shook his hand and left without another word.

Five minutes later he met Ensign, soon-to-be Lieutenant Åke Steelglove, and he had a hard time hiding his surprise at this amazing giant, a white-blond Finnish-Swedish version of The Hulk, but wearing the same camouflage fatigues and the same gold wings as his more human-looking colleague. Their greetings followed the same American drill pattern.

The central part of Steelglove's tale dealt with how he himself held on to the minisub, attached the explosive charge, set it, and then hung on for a moment more "like a damned flag" to a horizontal bar with one hand as he set the detonation timer with the other, wondering what would happen if he lost his grip—probably he would be sucked into one of the propellers and come out the other side "like KGB Stroganoff"—and how he decided to risk pulling the air tab on his life vest, and so he had popped up to the surface like a cork, which involved several very dangerous moments in itself, but had still been better than the Stroganoff alternative.

O.M. was glad he could finish the two interrogations in a single day, and he hastily said goodbye to the extraordinarily colorful Lieutenant Colonel Skip Harrier.

"Well, Colonel? Are the boys Russian agents?" laughed Harrier. He didn't seem to take this seriously.

"If they are, we're *both* Mickey Mouse," laughed O.M., pleased that for the first time he answered an American like an American.

"And now you're going home to kick some ass?"

"No, I'm going to London."

"I can understand that. Give those queer bastards a real raking over the coals for me, too—just kick the shit out of them."

"Well," said the Old Man cautiously, "I shall have a serious talk, anyway."

Nine hours' difference from the Mojave Desert, and it was two o'clock in the morning. In the biggest military complex on Lidingövägen in Stockholm, almost all the lights were off. The light of dawn was beginning to seep through the venetian blinds in the interrogation room, and the three men were unshaven and red-eyed.

Carl found it incomprehensible that they were trying to wear him down. The effect could only be the opposite; during two years of interrogation training at Sunset Farm, he had gone through times that would have made the Borgström fellow doubt his sanity.

Carl was sure he could withstand most forms of physical torture if the matter was important enough. And whatever could not be withstood—certain chemical substances that knocked out selected parts of the brain's activities, for example—could theoretically be defended against with a stream of babble, though they couldn't practice this realistically. But old-fashioned police interrogations, in which the interrogators constantly searched for little lies and contradictions, as Borgström was doing now, were an intellectual insult.

Carl had long since brought his anger under control. But the longer this amateurish nagging continued, the humiliation itself burned into him more and more.

Borgström had a rather transparent theory. Since Carl was a Communist from his school days, and since Communists were loyal to the Soviet Union, and since pro-Soviet youths were easy prey to recruitment, then Carl must have consciously applied to enter Swedish intelligence because, as a high-school student, he had already been a Soviet agent. Carl obstinately tried to explain the difference between pro-Soviet leftist organizations, an insignificant minority on the Swedish left during his adult life, and the more ordinary left that emphasized anti-imperialism. He was patient and calm.

But Borgström used every such explanatory digression to try to get him to admit that he was opposed to "so-called U.S. imperialism," which he was, even today. In which case, he said, Hamilton must be a supporter of Soviet imperialism.

Carl mentioned again that he had donated two million kronor to the collection drive for Afghans suffering from Soviet aggression. Borgström regarded this merely as a clever maneuver designed to make himself seem innocent.

He mentioned that he had landed the defecting Vice Admiral Koskov. But Borgström regarded this as mere proof that he was helping Soviet intelligence spread disinformation.

He mentioned that he had confronted a group of hijackers on his way home with Koskov and had killed two of them and disarmed the third. The hijacking had not happened by chance, and all reports and testimony from the French commission showed that Koskov and he had been its targets. But Borgström saw this as proof of what extraordinarily clever diversionary tactics the Soviets were prepared to employ. Besides, the so-called hijackers had been armed only with blanks.

Borgström moved on to claim that what Koskov had had to say had led to no concrete or operative results. Carl shook his head and smiled to himself. He couldn't tell Borgström about the very concrete operative results, which had the code name Operation Big Red. But he pointed out that the Russians had tracked down and murdered Koskov, that he himself was clearly in the dark about Koskov's location, and that Koskov was a strange kind of phony defector if the Russians murdered him just as he started to work.

Then Borgström started over again with Carl's leftist background, as if to make him good and tired.

And that's the way the interrogation proceeded, hour after hour, around and around, evening night morning afternoon. On Midsummer Eve Carl was allowed to leave the red building and return home; he was given back his keys.

He found his apartment completely demolished; it looked like the scene of an old-fashioned movie fight. The floor was ripped up in several places, the library fireplace had been taken apart and reduced to a pile of bricks and marble blocks, the kitchen was destroyed, and all his books had been pulled down from the shelves and the bookshelves torn out. His stereo was missing many components and didn't work. A few of his weapons were gone, too. The bathroom was ruined.

He took his toilet articles and went out to the kitchen and washed at the sink, where there was still running water.

If the upcoming election went the way it should, which at the moment seemed difficult to predict, then Peter Sorman would become the only foreign minister in the world with a black belt in karate.

It was a hobby, or rather passion, which his party colleagues (those who knew about it) had never been able to understand. And the colleagues who did not know that Cabinet Secretary Sorman spent several hours a week on peculiar exercises in violence dressed in white pajamas would never have believed it, or would have regarded it as the Conservatives' usual campaign slander.

Sorman was considered ice-cold, a man with absolute control over his emotions and his brain. On the whole, Sorman himself shared this view, and he related it to the concentration and contemplation that were an important part of the Asian martial arts.

He worked hard, harder than most other people, and he was considered cleverer than anyone else—an opinion that he also shared. So it was not unusual on this Midsummer Eve for him to be the last one still at work of all the top-level civil servants at the Foreign Ministry. The foreign minister himself, who was going to retire after the election and turn over his job to Sorman, had been fortunate enough to start his vacation several days ago.

As far as Sorman was concerned, it was doubtful whether he would have any time off for a Midsummer holiday. The children and his two former wives were already waiting on the island, and they had called him three or four times until he switched off his direct line.

In front of him on the rococo desk in his high-ceilinged, handsome old office lay three piles of documents. They were political time bombs which, if not disarmed, could upset the election campaign completely. Everything would be about "scandals" and "affairs" and the government's responsibility or ignorance and so on and so forth. This had been a pattern in recent years, and in numerous cases it was suspected that Säpo had been trying to influence the political climate by leaking information to the press. After the election they would castrate the security service.

It was Säpo's initiative that was suspected behind the latest scandal. A person "who was said to be among the most trusted in the ruling party's inner circle" had been caught by narcotics detectives in possession of cocaine. At home in his own apartment. At a party with political colleagues, journalists, and other politicians present. According to the conservative papers, several top Social Democrats were now suspected of drug offenses, and they reported that this had been going on for years, that these Social Democrats considered themselves outside, or rather above, the law. Many people had been arrested, including a civil servant on the Immigration Board involved with refugee questions.

Two of the people at the party, the civil servant on the Immigration Board and the person who was said to be among the most trusted in the Social Democratic inner circle had also, for largely incomprehensible reasons, been supplied with handpicked policemen as bodyguards six months before. Which naturally made the alleged offense of their host all the more peculiar.

Two matters had still not become public knowledge. The tip to the Stockholm police narcotics squad had come from Säpo. That was why they hadn't hesitated to pull a raid in spite of the partygoers' high social standing. The second factor was worse: the handpicked policemen were gay, and the two Social Democrats to be protected were also gay. Government-requisitioned prostitutes, in other words.

A story like this would be disastrous.

The least task on Sorman's desk—least in terms of volume of paper, anyway—was the second, concerning a possible impending spy affair: the Defense Chief had left a memo about reports originating with British intelligence concerning a member of Säpo and two military officers suspected of being Soviet spies.

It was difficult to judge what kind of political effect this spy "affair" might have. Sorman hoped the information would quickly be proved correct, at least in the case of the Säpo suspect. Then Säpo would have its hands full for a while, and the spy scandal could be used against it when it was time for the slaughtering knife after the election. As for the two military officers, the brass was investigating the matter internally before calling in Säpo. An understandable precaution. In addition, they were taking an exceedingly skeptical stance, especially regarding a certain officer within the most secret division of Swedish intelligence.

Sorman had quite a few documents dealing with Count Hamilton in the second pile on his desk. He had never met the man and didn't even know what he looked like, in spite of the fact that Hamilton, on various occasions, had been the cause of difficult situations for the Foreign Ministry. But Olof Palme had spoken highly of him and even given him a medal. In addition, he was one of the men behind Operation Big Red.

Hamilton and his colleagues had acted in the belief that their orders came from the defense leadership and the government. In actual fact, the now happily retired head of the navy had on his own authority, and almost in desperation, sent out the orders to initiate the destruction. Now the military brass were questioning whether the whole thing had ever taken place. Sorman smiled when he tried to imagine the embarrassment that must be flooding certain sections of the armed forces.

But he himself knew that Operation Big Red had taken place, after discussing it in a confidential conversation with the head of the Soviet government. Sensible decisions had been made on that occasion, marked to a high degree by the spirit of glasnost, you might say. One of the matters that had been agreed upon was absolute, reciprocal discretion.

The thought that Hamilton might be a Soviet agent was naturally improbable. The Soviet casualties in Big Red had clearly been much too great. So the spy crisis had nothing to do with this.

When Sorman took the third pile on his desk into consideration, though, the possibility of a connection arose. This third problem concerned two Swedish doctors who, as of three days ago, were being held prisoner by a group in Lebanon believed to be on the fringes of the PLO. Yasir Arafat had sworn by telephone from Tunis that the PLO had nothing to do with it and promised to put his resources at Sweden's disposal so the hostages could be freed.

But it was more or less a nonbinding promise. Sweden no longer had diplomatic personnel in Lebanon, and the sparsely manned embassy in Damascus couldn't be expected to make expeditions to the Palestinian refugee camps, or wherever else, to start direct negotiations with the PLO.

But with Count Hamilton it was a dramatically different matter, according to the documents. On two occasions he had worked with the PLO's intelligence service in the Middle East. Both occasions had had dramatic results, though the events were described with some measure of diplomatic caution. So Hamilton had a direct and well-developed relationship with the PLO, and right now he was personally in need of a demonstration of the nation's confidence.

If the imprisoned Swedish hostages could be rescued, that would be an extraordinary political asset for the government. It could take credit for a happy ending, and the story would contrast well with the upcoming drug scandal.

It was more than urgent to free the hostages. And Hamilton had nothing to lose.

Carl felt himself in chaos, both inner and outer chaos. His home had been demolished. They had even taken some of his liquor.

He sat in an armchair in the former library—or rather, he sat on the remains of a ripped-up cushion and drank half a tumbler of whiskey straight before realizing he didn't really feel like it.

Nothing could make him pull himself together. He should have been with his mother and relatives in Skåne. Maybe he ought to sign out a car and drive there. Maybe he wasn't allowed to sign out cars anymore; could he rent one? Could you rent a car on Midsummer Eve?

They had told him the apartment would be fixed up by his own department, but they were probably off for the holiday, and then there'd be summer vacation, of course.

He thought about calling Eva-Britt, but pushed the thought aside. Presumably she was working at rounding up youthful Midsummer celebrants, or else she had made holiday arrangements and was out at sea somewhere. It was beautiful weather.

He thought about calling the Old Man but wasn't sure he could do that, given the situation. He was thinking sluggishly, trying to stick to trivial things and small practical problems. He deliberately dropped the empty glass onto the stone floor so it broke, and he stared at the pieces of glass for a while.

When the telephone rang, he didn't want to answer, but few people had his number and it might be her or O.M. He answered on the fifth ring.

A haughty female secretary announced that Cabinet Secretary Sorman was expecting him, and that it was urgent.

He objected feebly that he was tired and unshaven and that it was Midsummer Eve, and when he heard himself he had the feeling that in some way he had short-circuited, that his brain was only functioning on reserve power. He had no resistance. A little later, newly shaven and with a clean shirt, he walked toward Gustavus Adolphus Square and the palace of the Foreign Ministry. He felt as if he was floating down the sidewalk like flotsam.

The guard had him down on a waiting list, and a secretary standing inside the bulletproof glass doors escorted him up to Sorman's office, which was very large and very bright and looked like a picture from a magazine article about how aristocrats lived in the old days.

In front of the ornate desk a chair had been pulled up, and Sorman first stretched out his hand for a firm handshake and then gestured toward the chair like a military man.

"Well," he said, leaning back against the blue velvet of his own chair and putting his fingertips together, "it's time we met. I understand you've had some difficulties these past few days."

A meaningless cliché and an implicit rhetorical question. Carl didn't reply, and when Sorman did not continue, the silence grew in the room, enhanced by the ticking of a grandfather clock.

"Yes," said Carl at last, "I've had a rather difficult time, yes."

"What is it they suspect you of, and do they have anything other than the Tristan report?"

"Is this an interrogation, and can I really talk about those matters here?"

"No, this isn't an interrogation. And I've read the entire Tristan report; we can speak freely."

"Of course they have nothing besides the Tristan report."

"Do you have any idea what it's all about? Does it have something to do with Big Red?"

Carl felt that he was beginning to wake up. He replied very slowly. "I have difficulty understanding how I can sit here and discuss classified information with someone whom I don't even know."

Sorman had not shifted. Now he gave a thin smile and templed his fingers again. "There were four of us in the government group involved with Big Red. I have discussed it with the Russians since then, and internationally the matter is over with. The reason I'm bringing it up now is because that whole chain of events should preclude suspicions of this type against you."

"I'm not allowed to mention the subject with my interrogators. They don't know anything about what you call the chain of events."

"Seems tricky."

"Yes. What's the reason you asked me to come here?"

Sorman didn't answer. Instead he leaned forward, pulled out a desk drawer, took out a diplomatic passport, reached over and placed it in front of Carl on the desk.

"Is that still valid?" asked Carl, neutral but sulky. His own old and very temporary diplomatic passport was not exactly revealing.

"Yes, it's still valid. From the bureaucratic point of view, you're still registered as an assistant naval attaché in Cairo, though it was a short tour of duty. Damned difficult to explain after the fact—certain of Commander Hamilton's actions and deeds, by the way."

Carl felt his annoyance and energy level rising as Sorman avoided getting to the point, whatever it was. He leaned back slightly and imitated Sorman's gesture of putting his fingertips together.

They sat in silence and stared at each other. Then Sorman seemed to decide to get to the point.

"I assume you've read the papers about our kidnapped doctors in Lebanon," he said, the tempo of his speech noticeably faster. "We want them home. The PLO has promised to help—Arafat himself said so on the phone today. Our diplomats in Damascus have limited contacts, but you are said to have had excellent relations with PLO intelligence. Are they still viable?"

"As far as I know, yes."

"Then we want you to travel on our behalf, to try to establish an indirect negotiating contact with the PLO alongside the official diplomatic channels; to try to locate the hostages, or to get us information about who or what group is holding them, and these people's connection with the PLO. The idea is to increase our negotiating leverage."

Carl forced himself not to answer spontaneously; Sorman's deliberately vague manner annoyed him. Instead he chose to win a little time with a question on a matter of form.

"So far as I understand," he began hesitantly, "I am not on duty. While this investigation continues I am technically on leave, but instructed to remain available. And by the way, I haven't read the papers for the last few days because I've been under interrogation—I didn't know anything about these doctors."

"You're on leave from what? From OP5?"

"Yes, naturally from OP5. That's where I work."

"All right, but you're getting this Lebanon assignment from the government—all the better that you're available."

"Do I have the confidence of the government, then?"

"Yes, to the highest degree. We regard the spy accusation as nonsense. We have full confidence in the importance of your contacts in Lebanon and in your ability to get us information that may be of great value."

"Do you think it's the PLO who's kidnapped them? It doesn't sound like them."

"No, you're right, and that's not what we think. But there may be some kind of connection to the PLO, and the more pressure we can put on them, the likelier that they'll put pressure on the kidnappers."

"Yes, but a diplomatic passport won't teach the kidnappers respect; from their point of view, if they can take one more hostage, all the better."

"The idea is not for you to seek out the kidnappers, and as far as your own status and safety are concerned, I don't need to give you specific instructions. You've heard it all before."

"I'm sent out by the government but I represent Sweden only if things go well. If it all goes to hell, then I'm a loose cannon out stirring up trouble and you're not responsible. Correct?"

"That's about it. Any objections?"

"Not at all. As you said, it sounds familiar. But I have a few questions that I don't know whether to ask."

"Then maybe you'd better not. By the way, I don't want you taking any weapons on this trip."

"Is that a direct order or a general wish?"

"If I were your military boss, I'd say it was an order. But, as you know, I'm not your military boss."

Carl stood up and walked straight across the room to the window. Sorman waited at his desk; Carl heard him make a short private call, saying that he would be through very soon and could come to the island within two hours.

Down on Gustavus Adolphus Square there was light traffic and almost no pedestrians. People were already out with families and friends on the islands or in Sörmland and Uppland. It was too late to go to Skåne, Carl thought. Then he turned around and stood leaning against the windowsill while he fired off a battery of questions. Sorman answered lightning-quick.

"If I leave today, when would I get there?"

"Tonight if you take a flight right away."

"First to the embassy in Damascus?"

"Yes. You'll be met at the airport."

"My escort will be going to Lebanon too?"

"Yes, a hotel somewhere in Beirut would be better than Damascus."

"Can I have equipment sent by courier afterward, and if so, when?"

"We can send a special courier tomorrow. What kind of equipment are you talking about?"

"Binoculars, shortwave radio, night-vision glasses, little things like that—I'm not talking about weapons."

"Give me a list now and I'll send all of it by courier tomorrow."

"I'll need a large amount of money, in dollars."

"How much and for what purpose?"

"Hard to say. At least twenty thousand dollars for bribes, and the accounting will come later. Will you issue my tickets?"

"No, pay for them yourself and bill us later."

"That is, if it goes well—otherwise I've been traveling on a private trip?"

"No comment."

"I have only one question more."

Sorman made an inviting gesture with his hand, but Carl hesitated. Sorman's earlier indirect conversational style had made him uncertain.

"If I'm lucky, I'll be able to contact people I know in the PLO. If we're even luckier, it will turn out the way you think and the kidnappers will have some kind of PLO connection. In that case, we'll probably be able to get our doctors out by ourselves, without any special diplomatic game with the embassy people." Carl broke off. He thought he had been fairly successful at ambiguous speaking himself, and he expected some general mumbling in reply.

Instead, Sorman stood up angrily and banged the desktop with the side of his hand in a curiously deliberate way—a gesture that puzzled Carl at first. "Under no circumstances should this involve unnecessary risks." He banged again. "You are there to offer expertise and support for the negotiations, not as some kind of Rambo. Do I make myself clear on this point?"

"Yes, perfectly clear," answered Carl, looking away.

"There can be no misunderstanding on this," continued Sorman with unabated intensity.

"No, none. And what may I offer the PLO if they help us?"

"Sympathy," replied Sorman curtly, dropping into his chair as if a storm had passed.

"Only sympathy?" asked Carl, feigning surprise from his position over by the window. "Won't that seem a little meager?"

"In your circles they say something like . . . how do you say it?"

"*I owe you one*—difficult to translate into Swedish. The problem is, they've already done quite a few favors for me."

"Offer them increased representation at the PLO office in Stockholm—they've been trying to get a visa for a secretary for a long time."

"That's still stingy. I'm going to be asking for important favors."

"Your assignment is hardly to conduct Swedish foreign policy."

"No, of course not, but the better the bargaining chips, the greater the likelihood of cooperation. It's purely practical."

"Then lie, in that case."

"I won't do that."

"I thought that was part of your job."

"Sometimes. Sometimes not, and this time not. As I said, I've gotten help before by making vague promises. My credibility is limited."

"Okay, offer them two things: increased PLO representation, and a renewed Swedish effort in the Nordic Council about trade restrictions with Israel."

"Can I guarantee both?"

"No, but you can make realistic commitments."

"What does that mean?"

"I think you'd better hurry up and catch your plane."

"The first is a specific promise and the second is an unspecified promise?"

"Something like that. You're flying via Berlin, I believe."

"East Berlin?"

"Yes, but the Russians won't fool with you. That affair is literally as well as politically buried."

"It doesn't seem like it, if they're trying to accuse me of espionage."

"How do you know it's them?"

"It couldn't very well be the British."

"When you get back, the whole thing will have blown over. Now

I'd better wish you happy hunting." Sorman picked up Carl's diplomatic passport, walked across the squares of sunshine on the Persian rug and to the door, which he opened with a pointed gesture.

They shook hands. Carl took his passport and stuffed it in his back pocket.

"And when you come back, maybe we could do a couple of karate exercise rounds," smiled Sorman as he let go of Carl's hand.

Carl stiffened. Had Sorman suddenly gone mad? He was amazed.

"Yes, well, you see, I'm very interested in the sport . . . black belt . . . chairman of the national association," explained Sorman, showing a remote hint of uncertainty for the first time.

"I think that would be *very* ill advised." Carl intended to be gentle, but this was absurd. "Before I leave I'll send over my list to the guard down there—the list of the equipment, I mean," he added. He smiled quickly, turned, and left.

Sorman walked thoughtfully back to his desk and gathered up the piles of documents. The whole thing was at least worth a try. Two rescued hostages could offset two minor "affairs" during the campaign. From now on he was off for Midsummer.

But what had Hamilton meant by "very ill advised" about the karate? He was rather offended.

The Old Man was sitting deep in a leather armchair in a smoky room in the vicinity of Trafalgar Square, where he hadn't been in years. In London it was four o'clock in the afternoon, but he was still on California time. He was dead tired and having trouble concentrating and trying not to yawn.

Sir Geoffrey was undeniably the total opposite of Skip Harrier. At first, he had firmly and almost arrogantly rejected any thought that Tristan might have supplied deliberately false information, and it was no good O.M. just showing that he was generally skeptical.

They had spent several hours in the office going through the entire Tristan report with regard to the Swedes, and Sir Geoffrey had not hesitated to invite O.M. to bring Swedish interrogators to England to check things out. But that was neither here nor there. Obviously there weren't mistakes in the British parts of Tristan's information, which could be checked again.

Now Sir Geoffrey, in a calculatedly discreet way, looked at the clock. O.M. had to decide either to take a dramatic step, which he had no authority to do, or else to say thank you and withdraw. It was Friday afternoon, and Sir Geoffrey had already, in passing, hinted at the social obligations (as he put it) that were awaiting him in Chelsea.

"Well, old friend, may I offer you a small one for the road before we part?" he asked suddenly, and the Old Man realized he must have given a start, as if he had been snoozing.

"Yes, thank you, a little whiskey and water on the side, please," he replied mechanically as he took stock.

Sir Geoffrey waved over a waiter and ordered quickly, then turned back to O.M., friendly as ever, the index finger of one hand resting on his cheek, the very picture of sympathetic concern with the unspecified quandary of Swedish intelligence.

"You and I have known each other a long time, Geoffrey, so you'll surely understand when I say that I must go a trifle beyond my instructions," began O.M. carefully; his fatigue was swept away by rising adrenaline.

"Of course, old boy, you have my full support, so 'shoot,' as our American cousins would say. Go ahead and shoot."

"Well, to get to the point—" but the Old Man was interrupted by the waiter holding out the silver tray with his whiskey and water. "It would be simpler if I started by asking whether you've heard anything about one of our young officers, who, for a reason I don't understand, is known as Coq Rouge."

"Of course, for God's sake! Northern Europe's most indiscreet intelligence officer, your own real-life James Bond. Who, if you'll excuse me, would *not* have heard of his exploits? Do you still have him in the company?"

"Oh yes, he's still with us. He's one of the essential ones."

"Good God, man! No wonder you're upset . . . that's really bloody hell." Sir Geoffrey had wiped every trace of polite disinterest from his face. "Go on, by all means, go on! Give me as much as you know, or think you can give me." He interrupted his excitement to order a whiskey for himself.

When the waiter had left again, the Old Man went on. "This very man took part in a big operation against the opposition—one of Sweden's best-kept secrets. This was some time ago: the political complications were detestable, for we almost wound up with an internal war at home, and found ourselves briefly facing an acute threat of foreign war as well." O.M. paused as he sipped his whiskey, and he wondered what dereliction of duty or crime he was committing.

"Go on, old friend, go on. This seems to put several things in a new and somewhat unexpected light." Sir Geoffrey was now intensely interested.

O.M. slowly put down his glass before he continued. "The thing is this," he began hesitantly, "that if the aforementioned Coq Rouge—"

"You mean Hamilton, isn't that his name?" interrupted Sir Geoffrey with an almost malicious smile.

"As I was saying," continued O.M. without concealing a certain annoyance, "if the aforementioned Coq Rouge were a Soviet agent, then our intelligence network would collapse in internal crises. It would take us years to repair the damage. The opposition would be more or less in control in Sweden, and could play us off against the politicians however they liked. In short, chaos. Our greatest defeat since Poltava—yes, I remember that you're interested in military history."

"Poltava, did you say?"

"Yes, neither more nor less."

"Frightfully sorry to hear that, old boy."

"Oh, don't talk like that, Geoffrey, and stop calling me old boy. We Swedes don't like it, and it makes us think that you're a bunch of homosexuals."

"In that case, my good man, I shall try to choose my words more carefully, old boy."

"Fine. We've known each other for twenty years, isn't it something like that?"

"Twenty-one, actually."

"All right, twenty-one then. It's not only that I'm naturally concerned about the consequences of Coq Rouge's alleged treason. It's that I have rather substantial proof that the allegation cannot be true." He took a deep breath. "Therefore, I want this Tristan broken in some way."

"Rather sticky, actually. He's been given asylum, amnesty, a new identity, pension, the works. Enjoying the fruits of an entire nation's gratitude, all that. All but inviolable, speaking bureaucratically. You must come up with something concrete. Otherwise I'm afraid that even twenty-one years is not enough."

"You need more details?"

"Mmm."

"It would be the worst breach of my pledge of silence ever."

"Alas, you can't even get the Victoria Cross for that. But actions against Tristan can't be carried out unless you convince us."

"What do you mean, 'us'?"

"Me."

"To you orally? No written report that could be diverted?"

"You know a promise like that is ridiculous. But naturally you have my word of honor. Shall we take a little walk, then?"

They rose and left without paying, for it was against club rules to rustle something as vulgar as banknotes among the leather armchairs and the green reading lamps and brass fixtures. Monthly bills arrived discreetly yet punctually, even to MI5's and MI6's secret addresses.

It was pouring rain, and the weather forecast was pessimistic enough to threaten, as usual, the Wimbledon tennis matches.

The Old Man knew enough about London to have brought his own umbrella, and the two umbrellas created a joint shield against observation as well as directional microphones, and every time they were within yards of anyone else, they stopped their conversation.

It took the Old Man two and a half hours at a slow promenade pace to convince his old friend.

Coq Rouge had accompanied a Soviet defector to Sweden, a certain Gennady Alexandrovich Koskov—who later "disappeared" mysteriously, according to vague Russian newspaper reports. A large section of the Koskov report had been turned over to British intelligence in slightly altered form: it had been the source for Sweden's many goodies offered in trade during the past few years. It wasn't the usual brilliant shake-up, as the Swedes had perhaps implied at the time. A single operation had produced the whole catch, and Coq Rouge had carried it out.

Further, Koskov's knowledge had, by indirect routes, led to Operation Big Red. Three underwater installations in Swedish territory had been blown up. Soviet casualties were somewhere between fifty and three hundred. Even the most cautious estimate clearly indicated a catastrophe.

What political consequences all this would have, in the age of glasnost, could only be guessed at. But under any circumstances, the Soviets would want, first, to ensure that the incident was never publicized, and second, to transform Swedish intelligence, where this information was housed, into a tangle of suspicions.

If one now looked at Tristan from this perspective, what had he actually sold? Three small fry in his own little agent network and two GRU colleagues at Aeroflot in London. Granted. But this was completely insignificant in comparison with the consequences of Tristan's information in Sweden, if it was correct.

At this point the Old Man thought perhaps Sir Geoffrey was reluctantly beginning to come over to his side.

"What were you hinting at as proof?" the Englishman asked at last, after they had walked for a long time in silence.

"Isn't what I've told you enough?"

"Brilliant analysis, convincing in itself, but I'd like proof as well. Just give me one more straw and you'll break the camel's back."

"All right," sighed O.M. "The purely physical evidence is of a medical nature. Coq Rouge was not alone in the operation—there were two others who dived along with him."

"By Jupiter! If you have more of those James Bonds, you ought to go into the film business."

"British humor sometimes seems to me hard to comprehend. Well, they dived under difficult circumstances and violated quite a few security regulations and so forth; in fact, all three risked their lives. The medical reports are available. The Russians have learned that Coq Rouge participated—"

"That doesn't seem very hard to figure out, considering Hamilton's merits, does it?"

"Don't interrupt me, old boy."

"You said 'old boy.' "

"Yes, to show my irritation. So, the Russians guessed right about Coq Rouge, but they didn't know about the other two or the medical reports. Their objective through Tristan was to make us, and the politicians, doubt it had all happened."

"You can never know exactly what their objectives are. But it seems clear that you were the targets of this *maskirovka*, not us. Confound it all!"

"Why confound it?"

"Because we've been through this before. We've had a stream of these phony defectors, and they've been confusing the issues for close to fifteen years. Always the same pattern. And now we've fallen for it again! Well, I've got to go home. Can you find your hotel, and are you staying in London for a few days?"

"Yes, as long as necessary. Early tomorrow morning at your office?"

"Unfortunately, yes. The way the weather is, my social plans will be rained out. We shall, of course, crack this, and the opposition will once and for all learn to keep their hands off our family relationship. Good night, old boy, sleep well."

"Good night yourself, old boy, and you can be sure I'll sleep well. Eight hours' time difference, you know, and damned uncomfortable in tourist class on one of those American carriers where you're treated like a baboon."

"Good Lord, are you flying with the Americans? And why not first class, at our age?"

"An old prejudice, apparently. I guess I'm old-fashioned—I keep thinking you're noticed less in tourist class. Even though it's all computerized nowadays. But I'll never fly an American carrier again—I promise you that. We'll see each other tomorrow?"

"Yes, shall we say eight o'clock? No, let's say ten. Either way we're not about to let this cuckoo bird go until we've squeezed out the whole story."

Everything swam before the Old Man's eyes as he watched gentlemanly Sir Geoffrey, impeccable to the point of parody, vanish in the rain.

He thought he had never been so tired in his life. And he had never put more on the line. He had spilled classified information—that could be called espionage, and in a way it was—in order to save his own hide.

But O.M. was a practical man, and he differentiated, now as always, between God's law and human decrees.

Ten minutes later he was sound asleep, half undressed on top of his hotel bed.

Four

It was Monday morning after a Midsummer holiday weekend that should have been the best one Samuel Ulfsson had enjoyed in many years. The weather had been uninterruptedly glorious; seventy-seven degrees for three days in a row, and the whole family together with children and grandchildren—their own little Midsummer pole, croquet on the lawn, misty carafes of gold and red juices, chives and pickled herring with Danish aquavit, and bumblebees buzzing around the hammock.

Nevertheless, it had been terrible from beginning to end. Sam had concealed his bad mood by saying it was so hard to get used to not smoking.

The first letter he opened at his office was the one that came by courier from the monkey house on Kungsholmen; as soon as he saw it he smelled disaster, since it was so thin that the message had to be brief, and a brief message by special courier could only mean trouble.

He was right.

Police Superintendent Stig Larsson, who had worked for more than thirty years in Säpo and who during the past ten years had been head of its so-called Russian Bureau, had been under interrogation practically nonstop for the entire Midsummer holiday, while at the same time they turned his home upside down. On Midsummer Day, the search of his house had brought results. Behind the bathroom medicine cabinet they had found a little homemade hiding place containing small objects that without doubt were disposable code keys.

Two hours later Larsson confessed. For ten years he had been supplying information to Soviet military intelligence, the GRU. At first the information and documents had concerned only his own area of operation—that is, Säpo's hunt for Soviet threats to national security within Sweden. He was refusing to tell them how and where the code keys were used, saying that he didn't want other, innocent people to get in trouble.

He had two weeks left to retirement. The Russians' code name for him had evidently been Peacock.

At the moment, they were exploring whether he would consider cooperating in exchange for immunity.

That surprised Ulfsson. It was a method that was not unusual in other countries—the exposed traitor escaping legal consequences in return for full cooperation—but would the Swedish government agree to it?

What would happen, for instance, if news of the bargain leaked? Which it was bound to do sooner or later, when the news spread to a larger circle at the monkey house. How would the government explain it, especially in an election year, when the moderates would blow their horns about political appeasement of the Big Neighbor to the east?

Well, that was the politicians' problem.

The real worry was that Tristan had proved correct in one very important aspect.

The Old Man called from Heathrow to report briefly that they should be able to clear up the matter quickly as soon as he was home. He sounded in a good mood, though it was hard to know why.

Borgström's report on the interrogation of Carl was, for the time being, nothing to worry about. It had produced nothing, and neither had the overinterpreting, overenthusiastic analysis that came with it. Borgström, as expected, had concluded that Carl Hamilton had been a Soviet spy ever since he was a teenager, that he had taken the well-known route of leftist infiltrators beginning fifteen years before, that he had deliberately applied for secret assignments along the familiar pattern, and so on.

But Tristan claimed that Carl had been recruited in California, which was long after the Old Man had hired him. And besides, Borgström knew nothing about Operation Big Red.

The question now was how they should proceed with the still unsuspecting Osprey, head of OP4, Colonel Michael Rindström.

Ulfsson was more and more certain that his summer was going to be one of excruciating work. He hadn't even dared mention it at home, where his wife was making plans for a vacation in Brindisi with a side trip to Venice.

The simplest thing right now, and the officially correct thing, was to shift the decision to the Defense Chief. As soon as he heard O.M.'s first report, it would be time to go to the Chief. He tidied up all the meaningless records confiscated from Carl Hamilton's home, fastened them into an A4 folder along with three hundred pages from Borgström's interrogation and analysis, and was just about to tell his secretary to lock up the folder when she knocked on the door herself. She only had a week left until vacation, and somehow you could see it in her face.

"Are you really busy?" she asked in a tone that suggested he should answer yes.

"That depends on what it's about. Would you lock up this folder for me? What's up?" he asked in return, easily, as if he had time for anything.

"It's some madman downstairs with the guard who insists on speaking with the 'IB chief' and absolutely no one else. Isn't that what special missions used to be called?"

"Well yes, some people still call it that. What does he want?"

"Apparently he won't say, but he claims it has something to do with the Soviet Union."

"The Soviet Union?"

"Yes."

"What about it?"

"That's what he won't say until he sees the IB chief, and I assume that you're the closest thing."

"Go down and let him in if he can identify himself, and ask Larsson or one of the others in there to sit outside in your office while he's here."

"Shall we tape the conversation?"

"No, let's see what it's about first."

Ten minutes later a man who introduced himself as Gunwald Larsson sat down in a chair across from the head of Sweden's intelligence service. And if the head of Swedish intelligence had been at all familiar with detective novels, which he wasn't, this well-known name would have surprised him, and the conversation might have had a less peculiar start.

"It really *is* my name, you know," the stout man assured him. He looked as if he had been doing heavy physical labor for most of his life.

"Oh yes . . . ?" Ulfsson said inquiringly.

"I mean, it's not a joke or anything," continued the man, who could see he would have to explain further.

"No, why would it be?" asked Ulfsson, feeling a little sheepish.

"I mean, because of Sjöwall and Wahlöö."

"What are you talking about? Who was it you wanted to see?"

"You know, the detective writers," continued the fat man, embarrassed.

"Detective writers?"

"Yes, the ones with Gunwald Larsson."

"Do you have something to do with them?"

"No, that's what I mean—I don't. But my name really is Gunwald Larsson," replied the fat man with growing nervous irritation.

"Yes, I believe you. But what does that have to . . . What was it you said those detective writers were called?"

"Sjöwall and Wahlöö. Maj Sjöwall and Per Wahlöö, but Per Wahlöö is dead."

"Dead?"

"Yes."

"But that wasn't what you wanted to tell me, was it?"

"No, of course not. I thought everyone knew that."

"I'm sorry, but *I* don't, anyway."

"Well then, that explains it."

"Explains what?"

"That you didn't react to my name. I have the same name as one of their characters, a criminal detective. But it's my real name."

"I see. Well, as I said, I have no reason to doubt it. You identified yourself when you came in downstairs?"

"Yes, of course. I'm Gunwald Larsson and I'm a director of the BPA Construction Company."

"Well, all right. What's this all about?"

"I want to see the IB chief."

"I see. Why?"

"I want to tell him in person."

"He's on his way home from London right now. Isn't there any way I can be of service, since we're sitting here?"

"Who are you?"

"I'm the head of this department. What you call IB—that's what it was called before—comes under me."

"So you're head of the whole shebang?"

"You might say that. But if we could try to get to the point now?"

"To the point?"

"Yes, get to the point. What was it you wanted to say? Was it something about the Soviet Union?" Ulfsson could feel his patience wearing thin, and he expected nothing other than the usual nuttiness, like the crazy telephone calls from more or less intoxicated citizens who came up with brilliant, foolproof methods for catching minisubmarines. And the man facing him didn't seem very intelligent.

The visitor hesitated for a long time before continuing, as if he was embarrassed. "Yes, well . . . I don't know whether this is anything important . . ." he began haltingly, but he had to continue because Ulfsson had decided not to prolong this foolish conversation with more questions. "And I'm a Social Democrat and always have been . . . and I had a lot to do with IB before, when I was in the construction business . . . Communists and things like that. Well, we've never had much respect for Säpo in the movement, so I thought—"

The man stopped short, and Ulfsson thought it might have something to do with his own visibly negative attitude. He decided to be friendlier so the meeting could end sooner. "Yes, well," he said, "we aren't involved in those kinds of activity anymore. If it's about Communists in the construction business, I'm probably not the right person to listen to your worries. But what is it really all about?"

"Well, um, I've just come back from Moscow. We've had a delegation there planning a lot of construction in the northern suburbs. And, well . . . as I said, I don't know whether this will interest you, but I thought that I wasn't going to go to Säpo, at any rate. I don't trust them. Do you?"

"I won't comment on that. Were you there as part of a BPA delegation?"

"Yes, for four days."

"So what happened? Did something unpleasant happen?"

"I don't know how to put this. No, it wasn't directly unpleasant."

"Then spit it out so we can hear what it is," said Ulfsson, impatient, and the other man cringed and squirmed in his chair. Ulfsson regretted his outburst at once. "Go ahead and tell me, tell me in your own words and I won't interrupt you. What happened?" he asked, his voice soothing.

The other man screwed up his courage before getting going. "Well, it's like this, but as I said, I don't know whether this is something that will interest you . . ."

Ulfsson clenched his teeth so as not to interrupt.

"But at any rate. The day before yesterday we were out in the Babushkin and Medvedkovo districts to plan some new buildings that we may sign a contract on next week. Well, at any rate. The trip ended at the Medvedkovo subway station, and we stood there quite a while waiting for a car—it would actually have been easier to take the subway itself, since it works in Moscow. Damn nice subway they have. So there we stood waiting, and it was raining too, and I was thinking that this was a hell of a way to spend Midsummer. But at any rate, a car pulled up across the street, a Volga with curtains in the back window, so I thought it was for us at first, but it wasn't. And it was a narrow street, so it wasn't so far away, and the guy who got out—on our side that is, he wasn't driving but was sitting next to the driver's seat. Well, the first thing I noticed was that when he stumbled—he stumbled a little as he was getting out of the car—was that he swore in Swedish. And then it was a girl who was driving. She looked like a hooker and she probably wasn't completely sober either. And he turned toward us—it almost looked as if he was about to go the wrong way because it turned out that they went into the building across the street. Yes, I recognized him. There's no doubt at all. As I said, I don't know whether this has any significance for you—maybe you already know all about it, but I didn't want to go to Säpo, at any rate." The man paused and started to rummage around for something in his wallet.

Ulfsson's irritation had vanished. "Who was it whom you recognized?" he asked softly in an unconsciously lowered voice so that he was almost whispering.

"Yes, well, it was Stig Sandström. You know, the spy. And I'm one hundred percent positive," replied the other man, who at the same time found what he was looking for. It looked like a couple of photographs.

"That's not bad. That's really not bad. What do you have there?"

"Well, you see, when the girl came out I took a picture."

"When the girl came out?"

"Yes, she wasn't the one who lived there. He did. She got in the car and took off. So I took a picture when she came back out."

"Do you think she saw you?"

"No, I don't think so. I shot from the hip, sort of, and it turned out a little blurry too. But later I took another picture because I saw the room where the light was turned on up there, and then I caught a glimpse of Sandström. I put an *x* next to his window."

The man hesitantly pushed the pictures over to Ulfsson. They were in color, of typical tourist snapshot quality. The first showed a young woman in her thirties heading toward a black Volga that partially obscured her. The other showed an entire building; the uppermost corner window was marked *x* with a ballpoint pen.

Mouna was somewhere up on the flat roof, rigging up an antenna in the middle of the laundry hanging out to dry. Carl had just finished adjusting the curtains so that the binoculars on the tripod could be aimed out through an open window without being seen from the spot he was watching. Everything had proceeded quickly and smoothly as soon as he had given the slip to the diplomats in Damascus.

He was munching on little pieces of cucumber and the mashed-chickpea paste called hummus, along with pieces of pita bread and olive oil on the side. It was, he now realized, the first food he had had in almost twenty-four hours.

He felt a kind of inner peace. He forced himself not to speculate why or allow himself to be surprised. No doubt it was simply that he had got going, that he was doing his job, and that the job was far away from Lieutenant Colonel Lennart Borgström.

The room was cleared of almost everything. In one corner a stack of mattresses lay piled on the stone floor. Near the window stood a table and two chairs. On the long wall opposite hung a machine-woven tapestry with motifs depicting an Arab or Persian rider on a thoroughbred at full gallop in the desert beneath the exaggerated gleam of a crescent moon. On one of the short walls were a couple of color photographs in gold frames; one was of Yasir Arafat, and the other, considering the black crepe around the frame, was evidently Abu Jihad, whom the Israelis had murdered in Tunis several years ago. That was all, except for a water faucet and sink on the other short wall.

A family of ten usually lived here but he knew nothing about how or where they had been moved. It didn't bother him either, because they had been compensated generously with plenty of the Swedish government's crisp clean dollars. Without a receipt, he mused.

Everything had been well organized, far beyond his most optimistic expectations. Rashid Husseini had had the same telephone number and had remembered the significance of the number sixteen when Carl had called him from Berlin. The number sixteen meant that he was coming to Beirut, and when he arrived thirty-six hours later, he was expected, and he went to the same hotel as last time and was picked up less than twenty minutes later.

The PLO knew where the kidnapped doctors were being held; at least Jihaz ar Rased, its intelligence service, knew. That's why he was now no more than seventy yards away from his goal less than a day after his first meeting with Rashid Husseini, the man who usually called himself Michel—perhaps as a concession to his Christian Lebanese mother, perhaps to seem less Palestinian behind the façade of his law office.

Carl had urgently requested Mouna as his operative partner, not so much because he knew her, nor because she was beautiful though her face was disfigured by burns, but because he had an unshakable faith in her professionalism. Her rank within Jihaz ar Rased was comparable to lieutenant colonel. Few PLO officers in operative duty achieved such a high rank before they were thirty, and certainly even fewer who were women. Her peers obviously had the same opinion of her capabilities.

"It's all fixed, hidden under the laundry, but we'll probably have to move the laundry around little by little," she reported when she came back from the roof and almost casually inspected Carl's setup with the binoculars before sitting down. More thoughtful than hungry, she tore off a piece of pita bread and scooped up some hummus.

Carl nodded silently, snapped on the transmitter, typed in a call signal on the keyboard, corrected a spelling mistake, and pressed the Send button.

"Are you transmitting in plain Swedish?" she asked in surprise, her mouth full of food.

"No, not because I think it makes much difference with Swedish in these parts, but the computer transforms the plain Swedish into code and then we transmit both high-speed transmission and pulse," replied Carl, his eyes to the binoculars.

"How does the receiver know which code you're using?" she asked with neither curiosity nor insinuation in her voice; it might have sounded like an objection.

"The receiver's computer transforms the code into plain Swedish, and then it appears on the counterpart screen up there. If they're awake we ought to have an answer within thirty seconds," replied Carl without taking his face from the binoculars.

"Swedish manufacture?" she asked in the same expressionless voice as before.

"Yes, I think so. It's called RA-195. It's quite common among specialist units in our armed forces."

"Range?"

"Halfway around the world under the most favorable conditions."

"Between us and Tunis?"

"Between you and Arafat, you mean? No problem at all."

"Can you leave it behind when you go home?"

"Leave classified Swedish defense matériel in the hands of Communist terrorists?"

"Don't be ridiculous."

"Yes, if I can get the other unit out of the Swedish embassy in Damascus, and if you can pick it up there."

"That can be arranged."

"Let's see how this goes first."

"Do you see anything?"

"Caught a glimpse of several people on the ground floor. Nothing upstairs—the curtains are drawn."

"That's where they are."

"You know that?"

"Yes, we know that."

The radio transmitter beeped and a short text appeared on the screen. First embassy secretary Ingemar Stjernstedt at the Swedish embassy in Damascus reported that reception conditions were completely satisfactory and that he would continue to await reports.

Carl wrote a short report:

Position on the outskirts of Ein el Hilweh outside Saida. Observation post established. Distance to the hostages and kidnappers: 70 yards. No sign of the hostages. Awaiting definite sighting. Will transmit every other hour until further notice.

Carl pushed the Transmit button, sending a series of coded little beeps out into space which, within seconds, would appear as plain Swedish words at the embassy in Damascus.

"What did you say?" she asked.

"That I'm in place and have the target in sight and await confirmation that it's the correct one."

"Will they believe that?"

"I don't know. It might sound too good to be true, and maybe it is; we'll see."

"Do they know who you're working with?"

"No, except that it's the PLO."

A new message appeared on the screen:

Do not take action of any kind. Report when definite confirmation is made.

"What did they say?" wondered Mouna.

"That I'm supposed to take it easy and that I should tell them if I see anything interesting."

"That sounds reasonable. They're negotiating in Beirut, you know."

"Yes, how's it going?"

"I don't know."

"Fill me in."

Carl leaned over to the binoculars again and smoothed out a stack of papers in front of him so he could take notes while he waited for Mouna to report. Until now they had been busy with practical questions and getting set up. Carl didn't know much about the actual situation, except that both the hostages and the kidnappers were supposed to be in the building over there, a building set higher up and apart from surrounding ones, so it would be difficult to approach without being seen.

Mouna spoke calmly and to the point, and she seemed completely candid, even including details that were not very flattering to the PLO.

Two cousins, Taheer and Abdel Kader al Latif, were responsible for the kidnapping. The four others in the building were their relatives or friends. Technically, both men were under PLO indictment, because two months ago it had been discovered that they had participated in a conspiracy against some of Arafat's military personnel; they had been called to Tunis to stand trial at PLO headquarters and were expected to go voluntarily. Instead, obviously, they were trying to obtain escape funds in the common Lebanese manner: kidnapping under the guise of some political motive or other.

Now they were risking a death sentence if they couldn't escape. They realized this, of course, and that's what was complicating the negotiations. Naturally, they wanted money, and they wanted some form of guarantee that they might get out of the Middle East. Yet whether they received such a guarantee or not, they would not be able to escape.

The situation was also complicated by the fact that the PLO's negotiator in Beirut, Salah Salah, was related to Taheer al Latif. Maybe that was why he tried to spread the idea that the Shiite Moslem Hezbollah, Lebanon's busiest kidnapping organization at the moment, was behind it all. The Hezbollah, furious because they either knew or understood who the kidnappers really were, threatened to expose how things stood, either to the Swedes or to a Western journalist. Arafat, also furious, gave Salah Salah direct orders to assure the Swedes that the PLO had the situation under control, and rejected an offer from Jihaz ar Rased to storm the building where the kidnappers lived. The Swedish hostages must not be harmed; Arafat had promised that to the Swedish government.

So, depending on your political sympathies or antipathies, you might regard the people responsible for the kidnapping as either PLO or not PLO.

Dusk fell quickly as Mouna finished her background report.

Carl rummaged around in one of his small, heavy suitcases on the floor, looking for more equipment. He wondered whether he should mention the subject they would have to talk about sooner or later, now that they would be spending days together in the same room.

She didn't ask any questions. She must have seen night-vision glasses and image enhancers before. He slid a pair of goggles for night vision toward her.

"Try them out. The focus button is in the middle of the aperture, same as binoculars," he said as he screwed on the big image enhancer above the tripod.

"Syrian customs. You didn't come by taxi, did you?" she asked curtly as she put on the goggles.

"Diplomatic passport—no customs. And a taxi is better than official transportation. I assume we'd prefer not to have any more kidnapped Swedes."

"Interesting equipment. We'd like you to have difficulties—for security reasons, if nothing else—in taking them home. The one you're looking at now on the ground floor is Taheer himself."

"The bald one?"

"Mm-hm. The guy in the background could be one of his cousins. So, what do you say?"

"You want to do business?"

"We always do business, as you know."

"I need new equipment—we can make a trade. They're going to eat, eh? Do they always eat at the same time?"

"Not always, but about this time, when dusk falls, seems reasonable. Then they stand guard outside in some way; they can't do that during the day."

"So they eat when it gets dark and, in the best case, they all are on the ground floor except for the one who stands guard outside?"

"In the best case, yes. One of them is on his way outside. Do you see what he has in his hand or under his jacket?"

"I saw the barrel, at any rate. An AK-47 with the butt folded up, I suppose."

They stared for a moment through the darkness, which wasn't dark for them. One of the men slowly opened the outer door and stood for a minute in the doorway before he said something to those inside and carefully closed the door behind him. He pulled the jacket hiding the weapon tighter around him and quietly began to walk around the building.

They both automatically noted the time and the individual.

"Shall we continue our business?" asked Mouna when the guard had disappeared around a corner and the others seemed to be eating, all together, in a room near the main entrance.

"Well," said Carl after he had finished his notes, "I'll need to borrow three things. Later I'll leave the whole mess behind, and you'll also get the other transmitter in Damascus if we can arrange it."

"What three things?" she asked curtly.

"Two easy and one difficult. A knife with a long blade of the bayonet type, and a knife with a short and preferably double-edged blade, the usual commando type."

"Those are the easy ones?"

"Yes, and now comes the difficult one. A pistol, preferably automatic and with night vision and definitely with a silencer. Can you arrange it?"

She sat in silence for a moment, and when she answered she didn't hide her sarcasm. "Is there a particular brand or a particular type that you prefer?"

"Yes," replied Carl, ignoring the sarcasm. "If I get to choose, then make it a Heckler and Koch MP5, the compact model, with a silencer and night-aiming device. How are your supplies?"

"The Germans aren't too keen on doing business with us. What's the most important?"

"That the weapon is silent, if I have to choose, but I have nothing against other brands."

"We have the absolutely strictest orders not to endanger the hostages."

"We who?"

"You and me, for example."

"I represent the kingdom of Sweden and you the republic of Palestine, don't we?"

"No, we are the ones responsible for military efforts here."

"That depends on how things develop. Better for us to prepare for any eventualities, don't you think? Better that I get the blame if everything goes to hell; then it would be us, Sweden, who's embarrassed and not you."

"But we'll get the blame."

"Not if I survive. Not if I die, either. It will be either one or the other, and if things go well, I'll give you the credit and you'll get some nice PR and everyone will be satisfied."

"You're in military intelligence now?"

"Yes. All that with Säpo is a long time ago, thank God."

"Thank God for what?"

"That I have nothing to do with them anymore."

"Some operations department within military intelligence?"

"Mm-hm."

"Rank?"

"Commander. It's the naval equivalent of major."

"He's coming back around the other corner now, do you see him? How long did it take? By the way, in that case, I'm your superior."

"He was gone for three minutes and seven seconds. Yes, you have a higher rank than I do, but we're not under the same command."

"Do you have the right to make your own decisions?"

"Within reasonable limits. For example, I have some right to negotiate politically, but I already told that to Rashid in Beirut. He seems to be taking up his position outside the main entrance now."

"Yes, he's opening the door and probably telling them that everything seems okay. When they're done eating, someone will probably change places with him. What did you tell Rashid? What business is there on the political level?"

"You help us. We get the hostages out. You get a new representative at the PLO office in Stockholm; yes, there've been difficulties about that. You get several vague promises of expanded political support from Sweden."

"Can we rely on these promises?"

"The first one, yes; presumably not the others."

"What did Rashid think of it?"

"Well, what the hell was he supposed to think? From your point of view the problem is that our diplomats already have grasped that you have something to do with all this. You have to help us, and we—our politicians, that is—don't have to offer much."

"Can we get help from you sometime? I mean, from the military?"

"That depends on what you ask for and whom you ask. If you ask me and it's something more or less legal, then yes, of course."

"They're changing places now. Did you get the time?"

"Yes. The cousins themselves don't stand guard, if my guess is right."

"No, they regard themselves as bosses. It's the four others who alternate between the prisoners upstairs and standing guard outside. Do you have influence in your organization?"

"I did until recently. Right now things aren't so good. But we'll see how it goes."

"I'll try to get your weapon if you promise me something."

"I'll promise when I see the weapon—it all depends on that, you see."

"What do you mean?"

"A silent weapon with night vision means two of them taken out before the others even know what's going on."

"One guard and the one who comes out after a shot to see what's happening?"

"Yes, that's one scenario. Without the night vision and the silencer, totally different arithmetic and totally different promises."

"I'll wait until tomorrow morning to put in the order. Something like that we'll probably have to get from up in Beirut, by the way."

"Might take time?"

"Yes."

"How long?"

"Twenty-four hours."

"Okay. Either the negotiations go well or else they'll take a long time. Is there any risk that they'll move the hostages?"

"No, I don't think so."

"Why not?"

"Because they don't want to get killed. If they think we know where they are, they won't stick their noses out unnecessarily. If they don't think we know where they are, they won't want to be discovered."

"You're good, Mouna, very good. Even at torturing friends."

Silence fell in the room. Now the terrible subject hung in the air between them. It was completely dark.

She moved over next to him, cautiously, pulling up her chair in continued silence. Then she unbuttoned his shirt and moved the palm of her hand over the five long scars that striped his chest. She buttoned up his shirt again, still without a word, and he had to wait a long time before she spoke.

"I read about the end of the story later. It all turned out well, anyway," she whispered at last.

"Yes," he whispered back, "since I was tortured, the terrorists believed the story when I got back. A great deal depended on that, actually. You were right, and you did the right thing. No hard feelings."

"You got all of them?"

"I think we got thirteen, but two escaped. I'd rather not talk about that; I never did like that operation."

"Why not?"

"Because in my damn naïve Swedish way I thought it was all a matter of getting as many of those German and French and Belgian terrorists as possible together in one place, in order to catch them and put them on trial."

"Yes, I think that *was* probably naïve."

"So we murdered them instead. Were you the one who tipped off the Swedish embassy in Damascus that the Syrians had me?"

"Yes, of course. Otherwise you might have disappeared or else they would have tortured you for real in order to find out how it all happened."

"Clever."

"No, not especially. But sensible."

The conversation died out, and she moved away from him. They returned to their surveillance, and during the next few hours they exchanged only short remarks related to their target.

There was something about Mouna he couldn't understand, and he wondered about the reason for it. She had never done anything he regarded as operationally unsound. She was totally rational; at least you could always see this after the fact. But "after the fact" and "in theory" are one thing. "In reality" is something entirely different.

When years ago Jihaz ar Rased had found out that German terrorists were in Damascus to plan destruction, or possible destruction, on an entirely different scale than European terrorists normally engaged in, Mouna had led an operation into enemy territory of such scope that you would have to look to British literature from World War II for similar accounts.

They had struck against the terrorists—and Carl—practically in the middle of Damascus, and then transported their prisoners through three or four Syrian military roadblocks in a stolen Syrian army truck.

It wasn't really all that hard arranging such a thing, but you had to have precise plans and reliable backup.

And later, when it turned out that one of the captured men was Carl—an officer from a relatively friendly power and possibly not a terrorist at all—Mouna had improvised her way out of difficulty as though it were as simple as in a classroom.

She had apparently trained for a few years in North Korea, whose intelligence organizations were unknown to Carl, but there was no doubt she knew the theoretical basics, and she wasn't a lieutenant colonel for nothing.

He loathed one part of this, however. It was logical and sensible, as in a classroom, but still detestable. She had asked him to kill the two West Germans to prove to the other Palestinians in her group that he was not a real terrorist. She handed him a bayonet and gave the order almost as if she were asking for more tea.

"Why did you ask me to kill those boys?" he asked at last.

The darkness and the long silence before his question made it twice as harsh as it would have been in daylight. But she still answered lightning-quick.

"To convince the others in my group. No one would question the command. They had to be executed, and you are an officer."

"I didn't like it."

"Who would have liked it? Do you think I would like it, or any of the others? What do you take us for? But there was so much at stake."

"There always is."

"Yes, for us there always is. We have to survive at any price, and you know it."

"Didn't you hesitate when you had to cut me up?"

"More when I had to shoot you. On the outer side of the thigh there aren't any big blood vessels; it wasn't dangerous. But through the body under the collarbone . . . well, people's blood vessels can be rather individual. It wouldn't have been good with a large artery in the wrong place."

"My arteries are apparently in the normal place."

"Yes, thank God."

"Do you remember what you said?"

"You mean before I did it?"

"Yes, right before."

"I said that I felt love for you and that it's not the same thing as being in love with you. That's exactly what I said."

"What does it mean? Is that a translation from Arabic?"

"Yes, but a good translation. I feel love for you rather like a brother."

"Lie down and sleep for a few hours; I'll take over here."

"Why?"

"I'll take this watch, you can take the middle of the night, and I'll take the morning while you sleep. Then you'll be fresh and alert when you have to set the machine in motion to get my goods tomorrow."

"Heckler and Koch MP5?"

"Preferably."

The Old Man felt like a criminal lawyer. The first part of his report was now written up, nice and neat—he had finally gotten the secretarial help he needed though it was vacation time—and the logical organization, step by step, was irrefutable.

There could be no doubt that Operation Big Red *had* taken place. Ensigns Steelglove and Lundwall had unquestionably dived to such a depth for such a length of time that they had risked their lives; it was probably worse than they themselves realized, though they knew of the danger. The medical attachments spoke for themselves. The testimony of the ensigns matched perfectly. The helicopter pilot's account agreed with both Lundwall's and Steelglove's reports, as did that of the commanders on the robot-boat 37 and HMS *Sjöbjörnen*. This independent testimony from various persons who had not known about the significance of the operation all spoke the same language: Big Red had taken place, and this could be firmly established despite the political ban on inspecting the wreckage sites. And it had resulted in many casualties, and no survivors, for the Soviet Union.

The second step in the proof was just as logical. There was no reason to doubt the authenticity of Koskov's report on even a single important point. A significant amount of information had gone to the British, for example, who had found no mistakes in the facts they could test. So Hamilton *had* transported a Soviet defector from Cairo to Sweden. And under extraordinary circumstances. O.M. smiled at his own understatement.

Hamilton had averted a hijacking attempt and then made use of the Swedish air force's Hercules plane to go from Cyprus to Stockholm. If he had been a Soviet agent, there would have been plenty of opportunities to fail during that transport home. On the contrary, the desperate Soviet attempts to thwart Koskov's trip to Sweden had not succeeded, primarily because of Hamilton himself. And Koskov was one of the most valuable defectors ever to come from the Soviet Union to the West.

Common sense dictated only one conclusion. Hamilton could not possibly be working for the Soviet Union, and the Russians had no knowledge of Lundwall or Steelglove.

Historically, the Russians had carried out successful diversionary maneuvers of this Tristan kind before. The irony was that they had learned the basics from the British during the Second World War, when they were allies, and about the most important methods and information from Western intelligence in the fight against Nazi Germany.

At least that was Sir Geoffrey's explanation.

It had started with Enigma and Double-Cross. Enigma was probably one of the best-kept secrets, and one of the most important, of the entire war. When by chance the British had stumbled upon the German code machine Enigma, they succeeded in deceiving the Germans about it by blowing up a truck so that it looked as though everything, including the code machine, had been destroyed. Then they were able to follow German military code traffic throughout the war, and to protect this secret power, at times they had to act as if they hadn't had access to coded information ahead of time. The bombing of Coventry—the Germans' first large-scale terror bombing on British territory—was such an instance.

Access to Enigma also meant that one hundred percent of the intelligence agents that the Germans put into Britain could be caught. Regardless of whether they slipped in by parachute at night or arrived by fishing boat on the Scottish coast, a British patrol was always waiting for them. Without exception a very simple offer was always made. Either they could cooperate from then on and help in sending back false information to their homeland, information supplied to them by British military intelligence; or they would be executed by a firing squad, as the rules of war prescribed in the case of military spies without uniform or designation of rank.

As the British might reasonably expect—O.M. wondered whether it was psychologically correct, and decided it probably was—about half of the captured agents chose to be shot. The remaining half cooperated, and presumably this Operation Double-Cross played an even greater role in Britain's victory than the official history of the war admitted.

And the Russians, as allies, had full knowledge of the extent and techniques of Operation Double-Cross. After the war, they cleverly and with great determination converted their knowledge into something you might call Operation Double Double-Cross. They sent a stream of phony defectors to the West, who then pretended to be traitors and actually palmed off so much disinformation—peppered, naturally, with genuine but unimportant real information—that something resembling total confusion developed. That was super *maskirovka*.

As the Americans and British began to suspect how things really stood, the Russians increased the amount of genuine information, the bait, and even reached the point where they nailed their own agents. MI5 and MI6 were in this way thrown into a state of virtual civil war directed from Moscow.

Worst of all was the period after Kim Philby and the other traitors fled back to Moscow in the late 1950s. Sir Geoffrey, with almost physical shivers, had described it as "confounded unpleasant," which in his vocabulary meant catastrophic. So naturally it would be "confounded embarrassing" if they were now forced to admit that the Russians had done it again.

There was one thing the Old Man and Sir Geoffrey had easily agreed on: they wouldn't approach Tristan in any way that would make him think they were suspicious but, on the contrary, would behave with a certain enthusiasm.

And almost exactly as both Sir Geoffrey and O.M. had expected, during two days of renewed interrogation carried out by British personnel who themselves had no reason to doubt his authenticity, Tristan was able to remember new, tiny, and seemingly insignificant details that they hadn't previously asked about the Swedish agents in the GRU.

For instance, Tristan now said that Carl supposedly had the code name Seahawk, although they had discussed Seal but for unknown reasons had rejected this less heroic variant in favor of the more flattering yet slightly absurd Seahawk.

That was perfect, and it followed the pattern. The Russians knew about Carl's American training with the Seal groups.

Regarding the agent in Säpo, Tristan now remembered, although with some effort, further details such as the fact that he first had the code name Peacock, which suited his behavior, and second, that he had had an affair with a Polish woman employed by the Orbis tourist bureau, and that he had been warned about it by both Soviets and Swedes. Peacock was supposed to have a summer place out on some island where his neighbor kept pigs, and it smelled far worse than peacocks do, which resulted in numerous complaints. Four years ago a Soviet case officer had paid a visit and as a joke demanded extra pay for physical hardship.

As for Osprey, on the Joint Chiefs' staff, on a certain occasion during his UN tour of duty he had been in a car accident while drunk. He had settled the whole thing secretly, so that neither the UN nor the Swedish authorities made trouble for him. But his Jaguar—the whole thing took place in some "English" country and he had a Jaguar for private use—had been damaged, and he had needed a lot of money to repair the car. The GRU paid for the repair, and that's how the recruitment was done.

Sir Geoffrey unhesitatingly agreed with the Old Man; *if* Tristan was a phony defector, then it was almost obligatory to check these supplements to his initial information about the Swedes.

So the whole thing was in a sense following a familiar pattern, with the difference that the Russians had chosen this time to take on a more or less allied Western country. Psychologically, at least, one could see why they had done it. If they could first make the British believe the story—reasonably the most suspicious intelligence service in the Western world toward Soviet defector provocations—then the Swedes would receive such conclusive evidence from them that they would buy the story too.

The premise was totally correct. MI6 was one of the intelligence organizations that most impressed the Swedes, surpassed only by the West German BND and the Israeli Mossad.

The whole thing looked good, the Old Man realized. But he thought it would be difficult to persuade his immediate superior, Samuel Ulfsson, on that point.

It turned out to be very easy. But when he presented his report—

Ulfsson let him continue without interruption for over an hour—an entirely different question happened to take up their time before the critical piece of the puzzle fell into place.

"Do you know where Hamilton is?" asked Ulfsson, as if he were changing the subject.

O.M. shook his head in annoyance and was about to start arguing again, but Ulfsson forestalled him.

"Well, I do. As of two hours ago. He's in Lebanon."

O.M. was stunned. He thought of Philby, who had disappeared to Moscow from Lebanon right after the British had exposed him.

"Sounds like a funny place to be on leave," he said, flushing Philby from his mind.

"He's not on leave," muttered Ulfsson impatiently. "I don't know what to believe, but Sorman apparently sent him there. I was in contact with our embassy in Damascus."

"What in heaven's name is he doing and what the hell does Sorman mean by swiping one of our people?" grumbled O.M. as he sorted out the stacks of reports in front of him.

"It's that kidnapping story. Sorman got the idea that Hamilton could help, and he sent him, officially on behalf of the Foreign Ministry and the government, as some kind of expert."

"Does Sorman know about our predicament?"

"You mean the suspicions about Hamilton? Yes, he does, but that's evidently no great obstacle. I don't understand the way these politicians think."

"Do we know anything more precise about what Hamilton is up to?"

"Oh yes. He's sitting there with a high-speed transmitter rigged up, in direct contact with the embassy, down in Saida somewhere, south of Beirut. He claims to be seventy yards away from the target."

"The target. You mean the kidnapped Swedes and their captors?"

"Exactly."

"Good Lord. Do they know what they're getting into?"

"What do you mean? They've undeniably gotten themselves a quick and efficient expert, if Hamilton's reports are correct, and they undoubtedly are."

"Yes, but I don't think Carl is quite in balance after . . . well, after what has happened here. The idea is for the hostages to be freed alive, isn't it?"

"I take that for granted. Sorman's idea was that Carl had good contacts with Palestinian underground organizations and so was better suited to make the type of contacts our diplomats can't make. He didn't sniff out where the hostages are on his own."

"Is he armed? Is he working with anyone?"

"According to Sorman's instructions he was not to use weapons, and there were no weapons among the equipment that was sent to the embassy in Damascus."

"What was there?"

"Radio transmitters, night-vision devices, things like that, but no weapons. What do you think?"

O.M. didn't dare say out loud what he was thinking: in the worst case, he knew, if Carl had pinpointed the "target" and the diplomatic negotiations were not producing results, Carl would resort to violence. He was quiet for a moment.

"I think, in fact, that poor Carl is both acutely and chronically out of sync," he began cautiously. "He isn't well, he's going around worrying about something he's been involved in, plagued by a bad conscience, to state it simply. And now when we come with our suspicions of treason on top of all that, I think he's capable of doing something very dangerous, almost like an unconscious suicide attempt or a mixture of that and, shall we say, proving he isn't a traitor. Something like that."

"Well, you're the psychologist. An odd sort of sideline for an intelligence officer. But there's not much we can do about it now."

"Oh yes we can. We can call him home."

"I think he would misunderstand that."

"You're right. He'd imagine we were going to throw him into Borgström's hands again."

"Yes, and he's not susceptible to lectures. Let's just hope it goes well. But I have two other items of news for you, one definitely bad and one that you may think is rather good. So . . . ?"

"Let's have the bad one first."

"The Peacock has confessed. He had code keys at home, hidden behind the bathroom medicine cabinet, and he has confessed."

O.M. turned cold and then hot. "That's undeniably very bad news," he muttered at last, in an almost resigned tone of voice. He dug out a package of cigarillos with white plastic tips. "Have you got a light?"

"No, I quit smoking, but I can get one," said Ulfsson, pressing a button on his intercom and ordering matches.

"It's the damnedest thing that you've quit smoking. I never thought it possible. And what a strange time to do it," said O.M. slowly, as he took the first drag on the day's first cigarillo.

"Sheriff," said Ulfsson.

"What do you mean, sheriff?"

"That's what your cigars are called. Are they something you picked up in the States?"

"No, I think these are Swedish, or maybe Danish. What was the good news, if there can be any good news after that?"

"Sandström is in Moscow. He's living there, and we have his address."

"What?"

"Yes, you heard right."

They started talking all at once. Suddenly everything seemed changed.

Gordon Ingram, thought Carl.

The weapon was approximately twenty-five centimeters long with the collapsible shoulder rest shoved into its metal grooves.

He had fired model number 10 on several occasions, and it was hardly a precision weapon. This one must be model 11, since the magazine contained .45 caliber bullets, an awkward caliber for an automatic.

He examined the bullets one by one, wiping each. They were .45 ACP of American manufacture, and no abnormal ones among them. The spring in the magazine seemed fresh.

The black-painted weapon had scratches in the paint here and there, but it seemed in good condition. He dismantled it and put it together again. The recoil spring showed no sign of weakness, and the movable bolt was without rust.

A single magazine, and it held thirty rounds.

Gordon Ingram exported his weapons to Latin American dictatorships primarily because the weapon could be hidden easily under clothing. It had a perfectly rectangular shape, and if you held your hand and forearm around the downward-pointed magazine, from a distance it might look like a small box or maybe a portable radio. Apparently the security police of the banana republics liked the weapon, but Ingram never had any great sales success in the Western market, and one of the reasons was probably the unnecessarily high caliber. Nine millimeters was standard in the West; that ought to be sufficient, and it was strange picturing this Gordon Ingram choosing the heaviest pistol caliber for an automatic.

The barrel was 146 millimeters long, and in the five-centimeter-long piece sticking out from the box was the whole explanation for why Carl was holding this odd American weapon in his hands. It featured five big screw threads, which were for the silencer, a smooth black cylinder that was longer than the entire weapon. In 1969, or was it 1970, Ingram's business had gone bankrupt, and he had developed the silencer instead, and models 10 and 11 were fitted with the new accessory without their becoming any kind of international success for that reason. It was incomprehensible how one of these peculiar weapons had turned up in Palestinian possession in Beirut.

It could only be used at close range. Well, that made things simpler; it eliminated a lot of possibilities; it made it easier to figure out.

Even if she had gotten hold of a Heckler & Koch, he would have been forced to take a trial shot in some way in order to make sure that the sight was working. Here you didn't need a sight, here it was merely a question of no more than a few yards' distance. Just about the same as with knives—there was no mistaking with knives.

The embassy in Damascus reported that the negotiations were in a crucial phase and warned him not to create any disturbance.

He replied with the message that the kidnappers were being observed and had been identified except for one young man; he had sent the names by radio. With regard to the hostages, he couldn't yet confirm that he had seen anything definite that could identify them correctly. He had only observed two pair of bound legs on a double bed. But two captured males combined with Jihaz ar Rased's reports ought to be sufficient.

The embassy confirmed his information about the identity of the kidnappers.

The kidnappers ate after darkness fell, with the curtains drawn, and they took turns standing guard. He decided which one of them would make the easiest target—the youngest one, who looked seventeen or eighteen years old.

When they ate, they all gathered on the ground floor and left the hostages alone. After they finished, one of them took food up to the hostages and another brought trays and silverware; the one who went up with the food stood guard.

The evening meal took about twenty minutes. That was the right time to do it.

The pistol that Mouna had supplied had no extra magazine. It was an ordinary Colt .45 (Skip Harrier's favorite weapon), but with only seven rounds in the magazine. The extra box of bullets with fifty .45 ACPs wouldn't make any difference. He had thirty, plus seven in the two weapons, and either that would be more than enough or else it would be disastrous.

He felt a kind of inner peace. He was not tired or nervous when he wrapped his hand around the knurled walnut exterior of the pistol butt—in his left hand, since he was holding his pen in his right. He had used up thirty sheets of paper. On another page he had collected crucial strategic information.

This might be the end of the line, and he felt almost content at the thought. He didn't want to go back. He didn't want to see Borgström's triumph and sweaty upper lip ever again.

Real people lived a real life when they were thirty-four years old. They had a family and people they loved, they had children with worries about poor grades in math or cross-eyes or trouble with their pals.

Eva-Britt was a real person. She had a bad complexion, she was nearsighted and a Christian and had never pointed a weapon at another human being, and she never lied except in the line of duty. If then.

The pistol was almost as long as Ingram's submachine gun if you didn't count the silencer.

Maybe Jihaz ar Rased had some special reason for only supplying her with American weapons. It had been at the cost of night vision and greater assault possibilities. Besides, maybe the diplomats would take care of everything.

If Salah Salah didn't watch out, he was likely to be cooked in the end in any case, and he probably realized this. Palestinians are usually quite realistic. The ones Carl saw through his image enhancer were going to die, too, sooner or later. If it was later, it would be a job for Mouna and her comrades.

She was breathing evenly and calmly, as if she were sleeping peacefully. Her burns made her even more beautiful, but he had never asked her about them.

She was from Gaza. Her brothers had been killed by Israelis who had blown up the family's two houses because they were somehow under the impression that the person they were looking for was part of the family.

She had escaped to Jordan, where Abu al-Houl had gotten hold of her, and later it had been North Korea.

If you felt as much hatred as she did, would it be easier?

He used to tell himself that he hated Näslund, the head of Säpo's counterterrorist unit, and he used to tell himself that he hated Uwe Dee, head of the West German antiterrorist commandos GSG9, whom he had hardly met except once, when they had drunk a champagne toast. Well, naturally they had seen each other before then, but that hardly counted.

The groove on the Colt ran just above the butt. It was better to grip it farther down when you cocked it, as on his own Beretta.

No, he didn't even hate Uwe Dee or Näslund.

It was meaningless to say that he loved Tessie anymore. Too much time had passed.

For Mouna he felt love, to use her own expression. And for Eva-Britt, whom he would probably never see again, and for the Old Man and for Lundwall and even for Steelglove.

Only colleagues, if you included Eva-Britt.

So he was sitting there with his eye pressed to an image enhancer, without feeling fatigue or aggression, reviewing his life.

It might be over. They thought he was a traitor. They would never be able to prove it, since it wasn't true; and since they could never prove it, they would never be sure; and since they could never be sure, he would be forced back into normal life.

What would he be then?

According to the cover, he was an executive in the real estate business, in neat clothes, who had once had radical opinions. He wasn't sure where the theater of his job ended and where he himself began.

There was no life beyond the big theater, at least no distinct life that he could imagine.

He ought to start wearing more comfortable clothes. And then what? He should sell real estate and take up some kind of philanthropy. And then what? He should refurnish his apartment, according to his own tastes. But he couldn't imagine what it would look like. He didn't know what his tastes were.

He probably ought to read more books. He probably ought to get rid of almost everything in the weapons cupboard, but not all of it. He needed to shoot for his peace of mind, for the sake of the concentration.

He should run cross-country instead of, morning and night, month after month, year after year, doing the standard exercises, the hundred most effective methods, using one's own body, of seriously injuring or killing a human being in another body, the human being who existed behind the sandbag with the almost worn-out human features.

Could he love any woman truly, the way he had loved Tessie? Could he learn about diapers and baby bottles as easily as new software? Were civilian computers anything he was suited to?

Colt Model 1911A was the name of the weapon in his left hand. In principle it hadn't changed very much since 1911, even though the screws in the knurled walnut grip of the butt on this particular one had a look that was new since the 1960s. The pistol might have been in Vietnam. It didn't come from a surplus warehouse; it had actually been used.

If he went back to Sweden and they threw him out, would he dare contact Eva-Britt again after what had happened that last night?

Was he crazy?

Those butcher murderers back home had been acquitted. Was he capable of chopping up someone? Without a doubt. If there was good reason. So was he crazy? Was that why he felt so calm right now, when he should be nervous?

He was possibly about to kill five people who were asleep, at least four of them seventy yards away, and it seemed to him like a mere technical or practical problem. Whether the diplomats succeeded with their negotiations or not made no difference. If the hostages were returned nice and easy, then the men over there in the building would live a long time, but it made no difference to him which way it went.

He had no personality of his own: he had a profession instead, a profession that had become him and that they were now going to take away from him. He was going to cease to exist.

Mouna was enviable. But she wouldn't take him seriously if he said that he wanted to stay with her group instead of going back home. She would think he was crazy, and he felt too much love for her to love her or to obey her.

He was thirty-four years old. Now it would soon be over.

. . .

"I don't know if you've met the Old Man, but you probably know who he is," began Ulfsson in a businesslike manner.

"Yes, we've met a few times, although no more than a few," replied the man. He didn't know why he had been suddenly forced to interrupt his vacation, and according to O.M.'s and Ulfsson's presuppositions or at least hopes, he had no idea he was Osprey, a traitor.

He was suntanned and wearing a checked sport shirt and had herring scales on his hands, and his clip-on sunglasses stood out like great eyebrows above his glasses. He was wearing sandals without socks. He was sitting calmly and comfortably, leaning back in his chair, and he was even splaying his toes. According to international terminology he was a brigadier general; according to Swedish terminology he was a four-star colonel in approximately the same tax bracket as a young reporter for an evening newspaper. And he was head of one of the most sensitive departments in the armed forces, OP4, responsible for, among other things, tactical countermeasures against foreign—that is, Soviet—submarine activity. His views were very Swedish.

The conversation would very soon become un-Swedish.

"It's a serious matter, and I want your spontaneous and completely truthful—for God's sake, your own sake, and our sake, truthful—answer to a number of questions," Ulfsson said with a smile, which seemed to O.M. highly forced. And Sam was searching for cigarettes again.

"That sounds really distressing. Just tell me what it's all about," replied the so-called Osprey.

"What contact have you had with Sandström over the years?" asked Ulfsson curtly, without a quaver.

Osprey immediately changed his posture. Unconsciously he straightened up. "Is this an interrogation of some kind?" he asked as he shifted. Suddenly he looked suspicious.

"Yes. And we're taping it," answered Ulfsson in the same tone of voice as before. "The question one more time. What contact have you had with Sandström?"

"We're talking about the spy?" The suspect was now sitting straight up and looking as if he missed his uniform.

"Yes, that's correct. We want you to tell us as much as possible without our asking questions. This is important, Lennart. I can't emphasize that enough."

"Damn, you sound so formal all of a sudden."

"I am formal. So—Sandström?"

"What should I say about him? This sounds embarrassing. What are you really thinking? Do you think I'm working for Sandström, or what the hell is this about?"

Ulfsson let the silence settle in the room. "We want you to answer our questions."

"You don't think I'm a spy, do you, damn it? That would be something! Ha! So that's why we never caught those devils. Those rumors, is that what this is about?"

"Don't force me to be more formal, please. It's bad enough as it is. Now just tell us everything that has to do with you and Sandström, how you know each other, everything." Ulfsson looked as if he might explain himself further but changed his mind at the last minute.

Osprey composed himself and started to talk.

It's true he had had quite a lot to do with Sandström. That he had not reported this to OP5 might later, after the fact, be embarrassing insofar as it was his responsibility to do so, but anyway it was many years ago.

They had both been majors, Sandström newly divorced and he himself a grass widower, and it was on Cyprus, during UN service.

There had been a lot of drinking, a lot of women. Not exactly something you're especially proud of afterward, particularly considering what Sandström turned out to be.

But yes, they had caroused a lot, and there had been women and booze, but nothing that . . . well, that made their messy private lives interfere with their duties. Except for some red-eyed mornings.

Sandström was a devil with women, you had to admit that. And the booze was cheap, and so on. Cypriot brandy was treacherous, by the way, slightly sweet and weaker than real cognac. People often drank it with ice and, well, it was easy to drink too much. They pulled themselves together when the wives came down on summer leave. They were only human, after all. Or men, anyway.

There wasn't much more to tell except that it was embarrassing afterward when it was learned that Sandström was a spy. But he hadn't seemed mysterious then. Had he been a spy already?

"Yes. He was already a spy. So far as we know. Tell us about the car," interjected Ulfsson.

Osprey froze. "What car?"

"The car, everything about the car," countered Ulfsson, mildly yet firmly.

"The Jag?"

"Tell us now. Whatever you say in your first version is the most important."

"Do you mean that I'm going to be . . . questioned, that I'm going to be questioned again after this?"

"Yes. Probably. So tell us about the car," continued Ulfsson in the same calm way, as if the whole affair were somehow trivial.

The man the Russians called Osprey took a deep breath. His brow had started to sweat.

It had been a Friday or Saturday night. They had taken a night off and gone to Limassol. Yes, it wasn't that far from Larnaca and Camp Victoria, maybe a couple of hours. There was a fish restaurant in Limassol and . . . well, it probably didn't make a difference, but it was called Christos. On the way home they had driven into a damned donkey cart with no lights. No chance of stopping, they just crashed. And it didn't have anything to do with liquor, but there was really no reason to drag in the police. Considering the liquor, among other things. So they paid for the donkey cart on the spot.

That was that story. The whole thing could be considered settled.

"You talk about 'we' without explaining yourself. Does 'we' mean you and Sandström?" asked Ulfsson.

"No, it doesn't. Do you have to know who it was and who was driving and all that?"

"Yes."

"It was me and the head of the battalion. On the way back, that is. Sandström had come along to Limassol but he found . . . he found a reason to stay there."

"Women."

"There's good reason to assume so, yes."

"So he heard about the episode later?"

"Yes, I told him about it."

"How did you get your car repaired?"

"Why do you want to know that?"

"How did you get your car repaired?"

"Well, I thought there was a rush."

"That's not an answer to the question."

"What the hell are you getting at? Investigating drunk driving while on duty over ten years ago—hasn't the statute of limitations expired?"

"Still not an answer to the question."

"Okay, I give up."

"Well."

"We, that is, I took off the dented front fender and later I had the car repaired with a new front fender ordered from England."

"Was it expensive?"

"I think it was."

"How did you pay for it?"

"Used up my savings, that's all."

"Where did you have your savings?"

"In the UN bank account. Shot the wad. If only I'd saved the fender. But they ordered a new one, and then there was air freight and one thing and another, and to be quite honest this is hell having to go through this right now, it's more than ten years ago—don't you realize that?"

"Of course. But whatever is buried in snow, you know . . . all your savings? Sounds expensive."

"Well, not *all* my savings. But it was extra-expensive, and besides, I wanted to exercise a certain discretion."

"Bribes?"

"That's not how they're viewed on Cyprus."

"You paid cash?"

"Yes."

"How much?"

"Approximately . . . well, do you want it in Cypriot pounds or how?"

"Makes no difference, just the total, preferably something comprehensible."

"Approximately fifteen thousand kronor, Swedish kronor."

"And you took it out of your account, your salary on deposit?"

"Yes, I didn't exactly have the money under the mattress."

"What happened to the car then?"

"When I went home I sold it. I'd lost interest, and besides, it had the steering wheel on the wrong side."

"Don't they drive on the right on Cyprus?"

"Yes, but the car was clearly of British origin, if you can say that."

"Thank you, that's enough."

"What the hell do you mean by that?"

"Exactly what I said."

"Are you crazy?"

"No, I hope not."

"Well, what's this all about?"

"I hope that you won't believe your ears when you hear."

"Have the Social Democrats come up with something like perpetual drunk driving for defense personnel?"

"No."

"I didn't think so. So what the hell is this all about?"

"This conversation has been taped and will be listened to by the Chief, among others."

"Turn off that damned tape recorder and tell me what this is all about, in that case."

"I think we can at least end our conversation for now," replied Ulfsson without even seeming to strain his self-control.

The Old Man thought Sam sounded pleased, and rightly so. A number of things were now clear. In any case they could now get proof whether he or Tristan was lying. But possibly one last question was needed.

"Did Sandström hear any talk about that car repair?" asked O.M. gently, as if out of pure confusion he was interjecting a completely unnecessary question.

"I think so. He was the one who recommended the repair shop to me," replied the man who would soon be stricken from the Tristan list of suspects.

Are we going to be saddled with a homosexual scandal, too? As if the cocaine business wasn't enough, sighed Peter Sorman.

It certainly wasn't his problem, since nothing suggested that any Foreign Ministry people had participated in "the Social Democrats' group grope." Or worse.

At a press conference earlier that morning the prime minister had drawn the lines of defense. The alleged top Social Democrat in the fuss had no political duties in the party and hadn't for years, since his main area of activity had been stock speculation, and the publishing of a gossip sheet of the finer sort called a newsletter, which cost a thousand kronor per issue. The fact that within his large network of contacts he had acquaintances dating from his earlier work as a Social Democratic reporter was not peculiar: he knew moderates too, indeed by now more moderates than Social Democrats.

The fact that the suspect had given a dinner party the week before at which a high-ranking police chief and the minister of justice were present had nothing to do with anything, since on that occasion, of course, no drug consumption had taken place. The minister of justice could not be blamed if one of her acquaintances had committed a crime. The political undertones coloring the events had to do with the simple truth of its being an election year, and the Conservative opposition being tempted to run a smear campaign as usual. No one in a responsible position had in any respect committed any kind of error.

The party obviously had nothing to do with the alleged crime. Judicial authorities would now investigate in the usual way, and the government neither could nor should get involved in police work.

So far so good.

But what about the question of how a suspected drug abuser not only could associate with police chiefs and ministers of justice but could also get a personal bodyguard handpicked from the Stockholm police? Since when had it been all right for Sweden's police authorities to give drug abusers bodyguards? And on what basis had the police guards been chosen?

The last was the unpleasant question.

The populist reporter from *Aftonbladet*, who always played the part of aggressive American muckraker at press conferences, had even asked if it wasn't possible that these handpicked policemen had certain personal characteristics that determined their selection—vegetarian eating habits, particular sexual inclinations, something on that order?

The prime minister had rejected the question scornfully, at the same time pointing out that this was under the jurisdiction of the police and not the government. But there had been snickering. Rumors were running wild.

The handpicked guards, according to the rumors, had qualified primarily because of their membership in a leather-and-whips club of the sleazier variety. And if that story was published in the press, true or not—Sorman didn't know or care—the election campaign would start off disastrously. The whole thing was disgusting.

There were only two stories that could now knock the impending group grope off the front pages and out of the tabloids. The first was obviously the Tristan business. The other was a resolution of the hostage drama in Lebanon. An hour before the terrible press conference the prime minister had asked the Defense Chief for a report. The military's own investigations had so far not indicated that the officers on the defense staff named by Tristan were spies. Of course, there was reason to be skeptical about the armed forces' investigation of their own people, but with great effort they had come to some partial conclusions. They had checked out the Koskov story minutely and had found nothing that would lead to its reevaluation; they had again gone over their so-called Operation Big Red and affirmed that it had taken place. This last would be almost comical if the situation hadn't been so serious. Like crossing the river to get a drink of water, thought Sorman.

And as far as Colonel "Osprey" was concerned, significant errors had been found in Tristan's information. The UN records showed an account withdrawal more than ten years old that showed he had paid for certain car repairs or whatever it was with his own funds. But it was still too early to draw definite conclusions.

At Säpo it was a different story. The police superintendent at the Russian Bureau had confessed, of course, and they had found evidence. And for once Säpo had demonstrated that they were capable of not publishing their secrets in the evening papers—naturally because publicity would harm them and not the government. But the fellow had been offered immunity in return for cooperation, and this was politically dangerous. At least he wasn't a Social Democrat—if he were, under present conditions, they would have been forced to sentence him. They couldn't afford another "covering up their own people" scandal.

What lay on Peter Sorman's own desk was, however, mostly about the Lebanon affair. The situation was critical.

The kidnappers had demanded a million dollars from the Swedes and had given a deadline. On the one hand there was the position "never negotiate with terrorists"; if one did, there would be criticism and trouble in the right-wing press. Though one could benefit by this: one could say that rather than sticking to harsh if theoretically sound principles, the government had decided to save Swedish lives, and so on. But what if the kidnappers came up with new demands, and what if they just took the money and fled, killing the hostages anyway?

Half an hour later the arithmetic was considerably simpler and gloomier. Yasir Arafat called again from Tunis and assured his "old friend" Sorman that the kidnappers had nothing to do with the PLO and would surely receive their proper punishment—two messages that seemed sharply contradictory. The PLO offered to escort the hostages to Beirut if they were released; and if the negotiations did not bring results, the PLO could, as a last resort, attempt a rescue by force.

Sorman firmly said no thank you. If the hostages died, Arafat would say that the rescue attempt took place at the behest of the

Swedish government. If the hostages got out safely, the PLO would take the credit—with all the extraordinary consequences this might have in Sweden during an agitated political season.

The embassy in Damascus then reported on the latest proposal in the negotiations at the Hotel Summerland between the PLO's alleged mediator, Salah Salah, and the Swedish diplomats.

The kidnappers were demanding a million dollars, as expected, but also the assistance of the Swedish delegation in leaving the Middle East—six people, preferably by plane, and with Swedish diplomats on board as insurance. For both political and practical reasons this was unacceptable. The only thing to do was to try to gain time.

But the kidnappers seemed to know that this was their only chance of survival. So they had set a deadline of twelve hours—after which they would draw lots for which doctor they would kill first, transmit proof of this in some way, and then set a new deadline.

Sorman thought of Hamilton. According to the latest bulletin, he was sitting only seventy yards away from the kidnappers' hideout. A Swedish rescue attempt? No, that didn't seem very clever. It would require Sorman to transmit some kind of message to him with this intent; if things went well the military would take the credit, and if things went badly, he and the government would get the blame. No, Hamilton's only assignment must be to tell the diplomats what was going on. Nothing else. One could only hope they were careful about what they told him in turn.

The message Carl received from the embassy secretary in Damascus was brief but specific:

> *The kidnappers have made an unacceptable proposal. Money and free passage with diplomatic hostages. The answer will be no. Deadline 12 hours. Report all observations of possible reactions and activities.*

Simultaneously one of Mouna's orderlies arrived with instructions from Tunis. They were to prepare for a rescue attempt. The Swedish government had agreed.

Carl tapped out an inquiry to the embassy as to the truth of this Tunis information. Several hours later a reply arrived from Stockholm via Damascus: the information was firmly denied. But there were no new instructions.

Then he and Mouna quarreled over who would eventually do what and about whether she should bring in reinforcements.

It took time to reach an agreement.

The main tactical problem was that they didn't know whether the kidnappers had primed explosives in the room where they kept the hostages. It's true that they hadn't seen anything to indicate this over the previous few days; for instance, it took only thirty seconds for someone leaving the ground floor to appear in the upstairs room, and that did not indicate the need for any kind of disarming. But it was risky to take a chance, and they therefore couldn't adopt the simplest plan: to kill all six at some moment when they were all downstairs, for instance during supper.

At dusk, one kidnapper returned after having been gone for six or seven hours, and for some time Mouna and Carl watched them arguing and discussing downstairs, more excited and nervous than previously. The conclusion was simple. The kidnappers had received, via Salah Salah, the negative reply from the Swedes, and now the question was how they would handle their deadline—twelve hours from when?

Carl and Mouna now had an easier time coming to an agreement; she requisitioned two cars, a taxi, and an escort car with drivers, but only two men as backup.

Two hours later, when it had grown completely dark, they began their work.

Mouna watched through the image enhancer as Carl left the house where he had stayed so quietly and walked up the slight hill to the kidnappers' building. Next to the front door was a big water barrel: he would wait behind it and launch his first attack from there, so that she could see what was happening. She in turn had radio contact with her two men sitting in one of the escape cars thirty yards away, but obviously they would observe strict radio silence until things began to happen.

When the guard came out the door Mouna felt her pulse increase to what seemed like the pain threshold, and she forced herself to take her eye away from the image enhancer for a moment and stare out into the darkness in order to convince herself that it wasn't really possible to see anything, though she was watching as if it were daylight. The guard loitered on the stairs for a long time. It looked as if he was not going to make his usual rounds—what would Carl do in that case? Presumably he'd wait until the guard went back inside, and then move on to phase two as if phase one had already been accomplished.

Sitting as a passive spectator was unbearable. She had no precise idea of Carl's capabilities, but this was something that looked easy only during practice: in reality the risks of failure were immeasurably great. The guard might start to walk around the building in the opposite direction, or choose the wrong way around the water barrel, or even strike a match for a cigarette. Carl, squeezed in tight and motionless against the water barrel, had taken off his goggles; he had the short knife with the black nonreflecting blade in his hand. The choice of weapon made Mouna realize how he was probably going to do it. A perfect method if he succeeded, but catastrophic if he misjudged by as little as an inch.

Suddenly the guard seemed to make up his mind. It wasn't the young boy this time, which irrationally relieved her, at the same time that she grew more uneasy, since this one seemed to be the stockiest one. He took three or four steps toward Carl's hiding place.

With a kind of delayed response she watched what happened then. At first it looked as if he just collapsed soundlessly into Carl's arms, after which Carl carefully laid him down on the ground. But she had seen the stabbing itself, at the lower part of his spine, at an angle from the side. Carl had punctured the man's aorta as well as spinal cord. Paralysis in that case was immediate and death came very quickly.

Carl put on his goggles again and waved in her direction that phase one was complete, which she already knew.

But he did not go toward the door; instead he vanished from sight, making a round of the building. She wondered why, but decided he needed to verify that the others were inside.

They had just finished their meal. But only Mouna could see that from her position at a distance, and it took Carl more time to take his bearings.

When he turned around the farther corner he was walking so that it was audible—impersonating the guard—and practically stomped up the stairs. Then he raised his submachine gun, released the safety, pulled open the door, and vanished from her sight. The subsequent events she could only guess at, based on the reactions of the two men she could see through the window sitting at the table.

Carl stepped straight into the room with his weapon at hip level and fired three rounds right through the middle of the man sitting with a gun in his hand. At the same time he shouted in English for the rest to get down on the floor, face down, and when they didn't obey he fired another three rounds through the back of the one closest to him, and an instant later the three remaining live figures were lying motionless on the floor with their arms and legs spread.

He moved around the room so that Mouna could see him and gathered up the three automatic weapons he could find. Then he moved the table away so that he had a clear view of the entire space. He hung his own weapon around his neck so that his hands were free and pulled the magazines out of the three Soviet automatic carbines, took out the cartridges, and placed everything in a clattering heap on the table.

The three on the floor were silent. He transferred his weapon to his right hand and searched them one by one, but none of them had any further weapons.

For the moment everything was under control. He took out a little walkie-talkie, pressed the button, and reported that phase two was over, and less than five seconds later he heard a cautious honking in the street, which meant she had transmitted the message to the backup group.

One of the men who had been shot moved a little. Carl must have missed his spine. He decided not to kill the man, but instead went over to the radio playing Koran recitations and turned up the volume.

Then he ordered the three surviving men to sit up against a wall—at a place where Mouna could see them—and to put their hands behind their heads. They obeyed slowly, moving almost in slow motion, but Carl decided it was shock rather than an unwillingness to cooperate. When they were where he wanted them, he pulled up a chair, turned it around, and sat down facing them with the now demonstrably as-good-as-silent Ingram pointed at them; the shots had been no louder than coughs. Presumably the Swedes upstairs had heard nothing but some scraping of furniture, some phrases in English, and now the wailing Koran recitation.

The two adult men looked more resigned than fearful, as if they didn't regard a visit from death as anything particularly unexpected. The boy was different—the one who usually took the first guard watch of the evening.

From now on everything ought to go according to plan without any big problems.

"Do you understand English?" asked Carl in a low voice so that he wouldn't be heard over the Koran.

All three of them nodded, the two older ones sullenly, the ones who were the al Latif cousins and would die later. The boy nodded vigorously, terror exaggerating his movements; he had a gentle, intelligent face.

"I am Swedish and the negotiations are now over," continued Carl, pausing for a long time to see whether they would break out with any threat against the safety of the hostages. But none of them said a word.

"We don't want any unnecessary bloodshed, just our people back. How you resolve your problems with the PLO later on is your problem, not ours," lied Carl calmly. "You over there," he continued after a moment, nodding toward the boy, "how are you related to these guys?"

The boy did not answer, but stared at the floor and looked as if he might weep. The man named Taheer replied, calm and without the least uncertainty in his melodic and surprisingly beautiful voice. "Karim is my son, and I offer you my life in place of his. Karim is only a child and has to do as his father says."

Carl let his gaze shift from one to the other a few times before he made a decision and continued. "We'll do like this," he began, with an effort not to sound unsure in any way. "Karim, you will go upstairs and free the hostages. You will take them to the car outside and you will come back here when the car leaves. You have to come back here or else I will have to kill your father. Do you understand what I'm saying?"

The boy nodded eagerly.

"That isn't good enough, Karim. You must repeat what I said in English. Do you understand?"

The boy nodded again but said nothing until his father hissed at him in Arabic.

"I will get the hostages, free the hostages, and go out with them to the car. They get in, the car leaves, I must come back here." The boy reeled off the items nervously.

"That's good, Karim. You will take them out the back way. They must not see any of us in here because then they will be afraid, do you understand?"

The boy nodded and then sat silently with his head lowered until he remembered to repeat the instructions in English.

"That's good, Karim. If we do this, my countrymen will get to Beirut and be free. You must come back here so that I know you haven't warned anyone. Do you understand?"

"Go out the back way with them . . . Shall I tell them that they are free?" replied the boy, who looked as if he were beginning to compose himself, beginning to hope to stay alive.

"Quite right, Karim. You will tell them that they are now going to a hotel in Beirut to meet Swedish diplomats. It's all over. And then come back here so that we won't have to shoot anymore. Don't try to run off, Karim, because there are more Swedes out there, who will have to shoot you if you run, and I will have to shoot your father and your father's cousin. Do you understand everything?"

The boy quickly repeated the instructions in English, and Carl nodded quietly after each item.

"Taheer, do you have any objections?" he asked, his voice significantly harsher.

"What are you planning to do with us?" asked the older cousin sullenly.

"The plan is for me to sit here and keep all three of you company for as long as it takes our car to reach safety. Then I will leave here and you will have to take care of yourselves as best you can. The only concern of the Swedish government is to free our hostages. We don't care about you. You've already paid the price to us." He nodded at the two shot men, lying completely still in their own blood on the floor.

"Your position isn't very strong," he added, turning on his little walkie-talkie to report that phase three was completed. "Remember now, Karim," he added, turning toward the boy again. "If you harm the hostages, or try anything stupid, then your father and your father's cousin will die first, and you'll be next. Understand?"

Karim looked as if he were about to repeat this last thing in English too, but Carl stopped him with a gesture and nodded to him to get going. At the same time all four heard a diesel Mercedes in front of the building.

As the boy left the room and his footsteps could be heard on the stairs, Carl turned off the radio and made a sign to the others to keep quiet. He listened intently. The faint mumbling of a conversation could be heard upstairs, but he couldn't make out the words. After a short while footsteps were audible on the stairs and cheerful voices; Carl heard several words in Swedish and suddenly felt incredibly relieved. But it wasn't over yet.

All three of them heard car doors slam and then the Mercedes engine receding. Karim returned and, hesitating only a moment, went and sat down next to his father and cousin, and after hesitating some more, he put his hands behind his head.

Carl raised his walkie-talkie and reported that they could now proceed to phase five. He regarded the three gloomily, wondering what they were thinking. They were alive, they were breathing, they were sitting there ten or twelve feet away, and presumably they were hoping. Sad, especially for the boy. He was a Palestinian, he was brave and made an intelligent impression, and he had just done what his father told him to do. What seventeen-year-old could be blamed for that? Mouna herself would have done what her father said when she was seventeen, and, just like this Karim, she could have sat here with her breast full of hope, while death was on its way.

Mouna knocked the prearranged signal and came in with her goggles dangling from one hand. She squinted a little in the harsh electric light. She was dressed in her camouflage field uniform, on her shoulders an eagle and a star. Her commanding presence made it clear who was in charge, and Carl almost stood at attention.

They exchanged a glance, and then she commandeered the American submachine gun by stretching out her hand and snapping her fingers.

At that instant the two men understood. They seemed to recognize her, and certainly her uniform. On her left arm she wore the field badge of the Palestinian intelligence service, and the number 17 indicated Yasir Arafat's personal guard.

Carl stood up and was starting to leave when Taheer let loose a stream of words in Arabic. Carl heard the Ingram's stifled coughing, three times four. Six plus twelve is eighteen, twelve rounds left in the magazine, he thought mechanically as he reached the outer door. He paused for a moment on the porch, looked up at the clear, starry sky, and took several deep breaths.

Then he went to the dead guard, threw him over his shoulder, and bent down for the automatic weapon on the ground next to the water barrel. The man's spine cracked and creaked; Carl had evidently made a perfect strike and almost severed the spinal column. That happened sometimes if you struck correctly, he remembered from practicing on doped pigs. He took the body inside and put it down next to the other corpses. Mouna was already upstairs looking for documents.

He sat down on the chair for a moment. All lay face down on the floor except Karim. The boy was lying on his back with eyes wide open. He almost looked alive.

If Karim had been the guard tonight, Carl would have stabbed him in the spine, of course. It had to take place in absolute silence, without the slightest scream. But this was something different.

Mouna came down with a bag in her hand. She raised her goggles with a meaningful gesture and turned off the light. Carl put on his goggles. The moonlight outside reflected brightly in Karim's eyes, which seemed almost accusatory.

Carl stood up quietly and followed Mouna out.

When they got back to their room, Carl sent the briefest of messages:

Hostages free after successful negotiations. Arrive Summerland in one hour. Dismantling the station.

They packed the equipment, which two of Mouna's subordinates carried off to a car at the back of the building where further forces had been waiting. Mouna had not told him until now that, contrary to their agreement, she had a reserve of an entire Palestinian company, twenty men.

Five

Except possibly in the case of his smoking, Samuel Ulfsson had always lived a life of moderation, and this even applied to his emotional life. In that sense he was very Swedish. He became neither excessively optimistic nor bewildered and pessimistic when unexpected news seemed splendid or catastrophic. Similarly he neither loved nor hated people he had to work with, though in his field there was no shortage of eccentric personalities. And in the steady stream of men, almost exclusively men, who sat in the chair across from him and held forth on their more or less secret, more or less well prepared missions, he seldom found occasion for personal sympathy or antipathy.

In that respect, Näslund was a dramatic exception.

Henrik P. Näslund was head of the central unit within Säpo that was supposed to track down spies and terrorists. Previously it had been called Department B or the B-Bureau, but now they had changed it to Department E and Näslund was its boss. And this central unit down at the monkey house on Kungsholmen was truly Sweden's most inefficient institution. Its foremost characteristic was that work assignments were never completed, and this meant, in concrete terms, that it never caught any spies. On top of that, Näslund was crude and loutish, and Ulfsson agreed with the people in his own department who disliked him intensely.

But this time Säpo had succeeded; the Peacock had confessed. And now they were negotiating with the Peacock about immunity and with the government about whether it could even do such a thing. It would have to be a deal between the monkey house and the government, and Ulfsson knew this didn't concern him, but the horrible Näslund was sitting there asking him about it.

"It's your business. You'll have to take it up with the politicians. We have no reason to get involved," said Ulfsson neutrally.

Näslund took out a steel-toothed comb and several times ran it energetically through his slicked-back hair. He always did this when he was thinking, and he was oblivious to the effect the habit had on people. "As you know, we also have excellent English contacts," he began, suggesting that he had something up his sleeve.

"Yes, of course. We keep to the intelligence service and you to the security service, and that's quite sensible," Sam replied evasively.

"Exactly," continued Näslund as he stuffed his steel comb back into his pocket. "Exactly. Our sources in MI5 are talking about an expanded Tristan report, about agents with the code names Osprey and Seahawk?"

"Seahawk?"

"Yes, the sort of sea bird that chases gulls and makes them drop whatever they have in their beaks, a kind of pirate of the air. I thought you knew about them in the navy."

"Well, yes, I've seen them. They're common at the outer islands and on the open sea. Interesting birds."

"Yes, but I wasn't going to discuss ornithology with you."

"You started it."

"Well?"

"What do you mean, well?"

"Have you found moles in the house too?"

"I don't think so. Of course, one never knows; you've had a couple of them in the past ten, twenty years, or maybe more like thirty."

"To whom do the code names Osprey and Seahawk refer?"

Ulfsson had an almost unbearable urge for a smoke. "This is the way things are," he began slowly. "The Tristan report does refer to two other suspects, but we have definite reason not to believe it."

"So Tristan is supposedly telling the truth about our man but not about your personnel?"

"Yes, that's the conclusion we're leaning toward at present."

"Evidence of suspected espionage is a matter for the Security Police."

"That depends how well founded it is. If it's not well founded, we can keep it in-house, and if you want to complain about that you'll have to go to the government, and I think we'll have the government's backing. As far as one of these two is concerned, in the defense ministry, the government has already given us a kind of verdict. Their conclusion is the same as ours."

"Concerning Seahawk?"

"Yes."

"Osprey is still uncertain?"

"I wouldn't say that."

"Why did you want to have these interrogations of our man about his relationship to Sandström?"

"Have you carried them out?"

"Yes, I have the reports with me. Your theories seemed to be right. But I have to know the reason."

"You mean the reason why we were looking for a connection between your man and Sandström?"

It was time for a certain limited honesty. "We think the information from Tristan is based on Sandström—in regard to your Peacock as much as our Seahawk and Osprey. With the significant difference that Peacock is a real spy. We have reason to believe Sandström is in Moscow, working for the Russians. A typical Russian operation; they want to create chaos for us."

Näslund sat in silence for a moment. It looked as though he might take out his steel comb again. The effort of his thinking could almost be smelled in the room.

"But," he said at last, "but it's hard to believe they would pin it on a real spy just to make you believe that you have a house full of moles. And this Tristan exposed his own spy ring in England. Someone more suspicious than I might almost think that you were trying to protect your own people from scandal. Are you thinking of negotiating for immunity too?" Näslund looked amused, as if he had finally seen through the scheme and could make a joke about it.

Ulfsson had to suppress an impulse to go along with him just to end the conversation. But he could see the headlines of the evening papers if the monkey house felt pressured.

"No," he said, annoyed, "we are certainly not negotiating for immunity. We've gotten much farther in our analyses, and as I said, for the most part the government shares our conclusions. Tristan's information is partly true and partly false. That's how it looks. If anything should change our minds, we shall naturally call in the police. At the moment there's no reason to."

"It's your responsibility."

"What is?"

"To go to the police with suspicions like this. It's our job to decide whether the matter can be dropped or not." Näslund looked ready to fight.

But for Ulfsson, only the bureaucratically sarcastic reply remained. "If you want to complain, go to the government. And if anything new turns up, you'll hear from us." He prayed for the conversation to end.

Näslund did not reply. Finally he opened his briefcase and placed a brown envelope on Ulfsson's very tidy, tobacco-free desk. Then he left with a curt nod.

Ulfsson slit open the envelope and read quickly through the interrogation report. Everything was correct. He sighed with relief and looked around for his cigarettes before he caught himself.

He pressed the button on the intercom and told his secretary to bring O.M. in from the far reaches where the old owl was waiting. But O.M. was already on his way, as if he had known how long Näslund would take.

Ulfsson moved from his director position over to the little side table under the painting of the army sergeant major and the forcibly conscripted boy. He placed Säpo's interrogation report in front of the chair opposite him, and at that very moment the Old Man came into the room. He had a surprisingly happy expression and his owlish eyebrows were raised.

"Since when are you opposed to cruel animal experiments?" he asked cheerfully.

"What do you mean?" Ulfsson wondered whether he was supposed to laugh at some joke he didn't understand.

"Haven't you seen it?" O.M. continued merrily as he picked up the documents from the monkey house. "There's a little political slogan pasted right above the button I press to find out whether I can come into your office or whether you're talking on the phone and I have to wait. It's against cruelty in animal experiments. In German. Well, I can see this is all in order, as expected. I suppose down at the monkey house they don't understand anything, do they?" O.M. was reading the documents, holding them close to his face, with his glasses pushed up onto his forehead. He had the habit of putting on reading glasses and then pushing them up.

"Well, I don't usually press the Wait button myself when I come in. Haven't seen anything about cruelty to animals. It was in German, you said?"

"Yes. But there's an even better political slogan above the code buttons to the slave corridor. You haven't seen that one either?" O.M. read quickly, as if it was mostly a matter of verifying that everything was as he had expected.

"You see, there's an English motto," he continued when he received no reply. "I think I heard it once but forgot it, wonderful, anyway— above the code lock. Haven't you seen it?"

"No. What does it say?"

"Something like this: 'Espionage is one of the world's two oldest professions. But in the other profession there are fewer amateurs and less immorality.' Quite apropos for today's activities, don't you think?" O.M. finished reading and put his reading glasses back in his jacket breast pocket.

"No, I haven't seen it. Yes, you might say that."

They quickly summarized the situation:

First, Sandström was working in Moscow. The report from the monkey house confirmed that. The Peacock had had a visit from him during the very summer when the pigs were there.

So the Russians had blown one of their own agents, but one who was just about to retire and lose his usefulness anyway. They had had to make Tristan believable in order to make the Defense Ministry get rid of Hamilton, throw itself into self-tormenting chaos, doubt that Big Red had ever taken place, and possibly conclude that the information from Koskov was unreliable.

Second, Sandström, fully employed in Moscow, was going to be a bother and a financial burden for years to come. They would have not only to reconstruct his knowledge of strategic information, but also to go through his whole damned circle of acquaintances in the Defense Ministry and police in order to arm themselves against new provocations.

They could, of course, let the Russians know that they knew Sandström was working for them. But that would solve only minor psychological problems and only temporarily stop fabricated espionage accusations.

One unpleasantness was that all of this would take resources and money. Money they could get from the Defense Chief, but he would have to get it from the politicians. A well-founded suspicion that Sandström was an official of the GRU in Moscow was not enough to make the politicians pay. They would need proof.

"We could photograph Sandström—we have his address and everything, after all," said O.M. suddenly, starting to look for a cigarillo but changing his mind when he remembered his boss's difficulties with smoking.

He explained quietly: they could kill several birds with one stone. First of all, it wasn't exactly the kind of assignment you could give to a pensionable officer in the military attaché's office. Second, it might be a nice idea to let Carl take on this totally calm, pleasant assignment, so far from the troubles the boy had been involved in lately. Third, this would show the Russians that their provocation had gone completely to hell. You don't make someone you think is a Russian spy your attaché in Moscow.

If you thought about it, O.M. argued, it was uncomfortable keeping Hamilton in the covert division at the moment. It might be useful for him to spend some time in Moscow—and in fact wasn't it Sam himself who appointed naval attachés?

All this would demonstrate, not only to the Russians but above all to Hamilton himself, that the Defense Ministry had unshakable confidence in him. The Chief could make this point, couldn't he?

Ulfsson was thinking, and O.M. showed no inclination to rush him. What were the drawbacks? It was unlikely the Russians would go after Hamilton, since a sensational Swedish loss would involve dangerous publicity, including Big Red, which the Russians wouldn't want at all. Yet merely to reinstate Hamilton in the secret service was complicated, given how inflammatory the situation was. Still, they were expecting new personnel in the operations department, and it would be better to let them get settled in peace and quiet without having to think about the Russian field personnel in Stockholm who were constantly shadowing Hamilton.

If they got data on Sandström in Moscow, it would solve many practical and financial problems. Yes, that was a good idea, even a brilliant idea.

"I see that you're fond of the boy, aren't you?" asked Ulfsson, not revealing what conclusion he had drawn.

O.M. sighed heavily. "Yes, I'm very fond of the boy. Not only because his whole enterprise was my idea, but also because we have a certain human responsibility. He's been through a lot in the last few years."

"How do you think he's doing?"

"Hard to say. In some way it's part of his personality to tune himself up to a superhuman level when he's on assignment—he becomes one of his own supercomputers. But it takes a heavy toll, and between jobs he sinks into brooding and the blues."

"Do you worry about him?"

"Not if he's working, but when he's not working. Well, that is . . . what he calls working. He doesn't think much of doing paperwork."

"But he handles it well, actually."

"Yes, I should think so. He has more education than any of us, and besides he's quick-witted. No genius, but quick-witted."

"So this way he'll get both a vacation and a job in Moscow, is that what you mean?"

"Yes, and we'll get the job done and it will solve a lot of problems. It's your business now to convince the Chief."

"What would you have done in your day, when you were the one who had to do that?"

"Usually I told him after the fact. But I never appointed military attachés, and that's your heavy obligation. Do you think there will be complaints from the foreign service?"

"Naturally. How old is he?"

"Thirty-four, rather young for a captain."

"Captain?"

"Yes, I thought you should suggest that. The Chief can make decisions on extraordinary promotions. As a simple expression of the Defense Ministry's appreciation. In addition, he'll be stylish at dances—I mean with the Legion of Honor and all that."

"Is the government going to buy this? The defense minister has to approve new military attachés."

"They've already sent him to Lebanon as an assistant naval attaché. The hostages were released last night, so he'll be coming home."

"Yes, it went smoothly in the end. So, let's see. We have to assume that he'll agree to this without complaint or the kind of complications he usually causes. Then I think I can get the Chief to buy the idea."

"And the foreign service?"

"That's the Chief's problem. It's usually all right once he's made up his mind."

"And the Russians?"

"What do you mean, the Russians?"

"Well, they have to approve the new naval attaché, too, don't they?"

Ulfsson burst out laughing. It was hard to imagine the Russians having any opinions about Carl that they could express openly, glasnost or no glasnost.

. . .

Mile-high, cathedral-like cumulus cloud formations loomed over Småland. Looking down through a dizzying open rift toward the earth, Carl caught a glimpse of the Öland bridge. The plane from Damascus had entered Swedish airspace.

He leaned his head against the window and looked at the cloud formations, trying to empty his mind. Soon it would all be over; in only a few hours everything would be over. One last item to take care of and then the operation would be finished.

He could see her clearly in front of him. She was sitting with her knees drawn up under her chin down on the rocky beach. Someone was fishing close by with a long rod and sinker; he had never seen any of those fishermen catch anything and didn't even know what kind of fish they were after.

She was wearing a nurse's uniform and he was in jeans. They had taken a round through the hospital area in the refugee camp, and he had made occasional notes, pretending to be a journalist. He still had the notepad in his hand when they sat down on the beach.

The heat of the sun made the skin on the burned side of her face reddish and taut. He had had a hard time bringing up the subject: what was done was done, after all, and nothing could be changed. Finally he asked a single word: "Karim?"

She sat in silence with her hands clasped around her shins and her chin resting on her knees. It was impossible to imagine her in the multicolored camouflage uniform with the lieutenant colonel's insignia and the Arafat number 17, which looked like the Roman numeral IV. But her work, like his, consisted of pretense, and she was very good at it.

She hesitated for a long time before answering, perhaps because she wanted to appear to be thinking about it, as if out of humility, as if not to show how easy it was for her to answer.

The Israelis, on average, shot one Palestinian a day in the occupied territories. Strategically and tactically, the intifada, the uprising, overshadowed everything else in importance. She began at the end of the story. If some madmen whom people, rightly or wrongly, associated with the PLO chose to kidnap and possibly murder Swedish doctors, of all people, then the intifada would be irreparably harmed. The crime was treason, and the sentence had been passed by the PLO's leadership in Tunis. That's the way it was from a purely legal standpoint, and it was quite simple. As far as Karim was concerned, naturally it was sad because he was young. But all of them were traitors; they were not PLO. People who sabotaged the intifada were guilty.

And besides, the end for him would have been the same no matter what, maybe a little later or maybe less neatly, but the same.

Carl did not answer. He tormented himself for a while with remembered images, in slow motion and in color, while the actual course of events, when they happened, had moved more quickly than normal and in black and white. At the very moment when he killed, the action was free of extraneous observation or emotion; it was like driving a car very fast, with a kind of concentration on doing the right thing the whole time, but no terror, no excitement, no feeling. But looking down at Karim's wide-open eyes after he had been killed, that he would always remember—in color and slow motion, crystal clear.

Mouna started talking in a brisk businesslike tone, as if to rescue him from sorrow and passivity. How well she knew him. First there were the small practical details. He could turn in the other radio at a Palestinian souvenir shop in the Hammediyah bazaar; yes, he'd find it all right, he'd been there several times; and he would return the pistol when they took care of his transport to Damascus.

And then there was the political price to pay.

He made no objections; he supported the Palestinian movement and always had, as long as they had known each other. He would do it.

She dodged him when he tried to get personal. She was married to the revolution, she said; she had a position that meant that every day she risked being killed, she couldn't be a mother and mate under such conditions, and besides, she couldn't imagine herself as an obedient Palestinian housewife.

She managed to make him laugh, and then she stood up. It was time to go to Damascus, she said.

Carl gave a start as the plane bounced heavily on the asphalt runway and he saw the gleaming aluminum terminals rush past.

As he waited for his suitcase—it now contained only some dirty laundry and a few clothes better suited to the field than the ones he was wearing as a traveling Swedish diplomat—dreamlike feelings came over him. It was summer, and stuffy in the arrivals hall. The Swedes on vacation—nice, law-abiding taxpayers who were people just like himself—were stranger to him than Mouna and her soldiers. He hadn't had the nerve to ask whether he could stay with her group.

Down there on the beach it seemed so clear that he was a different sort, a nice sort of Swede. But here among the actual nice Swedes, things were turned around again.

He took the green line through customs and the officials didn't even give him a glance; for once he had nothing with him that would interest them.

He took a taxi straight to the Foreign Ministry and, since the cab had a telephone, called ahead to announce his arrival. He watched the Swedish summer landscape slipping past with its grazing cows and red barns and stone churches, thinking about nothing at all.

He left his suitcase with the guard and went up to Sorman alone. He pressed the button, which instantly lit up red. He paced back and forth on the soft Persian carpet of the summer-silent corridor, and then sat down impatiently on one of the creaky rococo chairs beside a little black marble table with gilded legs and wooden trim. A secretary came out and gave him a cup of coffee in a white plastic mug, with three gingersnaps on a little blue napkin that barely covered the plastic tray. He gave her twelve thousand-dollar bills without saying anything, as if it were a joke. Then he explained that he was supposed to account for his travel money, and he wanted a proper receipt. She stared at the bills as if they were something unpleasant that did not belong in the Foreign Ministry; but at least they were clean and unfolded and had no trace of bloodstains or other nastiness, he thought. She went off holding the bills out in front of her between her thumb and forefinger as if she would have preferred to carry them with tongs.

Then the waiting signal screeched and turned to green, and Carl stood up and went in through the tall white doors that led directly to Peter Sorman's office.

"Welcome home and have a seat. The trip went well, I hope," said Sorman coolly and formally with a gesture toward the blue velvet chair in front of his desk. They didn't shake hands.

"The hostages have come home and everything is fine, I understand?" asked Carl. You had to start somewhere. Now the political price had to be paid, and he found to his surprise that he didn't dislike exacting it.

"Yes, all's well that ends well," Sorman confirmed with a smile that wasn't a smile. "Everything went very smoothly in the end, it seems."

Carl gave a brief, uncontrolled, and apparently unmotivated laugh. Then he waited a moment.

"The hostages were freed through a joint effort. I went in with an officer from PLO intelligence and carried out the rescue. The PLO explicitly asked me to tell you this, so that from now on you know exactly how it happened. The way the situation was, there were no other possibilities. Time was running out, the terms were unacceptable, we had them under surveillance, and they seemed nervous. We carried out a rescue by force. And that's what I'm supposed to tell you, which I hereby have done."

Carl leaned back. He enjoyed seeing how Sorman lost control, how his mind was racing. His exertion was evident, and Carl regarded him with inner amusement.

"You freed the hostages by force?" asked Sorman at last.

"Yes, that's correct. There were six kidnappers. It wasn't a large organization."

"What happened to them?"

"We shot them."

"All six?"

"That's correct."

"Did you participate in that?"

"Yes. I went in first. I took out a guard and then I killed two more of the men inside and took control of the situation. I had the hostages released and taken away. Then the PLO personnel came into the picture. Tactically, it was a well-orchestrated operation: we had, of course, studied the situation for several days before we went in."

"What happened to the other three?"

"The other kidnappers?"

"Yes."

"PLO personnel executed them after the hostages were led to safety."

"Did you participate in that too?"

"No. But I helped to clean up afterward, naturally."

Carl was enjoying this, and for his own part felt not the least bit uneasy—partly because he knew there could be no action against him given the risk of publicity, and partly because he didn't care.

Sorman had begun to sweat. The news was certainly simple and concrete, yet not so easy to understand. They sat silent and unmoving for several minutes.

"Was there ever any danger for the hostages, in your opinion?" asked Sorman eventually, his jaws clenched. He began to look aggressive.

"No, no, not so far as we could judge. We went in when we knew that all six kidnappers were on the ground floor of the building. The hostages were on the upper floor, so during the confrontation they were completely safe. And they never knew what happened."

"Why not?" snapped Sorman.

"I heard them talking to each other rather cheerfully as they left, and they didn't see the mess I was in at that point. If they had, or even suspected it, they'd have sounded different. They probably thought your diplomatic initiative had finally done the trick." He couldn't avoid a slightly ironic tone.

Sorman glowered. "Wouldn't they have heard something of . . . of the killings? It's hard to imagine they didn't."

"Not at all," said Carl easily. "I used a good-quality weapon with a silencer which the Palestinians supplied me with. And the three executions, as I said, did not occur until they were gone; besides, they too were done with a weapon with silencer. So it's only you and me who know about this—here in Sweden, that is."

"Why the hell are you telling *me* about it!" shouted Sorman, raising his voice for the first time.

"Because the PLO personnel expressly asked me to. As you know, I owe them a favor for their help, and now I've paid them according to our agreement. I've accounted for the money with your secretary. Some of the equipment was left there."

"Weapons?"

"No, as you know, I took no weapons with me, as per your own instructions. The PLO supplied the weapons. What I left was technical equipment, for night vision and things like that, nothing remarkable and nothing classified."

Sorman stood up with what looked like some effort—Carl observed how trim for his age he was—and went over to the window where Carl had stood when they had last met. Carl waited, curious to see what the politician would do next.

At last Sorman turned around, leaning against the windowsill with both hands behind him.

"First of all," he said firmly, "this damn well had better not get out."

"No, that's obvious. I have no such plans," said Carl with a little smile. What did the man think—that he was going to run straight to *Expressen*?

"Secondly, it stops here between the two of us. I won't take the matter further to the government, and you won't take it to the defense leadership. Can we agree on that?"

"Of course," lied Carl, who didn't believe the man for an instant.

"Thirdly, I wonder what you're up to at OP5. Weren't you the one who was involved in that hijacking last year?"

"Yes, that's right. We had to get that Russian back to Sweden at all costs; those were my instructions and I obeyed them."

"And killed two hijackers and took a third prisoner?"

"Yes, fortunately."

"Now I'm wondering whether you have some kind of . . . whether here in Sweden we are dealing with some kind of intelligence officers who have the right . . . who are 'licensed to kill'?"

"No intelligence service in the world issues any kind of special license. The English do talk about some ancient royal prerogative that gives them the right to do anything in the nation's interest."

"And what is your prerogative?"

"I have none. If an operation like this one goes well, neither you nor anyone else complains."

"And if it hadn't gone well?"

"Then it would have been my problem to come up with explanations and make apologies. Should I have let them kill our hostages rather than make use of . . . I think you politicians call them 'unconventional methods'?"

"No snide remarks, if I may ask. This is nothing to joke about. If you think you can run around the world killing people, it's only a matter of time before you bring down on our heads some sort of political catastrophe. It was bad enough with those hijackers. You know that."

"Yes, but things turned out well, and they did this time, too. There's no reason to believe we shall ever land in that type of situation again. It's not exactly routine, may I point out."

"How many people in OP5 have your capabilities?"

"I'm not sure I understand your question."

"Let me put it this way. How many people could have carried this out the way you did?"

"Three."

"Three?"

"Yes."

"Including yourself?"

"Yes, myself and two others."

"Do you have any special kind of training, and if so, who made the decision to give it to you?"

"Yes, we have special training. As far as who made the decision, you'll have to ask the defense leadership about that. I'm not authorized to say."

"What the hell are you telling me?"

"You're asking about classified military information which I don't have the authority to divulge. You will have to ask the Defense Chief or someone else."

"I regard that as impudence."

"It's not meant to be impudent. I am no longer in diplomatic service, so far as I know." Carl took his diplomatic passport out of his back pocket and tossed it onto Sorman's desk.

Sorman nodded, as if confirming something, or as if he had thought things through and had found his thoughts to be correct and wise.

"Not a word—everything stops here between us," he said after a moment and put out his hand for a handshake.

"Everything stops here," confirmed Carl, rising to shake hands.

On the way downstairs he felt like a balloon that has been untied so that the air rapidly rushes out. Now it was all over.

Sorman had not asked about the kidnappers' identity or allegiance, as if the matter was of no significance, so he hadn't had to lie. The matter was clear: the PLO had done Sweden a favor; Sweden was indebted to the PLO. And it was all over.

He felt powerless when he picked up his suitcase with the guards, but he decided to go home anyway, possibly with a little detour, for the thought of his destroyed home was distasteful—if it really was his home and not just a cover for a spy who was supposed to look as if he were living the normal human life of a real estate wheeler-dealer.

He took the route around the Foreign Ministry out along Strömmen, down to Riksbron, and he stopped for a while to watch a fisherman with his net in the stern of a green-painted boat. When the net was pulled up, a big shiny bream lay in the bottom of it, and the other spectators around Carl started to applaud.

He felt sorry for the fish who was dying to the applause, and he asked himself: Who would eat a dead bream? How did you even cook bream?

He went over Riksbron and under the walkway that connected the two houses of Parliament, closed for the summer and until after the election—unless some scandal came up or had to be covered up. He wasn't up to date on the news.

At the tobacconist at the head of Västerlånggatan, where the stream of shorts-clad tourists grew denser, posters for the evening papers screeched about the successful resolution to the hostage drama in Lebanon. There were big pictures of the doctors reunited with their families. He looked at the two men and their wives and children. He hadn't seen them before, even though he had been only a few feet away from them, only a day or two earlier. Real people, real families.

He bought a paper—the conservative one, which usually reflected Säpo's opinions—and continued up Västerlånggatan, but changed his mind halfway home and settled down on a park bench outside the Stock Exchange to read the paper next to a couple of middle-aged drunks smelling of piss.

The front page was dominated by reports on the hostages. Nothing there that shouldn't have been. A few vague references to secret (and successful) Swedish diplomacy.

Then followed several articles under the headline SOCIAL DEMO-CRATS' COCAINE RING, but he couldn't make sense of them. It seemed completely crazy. Was the government supporting personal favorites among the Social Democratic elite who, for unknown reasons, had handpicked special policemen as bodyguards?

He wondered what "unknown reasons" meant, but it neither in-terested nor concerned him. He folded up the paper, stuffed it in a garbage can, and continued homeward, suppressing the thought of what was waiting for him and brooding instead about Cabinet Sec-retary Peter Sorman.

One of the government's most dedicated men, one of the few who knew about Operation Big Red, one of the most important politicians in Sweden, one who never participated in mudslinging itself. And a total cynic.

Sorman didn't care about the doctors on the front page that night; he did care about political success. He had no objections to the deaths in Lebanon—true, he didn't know about Karim—but he knew it wouldn't be good to have it known that anyone but Swedes had resolved the crisis. Maybe that's how you were after thirty years in politics or, for that matter, thirty years in the secret service. Carl had spent more than ten years in the secret service, and that had already stripped him of his personality and made him into a wandering actor and a murderer. Almost half the people he had murdered were

Palestinians—if you didn't count an unknown number of drowned Russians.

He forced himself to think about the word "murderer." There were about half a dozen euphemisms in the jargon—everything from the Russians' almost poetic "specialist in wetwork" to the Americans' more direct "hit man"—which all meant the same thing.

Perhaps, he thought, he should become a policeman instead, a real police officer like her. No, any police job would lead back to the monkey house on Kungsholmen. He had to think of something completely different. What if he boned up on finance and established a cultural foundation with all his money—annual concerts, baroque music with period instruments, things like that which were seldom done because of the cost. Or a foundation for young political artists. Painters always needed money when they were political and wouldn't paint portraits of the royal family, as one of his former friends from Clarté did.

He couldn't get away from his money, and money ought to be used for good causes. Presumably for better—no, not better, but more lasting—causes than the Afghan liberation movement, to which he had donated all that money the year before. Now the Russians were pulling out, and of course it had nothing to do with his donation, even if it had reached the right address. He couldn't escape from the money. And he shouldn't just let it sit there making more money, which it could do all by itself.

At his door on Drakens Lane, he had to make his way past workers pushing wheelbarrows over wooden planks and piles of bricks and other construction debris. There were flowers on the windowsill on the first landing—they looked as if they needed water. He stopped and unconsciously, automatically touched his left side; yes, he was unarmed.

No, he thought. No, it's over. A normal Swedish man has the right to walk unarmed into his own home. He went up the stairs. At the top, as expected, the builders were working in his own apartment.

Lallerstedt was supervising the work force. He was standing in the middle of the apartment and commanding as if on the bridge of a ship, which is where he belonged.

Commander Lallerstedt was Carl's immediate superior in what was euphemistically called the special missions department, and he was, as usual, red in the face. Carl set down his suitcase and looked at him with amazement. A real naval officer, thought Carl, and yet he's *here*.

"Good thing you're back, Hamilton!" shouted Lallerstedt, retaining his tone of command. "We're in the process of cleaning up, as you can see. Wanted to be here myself so that nothing unnecessary would be built in, if you know what I mean. How've you been, you son of a gun?"

"Pretty good; a little short on sleep, is all," replied Carl, astonished.

"Damn good thing you turned up!" Lallerstedt continued shouting until he realized he didn't have to. "Did everything go all right down south?" he inquired more normally.

"Yes, the operation went fine. What the hell are you doing?" Carl had not gotten over his amazement.

"Restoration of an officer's apartment. Routine. What should we do with the room we can't get into?"

"That depends on whose workers these are."

"The Defense Ministry's."

"Then I guess I can open it, but it isn't damaged much, and it doesn't have much more than—well, you know what I mean."

"Yes, those cartons over there that we haven't opened seem to contain various items, or what should I call them?"

"Items?"

"Yes, which presumably belong in your locked domain. Could we go inside? I seem to think you have a telephone in there."

Carl went over to the big oak door and opened it; when the steel door behind was revealed, he punched in the combination on the electronic lock.

"I changed the combination after the monkey gang was here," he explained.

The floor was torn up at the corners; a window shutter behind an iron grating had been ripped off; the punching bag lay like a slit-open seal in the middle of the floor. Otherwise everything was almost undisturbed.

"Must be hell having people rooting around like this in your home," pondered Lallerstedt courteously.

"Yes," said Carl, "it is. The telephone is on the wall over there next to the weapons cupboard, but it's bugged, of course."

"Oh, I don't think so," said Lallerstedt, punching in the seven digits that Carl anticipated. "Seahawk is home now . . . Yes, so it seems . . . I'll pass on the message . . . In half an hour. Yes, I understand."

"What did Sam say?" asked Carl tonelessly as he looked at one of his targets at the far end of the room. He hadn't taken it down as he usually did after practice, and one of the shots was outside the 10. He felt oddly embarrassed, as if Lallerstedt had noticed it with disapproval.

"You're supposed to go to the Chief's office, and I'm supposed to recommend your uniform," said Lallerstedt with a twinkle in his eye.

"What do you mean, uniform?" Carl was mystified. "Are they going to slit the epaulets off the shoulder boards, like the old days?"

"No, quite the contrary, I would think. The Chief and Sam are expecting you in a half hour. I'll hold down the fort here at the restoration station."

"You know I only have a dress uniform that's a little too small. And besides, I wore your pants," muttered Carl. He forced himself not to speculate about the imminent meeting.

Lallerstedt was amused. "Then it will have to be civilian clothes, but it probably wouldn't hurt if I suggest that you shave first."

"What did you mean by Seahawk, by the way?"

"Seahawk? That's the Russian code name for you."

"What the hell is that supposed to mean?"

"I don't know the details, and you'll be getting them from the Chief himself or from Sam. You were supposed to have been an agent called Seahawk or something like that. But it's all over and done with, so you can stop being nervous. Do you know what Seahawk means, by the way?"

"I know what a seahawk is, but is it supposed to mean something special?"

"Oh yes. Go get shaved now and see about putting in an appearance, and I'll continue with the fortifications. This is on the Defense Ministry's account, you know. You can probably replace the destroyed furniture by requisition later on, and we'll pay for it."

Carl went into the kitchen, where there was water and they hadn't started working. He shaved and changed his shirt and left without saying goodbye to Lallerstedt, who was busy again with the workers. He went down Skeppsbron and past the Grand Hotel before he realized that he shouldn't arrive late and sweating, so he caught a cab.

The Chief looked solemn and formal.

Carl noticed that first. His next observation should have been the first, and it concerned who else was present. On either side of the Chief sat Sam and the newly appointed navy chief of staff. And they were seated in the low armchairs at the side of the room instead of at the big conference table where they had been last time.

Carl went around the circle and shook hands with them in order of rank, and when the Chief sat down, the other three did too, Carl last. He was uncertain whether military protocol prescribed this, but it couldn't be wrong, anyway. He felt completely neutral inside. Nothing surprises me now, he thought.

"Yes, this was a terrible episode . . ." began the Chief, clearing his throat.

Why had Sam put on his uniform? Carl wondered. He never did that except on official occasions and for newspaper interviews.

"But," continued the Chief, adjusting his glasses, "we've arrived at the light—we've reached the end of the tunnel, you might say. First of all, Hamilton, as head of the agency, I must offer our apologies for the unpleasantness this incident must have caused you."

Should he say anything? He decided not.

"And so, and so, to make a long story short, well, you'll get the details from Sam later on, so, in consultation with the Old Man, I have decided on your promotion. This should not be considered an attempt on our part to smooth things over. What was done had to be done. But you should regard it as a sign of our esteem for your extraordinary service and our unwavering confidence in you."

The Chief suddenly reached for a document lying on the table in front of him and stood up. Carl stood up too, instinctively, when he saw that everyone was about to rise.

"I now," said the Chief, handing him the paper, "have the great pleasure of presenting this letter of appointment from the supreme commander to our youngest captain to date. Congratulations!"

Carl had no time to think about the meaning of this. Everything was about form. He accepted the document and was about to salute, but shook the Chief's hand instead and then that of the navy chief of staff and then Sam's. Yes, well, apparently this was the protocol; and when they had congratulated him with manly handshakes, they all sat down again and an enlisted man brought in a tray with glasses of wine.

"There's just one thing that I'd like to ask you," said the Chief when they had been served. "*Skål*, by the way. *Skål*, Captain!"

Carl toasted his superiors according to rank and then they drank in silence and looked at each other as Swedes do before putting down their glasses. German wine, *Spätlese*, probably Rheingau, quite good, thought Carl, chasing away a number of German memories.

"Well, ahem, that is," continued the Chief, "when you read your documents you'll see that we've made a certain reorganization. As of next month you will be our resident naval attaché in Moscow." He smiled at the surprise, for now Carl was truly dumbfounded.

"Does the Defense Chief think the Russians really have such a sense of humor?" he asked at last, and the others laughed.

"It's not a question of humor. They have to realize once and for all that the whole thing with Seahawk didn't work—an apt code name, by the way. But something very important is at stake, and you'll get the details from Sam later."

Carl looked at the Defense Chief. Was he the object of some sort of psychological warfare? The expressions of the other men lacked the tension they would have betrayed if that were the case—or had a final insanity overcome him? He looked at his hand, which was still holding the glass with the amber-yellow fluid—yes, it was probably a *Spätlese*.

Then the Chief rose again and the other men stood up too. He held out his hand to Carl and winked and repeated his congratulations, and the navy chief of staff said the same, and then Sam signaled discreetly to Carl that it was time for them to leave, whereupon the newly appointed captain and the commodore, showing the proper respect for their superiors, withdrew.

"What the hell is this all about?" asked Carl as soon as they were out of the room and had started down the corridor to the other end of the building and their own domain. Carl had to walk one step behind Ulfsson, his superior and commanding officer.

"How's your Russian?" asked Ulfsson cheerfully over his shoulder.

"Pretty miserable. I know the five or six hundred most common military expressions, things like that, and I assume I can order borscht without being misunderstood, but I've probably forgotten everything else."

"Doesn't matter, we have intensive courses, and you've got a month." Ulfsson was still cheerful.

"But what the hell is this about?" persisted Carl. They had almost reached the code-locked entry to their own regions.

"Sandström. Wait till we get to my office."

Ulfsson thought he knew precisely what Carl's assignment was in Moscow. But he didn't.

Six

Yuri Chivartshev was living through his most nerve-racking week ever since he had come to Stockholm as head of the Swedish station.

Somewhere Operation Reorganization had gone wrong, and the end of the mess was far from sight.

Within Säpo, the first target, everything seemed to be going right. They had been weakly represented in the Russian Bureau, with the Peacock heading toward retirement and virtually phased out; it wouldn't have been good to have him as an active retiree when he could no longer easily get at information. Now the situation was improved: the Swedes would set things in motion and investigate themselves, as usual, and then they would make cosmetic changes and shuffle people around. Since all Swedes, even Security Police officers, are employed for life, the responsibility for anti-Soviet activity in Säpo would end up being transferred to new people, with good qualifications, from different departments. Conditions would be good for a GRU informer to move into the discredited and suspect bureau.

If Zentral hadn't bitten off more than it could chew, everything would certainly have gone according to plan. But some of the Moscow desk strategists had evidently decided to kill two birds with one stone by striking at military intelligence at the same time.

The conditions were theoretically simple. In theory it was a brilliant *maskirovka*. But the Tristan plan had had political and psychological weaknesses. It was politically wrong to dredge up questions about the Swedish intervention against Chichagov, Bodisko, and

Apraksin; it risked publicity and deteriorating foreign relations, which might enrage the political leadership and be regarded as sabotage against détente and glasnost. Psychologically the operation was even less well thought out. A report from Aeroflot confirmed that the Old Man himself had taken off on various trips—to California and London, in tourist class, strangely enough—and it wasn't hard to figure out why he went to the bother. Moreover, whatever it was that Hamilton had been involved in with the SEAL people, the CIA wouldn't give up until everything had been checked out.

The weakness was that Zentral didn't know enough about Hamilton's actual purpose in the United States. The only thing they knew for sure was that he had received that special medal: the wings with a claw clutching a trident.

Chivartshev sighed. He was the one who had gotten that information, and at the time he had been pleased about it: snapping the color photo of Hamilton as he came out of the French embassy, blowing up the detail of his chest with the line of medals. Chivartshev remembered the wind sweeping aside Hamilton's cloak so his chest was exposed. Later some clever functionary in the Moscow information unit had confirmed the interesting scrap of information about Hamilton's training in California.

If only he had snapped the photo a few seconds later, then everything would have been better off. It had been a terrible mistake to try to discredit Hamilton, though it was easy enough to want to destroy the department where he worked.

But this wasn't something the Swedes could fall for.

So the question was, what conclusions *had* they drawn? What was Ulfsson thinking? What was the Defense Chief thinking? And the Old Man? This might all end very badly, but it was too soon to do anything except hope that the Swedish defense brass would refuse to reveal what they thought of Tristan. Meanwhile there was the question of Hamilton himself.

Moscow was demanding some sort of analysis, which they claimed was urgent because of the formality of having to recognize Hamilton as a diplomat. Why? That was the first question. And were there objections? That was the second. Chivartshev could only guess, and guesses were not what he usually filled his reports with.

Why would they take Hamilton out of the secret service and make him part of open intelligence? And why send him to Moscow, of all places?

Obviously he had the kind of training that could be put to best use in Moscow, for he had certainly been educated to consider the Soviet Union the primary enemy. But how could he return to undercover work as an attaché? Was he regarded as the Young Turk heir apparent to military intelligence? After all, both Samuel Ulfsson and the Old Man would be retiring soon, the Old Man in several months. No, he was too young and his experience too limited. Anyway, most countries never made field personnel into bosses, though you couldn't tell with the Swedes.

Was there some underlying joke? Could choosing Moscow be an arrogant gesture, as if to say, Here you see what your provocations were worth. We would never send anyone with the shadow of suspicion on him to Moscow. No, that was a British way of reacting, not a Swedish one.

What about an official Russian objection to Hamilton's presence in Moscow? The Swedes now had at least one man who could be deported in exchange if they decided to deport Russians from Stockholm—as the result of a leak about Peacock. The Peacock's most recent control had left Sweden two months ago, and previous ones were all over the place, though none in Scandinavia. But that didn't rule out the possibility that the Swedes might want to deport some Russians, as they usually did when politics and publicity demanded it. So that was a disadvantage. Of course, it was offset by the obvious fact that Hamilton in Moscow offered interesting opportunities for the Russians, which would make it difficult for the Swedes to take action against Soviet personnel in Stockholm. Hadn't they thought of that? No, apparently not. They were compartmentalized: the military thought only of military matters, and politicians only thought about political ones, and they were actually proud of this crazy system.

Would Hamilton, so used to covert action in the field, be able to adapt to legal embassy reporting? It'd be interesting to see whether he took risks. Perhaps they might be able to approach him outright sooner or later. Highly improbable, but not to be ruled out.

In any case, they should accept the new Swedish naval attaché without raising an eyebrow.

Chivartshev called in his personal cryptographer. He prepared to send a brief message to Zentral.

· · ·

Captain Carl Gustaf Gilbert Hamilton had a very strange week. In addition to the time he spent at defense headquarters—where, to his surprise, they welcomed him as an ordinary colleague in the service and where they gave him some diplomatic training—he spent four hours a day in the language laboratory and pestered his now equal-ranking colleague, Lallerstedt, about matters of uniform details and naval jargon among gentlemen.

One important question was in what order service ribbons should be arranged on the left breast of his uniform. They couldn't be placed in one row, because you couldn't put more than three ribbons in a row. The honors most important to yourself had to be closest to your heart, followed by any possible commander's ribbons.

There was only one patriotic solution. In the first row, Carl placed the blue and yellow ribbon of the King's medal for bravery in the field, then the carmine-red ribbon indicating the Commander's Medal of the Legion of Honor, and then the Commander's Medal of the West German Bundesverdienstkreuz.

On a second row directly underneath he put the other ribbon for the King's Medal for bravery in the field.

On his other breast would be the SEALs' golden wings; there was no reason to keep it secret from the Russians, since they already knew about it.

Few if any captains of the Legion of Honor would have placed that honor second. Every West German officer who saw his own honor at the outer end of a row of ribbons would be offended. But to wear the Swedish honor first was as natural for a Swedish captain as for a Soviet sea captain second class to place the Order of Lenin or the Red Banner or the Red Star medal closest to *his* heart.

The arrangement was irreproachable in its arrogance.

As far as the subject himself, the traitor Sandström, Ulfsson thought that no particular studies were called for: that appearance and address were sufficient. But Carl did not share this opinion.

Most important, however, was preparing for Moscow and for maximum freedom of movement there. A little Lada—with diplomatic plates, to be sure, but still a Russian car—would be more feasible and discreet for getting around Moscow than a conspicuous Volvo. The quickest way to get a Russian car delivered to the Swedish embassy in Moscow turned out to be via Finland.

On the whole this was a nice assignment, like a change of profession, and presumably more realistic than becoming a policeman or philanthropist. It put Carl in a good mood, and he tried to look on developments cheerfully; at least he was being kept busy with ridiculous projects that made one believe that this was the way real people prepared for real trips.

In this mood he signed out a car and went down to Kivik to visit the Old Man, who wanted to see him for a few summer days.

The apples were beginning to show. The Old Man seemed to have a million unripe apples to worry about, and at first he talked mostly of insect pests and leaf rust that he thought was connected to pollution in Poland. At the mouth of the Weichsel—yes, everyone else called the river the Vistula, but the Old Man had been brought up and educated during the German era—the beaches had been closed and the big resort hotels stood empty, even the wonderful old hotel in Sopot, where he had often stayed in the days when intelligence work was characterized by gentlemanly sportsmanship. Now death flowed from the mouth of the Weichsel, and on the beaches were posted signs warning you not to swim at the risk of your life. It was right across the water from Kivik.

The topic of ecological disaster finally exhausted, the Old Man—snorting with laughter, with his eyebrows raised high—brought out some of the day's papers and read them aloud to Carl, who as usual in the evening was tending the fire.

A few days ago, reports said, Cabinet Secretary Peter Sorman had had the pleasure of making a statement at a press conference. Conservative journalists asked questions about negotiating with terrorists and whether Swedish diplomats were really doing their jobs, and so on.

That wasn't so strange. The strange thing was that Sorman, for the first time that anyone could remember, had gotten upset and lost some of his self-control. He had stated cryptically, "A Swede in diplomatic service, at the risk of his own life, went into a part of Lebanon where there are practically bounties on a white man's head, and got the two doctors out."

In the flurry of speculation, journalists proposed three candidates for this mysterious Scarlet Pimpernel drama: Ambassador Rolf Gauffin, who had been in Damascus and Beirut, was the narrow favorite over Ambassador Ingemar Stjernberg and Embassy Secretary Belius. All three had made appropriate, properly mysterious and properly modest comments on the Swede "in diplomatic service." (No journalist noticed the nuance: a person "in diplomatic service" could be someone other than a diplomat.) "I don't think anyone can actually say who Mr. Sorman is referring to," said Ambassador Gauffin. "In any case, I can't tell you anything." Belius claimed he had been in Damascus by coincidence and had no further comments. Ambassador Stjernberg referred them to the Foreign Ministry or to Sorman himself, and had no additional comments. The vacationing foreign minister, finally tracked down, would not comment on the rumors except to say, "Peter Sorman was obviously provoked at the press conference, and the point of secret diplomacy is that it should be kept secret."

"Great, no?" chuckled O.M. "Now that it's an election year they can make a scandal out of anything. You were there. What really did happen? I'll put a fiver on Gauffin."

"Do you really want to know?" asked Carl without turning around. He was still preoccupied with the fire. O.M. had his logs on an iron stand that was supposed to be practical, but it meant the fire was always going out.

O.M. didn't reply, and Carl did not turn around. The crackles of the burning logs filled the room. O.M. went out without saying anything, and Carl cautiously moved over to the sofa. It was dusk, just the time when you have to decide whether to turn on the lights. Carl preferred the dark.

The Old Man came back with a bottle of his home-distilled, illegal apple brandy and two glasses, and Carl understood that he did want to know and that it was going to be a long evening.

"I had thought we'd go down to the beach," said the Old Man innocently as he filled a glass and passed it to Carl, then poured one for himself. "But," he continued, raising his glass to Carl, who could no longer see his eyes, "I realize we are going to have a long evening. *Skål*. So. What happened?"

"The PLO and I rescued the hostages and sent them up to the Hotel Summerland in Beirut. We used silencers on the weapons, so the doctors had no idea what happened. The diplomats didn't either, judging from those reports," replied Carl in one long breath. So then everything was said and the gates of hell were opened anew. He thought he had successfully closed them.

O.M. sat in silence, swirling his glass. Carl expected a series of inescapable questions.

"The hostages were aware of nothing?" asked O.M. with a sigh, sounding dutiful about asking.

"Right. Nothing." Carl took too big a gulp of the homemade Calvados, which smelled of fusel oil and almost made him gag.

"How many kidnappers were there?" continued O.M., motionless.

"Six."

"Any survivors?"

"No."

"You did it?"

"Three of them. I went in first—it was Sweden's responsibility, so to speak."

"Unpleasant?"

"Yes. Very. Not then, but afterward."

"Anything in particular?"

"One of them was a boy of sixteen or seventeen, and he was executed afterward, after the Swedes had been taken away."

"You did it?"

"No, damn it. The PLO. I did the break-in."

"How many did you kill, then?"

"Three, I said."

"Yes, yes. But I mean, that was all during the raid?"

"Yes."

"Then the others are not your responsibility."

"That's what their commander said, too."

"You don't share that opinion?"

"Of course not."

"*Skål.* It probably *is* going to be a long evening, as I feared," said the Old Man, sighing again. Soon they were sitting in the real dark, and neither of them wanted to turn on the lights.

The Old Man started in the 1940s.

One time in Italy, in a place where there were high reeds, he had for the first time drawn a weapon with the intention of killing another human being. It had felt so unreal; the sun was shining and it was daytime and the insects were a bother. But there hadn't been any other way out. Otherwise a large part of a partly Swedish network of Western agents in the East would have been ripped apart. It was either this man fleeing through the reeds or ten other people on the other side.

Afterward, when the men gathered around the fallen prey as if it were an ordinary hunt, everybody had psychologically shielded themselves from what they were looking at by talking in hunting terminology.

No matter how much you tried to speak sensibly about something like this, you could never escape the truth that reason and logic were one thing and feelings quite different.

Carl interrupted suddenly. "Sometimes I feel as if I'm going mad," he blurted.

"That's a healthy reaction." The Old Man's resort to jargon would have seemed absurd if Carl hadn't known that he was trained as a psychologist.

No rational person could kill someone at close range without asking questions, O.M. went on. Perhaps it was different in wartime, especially when far away from the enemy. Then the assignment became abstract, as when pilots leave it to computers to work out where the bombs should be dropped. That's the way it had been in Vietnam, for instance. On the other hand, lots of Americans in the Special Forces came home with serious psychoses, though none of them had killed half so many people as a single bomb load might have. It was normal, it was the opposite of madness, to torment yourself with reproaches afterward. The play of circumstances had placed Coq Rouge on the firing line on more occasions than could reasonably have been anticipated, but on the other hand, maybe it wouldn't happen anymore.

"Where does that Coq Rouge nonsense come from?" Carl was suddenly curious on this point and felt a certain weariness with the sermon.

"It's something Näslund came up with, I think," muttered O.M. He was put out by the abrupt interruption, and lost his rhythm.

"Näslund? He doesn't know French, does he?" Carl persisted.

"No, but he was in Paris for some meeting of the Kilowatt group—yes, before the final phase of that Israeli action in Stockholm—so some French colleague probably gave him a hand."

"He was sitting there gossiping about his personnel?"

"Yes, I assume so. Those policemen can never keep their mouths shut."

"But what does it mean? Is it a nickname? What does it refer to?"

"Damned if I know, but if we could get back to—"

"No, I'm curious. And how many people know about it?"

"A certain number in the monkey house on Kungsholmen—that's where it spread from—and then all the computers in the world, at least on the Western side. It refers to, well, a red rooster. There's a song from the Spanish Civil War, you know—red means socialist and a rooster is someone who fights."

"Or else red means bloody," remarked Carl gloomily.

"No, that would have come later, in that case. Do you know how many people you've killed, and does it have any importance—the number, I mean?"

"Of course I know, and of course it's important. Four Israelis the first year in Stockholm when I was working in the monkey house. Two plus one West Germans the year after, in Syria and Hamburg. Then it's a philosophical question how my intervention in what happened in Hamburg should be regarded—twelve were killed there at the same time. Last year two Palestinians and a completely innocent Polish immigrant. And now three Palestinians. That makes five Palestinians, four Israelis, and four Europeans."

"Finished?"

"What do you mean?"

"There's a dramatic error in your count, and that fits in with what we were talking about."

"You mean last year?"

"Yes, of course. You and Steelglove and Lundwall drowned between fifty and three hundred Russians when you blew up their underwater installations. Why not the same guilty conscience about them? I mean, it's hardly some kind of racist evaluation, is it?"

"I'm used to not thinking about it. It's only with you and Sam, and maybe with Steelglove and Lundwall when they get home, that I can talk about that."

"Don't try. It was a regular act of war, and that's the way the three of you thought of it. That's the difference—it's not very rational, but that's the way we think and feel."

"You don't think a man can be tormented by killing in wartime?"

"Yes, of course. I don't think you would have done very well under Skip Harrier in Vietnam."

"Did you meet him in California? What did he say?"

"Well, he said quite a lot; among other things, he spoke very well of you. Something along the lines of 'I just love that boy and don't you fuck with him because if you do I'll cut off your balls.' Mm, along those lines. I'm not sure how you'd put that in civilized language, but it has to be interpreted as an expression of great esteem. How would you translate it?"

Carl burst out laughing. It was the first light moment since their conversation had proceeded into darkness.

"Something like this. 'Commander Hamilton seems to me a particularly upright young officer, and I would find it remarkable if you, on the flimsy grounds that you have indicated, Colonel, sir, would even consider making difficulties for him.' Americans are rather more direct than we are."

They laughed together, relieved. The Old Man disappeared to get a bottle of white wine; Carl noticed that he turned on a few discreet lights when he came back. It would be better to see each other clearly from now on.

"I can see you're no great lover of homemade Calvados," O.M. apologized. "But tell me, how did things go?" He poured the wine, and they tasted.

"You mean in Saida?"

"Yes, during the break-in itself."

"You want the chance to make excuses for me and say that anyone would have done the same, and so forth."

"Not necessarily," O.M. lied calmly, "but *was* there any other choice?"

"No, they had made impossible demands. They wanted transport out of the country under our diplomatic protection, since otherwise the PLO would execute them, as they well knew. There was a big risk they would kill one of the Swedes, as they threatened. We had them under surveillance while they were arguing about what to do. And the deadline was very close."

"Did you have them bugged?"

"No, we didn't have the equipment, and besides, it probably wasn't worth the risk; we had a good observation post and they weren't aware of our presence. But what we saw was alarming enough. We knew their routines. We knew when they would all be together eating supper."

"And that's the time you picked for the strike itself?"

"Yes. We couldn't wait another day. The hostages were upstairs from them, and they were all downstairs."

"Good. And then?"

"We had night-vision devices and used that advantage. I approached the building, observed by my assistant. Then I took out the guard, who came out to patrol according to routine. Afterward I went in and shot two of them, took control of the situation, and then called in my Palestinian backup."

"How did you get the hostages out and how could they not realize what was going on?"

"I sent the boy upstairs to bring them down to a waiting car manned by Palestinians, and then ordered him to come back inside."

"Why didn't he take off?"

"Because I was pointing a forty-five-caliber automatic at his father and his father's cousin while he carried out his assignment."

"Brilliant! Perfect! Straight out of an instruction manual! It's incredible how simply something like that can be done with small units instead of in the German style with a lot of noise and commotion. An excellent effort, Carl. I really must congratulate you."

O.M.'s enthusiasm seemed rather exaggerated, but from what Carl knew of him it might very well be genuine.

"I think you want me to make excuses for myself again," said Carl slowly after a long pause. "But this is the way things are. With each individual case, we've wound up in discussions like this. And each time, it's turned out that everything happened the way it had to happen, there were no alternatives, and fortunately I managed to do precisely the right thing in the right situation. No, I'm not being ironic. And each time, I have, in the end, actually come to the conclusion that you're probably right. But the thing is, there are too many cases to talk about coincidence anymore. I've become some kind of lawful murderer for the Swedish state, and that's the heart of the problem, the end result."

It was O.M.'s turn to be silent for a while, and then he changed the subject.

"What do you think of your new job in Moscow?" he asked, betraying none of his great unease.

"Great," replied Carl quickly. He smiled reassuringly. "Really great, as a matter of fact. I'm a diplomat and semicivilian and have strict instructions not to take any weapons in my baggage, and that suits me fine. I'll get to learn a lot about the Russians, and I get to play the officer and gentleman. The assignment itself is easy if things go well, and impossible if they don't, so there's not much to worry about."

"How are you planning to do it? At close range or from a distance? And how long are you thinking of waiting?"

"When I take a picture of that devil, you mean? At close range, absolutely not lying around and waiting with a telephoto lens somewhere—I don't think that would do in Moscow. At close range after a few months, after the Russians get used to me."

"How will you do it close up? You can't wait outside his door or at GRU offices."

"No, of course not. I'll go over to his apartment some weekday evening, look to see whether there's a light in the window, and if there is, then I'll go up, open the door, march in and say hello politely and tell him that I'm from the Swedish embassy, and invite him to come home with me if he's tired of Moscow."

"I'll be damned," said O.M. His eyebrows rose to the owl position. "Do you plan to knock first, or what? And what are you going to do about the front door of the building?"

"In newer apartments in Moscow they've started installing code locks of the Western type. I have a gadget for it. Ordinary Russian door locks are somewhat similar to the Abloy type, only simpler. You can open them with a hairpin, like detectives in the movies, if you want to."

"So you walk right in and make a little conversation while you take his picture, as if in passing?"

"Yes, something like that."

"And if he doesn't like it? I mean, what if he's armed?"

"I'll still be able to take the picture, and then I'll leave, but it's more likely that he'll get into conversation with me. Which I can record, by the way."

"Hm. And how will you live in Moscow up until zero hour?"

"As if I were a rather careless young diplomat who, more by luck than out of competence, always acts according to the law. I go to the pubs too much, and my tongue's a little loose, and I seem as if I've been expelled from the job I really wanted. I hint that I've somehow gotten the boot, and that Moscow is a kind of punishment. If we're in luck they'll try to approach me, and that would be great."

"And then you won't refuse them right away?"

"No, but of course I won't do the opposite either. But it won't be so easy. The Russians aren't stupid."

"Your plan seems a little thin, I must say."

"Maybe, but there's plenty of time, and I have to get to know the city and get used to the new job. It's only a question of a brief little moment of surprise, and then the matter is done."

O.M. brooded for a moment before changing the subject again.

"What do you have in mind after you come home?" he asked.

"I don't know. Luckily I'm no longer good for covert work in the field—I don't like it anymore. We'll have to see."

"Lallerstedt is going to quit in a few months. He wants to go back to sea, and that's where he's undeniably best suited. Would you be able to take his job?"

"That sounds like a trap."

"Not at all. But I promised Lundwall that when he came home his boss would be Carl Hamilton. Commander Carl Hamilton, I said, but captain would do just as well."

"It's a little unexpected."

"Yes, but you know, we have to take care of our house. I'm retiring soon, Sam too, and we have to look for fresh talent. The boys have to have someone who can protect them when they come home—you can appreciate that, can't you?"

"You want me on the inside, and more computers than knives from now on."

"Yes, something like that. I think it would suit you too. Above all, I think it would suit our new green lieutenants."

"When are they coming home?"

"While you're away, I assume. We'll get them stabled and bridled before you get back."

"Doesn't sound so bad."

"No, it doesn't. But before we go to bed, there's one unpleasant thing I have to tell you about."

Carl stiffened. If O.M. said "unpleasant" it was not likely to be an exaggeration.

"I found out yesterday," he continued heavily. "Since the Americans got part of the Tristan report from their London cousins—well, nothing else could be expected—they weren't satisfied with Harrier's and my conclusions, or even with the new information they probably got from London."

"New what?" asked Carl with a crack in his voice. He suspected something *very* unpleasant.

"Yes, from Sir Geoffrey Hunt at MI6. Well, the Americans decided to leave no stone unturned until they'd gotten to the bottom of everything. So the DIA and the FBI, too, I presume, dragged in a lot of your friends for rather harsh questioning, carried out under what they themselves call 'duress.' A peculiar euphemism." He stopped. Carl was already getting the point.

"Tessie?" he asked. He already knew the answer.

"Yes. Teresa O'Connor."

"How?"

"Three or four days in a basement somewhere. The standard American procedure when it comes to exposing a Russian agent—you know."

"Yes, I know. Say no more. They got to do it to us so that we could practice techniques for resisting interrogation. I know their whole program," Carl said miserably. "She's the person who has been closest to me in my whole life."

"I know that," said the Old Man quietly.

"That baboon from the DIA going at Tessie for three or four days—" Carl couldn't go on, overwhelmed by a note of simultaneous sorrow and rage.

"You understand, Carl," said O.M. gently, even sadly, "it's Sandström doing this to us. And this is only the beginning. This is the way things will go on."

Carl seemed barely to be listening, but O.M. knew he had heard him.

"Well, now we'd better go to bed. Early breakfast tomorrow." The Old Man stood up.

It hurt inside. He felt cruel toward a man he had learned to care about like a son.

But it had to be done. Like a swift surgical operation. Sometimes it was necessary to cut even the ones closest to you.

Neither of them slept that night, or so they thought, anyway. And the light of the summer morning came very early, for it was only the beginning of July. Too late in the year for nightingales, though, and nature was silent.

When Carl went to the usual guest room, with windows facing the slope of the garden—as if the rooms were a sentry box from which he was supposed to listen for the slightest crunching on the gravel pathway from the gate—he knew he wouldn't sleep. Tessie came to him, Tessie whom he had loved when he was a real person and had loved as a real person does.

Music came to him, sudden and loud, as if he were really hearing it, not just within his head. It was something from long ago, something on a seventy-eight with static. It was Horowitz playing the Liszt *Funérailles*, but it was actual funeral music, funeral music with march segments, as if a hero were being buried who been decorated with the Legion of Honor, for example.

He tried to be amused and he tried to feel cynical, but then she came back in the middle of the music, being interrogated by the gorillas from the DIA:

"Okay, you little commie slut, this is no game. Chicana or not, don't think you're a damn American.

"He must have told you, he probably told you that he was a commie—you've already admitted that, haven't you?

"You don't just fuck commies, do you? Are you just a damn commie whore? What did he tell you about his work for the Russians?

"The poor and the oppressed, is that right? You can shove that up your ass, baby. When we're finished with you, you might not have much ass left.

"Whatever suits us, little miss lawyer, little commie-fucking lawyer who's going to throw the U.S. Constitution in our faces. Baby, we are the U.S. Constitution. What did he tell you? How did he phrase it the first time he said that he was working for the Russians? How did he recruit you? Was it with talk about the poor pitiful Chicanos or illegal Mexes?

"Don't try it. We know that you worked with Mexes. Don't like capitalism, huh?

"You knew that he was a Communist and you still fucked him?"

Horowitz went on playing the *Funérailles.*

Carl wept. But it wouldn't stop—not the music or the gorillas' interrogation—but kept up for what seemed like days.

The Old Man lay in bed and thought mostly about his free-thinking mother from Småland. What would she have thought of her son now? Would she have said that you must always fight against the Evil One, regardless of the personal price you pay for that perseverance?

Yes, he hoped so. You should never give in to evil.

Carl would get over it. It would be easier once he started working. He was like a fighter plane that takes off with afterburners blasting and retracts its landing gear and climbs almost straight up to the heights where the battle will take place, and then the rest is all reflexes and computers.

Carl's hatred would help him. And it would help Sweden.

And afterward he would become a sensitive and incomparably experienced boss for the as yet unbroken mustangs from California.

It was right.

It wasn't easy, but it was right.

But the summer night was silent and the wind was still and there was no chance in hell of sleeping.

His mother would not have liked this last thought, at least not the way he formulated it.

. . .

They were both red-eyed at breakfast, and the Old Man joked un-successfully about the quality of Kivik's homemade Calvados. Neither of them had any appetite.

And when he asked Carl to come down to the beach to see which of the two spots had finally been selected for the summer barbecue, it didn't even occur to Carl that this was the usual trick to talk with no risk of being overheard.

"As you can see, it's the place you suggested yourself," said O.M., pointing with a leather-bound book he had brought with him.

Carl nodded. "Yes, it's more sheltered here among the trees. The place by the cliffs is better for swimming on sunny days, but this is better if you want to sit down and eat and things like that," he replied, obediently and mechanically.

They sat down on one of the split logs that served as a bench for the rough oak table near the stone-lined fireplace. Sunlight filtered through the ash leaves and hazel thicket. They had the sea behind them, with a gentle, sleepy swell. There was a faint breeze.

"You don't think the Russians are especially vengeful nowadays, do you?" asked Carl.

"No, it doesn't fit in with glasnost and all that. Under Stalin we wouldn't even have dared try something so insolent. But hasn't Sam been over all this?"

"Yes, of course. Of course he has."

They were both deliberately casual. But Carl's thoughts were on something entirely different, and O.M. knew it. He took a deep breath and poured salt on the wound. "Sad story. And from what I understand, it was a rather nasty interrogation," he said carefully, almost neutrally, as if he were talking about a triviality.

"I know," snapped Carl.

O.M. paused. "Sandström may do this to us again, you or me—well, maybe not me—but many others. As long as he's working over there, and that will be ten or fifteen years, we'll probably be hassling with this." He sighed.

"Well, I'll photograph the devil, at any rate," said Carl cautiously. "Couldn't we burn him alive later?"

"You mean leak the picture to the press?"

"Exactly."

"Can't do it. I mean, it would certainly be effective to burn him alive (great term, by the way), but we can't do it."

"Why not?"

"The government. Sorman and all of them."

"They wouldn't go along with it?"

"Of course not. Politics, foreign relations, all that, you know."

"So a little extra in appropriations is the only thing we can get with a picture of him?"

Now O.M., decided to stick in the knife. He took a deep breath. "My dear young captain, as the Russians would say, I must remind you that you are entering a perpetually mobilized unit. For us there is no war or peace or anything in between—we are always at war."

Carl certainly understood, but the Old Man wasn't sure about that, so he continued as he had planned during the night. "Do you like poetry?"

"No. I haven't read it since school," said Carl, equally blunt.

"Fine," said O.M., "because I'm going to read a poem to you that has meant more to me during my entire professional career than any text or report I've ever read. You should bear in mind when the poem was written; it's by one of our Nobel Prize winners and the year is 1940—well, that's what it says in the book, but it was probably written as early as 1939." And then he opened his leather-bound book to a place where he did indeed have a permanent marker.

"The poem is called 'New Weapons,' " he said curtly.

He waited for a rushing in the crowns of the ash trees overhead to pass, and then he read, slowly and somewhat ponderously, as the text demanded:

> Wipe the worry from your brow
> and go out in the fray
> to overpower the violence
> the struggle of your mind is done.
> In the weapon-play of the spirit
> no victory can be won
> against him who blindly denies
> that spirit exists.
>
> The barbarian selects his weapons;
> you must choose as he does.
> When the wild animal opens its jaws
> it is not the mind that must speak.
>
> Raise the spirit's mighty fortress
> in this world of danger
> and crush the serpent's children
> beneath the human animal's foot.

Only fools believe that goodness
is not born to bear a sword
even if evil must bleed
and sully a whole world.
Be certain! If you do not defend
your beliefs now in battle
then no morning star
will consecrate a new day.

He closed the book and waited.

Carl looked down at the ground with his jaws clenched. "Pär Lagerkvist, right?" he asked hoarsely.

"Yes, that's right."

Carl was suddenly calm. "Is it a direct order?"

"Yes. One of my last. I'll be retired when you come home," replied O.M. His mouth was dry.

"Is that all?"

The Old Man had to run his tongue around in his mouth before continuing. "Yes, with one restriction. The restriction . . . is that you do not submit a report to Sam before you come home."

Carl sat for a moment, drawing a circular pattern in the sand with a twig.

Then he suddenly looked up, his eyes very blue, and he gazed at O.M. for a moment with a look that was more melancholy than fearful. "The order is understood and will be carried out," he said.

O.M. felt a rush of exceedingly contradictory feelings. "That business about your not being allowed to have weapons with you—would it pose any special difficulty that we might possibly take care of?" He cursed the bureaucratic language when emotions needed to be so finely tuned.

Carl looked searchingly at him, almost amused. Then he rose to his feet. "No, not at all. It's of no importance. What we've been talking about is not a technical problem but a moral one."

He started resolutely toward the house. O.M. caught up with him, and they walked in silence through the rows of apple trees.

"You'll have to excuse me, but I have to go back to Stockholm. I didn't read up on Sandström. Now I have to get to know the fellow," said Carl lightly, as if from now on he had only minor practical problems.

The Old Man decided that he no longer understood him.

2

Moscow

Seven

The heat wave made it possible. According to the newspapers it hadn't been this hot in Moscow in August in a century. So he could dress in jeans and a short-sleeved cotton shirt instead of formal diplomatic garb, and it was natural to spend a few hours in the cool vault of the subway.

He was careful to move slowly and visibly, lingering at the stations, walking along the platforms and letting himself be impressed, and look impressed, by the marble, the polished granite, the crystal chandeliers, and the paintings, half of them depicting heroic passages in the history of Soviet power and half the great authors and poets of Russia. It was beautifully clean, without even a candy wrapper on the stone floor, and it was impossible to trail someone who didn't want to be followed.

He kept the subway map in his hand, manifestly a tourist—a look that was more difficult than it seemed. For among the eight million passengers who thronged each day through the system of 136 subway stations (according to his count), half a million of them were young men in shirts and jeans. In two hours three people asked him in Russian for directions, or what line they should change to.

The trains came every few minutes, and in the corridors leading from one line to another the currents of people moved quickly, constantly swirling past him. So one fine day or evening he would be able to vanish down here into the infinite rolling sea of humanity on their way to millions of different destinations, and after a few hours going hither and yon ride to the last station on the Kaluzhko-Rizhskaya line. The only drawback would be the eight stations in a row after the change at Prospekt Mira.

Since Russian agents in the West always used the subway, their suspicions might be aroused if he practiced too often. He would stay away for at least a week. The main thing right now was for them to be able to keep up with him if they were following him.

He strolled from the embassy on Mosfilmovskaya up to the university on Lenin Hill, where newlyweds liked to have their picture taken with a view over the city. He admired it himself for a while, leaning with his hands on the stone balustrade. The hazy heat and the twilight made visibility poor, but he could see at once the big red five-pointed stars below, by the Kremlin. The people around him looked young and happy; they were mostly newlyweds with their friends. Where were the in-laws? He would ask someone at the embassy about that.

He sauntered off toward the university subway station, unfolding his map and studying it before he went down into the Kirov-Frunze line.

There was a military academy in Frunze, where one of the groups of students was the future elite of the GRU.

It was clean in the subway cars, which were laid out like the New York ones, but there were no graffiti and no threats or terror or wary atmosphere. Most of the people traveling alone were reading books or newspapers, as likely Pushkin or Gogol as the sports pages.

Carl had a hard time feeling that he was the enemy, and he did his best to suppress the circumstance that made him so, the reason why he was in their city in the first place. He was their enemy; he was the enemy of the happy young people on the hill by the university; he was the enemy of the old man across from him with the medals from the Great Patriotic War—he spotted the Order of Lenin—who asked him something he couldn't answer; he was the enemy of all the subway passengers reading their books; and the enemy of all men in uniform, of course, who made up a goodly portion of the crowd. At least half of the officers he met were his superiors, as if major were virtually the lowest Soviet rank; they were mostly career officers with desk jobs, which you could tell from their medal-less uniforms.

He noticed a small group of cocky paratroopers with their blue berets pushed back on their heads. They were different, wearing a number of honors that showed they had distinguished themselves in combat.

Afghanistan, then. Paratroopers in Afghanistan—superpower against simple, armed peasant boys.

He saw that he was at the end of the line and stood waiting for the train at Turgenevskaya, searching his subway map until he realized that he could transfer at Kirovskaya on the same orange-colored line on which he had started.

A train arrived, and as it stopped he saw the national seal of the Soviet Union on the side of the car drawn up in front of him.

He stared at it mesmerized. It was the first emblem he had seen on his arrival in Moscow that morning, on the peaked cap worn by the officer at the airport who had so gravely and expressionlessly studied his passport for so long.

He had thought the map on the seal was supposed to depict the Soviet Union itself. But now he could see, right in front of him on the almost military-green subway car, that the map showed half the entire globe, with the Soviet Union, Africa, and Europe; North America was a tiny dot on the horizon up in the northwest. Under Africa the shining sun was rising—surely rising and not setting.

Two sheaves of grain embraced the world, this special world, and they met at the top of the circle. Above was the red five-pointed star and the initials CCCP. Nothing odd there. Nothing odd about the circular sheaves intertwined with red ribbons farther down, or the hammer and sickle at the bottom.

What mesmerized him was at the center. Almost exactly in the middle, between the hammer and the sickle, lay Sweden. The hammer was resting on northern Norway, and the rest of Scandinavia lay in the enclosed center.

The train left and the image vanished. He walked slowly and resolutely over to the transfer point at Kirovskaya, noting to his surprise that one of the stops was called Dzerzhinskaya. The train passed under Dzerzhinsky Square—so he was passing directly under the KGB.

The heat struck him like a wall at the top of the long escalator with the rows of innumerable lights on pillars—lamps like torches. He played around with his street map a little and dawdled as he read the street signs until he saw an ordinary, quite undramatic arrow pointing to Red Square.

When he came to street level and set his foot on the soft asphalt, the very first thing he saw was St. Basil's Cathedral, brightly illuminated.

It was as though he didn't want to go to it directly. He walked along the entire wall of the Kremlin, crossing the street since it was late and the traffic was light. No tail could avoid being seen when he jaywalked instead of using the pedestrian tunnels. He noticed a couple of cigarette-smoking policemen in light-blue shirts, but they didn't seem to be paying attention to him.

He walked down through Alexander Park and past the Tomb of the Unknown Soldier, where a bluish flame flared up in the center of a five-pointed star. Suddenly there were very few people around. Maybe this was because of the heat—his shirt was sticking to his back—or the late hour? Maybe both.

Beyond the eternal flame stood big black stone rectangles engraved with the names of Soviet cities, and he spelled his way through Smolensk, Kiev, Leningrad, Stalingrad, and so on down the row before he realized that the rectangles were sarcophagi. On top of "Smolensk" lay a little bouquet of flowers left by someone's family.

Down by the river and along the high wall he found himself completely alone. He was careful not to look behind him, and he walked slowly, as if out for a stroll.

Which he was.

After he had walked for a while along the river he saw the contours of St. Basil's Cathedral appearing in silhouette against the spotlights: there was no further detour. He walked up the hill to the sidewalk closest to the wall and gazed at the extraordinary sight—one of the world's most familiar shrines, and in that uncanny way it looked in real life exactly as it did in pictures. Except that he was so close that he could see the individual red bricks. He kept walking.

Suddenly a guard shouted at him.

He stopped and stood still, holding out his arms from his sides. But the threat was no threat. He was at the big entryway to the Kremlin and a few feet in front of him hung an iron chain marking a cordoned-off rectangle extending from the gate.

He signaled apologetically to the guard, and then he cut across in front of the cathedral, stopping for a moment to look up at the multicolored onion domes. He turned and walked for several minutes until he found himself in the exact center of Red Square. It was completely deserted, as in a dream, and he was sweating heavily.

He thought, It's a very nice, warm red they've found for the big five-pointed neon stars.

But this was crazy. This *was* Red Square in real life, and this *was* him, out on the deserted cobblestones painted with rows of colored lines for the parades.

Two men were standing guard outside Lenin's mausoleum—the only people in sight—and he crossed over toward them, stopping at the iron chain a few feet in front of them.

They were trying to be motionless, which is all but impossible, and they looked young—from their badges it was apparent they were cadets of some kind.

And now in front of them was this solitary tourist, studying the details of their uniforms and the shiny tips of their bayonets, and this one tourist was supposed to be their enemy.

Up in the tower with the black-and-gold clock a clattering signal began, and when Carl looked around he saw the change of guard approaching at what looked like a Nazi parade march. With much to-do and deadly serious stomping, the two guards were relieved and goose-stepped off, and the two new cadets stood stock-still on guard next to the embalmed Lenin in his glass case.

The whole changing of the guard for the benefit of a single spectator. Who was their enemy.

He walked back to the center of the square and took a deep breath of the warm night air.

All of this is very beautiful, he said to himself. No, very impressive. I'm overreacting, he thought, because I can't believe it's real. Not photographs, not a movie; I'm breathing and sweating and standing here and looking up at that green copper dome—no, probably just ordinary painted sheet metal. Above the dome fluttered a silky red flag with the hammer and sickle, spotlighted against the black sky and waving beautifully, as if being blown by an aesthetically and politically correct wind. Once, in Clarté, he had burned a flag like that, along with the Stars and Stripes, at a demonstration. Here was the original itself.

Until several months ago, Moscow was the last place in the world Carl had ever thought he would find himself.

Then his mood changed. With sudden determination, he started across the cobblestone square in the direction of the subway. But right below the museum, a much too convenient taxi appeared, the only car in sight.

He waved the yellow Volga over to the sidewalk, got into the back, and gave the address of the Swedish embassy at Mosfilmovskaya 60.

He expected he'd have to repeat it, having no faith in his elementary Russian.

The taxi driver did not reply or change expression in any way; he drove off at once in what seemed to be the wrong direction.

After several minutes, Carl realized that they were in fact driving in the direction of the KGB. Practicing his Russian under his breath twice before saying anything out loud, he asked the taxi driver, "Did you understand the address? Are we really going in the right direction?"

"Yes, of course, but I have to go around in order to get to the right street. Certainly. The Swedish embassy. Three crowns. Ice hockey. Maybe you know Tumba?"

And then the taxi swung around an enormous gray building with granite pillars and headed in the right direction. Carl chatted along about Russian ice hockey and how good it was. We Swedes admire Soviet athletes. I lived in the United States but I still prefer European hockey as we play it in Sweden and the Soviet Union. And so forth.

The taxi driver who had turned up so conveniently seemed to understand his Russian and to share his view of ice hockey. If he was a member of the opposition, he would report that Carl had lived in America, which they already knew. That was all right. He had no intention of hiding anything from them, nothing except the operation itself.

True enough, on the embassy building were three large gold crowns; he hadn't noticed them before. He waved the taxi on around back, past the Soviet guard who stopped the car and looked in the back seat before they were allowed to proceed to Building E.

The taxi driver had not had his meter running, and he now demanded ten rubles, probably three times too much. So he must be an ordinary, honest civilian taxi driver, Carl thought as he took out his little packet of red ten-ruble bills that he had signed for earlier in the day. He peeled off a bill and handed it to the driver, who had a hard time controlling both his joy and his astonishment at the quick negotiation.

"I'll rip *you* off someday," Carl said cheerfully in English as he slammed the door and walked past the tennis courts and around the corner to his apartment.

It was completely Swedish and completely bugged, like everything else in the embassy compound. The housing commission had furnished it with birch furniture from Ikea and Pakistani rugs—everything that might pass for a normal apartment for a minor diplomat. It felt like a hotel.

But the norm for a new arrival was obviously to bring along one's own furnishings as well as a wife and children. Carl was the only unmarried diplomat at the embassy, and probably one of the very few military attachés in all of Moscow who was alone at night.

That was fine, just fine. It would give them something to keep them busy.

He lay down on top of the crocheted bedspread, kicked off his shoes, clasped his hands behind his head, and looked up at the white Swedish ceiling.

You can't get at my thoughts, he thought with a certain triumph.

He had brought not a single document about Sandström with him, not even the photographs, nothing. He had everything in his head for the months to come.

It was on the eighth floor, all the way over in the left-hand corner. There were six windows in a row before you reached the balconies, if you started from the farthest corner.

The building was grayish white, had probably once been white. The building next door was more modern, red brick with eight little balconies at the very end, toward the gable near Sandström's building. Three phone booths stood against the red brick building. All this would be visible as soon as he came out of the subway station. The pictures had been taken from that position. Up on the roof, between windows four and five, there was a red and white antenna that had concerned them a great deal at first, but later the technical experts had determined that whatever it was it had nothing to do with Sandström; the apparatus was too ungainly for that.

No, he would not forget this.

Sandström himself was no problem, other than possibly the problem of underestimating him.

He had abused all his women; he preferred strangulation and slapping. The battering might go on for a long time, but in spite of his recklessness, which each woman in turn had attested to or recounted under interrogation, he had never harmed them except to give them bruises on their throats where he tried his stranglehold.

He had been a boxer in his youth but stopped after he was knocked out for the first time. Once he had been in a bar fight on Cyprus and taken a good beating.

His weapons record was brief and included only what was covered by normal Swedish military duty.

All things considered, the man was defenseless so long as the opponent was not a more or less intoxicated woman; his violence always appeared in connection with alcohol.

His medical history included everything from a possible tumor on the pituitary gland to a tendency toward mythomania; as reason for a petition for a new trial his lawyers had implied insanity. On several occasions he had fallen and knocked himself out, lying where he fell for as long as thirty hours before he was found, and this had led to hospitalization.

On the other hand, he had spent seven years sober in two Swedish prisons, and during the last two years, probably while he was planning his escape, he had realized he could seduce that poor woman all the way into marriage and onto the Finland ferry.

Carl assumed the wife was not in Moscow. He doubted she was in the apartment either. Sandström's taste in women leaned to the eelskin-sheath type more than to decent females, to put it in police jargon, and the wife was a decent female.

Or had been. He presumed that Sandström, under sober and orderly circumstances, had tried another of his strangleholds on her.

It would lead to complications if she were at the apartment. There shouldn't be any witnesses. One possibility was to offer her a lift to the Swedish embassy afterward. But no one, except maybe her and her family and the press, would want that solution. She would come home, she would be put on trial—Carl smiled at the thought of how Peter Sorman would handle it.

No, there should be no witnesses.

Sandström's spy story was almost ludicrous. Until his escape to Moscow, the man had been a walking series of failures.

He had dropped out of high school. He had finagled his way out of the draft and into the coastal artillery, and then he dropped out of that too after only ten months—the shortest possible contract time, corresponding to the shortest possible military service.

When he applied to the police academy he was, of course, accepted. He got married after he became a police officer, and his marriage naturally failed, and he ended up with alimony payments and living in a little run-down apartment. Then he applied to the naval academy, was naturally accepted, and when he graduated as an ensign in the reserve, he became a policeman again, drove a patrol car, and handled apartment burglaries and suicides.

His application for UN duty was naturally accepted, and he roamed around Cyprus, by now a lieutenant; at that point some genius talent scout in Säpo had caught sight of him—for all the wrong reasons, you might say—and recruited him as an unpaid snitch with promises of putting in a good word for him if he later wanted to apply to the company.

Back from Cyprus, he applied to the police section assigned to foreign residents, and was naturally accepted. And he sat and listened to American deserters from the Vietnam war, which he must have been just as ill suited for as for the job in Säpo. Which is where, against all common sense, he was accepted the following year. Straight into the Russian Bureau. All the many warning memos about the unbalanced UN officer disappeared at Säpo.

In Säpo he constantly arrived late and forged surveillance reports when he missed his relief officers. He got caught but was not kicked out. Memos about this, too, disappeared mysteriously.

He fled to another UN tour of duty and became, once more against all common sense, a security officer. That was when he was most likely recruited by the Russians, or he sold himself to them—six of one, half a dozen of the other. A classic security risk.

When he came back from his second UN tour, he applied for a job in the security department of the Defense Ministry, which should have made all the alarm bells go off at once. But the then head of JCS/MS, a captain—a fellow who was later given the boot, being an alcoholic who made a fool of himself with political espionage at an annual convention of reservists—hired him. Against all common sense. Still, the captain had checked with the company first, phoning the head of Säpo himself, at that time a known madman, the Mail-man's predecessor in the job; and the madman—who was later kicked upstairs, having embezzled, and promoted to provincial police commissioner in proper Swedish style—gave Sandström an excellent reference.

Since the head of JCS/MS was continually drunk, Sandström's work was like stealing candy from a baby. He had a copy machine right outside his office, and he had the right, as an officer in the Defense Ministry's own security service, to look at practically any classified document in the department.

In addition, the drunken captain forgot to lock his safe whenever he went on vacation, so of course the spy copied everything in it before he locked up the safe himself. It was hard to know whether to laugh or cry.

Oddly enough, Sandström was later kicked out of JCS/MS for skipping work too often. It must have been the GRU that didn't know whether to laugh or cry at that point.

But of course he got his old job back in the company, whereupon he immediately took a leave of absence for a third UN tour. In the Middle East he boozed and fought—exclusively with women, it appeared; strangleholds on one after the other. His case officer at the GRU station in Beirut was Sergei Alexandrovich Yermolayev; comrade Yermolayev couldn't have had an easy time of it.

He tried to blackmail a Swedish general, who wrote a number of scathing memos—which again disappeared at Säpo.

Next he assaulted a woman in Stockholm, who went to the police and turned him in for assault—and espionage. He was apparently in the habit of telling all his women that he spied for the Russians. Säpo interrogated both him and the woman, and then decided that there was no reason to accuse Sandström of espionage charges solely on a woman's word. However, the part about assault wasn't too good, so as a small reprimand he was moved from the Russian Bureau to a surveillance division, where he acquired even greater insight into the work of Säk; for instance, he was able to warn the Russians that one of their own intelligence officers in Sweden was planning to defect. The Russian vanished home to the gulag.

New tours to the Middle East, new incidents of alcohol and abuse of women, new reports back to Säpo from furious UN officers. These memos disappeared.

Then, in 1979, he was caught by Israeli intelligence, who happened to interrogate him under dramatically different circumstances than he was used to. He confessed to everything. He was sent home, put on trial, and jailed. Nothing else until he escaped.

Carl read more than five thousand pages of documents about all this. One thing was clear: Sandström had had protection. Someone in Säk had destroyed all the reports of his being a security risk; someone had hired him, for the Russian Bureau of all places, while he was still on work probation; someone had taken great risks to protect him, had time after time stashed away the warning memos.

This would fit nicely with the Peacock, the head of the Russian Bureau, after all—Sandström's eternally forgiving and indulgent boss.

Had the Russians decided the Peacock was burned for all practical purposes? Had they so overestimated the Swedish Security Police that they thought Säpo could tumble to Sandström's obvious protector? No such person would last for a minute in the GRU or any other Western security and intelligence organization, after all. Only in Sweden would someone like that survive; only Sweden had obvious madmen running sensitive departments in military and civilian security.

So if the Russians had learned that Sandström's protector was not being investigated, they wouldn't have believed it. They would have thought it was some extreme stratagem; that's what they were used to.

Perhaps they imagined the Peacock had already been caught. Were they being supersneaky, to burn an agent who they thought was already burned?

If they only knew, laughed Carl to himself.

The most disturbing conclusion was that the Russians controlled the recruiting policies for the monkey house on Kungsholmen. That would be mind-boggling. Yet they hadn't recruited very wisely with Sandström. An obvious security risk for his own country is likely to be just as great a security risk for the other side.

And it was all but unbelievable that they had fitted him into any kind of intelligence work. How had they trained him? Drugs and hard exercise? Basic training all over again and jogging every morning and no women, other than selected women who were impossible to strangle?

Pointless to speculate. They had done it; they had placed him in strategic, analytical operations service; they had sent him to war against Sweden.

The next morning Carl started his plan. He pulled on some lightweight exercise clothes and loosened up for several minutes on the Pakistani rug in his living room. Then he jogged out through the gate, around the building past the tennis courts and the parking lot and up past the guard, who would now probably note the time.

He ran down along Mosfilmovskaya at approximately three-quarters speed but tried to find an even rhythm so that it would look real. No reason to transmit correct physical data. Besides, it would be sensible not to deteriorate too rapidly until later, when he would have to start running with a hangover. He felt intense discomfort at the thought. He had never done sports with a hangover, and only a few times in his life had he even experienced that unpleasant condition.

He ran down the long, wide street, all but empty of pedestrians, for twenty minutes before he turned around; at this moderate speed, it ought to be about six kilometers.

From now on, he would make his turnaround point near the two big chestnut trees past Mosfilm's side entrance, and his original time of twenty minutes would worsen little by little.

But now, when he was presumably in the best imaginable shape, before brooding and gloominess and exaggerated boozing began, he could afford to pick up speed a little. His return time was eighteen minutes.

So. Thirty-eight minutes was the time that he would never again achieve.

In spite of the early hour, it was already hot, and he was sweating as he approached the embassy with its three crowns and its hideous black steel sculpture that was supposed to be art. Again he felt revulsion and discomfort at the thought of doing all this with a hangover. And it would have to be vodka—which he almost never touched. It was a chemical substance or an anesthetic, not a real drink.

He showered and changed into a gray suit with a light-blue tie and white shirt with a discreetly thin blue border on the collar. The very picture of a younger Swedish diplomat, he thought.

There was food in the refrigerator from an unknown benefactor. He wasn't hungry at all—was it the heat or disgust with the alien habits he was about to acquire?—but he could do with some juice. He hesitated at first, but the container was Swedish, stamped with a date and unopened, so he took a glass from the cupboard and drank half of it. The glass still had a little sticker on its base from its manufacturer in Småland.

At five of nine he went up through the compound, past the bungalows where the higher-level diplomats lived, and around to the main entrance. A young male receptionist sitting behind bulletproof glass asked for his identification and then told him in a military tone of voice to wait. From the interpreters' school, thought Carl. The younger security personnel probably come from the interpreters' school, speak good Russian, and are going to interrogate prisoners of war.

He was allowed to pass through the double security doors to the embassy's main floor. He stood on the flagstones in front of two glass cases displaying some kind of Swedish glass art—the usual illuminated egg in one case and a fantastic cat, or tiger, with a much too long tail in the other.

Then his boss appeared, coming down the curved staircase with the brass balusters and hardwood banister. His boss for how long? Two months? Four years? Tasteful, cold, very Swedish, thought Carl. Do I look like that? Do I have such perfect good taste? What sort of taste do I have?

The man reached the bottom of the stairs and put out his hand. "Welcome to your new job, Hamilton." He wore glasses and was in his sixties.

"Good morning, Colonel Nordlander." Carl was very proper and reserved.

"Oh, we can drop the titles. The defense contingent is small here. Can't keep up that kind of thing. How was your trip?" He made a welcoming gesture toward the stairs, and Carl followed him a half step behind.

"Fine, thanks. Strange feeling being here."

"Have time to get a look at the city?" They arrived at a pale, varnished door with the combination lock that led to the closed department.

"Yes, I walked a lot, and rode around in the subway for a while. I got here yesterday." Carl studied the combination lock—a Swedish brand, easy to crack.

After a brief tour, with Carl introduced haphazardly to whomever they happened to run into, another combination lock: then they were inside the inner closed section of the closed department. Carl inspected his office. Like any other Swedish office except for the safe and the fancy computer terminal.

"You know about gadgets like this, I'm told," said the colonel, nodding at the computer screen. "Is the equipment all right?"

"Seems to be," said Carl, feeling trapped. "Yes, this is great; we should be able to make something of this."

"You know about these things, I'm told."

"Yes, it's one of two things I'm good at."

"I see. What's the other thing?"

"Covert military intelligence service. The Russians call it illegal."

The colonel visibly stiffened. "Let's go into my office," he said curtly, and they went into the room next door. It looked more personal, decorated with family pictures, photos of dogs and boats.

"Well," began Nordlander, fumbling for pipe tobacco in a pouch in his jacket pocket, "first of all I want to welcome you. From what I understand, your primary assignment here is to put some order into our data. But before I continue, let me first say that we assume that everything we say here is or could be overheard."

"You found a lot of bugs several years ago; haven't you swept the place since then?"

"Yes, a number of personnel . . . but they were from Säpo, you know."

"I see, like that." Carl was resigned.

"So, let's keep it in mind from now on. Can't computers be bugged in some way too, by the way? I mean, aren't there certain risks in transferring the archives onto computer?"

"Yes, of course, but . . . do you have a bugproof room?"

"Yes, we have two conversation bubbles in the hall—didn't you see them? Right near the entrance to the department."

"Then maybe I'd better explain certain technical aspects there later."

"Fine." Nordlander was efficient and brisk. "Let's move on to the welcoming lecture on morals. What I'm about to say I am obligated by the service to say, is that understood?"

"Yes, I understand."

"Good. So. It's an exception when we have unmarried personnel here. You're probably the only one and . . . as a matter of principle, all fraternization with Russian civilians, with any Russkies at all, is against the rules. On the map of Moscow there's a red circle, and if you want to go outside the circle you have to give forty-eight hours' notice, and you must do this regarding any possible visitors also. It's important to stick to the rules, especially the ban on photographing. Taking notes is allowed. When we travel, we usually take our wives along—not just for . . . well, you know—but also because it's clever to have a witness along if any dispute should arise about what happened or did not happen in certain situations, you know? In your case we will assign one of our young male interpreters as a traveling companion. You understand. As far as your time off in Moscow is concerned, we don't get involved in what you do, but you *are* a diplomat and you represent Sweden. Exchanging money on the black market or any transaction of that sort is unthinkable. Not only must we stay away from anything illegal, but there are sometimes provocations with women and—"

"Excuse me, Colonel, may I interrupt?" said Carl. He worked hard not to show his impatience.

"Yes, of course."

"I have had five years of special training in military intelligence, and I've been active within the covert sector for almost as long."

Nordlander had not lit his pipe, which he had been tamping slowly and meticulously. Now he lit it slowly, appearing to ponder this implied reproach. He decided on a hesitant smile.

"Okay," he said, "to hell with this. In principle you have received the moral lecture prescribed according to regulations. Now let's go to a conversation bubble so we can hear something about the technical side of things."

They walked down the corridor, and at an inconspicuous door the colonel opened the seven-lever tumbler lock and they entered a heavily insulated room furnished with nothing but a small round table with two chairs, over which hung a large plastic canopy.

Sitting under this peculiar plastic shade was like being under a cheese bell. The colonel changed both his tone of voice and his attitude.

"To continue with a bit more of the moral lecture," he began firmly, "I've learned that you are very well qualified in so-called illegal activity. Permit me to point out in no uncertain terms that in Moscow we do not engage in illegal activities. There's no sport in bending the rules, and there's no reward for getting information illegally. Understood?"

"Yes, understood," replied Carl calmly. "I'm not here to make a fool of myself, and I understand what the job entails in general. And to avoid any misunderstandings—well, I don't know how much you've been briefed, but I have no weapon of any kind with me and have no intention of obtaining any."

"I should hope not. We are always unarmed, as you know. Well, what about the program?"

Carl launched into a lengthy explanation. From what Sam had told him, he knew that all intelligence reports from Moscow had been arriving haphazardly in Stockholm and were of widely varying quality, due to lack of organization and processing at the Moscow embassy. And the Defense Ministry was therefore burdened with processing problems, sifting out new information from old, and so on—a diplomatic way of saying that the military attachés in Moscow were preoccupied with their comfortable lives, with sitting in their offices and spelling their way through *Krasnaya Svezda* and other military journals, and then writing vague summaries.

Systematizing this nonsense, which would be Carl's primary assignment, required clever new programs for processing on-site, both easy to manage and satisfactorily secure.

What he had in mind was as follows, he told Nordlander. All information would be classified into one of three groups: red for the most sensitive, orange for interesting but open, green for purely archival material. All red material could be entered only if one signed on to certain special programs requiring a separate power source not connected to the regular network. This purely internal information could be found only when it looked from the outside as if the machines were shut off or the plugs were pulled.

With each report, they could ask the system what had been previously reported; duplicate reporting would be avoided and one could look directly at what was new. This would make things easier for the processing unit back home, and make their own information more systematic and easier to grasp. And once the program was set up it wouldn't take long, even for someone who had never worked with computers before, to learn to ask the system questions and enter new data.

"That's my official work assignment, and I plan to carry it out," he said earnestly. Regardless of the hangovers, he thought to himself.

They left the bubble and went back to their offices. Carl had a look at some of the papers he had to classify. He was supposed to begin with the most recent and work his way back chronologically; it would certainly take at least a month before any kind of working system was ready. But after that it would go much faster, he assured the colonel.

He learned additional information. First, he was supposed to go in and say hello to the ambassador in about three minutes; second, on the following day, in uniform, he would be accompanied to the Directorate for Foreign Affairs of the Soviet Armed Forces, to be accredited.

Ambassador Thunborg's office was spartan in its severe, muted Swedishness: the pale leather sofa and armchairs; the low, bare wooden coffee table; the two white side lamps; the light-blue wall-to-wall wool carpets. The unostentatious desk was of teak with slightly rounded contours, neither cluttered nor autocratically bare. A single lamp with a round white shade illuminated the papers, and in front of the desk were two visitors' chairs made in the same expensively simple style. Everything was reserved and deliberately soothing, and only the incomprehensibly abstract paintings struck a discordant note.

The ambassador was in shirtsleeves, his tie loosened. He shook

Carl's hand with an expression that mixed stern irony with resolute friendliness. He was a very short man; perhaps he compensated for the lack of stature with a certain force in expression and voice. He spoke loudly and confidently.

"Have a seat, Captain. First of all, welcome to your new job. Of course I hope it will be accomplished to the satisfaction of all parties."

Not all parties, thought Carl, but you don't have to know about that. "Of course. I hope so too."

"Now, to get to the point." Thunborg leaned forward energetically with his elbows on the desk. "I have tried to understand the purpose of your enterprise. I'm not without contacts, as you realize and . . . let me point out that we assume everything we say in this room may be overheard."

"Yes, I understand," replied Carl. He crossed his legs and waited for the next moral lecture.

"Well, even with our hosts possibly listening, I want to say that I don't quite understand the haste in getting you here. You have a record of a certain kind that . . . that would not be well received in this city. You understand?"

"Of course. But I have just changed jobs."

"I see. I talked to my old friend Peter in the Foreign Ministry."

"Peter Sorman?"

"Yes. He made it sound as if Moscow was the minimum distance he wanted to keep you at. He complained that we had no representation in Ulan Bator. As you might realize, this is rather disturbing."

"Yes, I can see that, and I also understand what Sorman was getting at. But that has no bearing on my service here."

"What was he getting at?"

"I promised him not to tell anyone about it. But I can say this much: it has to do with my previous service."

"Hm. You've participated in a number of rather spectacular efforts, haven't you?"

"Yes. But now I've been burned and can't work in operations of that type anymore, and that's why I have a new job in the legal sector."

"Exactly what are your intended functions?"

"I explained it all to Colonel Nordlander, in the conversation bubble. In general, I can say that it involves systematizing intelligence data here and developing a computer program, which is what I was trained for."

"In the Defense Ministry?"

"No, in . . ."

Carl sketched the three letters U-S-A in the air, and the ambassador nodded thoughtfully before he suddenly raised his objection. "But can't computers like that . . ."

He pointed up in the air and then at his ear.

"Yes," replied Carl coldly, almost hostilely, "that's the problem I'm planning to solve. I've explained the general outline to Colonel Nordlander. In the conversation bubble."

"Well, let me repeat one thing at least," continued Thunborg. He returned to his offensive position, leaning over the desk with his weight on his elbows. "I don't want to hear about anything in Moscow that's even reminiscent of your former activities. We don't want any expelled Swedish diplomats or anyone who might be in line the next time we throw out one of theirs."

Carl was completely sincere. "No, no! I'd regard it as a serious failure if I were expelled. And I haven't come here to fail."

"Fine," said Thunborg. He stood up hastily, and seemed to be struck with a sudden, acute difficulty in breathing. He took a little bottle out of his pocket and sprayed it into his mouth. Carl pretended not to see anything.

"It's . . . just . . . as maybe you can understand, considering what's written in certain . . . reports about you, natural . . . to be a little suspicious, or shall we say . . . cautious at first. But you are . . . most welcome, and I wish you success . . . here."

Carl went back to his office. He had not gotten the entry code from his boss the colonel, but he had an approximate memory of the colonel's finger movements, and it took him less than thirty seconds to force the lock to the closed department within the closed department. No alarm sounded.

That was disquieting; maybe he ought to speak to someone about it.

He got various stacks of report folders and carried them into his office, where he sorted them and entered data in the computer. Everything that would be classified red he locked in his safe, and everything else went one by one into the computer. If the enemy tapped in, fine: they would get a detailed picture of harmless and primitive Swedish information gathering.

The red material would have to wait until they had discreetly solved the problem of the reserve power source.

He skipped the lunch break and continued without interruption, almost maniacally, until five o'clock, and then, after some hesitation, for a few more hours. This might be one of his few healthy workdays, unpoisoned by liquor, and he wanted to get as much done, and done right, as he could at the beginning. He had little experience with how alcohol affects the mind, and he was uneasy.

At his apartment, he showered and changed, and was just about to throw himself into the first self-destructive evening when Colonel Nordlander called and invited him to a welcome-to-Moscow dinner.

Naturally he accepted, and naturally it was a very Swedish officers' dinner with more than modest liquor consumption, but Carl, almost gratefully, knew it was all right for him to say no, thanks, to a second cognac with his coffee.

The colonel lived in one of the embassy's split-level bungalows, and arriving there was like stepping into a villa somewhere in Djursholm. Indeed the whole evening, and not just the furnishings, was totally Swedish, with the conversation focused on an array of totally innocent topics.

Later Carl would learn that this was the style of work in Moscow: everyone took it for granted that they were always bugged—though that was actually unlikely. How many diplomats were there in Moscow? Between six and seven thousand? Listening to several thousand conversations every evening in the diplomatic corps alone would call for at least thirty thousand eavesdroppers—and add to this all the tourist hotels and foreign journalists and visiting businesspeople who added up to perhaps twice that. And what about systematizing, reports, translation, analysis, and filing? God, so much chatter to listen to!

Still, you had to admit that they were just as good at spying as at ballet, classical music, or ice hockey. Yes, and as in ice hockey, they didn't always win, though they were very good. It was the same game in the West, and occasionally someone else won, sometimes even Sweden. He had to believe this or he couldn't do his job.

The next evening Carl began his descent into dissolution. He had the department secretary reserve a table somewhere really Russian and nice since he had never eaten Russian caviar, and so on. Nothing odd about that.

It was like a dream, as his first evening in Red Square had been.

The dining room of the historic, classic National Hotel was a traditional, old-fashioned place with a wonderful gold and pale-blue ceiling and white linen tablecloths and large windows with a view of Red Square and St. Basil's Cathedral.

The dining room was up one flight of stairs, and on his way down the corridor with the thick, drab red carpet he could already hear the piano music.

It was Mozart's "Marche Turque," and when he entered the dining room, he saw at the far end, beyond the window table to which he was escorted, a grand piano and a very tall woman playing; she had glossy black hair and thick dark eyelashes that somehow deadened her eyes. The Mozart ended and she switched to a festive Chopin polonaise.

Carl lost himself in the view through the thin tulle curtains. Out there the heat and the evening sun on the Soviet flag, fluttering perfectly, on the peak of the Kremlin roof; and here inside crisp white linen, cool, heavy silverware, and Chopin. He tried to study the menu—pages and pages of dishes whose names seemed suspiciously familiar, downright Swedish, and others that were impenetrably Russian.

A waiter recommended caviar and a few smoked-fish hors d'oeuvres, and Chicken Kiev for the main course with champagne; Carl didn't yet know that this was all the restaurant had, never mind the menu. The only issue was whether to order ordinary champagne or "gold" champagne, whatever that meant. He ordered the gold because it sounded expensive and more ostentatious.

When his order had been taken he again listened to the pianist—now switching from Chopin to movie music of some sort. There were a few chords, a hint, of *Dr. Zhivago*. Ah. "Lara's Theme." Still forbidden, or at least frowned on, but the pianist had insinuated it so discreetly into the medley that you could scarcely notice. He gave her a smile of recognition as she looked up, and she quickly looked down, with a hesitant smile that meant something, although he couldn't say what.

When his champagne arrived she was back with Mozart, this time the variations on "Twinkle, Twinkle, Little Star."

He gazed at the champagne bottle standing in the middle of the table, without an ice bucket. It had a flat bottom and was made of light-colored transparent glass with gold-colored foil around the neck and a brown label. The cork was white plastic. He spelled his way through *Sovietskoye shampanskoye. Zolotoye?* "Golden" or "of gold" or something like that. "Gold champagne" with a flat bottom.

Tsar Peter or Nicholas had once ordered special champagne from Louis Roederer, insisting that the bottles be light-colored glass instead of dark green and with flat bottoms. The brand was still available in duty-free airport shops here and there around the world for thirty or forty dollars. He had never tasted it, since he wasn't fond of champagne, which merely reminded him of awful parties.

He hesitated before he started drinking, as if he wanted to retain his normal state for a few more minutes. His glass had a pattern engraved in the crystal and a gold rim. He held it carefully, with due regard to the precious fluid. Well, it looked good enough: fine little bubbles in even streams and a pretty color.

He glanced out toward St. Basil's Cathedral and then shifted his gaze and raised his glass to the pianist, who had finished the Mozart and was preparing to leave. The wine was somewhat sweet—*polusukhoye*, on the label, had to mean semidry or semisweet—but she smiled as she went past; her sheet music was still lying on the piano, so she'd be coming back.

The waiter arrived with a large garnished platter with smoked salmon, smoked eel, and something that looked like boiled ham. In the middle was enthroned an iced glass bowl with a substantial helping of caviar, with sour cream and blini on the side. Just as it should be.

"What does *polusukhoye* mean? I think the wine is too sweet . . . uh, *trocken.* I mean, this wine *nyet trocken,*" he said in his broken Russian.

"You can get a bottle that is quite dry, sir," replied the waiter in German.

"*Khorosho,* give me a bottle of that," Carl persisted in Russian.

"Do you want me to take this bottle away?" asked the waiter in German with surprise.

"Correct. Do it immediately," answered Carl in his presumably somewhat military domestic Russian.

"But we've already opened it . . ." the waiter pointed out, looking puzzled.

"No problem. Put it on my bill, but just give me a *trocken,*" insisted Carl, still in Russian.

The waiter shrugged, made a face, and carried off the bottle.

From now on you'll remember me, my friend, thought Carl, taking a cautious sip.

He nibbled thoughtfully on a radish before digging into the caviar in earnest. When had he last eaten caviar? It must have been sometime in his childhood when his father wanted to show off and demonstrate that some people happily ate more expensively than others. Carl had not seen his father for the last five years of his life; the old man never forgave him for "that Communist stuff," and tricks like burning the American flag and getting his picture in the paper, which their relatives might see.

The new bottle of champagne, classified *igriskoye*, was better, but it still tasted of something chemical. Anyway it wasn't too sweet for the salty, metallic flavor of the caviar.

What looked like boiled ham must have been sturgeon. It was delicious, and Carl's mood improved. He took big gulps of champagne now and had more of the fish. He was already training himself to drink wine at a different pace.

When the pianist returned he broke into applause for her, so that both she and the other people would notice him, and to his surprise a party of Finnish businessmen at the next table clapped too. She bowed slightly and seemed to be blushing. She wore totally flat shoes, no doubt because of her height, and no rings on her fingers. She was pretty, really.

He drained his glass of champagne in one swallow, nearly gagging. He had to tackle the Kentucky fried chicken, Russian style. With *champagne*? The woman was playing ragtime, lightning fast and technically perfect, but with little feeling; it seemed wrong, as when a diva sings a popular song with operatic phrasing. He supposed she had studied to be a concert pianist and was moonlighting to make money, just as in any Western country.

He searched his memory for a nice long passage from a Mozart piano sonata, since she seemed to return most often to Mozart. Not too obscure but not too famous either. He ought to be able to make use of her.

He called over the waiter and asked in German how he might request a piece of music, whether it was customary, and whether he should pay for it.

The waiter explained sullenly that he didn't have to pay the pianist, but implied that he himself, for a reasonable remuneration, would take her a note.

Carl wrote down his request on a scrap of paper and gave the waiter five rubles. That was an extraordinary sum if they took the official rate seriously of two dollars to the ruble.

She was playing something Russian, he guessed Rimsky-Korsakov, when she received the note with a whisper from the waiter; she nodded and turned toward Carl with a smile that seemed rather forced.

Carl refused dessert but, just in case, he asked for an extra glass of champagne. The waiter cleared his throat and, discreetly indiscreet, bent forward to explain in a whisper that was not a whisper that the staff was not allowed to sit with the guests, and that this applied to the pianist as well.

In that case, Carl asked, how might one invite the pianist for a glass of champagne? The waiter immediately offered his services to arrange everything—she would be done in about half an hour.

Carl took out another five rubles, which he pushed across the table, keeping his hand on the bill until he had finished his message; he asked the waiter to deliver greetings from the admiring guest, Count Hamilton. Would the title make a negative or positive impression? It was the first time he had introduced himself in that manner.

The waiter looked more respectful than hostile at the far from socialist introduction, snatched up the bill, winked reassuringly, and slunk away.

She was beginning the Mozart he had requested, and she was using no sheet music. He assumed a quietly listening expression and gazed firmly at her without interruption as he sipped at his wine. There was still a good bit left in his second bottle, and he was starting to feel drunk.

She gave him a flirtatious look, and he modestly lowered his gaze and blushed. Not so much because of her as because he was doing everything wrong, systematically wrong. It wasn't all that easy to behave like the most reckless and indiscreet attaché Sweden had ever had in Moscow, but it was absolutely necessary.

When she finished the Mozart he clapped vigorously, carrying most of the diners along with him. Dusk had begun to fall beyond the windows, and the red stars on the Kremlin's tower were glowing bright red.

Before she had started again, the German-speaking waiter rushed over to her; their brief whispered conversation ended with her seeming to confirm something with a nod. After a diversionary errand at another table, the waiter came back to Carl. He had arranged for a bottle of champagne, gold and very dry, in the bar farther down the corridor, she would finish playing in twenty minutes, and it would be good if Carl went to the bar ahead of time.

He asked when she might be playing again—in two days' time, it turned out—so he asked to reserve the same table for the same time then. That apparently wasn't done, because you had to reserve tables via some higher bureaucracy, but for a hinted remuneration it could be worked out.

Carl nodded and asked for the check, which turned out to be for close to ninety rubles. How expensive or cheap was that? He paid with one hundred twenty rubles. Twelve small red ten-ruble bills from his stack. He had to throw money around, and it had to be legal tender.

He finished off the champagne, which demanded a certain effort, waited for a pause in the music, applauded, bowed briefly to the pianist, and left.

The waiter hurried to catch up with him at the door. *"Danke sehr, danke, danke, Herr Graf,"* he croaked effusively, walking him out to the corridor. Whispering, he pointed down the dark hallway toward "Vostok."

Vostok turned out to be a single gloomy little room with dim lighting and a glass counter at one end. Near the entrance a sign was posted stating that only Western currencies and the most common credit cards were accepted. Carl remembered with relief that he hadn't cleaned out the credit cards from his wallet. He had assumed they'd be useless in Moscow, but how wrong he was!

On one of the brown plastic-topped tables in a corner stood an ice bucket with a bottle of champagne and two glasses. Only a few other tables were occupied, mostly by women. No doubt prostitutes, he thought, and what did they do when they had to pay? Did they have the right to possess Western currency? Or was he now seeing for the first time the KGB's and GRU's famous "swallows"? If they were swallows it'd be easy for them to bypass the guard at the front desk and pay for their mineral water in dollars. What a forlorn place.

Carl took a deep breath. Time for the men's room, down the corridor. It felt as if he got rid of at least one of the two wine bottles; he splashed his face with cold water and placed a ruble note on the little plate near the exit where others left small coins. Everybody on the staff at that hotel would notice him.

He took several more deep breaths on the way back to the dreary bar. He could still hear piano music coming from the dining room. He walked boldly and with renewed self-confidence to the table with the champagne bucket.

He had a hard time believing that a woman who had learned how to play the piano like that could be a prostitute or could work for them. Still, it was odd that she had accepted his invitation just like that. He pushed aside the problem—for the time being, it made no difference. His role was to pretend to be reckless, and so far so good.

Suddenly she came sailing in through the door—such long strides!—her sheet music under her arm, and straight up to his table as if she'd known where he'd be sitting. She extended her arm in greeting with a motion that made him think she expected him to kiss her hand, which he almost did.

He came around the table to pull out her chair. "Irina Dzerzhin-skaya," she said.

Carl froze. Was this a bad joke? Had he already been found out? But he suppressed his curiosity about her name. "Forgive me for being so forward," he said, smiling, "but the impulse was irrepressible and you never get an answer if you don't ask." He twisted the plastic cork from the bottle and filled the two glasses. "To your wonderful music," he proposed.

"To the whole world's music," she responded.

"The whole thing is simple, purely routine, in fact," said Commodore Gustaf Hessulf, brushing off a nonexistent speck of dust from the crease in his trousers. "We'll be met by a commodore and a lieutenant and there will be some small talk about the heat in Moscow and the Scandinavian climate and the fact that Leningrad also has white nights just as we do in Stockholm—they assume that all Swedish officers come from Stockholm. And then a soldier will come in—well, a sea man at any rate—with some coffee, and then we'll shake hands and you'll be accredited. Purely a formality."

"They won't offer vodka?" Carl wondered.

"Oh no, vodka is largely forbidden since Gorbachev, though sugar and yeast production is supposed to have doubled in order to meet the new demand."

"Do they increase production if demand increases? That goes against a planned economy."

"Yes, yes, but perestroika, you know. Well, I can't say that for sure because there doesn't seem to be any sugar or yeast anywhere in the Soviet Union, but apparently it's least noticeable here in Moscow."

Carl felt sweaty and uncomfortable in his buttoned-up uniform, and the gold braid aiguillette around his left shoulder made him feel rather operatic. The Volvo was stuffy and had no air conditioning. That morning, it hadn't been as disgusting to run as he had anticipated, but he had only just begun.

The commodore looked sideways again at the service ribbons on Carl's left breast. Carl had noticed that he hadn't been able to mask his surprise when he had first seen them, and now he was at it again.

"Are they genuine?" Hessulf asked doubtfully. "Masquerade items are not permitted, you know."

"Yes, I know." Carl was as relaxed as he could be. "But I have the Chief's permission to wear foreign as well as Swedish distinctions. And they're all in the proper order."

"Is that the Legion of Honor?" asked his superior, unable to hide his astonishment.

"Yes, the commander's medal," said Carl in as ordinary a tone as he could manage.

"But the Bundesverdienstkreuz—you haven't been stationed in Germany or anything like that, have you?"

"Yes, actually, I had several German assignments a couple of years ago."

"Well, still, you haven't been in service for twenty-five years or anything like that . . . I mean, that blue-and-yellow," continued the commodore, squirming.

"No," replied Carl in the same amiable offhand tone, "that's not the medal for service, as you can tell. It's the King's medal for bravery in the field, and it's supposed to be placed closest to the heart, isn't it?"

After this, several kilometers passed in silence before the commodore and his surprising new attaché arrived at the Directorate for Foreign Affairs of the Soviet Armed Forces. The offices were in an idyllic little pistachio-green building on Yaniseiva Lane, located both literally and figuratively speaking in the shadow of the General Staff's mighty, power-emanating white marble building with its black wrought-iron decorations and sculptures.

It was hard to believe that the two worlds belonged together. The wooden door of the little nineteenth-century building creaked as they stepped inside. They were met by several extremely polite cadets who were supposed to take care of their nonexistent outer garments—the heat wave was unrelenting—and escort them to the reception room. There, the cadets announced them in sonorous tones to three elderly naval officers in full regalia awaiting them, a vice admiral and behind him two commodores.

Carl stared as if mesmerized at the vice admiral's uniform, which he immediately recognized. The same uniform as Koskov's, whom they had murdered. And whom Carl had accompanied from Cairo to Stockholm with a great deal of trouble of exactly the kind that Peter Sorman despised.

They greeted each other with salutes and handshakes in the prescribed order—one of the commodores turned out to be the interpreter, probably the highest-ranking interpreter that Commodore Hessulf had ever seen—and sat down across from each other at a large polished table set with mineral water bottles and crystal glasses. The cadets poured as if it were expensive wine.

The vice admiral broke into very rapid and very congenial-sounding Russian, talking in a loud voice and chuckling. What was this? The translation that followed revealed even more astonishments than the two Swedes could have imagined.

"Mr. Coq Rouge! Or we can be more formal and say Captain Second Class Hamilton! On behalf of the Soviet Ministry of Defense and in particular on the behalf of the Soviet Navy, let me welcome you to Moscow. It is with the greatest interest that we observe that you have now transferred to the diplomatic service, and we regard it as an honor that the Swedish Navy has sent one of its most qualified intelligence officers to our capital. As you know, Captain, the relationship between our two nations is now better than it has been in many years. Don't you agree with that, Captain Second Class?"

"You'd better try to answer," whispered Hessulf with a little poke at Carl's elbow.

"Sir . . . or rather Vice Admiral," began Carl in English very carefully, "I am, of course, in complete agreement with you. It is with the greatest optimism and satisfaction that we are watching not only developments within your country but also the improved relations between our two nations." He let out his breath and exchanged a rapid, controlled glance with Hessulf while the translation, which was most likely unnecessary, took place.

The Russian responded almost immediately with another question, which made the two Swedes think they were in a bad dream.

"At what are you planning to direct your espionage here in the time ahead?"

This was a question that was light-years away from diplomatic etiquette and equally removed from Carl's idea of a formal conversation with formal Russians. The old salt laughed as he waited for an answer.

"I have given up that type of intelligence activity, and I now intend, as best I can, to complete my assignment as a Swedish diplomat here in your capital," replied Carl stiffly. Where would this lead?

"All right, all right," laughed the Russian and then switched, as Carl had anticipated, into surprisingly good if thickly accented English. "But in what objective are you going to take a special interest while you're here? Just tell me, because we might like to help you."

"Normally I would count on an occasional visit to the Baltic republics, for reasons I don't have to set forth, but since you ask, I can tell you that your installations in Murmansk would be most interesting to visit."

The admiral burst out in a long, thundering laugh, and after some hesitation his two commodores followed suit.

"You have spirit, young Captain Second Class, real spirit! As far as Murmansk is concerned, it's rather the same thing as with your Muskö base—we only let old gentlemen of rank with lots of gold insignia visit that kind of place, old gentlemen who don't see as well as young captains. Let me also point out that the Soviet Union's chief of staff has visited Muskö, and one of your old generals has already been to Murmansk. Any other suggestions, young man?"

Carl hesitated, but the temptation was irresistible.

"Sir, if Murmansk is reserved for elderly flag officers, I would settle for some less strategic installation that's part of your network of minisubs and diversionary groups. We in Sweden have been asking ourselves quite a few questions on that subject." Carl smiled. The situation was totally grotesque—dangerous and comical at the same time.

This time all three Russian officers chuckled. The admiral sipped his mineral water, and all the others at the table copied him.

"As you yourself have pointed out, young Captain Second Class, the ties between our two countries have been improving over the past few years. It is our most sincere hope that this positive development will continue. Thus, I will not reply to your jokes, which I am, however, willing to accept as jokes. Still, I welcome you to our city on behalf of my and your two colleagues. I hope that you won't hesitate to ask us for assistance; we are at your disposal. It would be a pleasure to meet you under more informal circumstances—I hope that you have nothing against that."

Carl had no idea what the proper response should be. But he knew what the admiral was getting at about the two commodores being his colleagues. One of them wore the red ribbon of the Order of Lenin with four narrow yellow rows followed by the Red Star among the honors nearest to his heart; the other had, in addition to the Order of the Red Star, something in blue and silver, which Carl thought meant bravery in the field. And since "field" in this case could hardly be Afghanistan, where the Soviet Navy had no representatives, it might well mean the Baltic Sea. What a devilishly contrived irony, and how congenial!

"I am flattered by your kindness, Vice Admiral, and if you invite me, I would be happy to come, though I would have to ask the advice of my superiors at our embassy first," replied Carl hesitantly. He felt ill at ease as a diplomat.

The admiral stood up, and everyone else rose as well. They shook hands again according to rank, but it wasn't entirely over yet.

At the door, one of the Soviet commodores tapped Carl on the right side of his chest. "SEAL. Very good. We have that kind of thing here, too, and they are also very good." He winked, laughed almost heartily, and shook Carl's hand again.

"That was the damnedest thing. I don't understand any of it," sighed Commodore Hessulf when they had again squeezed into the oven-hot Volvo. "Not one bit of it. I have never witnessed such un-Russian behavior. Either they or I have gotten sunstroke in this damn heat."

Carl was busy trying to roll down his window, which didn't seem to work.

"What the hell did he mean by 'Mr. Coq Rouge'?" asked Hessulf as he unbuttoned his uniform jacket and effortlessly rolled down the window on his side.

"No idea," said Carl brusquely. He was irritated by his window refusing to budge. "Makes me think of a song from the Spanish Civil War."

"The Spanish Civil War?"

"Yes, the red rooster and the black rooster. The red rooster is on their side—some sort of compliment, I assume."

"Are you supposed to be on their side?"

"Hardly. It might be a reference to my politics during my student years, but I was exceedingly anti-Soviet then."

"Well, what a damned mess. And you're certainly mischievous—inspect the minisubs, eh?"

"I was just trying to adapt to their hearty raw tone, and they didn't seem very bothered by it. Besides, they started it."

"Well, that's true. But I'll have to report all this to the ambassador."

"Did I make a fool of myself?"

"No, I wouldn't say that. Personally, I think it was fine that you paid them back in coin, but their behavior today was unprecedented—and they stepped up the level, too. A vice admiral and two commodores. Jesus!"

Carl could imagine an explanation for it. But he kept his speculations to himself. The colleague who had tapped him on the wings and called him a "SEAL" had passed on an open greeting, but what did it mean? Either, Old grudges are forgotten because we know who you are. Or else, We know who you are and you'd damn well better watch your step. Carl decided cautiously to stick with the latter interpretation.

"How's it going with the computers?" asked Hessulf, pointedly changing the subject.

"Fine, thanks. In a few weeks or so I can start giving you gentlemen private lessons, so we can get the system going with three pairs of hands."

"Oh hell, I'm too old for things like that, and I don't understand a damn thing about it. I don't think our dear friend from the outfit is much younger, for that matter."

"The outfit?"

"Yes, the boys in green, the ones in green uniforms, you know. The outfit."

"I see. But don't worry, as soon as the program itself is in operation it will go like a dream. You'll be surprised at how easy it is."

"Doubt it, but I hope you're right."

The car stopped at a red light, and the heat poured in like gruel through the open windows.

They had videotaped the meeting. Carl was quite certain of this since the camera over the doorway, not well hidden and pointed straight at the two Swedes, had moved a couple of times. The angle seemed to indicate that they were primarily interested in Hessulf. What would they accomplish by recording the reactions of Commodore Hessulf to their playful provocations?

Maybe they wanted to see whether Hessulf would be upset or amazed, whether he knew or didn't know who Carl was, whether Carl was in Moscow to continue his old line of work or to switch to something new.

In any case, he wasn't going to say anything about the camera. Things were disturbing enough already. He was here now, and he was here to prevail against them. Even if there was a risk that the personal price would be too great.

Carl rented a little Lada 1600 from Intourist, and every day for the rest of the week he took a practice drive for several hours at the end of the workday and before the restaurants got busy. He had to learn about Moscow's traffic; every city has its own kind of traffic.

Typical for Moscow was high speed, lack of regard for drivers in less impressive cars, and lack of regard for pedestrians. Carl adapted to the lower range of the high speed. On the largest avenues traffic was sometimes up to sixty miles an hour.

And he learned about the special lane—like the "cream lane" that Stockholm's city council wanted to set up—used not only by the party bosses' cars with black curtains in the back but by cars with significant codes in the license-plate numerals; an elderly man in his undershirt with a fishing rod sticking out of the side window of a little Lada or Volga was not just an ordinary citizen overcome by glasnost. And diplomatic cars with red plates could also drive in the "cream lane," as well as taxis and cars with the yellow plates that indicated membership in a trade commission or the like.

First he had to get used to the natural driving rhythm, and then he had to learn to get around; for instance, to get from any point in the inner city by the quickest way to the Swedish embassy, which wasn't always easy. The embassy was rather isolated and on the opposite side of the river from the area north of Prospekt Mira that was his ultimate goal.

He didn't drive outside the inner city but stayed within the network of spoke boulevards radiating out to the inner circle. He learned to orient himself with the help of the seven tall Stalin towers; they were excellent landmarks.

They were surely watching him during these drives. They would surely grow suspicious; that's why he wouldn't use his own car when the time came, but the subway—first his car, and then park it quickly and go down into the subway. Especially since they'd probably attach a little radio to his car so that they could locate him at all times.

But maybe they thought it was mere restlessness and curiosity about a new workplace, or reflexive behavior on the part of an intelligence officer.

Since he always had to drive the car back to the embassy before he went off to town to booze, he walked a great deal, and as a pedestrian he got an entirely different view of Moscow. Its architecture radiated power and made the pedestrian feel small; oddly enough, he felt much smaller here, on one of these wide avenues, than in Manhattan, under the towering skyscrapers.

First of all, the streets were disproportionately wide; you could never cross them in the ordinary way but had to find the underground passages at the street corners. Second, many of the buildings along the biggest streets were constructed with very high street-level stories, so that the entryways made the buildings look as if they had been constructed for giants. And lastly, the sparse but terrifyingly fast motor traffic made the distances seem greater. That's more or less how it worked psychologically, whether intentional or not.

But it was also possible to find the opposite. Not far from the General Staff's teutonic white marble building near the Arbatskaya subway station, Carl found Arbatsky Street, the gathering point for Moscow's street artists, a pedestrian street where the people of Moscow thronged to listen—their astonishment mixed with fear—to the protest singers. To Carl they seemed third-rate punk-rockers, and he couldn't understand what the lyrics were about despite all his brushed-up Russian. He consoled himself in observing that most of the middle-aged spectators seemed as puzzled as he was. The applause at the end of every number was hesitant and reserved. But not a policeman as far as the eye could see, at least not in uniform.

He should be able to use the pianist in some way, whether she was working for the KGB or not. If she was, he could turn it to his advantage somehow.

He pondered this during the two hours it took him to make his way forward in the endless line to see Lenin.

There was a special line for special people, like the ones at certain discotheques and restaurants in Stockholm where they let big shots on the pop music scene and their real or alleged friends in first. But for almost sentimental reasons—so as not to betray his younger days, his very young days—he didn't want to visit Lenin like that. He wanted to stand in the endless queue.

Once he had stood in a similar line on a little island south of Manhattan. It took two hours to get inside the Statue of Liberty and up to the narrowest parts of the spiral stairway where they had to go single file, and at last he stood in the head and looked out through the Plexiglas-covered slots in her crown. They didn't give you much time to look, and picture taking wasn't allowed, but millions of Americans went there anyway.

The line moved quickly toward the end, and he almost missed the mummy itself, his attention caught instead by the insignia on the sleeves of the elite soldiers standing guard; he still hadn't figured out Soviet insignia, even though a placard depicting them was posted in the office next door to his, in the embassy's closed department within the closed department. There lay Lenin in his glass case, sleeping in a suit that might have been bought at the PUB department store in Stockholm, and then Carl was out, having seen what millions of Soviet citizens saw each year.

The heat struck him like a wall, and he decided not to walk to his meeting but to take the subway instead. He had memorized the subway system station by station, line by line, concentrating particularly on all the transfer points between the yellow Kaluzhko-Rizhskaya line and the gray, brown, orange, green, and purple lines.

He sifted through his memory. He should get off at Oktyabrskaya on either the brown or yellow line. If he took the Kirov-Frunze line from Prospekt Marksa to Kirovskaya, changed to the yellow line to Turgenevskaya and continued to Prospekt Mira, then the brown line would take him from there in a semicircle down to Oktyabrskaya.

That was one of four or five alternatives.

He went over it all in his mind step by step as he put his five-kopek coin in the slot, which changed from red to white—shouldn't it be the opposite, from a purely socialist point of view?—and took the escalator underground; the depth at which Moscow's subway was located, which was considerable, was kept secret because the subway is regarded as part of the city's defense system.

Inside the subway car, he discovered a map above every other doorway. Good. He wouldn't have to memorize everything; it would be enough to have an approximate picture and a good routine knowledge of the transfer points.

But he still had to make an effort to ride so that a tail wouldn't lose him. It was essential that they always be able to follow him. Up until a certain moment. Still, he picked up the pace so that his behavior wouldn't seem too unusual when that certain moment arrived.

Once again, he went through the unpleasant associations that required him to think of these people as his enemies, or rather, would require them to think of *him* as *their* enemy: the Western spy with treacherous plots against peace and the Soviet state. That was what *he* was.

The trains arrived and departed in perfect four-minute synchronization, and in spite of the detour he had chosen, in less than half an hour he was at his station.

Again the heat and again the sticky shirt against his back. He was wearing lightweight white linen pants and a short-sleeved cotton shirt, which probably identified him as a Westerner to more sharp-eyed Muscovites, who without hesitation spoke English or German when they approached him about exchanging money. Of course he said no, thanks; he would never commit the smallest crime, not even driving under the influence. Above all not that, since several Soviet intelligence officers had been expelled from Sweden for just that reason, and they couldn't be allowed their revenge at his expense. And there could be no question of changing money on the black market, and if greed was imminent—he knew you could get four times the amount of rubles per dollar, so that one of his eighty-ruble dinners would cost only ten dollars at the black-market exchange rate—he reminded himself that he would take everything out as expenses when the whole thing was over. And if he couldn't, it still made no difference, since living expensively in Moscow was still cheaper than his routine in Stockholm.

She was supposed to be waiting at the boat rental place in Gorky Park, but he arrived ten minutes early. He suppressed an impulse to walk past their meeting place and look it over: he was *not* a spy, just a reckless young Swedish diplomat who had broken with his own country's security regulations.

Instead he walked down to the Pushkin Embankment below the park and sat in the shade of trees he couldn't identify—he was quite visible, still an easy subject for observers. And they would get used to that.

First, he would try to get into her circle of friends, expand his inappropriate acquaintances. If that worked out, he would also try to initiate some kind of romance with her. Even if she wasn't working for them yet, the chance was good she would soon be forced to.

The question was how he should behave with the hotel prostitutes. It was probably a criminal offense to engage a prostitute, even though officially they didn't exist. But wouldn't the Russians merely cheer at his weakness instead of making a diplomatic issue out of it? Probably. But you never could tell.

Out on the river, long boats full of tourists packed on three decks passed by. The stone embankment slanted directly down into the water, as if to receive amphibious vehicles, he thought. At the far end a group of children and teenagers were swimming.

He thought of the Old Man and the pollution that made swimming near the mouth of the Vistula deadly. Did the Russians have no deadly rivers? He shouldn't contact O.M., not even by diplomatic mail, not even to convey his opinion that Sandström must have a protector in Säpo. Nothing he ever said or did should have the slightest connection to Sandström. Until a certain moment.

The traitors back home would have to wait until later; his building custodian was still running around loose, a Soviet informer allowed to drift aimlessly. He had sealed up his apartment and entrusted his plants to Lallerstedt because he didn't want to find them dead when he came back.

Why did she want to meet him in Gorky Park? Did she want to lead him to believe right from the start that he was being taken out far enough to be safe from eavesdropping? As if being in a boat out on a little lake would prevent that.

It made no difference. He would find a way to use her, whether she was working for them, was going to work for them, or would never work for them.

On top of everything, her name was Dzerzhinskaya; that seemed like the same black humor that the intelligence bosses had had at that meeting in the little green palace.

The rowboats cost only a few coins to rent, and there were two different colors—pink and green. Giggling, she chose a pink boat, saying it went better with her dark green cotton dress. He rowed slowly under the big willow trees and calmly began to chat, questioning her as if conversing only about music.

Yes, she had finished her studies. She was thirty, and now it was a matter of getting into the concert circuit.

She trailed a slender long hand in the water. Yes, her name was really Dzerzhinskaya. No, no relation to the square where there was a statue of a Dzerzhinsky. She laughed.

"Don't you know who Felix Dzerzhinsky was? He was the founder of the secret police. The KGB is in that big yellow building there, always has been. Everybody knows that. Before glasnost, I guess I wouldn't have dared say it out loud."

No, if she had had family—with that kind of connection, her situation would have been quite different; then she would not have been a refusenik.

Carl went on rowing. He pretended that he didn't know the word.

Well, a refusenik was a person who requested an exit visa but was turned down. Of course it was a big risk to request an exit visa since so many people were turned down, usually for completely incomprehensible reasons, and you never knew beforehand. And once you requested an exit visa, the ground sank under your feet.

But a musician who was not thought to be good enough to be a soloist had no future in Russia—she said "Russia," not "the Soviet Union." She had thought of moving to Finland and working there. Of course you officially had to request an exit visa for Israel, but once you got out, you could choose for yourself. She had relatives in New York and in Canada who had emigrated in that way.

A refusenik's family could have a difficult time. There was no danger for her parents because they were both scientists, her mother a physicist and her father a doctor, but the situation was problematic for her brothers and sisters.

Glasnost might have changed many things in Moscow, but for the Jews everything was just the same, and there were plenty of Jewish jokes about that.

She didn't say it openly, but he understood that having foreign contacts didn't make things worse for her. Rather, her non-Jewish friends had begun to keep their distance, and foreign contacts could actually be an advantage. Possibly she speculated that acquaintance with a Swedish diplomat would protect her rather than harm her.

Symbiosis, thought Carl. She wants to use me and I want to use her. How will this end? A love affair, vague promises of helping her get out, or of marriage?

He changed the subject and talked about his impressions of Moscow and the traffic in Moscow and what kind of car he drove.

"A coincidence! My father also has a Lada 1600, but I drive it more than he does."

Carl rowed on. Only a few rowboats were out on the lake—most of them were tied up in long green and pink rows near the shore—and in almost every one a young man was rowing with a young woman in the stern; it looked like a traditional way to start a romance in Moscow.

"I would be very pleased if we could go to the theater together. My Russian is not good enough for me to go alone," he said shyly. There was suddenly an entirely new possibility. The combination of her car and Russian theater might create an unexpected solution. Naturally they had a splendid opportunity to blackmail her, and it would be incompetence on almost the Säpo level not to exploit that opportunity. She would be forced to become their informer if she wasn't already, and that suited him perfectly.

"I am very fond of the theater," she said.

Eight

Yuri Chivartshev had several reasons for being in a bad mood. It had been raining for a week; it looked as if it was going to be an early, cold, and wet fall in Stockholm. The Swedish election was approaching, and in all likelihood it would cause problems.

In addition, he had been forced to call in the KGB, and that was something that went against the grain. Instinct and tradition taught one it was best not to have anything to do with the KGB, and above all you should never be in its debt. But information from the innermost circles of the Swedish government was a KGB area of responsibility. And, unfortunately, they had such reliable channels that their information almost always turned out to be correct, so sometimes it was impossible to do without them.

The Swedish government had finally agreed to grant immunity to the Peacock—a formal decision made by the minister of justice and then supplemented by the chief public prosecutor, agreeing on behalf of the prosecuting authorities. Documents had been drawn up— "classified," naturally.

Chivartshev knew that the news had leaked out quite widely within Säpo and that there was a good deal of grumbling at the top. But when the Peacock started fulfilling his part of the bargain and started reporting how he acted as that poor sap Sandström's protector, on occasion on direct Soviet instructions, the leakage would get out of control at the so-called madhouse, or was it monkey house?

The Conservatives would go to their reporters at *Expressen* as usual and plant the usual information, and there would be the usual election scandal about the socialist government protecting spies. The Säpo lackeys might even drag in their claim that military intelligence was also protecting exposed Soviet agents, and then the military would have to say the Tristan episode was a Soviet provocation.

How much would all this demoralize the Soviet network in Sweden and make recruiting operations more difficult? It looked as if the Soviet Union sold its own agents. The worst kind of marketing imaginable, to put it in Western terms.

Should they get some of their own people in Säpo to leak a different version, about how their own wondrously intelligent work had revealed Sandström's protector? There were plenty of useful idiots among the crowd of Säpo journalists who could spread this disinformation; it was tempting, and might be quite effective.

Except how would it affect the election? It was a KGB job to keep track of that. But a new Conservative government might stem the flow of information from the inner circles, unless the KGB was using only electronic means. Not likely. So it wouldn't want scandals that helped the Conservatives, and from the GRU's point of view, too, a Social Democratic government was, of course, preferable.

In the end it depended on what certain people in Säpo decided was publishable. It wasn't until they took this step that possible countermeasures could be evaluated. Only ten days were left before the election, so Säpo could be expected to make its move very soon. All right, then—it was time to prepare the counterpublicity: a campaign about how Säpo's tremendously intelligent work had exposed the Peacock, without which the government could not ever have imagined the part about immunity, and so on.

That would have to do. The newspapers would have plenty of material to make scandals and headlines from.

Chivartshev closed the thick folder with the handwritten title on top, "Case D-46/71: The Peacock." He hadn't made much of a decision, but at least it was a decision.

He scribbled several notes before giving the evening's orders, and locked the Peacock folder in a tall safe on the other side of his office, hoping he would not have to see the case on his desk in the near future.

He had another thick report, this one from Moscow, to devote the rest of the afternoon to, and he was surprised at its bulk. Hamilton shouldn't be the cause of so much paper; it wasn't like him.

Chivartshev placed it in the middle of his desk blotter and went over to the window. He looked out at the rain toward the blue neon sign across the street—northern Europe's most anti-Soviet publication.

He ordered a glass of tea from his secretary, and waited until he left before sitting down with the Hamilton report.

Even the first page had him raising his eyebrows.

The young captain was carousing in Moscow. Surprising, to say the least. He was out almost every evening, eating fancy dinners, throwing money around like the worst black marketeer, and frequenting the bars at the Intourist and National hotels.

But every banknote he'd used that had been inspected had come from official sources via the Swedish embassy.

He was most often drunk when he walked home; he never drove while drunk.

Chivartshev smiled to himself; no, it was clever not to drive under the influence when you were an intelligence officer. As opposed to some others, whose names he would rather forget.

Hamilton was fraternizing with prostitutes, both those in the service and those who, well, whose work could be regarded as an expression of perestroika and individual initiative. But he had never gone all the way, so to speak, even though he had bought drinks for them on several occasions. The prostitutes gave a consistent picture. He was undeniably on the verge of talking too much. He had told them that he was a military man, that he had had a number of exciting jobs abroad, that intrigues at home had meant that they had sent him off on an idiotic job far beneath his abilities, and that he longed to go home.

On two study trips, one to Leningrad and the other to Kaliningrad (how could they have given him permission to travel there?), he had had a sweet young boy from the Swedish embassy along with him.

Chivartshev speculated over whether the charming young man might possibly explain Hamilton's unwillingness to sleep with prostitutes. He pushed the thought aside. There ought to be some limit to the Swedish tendency toward such filth. It was an unpleasant thought that such a prominent colleague might have such inclinations.

Besides, this speculation was contradicted on the following pages, which dealt with Miss Irina Dzerzhinskaya—funny name, by the way; she couldn't be related to old Felix, could she?—and her obviously quite intimate relationship with young Hamilton.

They were seen together frequently. He often dined while she was playing at the National, he had visited her home on several occasions, even once when her parents were not there, and they went to performances at various theaters a couple of times a week.

Hamilton's work at the Swedish embassy, as far as could be determined, was primarily technical, and it was hard to imagine how he was handling it considering the disturbingly high alcohol consumption. He often wandered through the streets alone, seemingly aimless (and they had taken great pains to discover any pattern or goal); he devoted himself to tourist activities, went to the parks, took the subway, or drove around in a car. As far as they could observe, he had made no contact of interest to Soviet security—though he *had* made some remarkable contacts from the security point of view of his own country.

Were the Swedes throwing away one of their best operatives on a meaningless bureaucratic, technical assignment in Moscow? Were they trying to make him bitter and vengeful, and was he really drinking too much?

It looked too good. Hamilton had proven himself to be an extraordinarily capable officer. Could his morals really fall apart so quickly?

Zentral was leaning to that conclusion. They had already authorized certain actions; they had, among other things, hired the pianist. She had her exit visa to think of, after all.

But they were also considering the thing with the young men as an alternative. They could assume that if Hamilton had been banished to Moscow because he was unwelcome at home, then he would presumably not be sent back because of bad behavior—an old-fashioned case of extortion, perhaps?

Chivartshev shook his head. There must be some mistake. First of all, that method was more suitable for less security-conscious and more prestige-bound persons. Second, it was all wrong psychologically: Hamilton would be deeply offended if anyone tried to blackmail him as if he were a simple salesman.

A direct, open approach would be much better. But then they would have to wait at least six months, or even longer. But the way Hamilton was behaving, there was a risk that his superiors would send him home, and then he'd be out of reach.

So wait and see for six months, follow developments, and then choose the direct approach instead of a provocation.

That was the answer to Moscow's direct question.

But it didn't feel right. How could such a professional spy commit so many classic errors at once? Why was it that in some senses he still was able to maintain his good judgment? For example, never committing the smallest infraction of the law.

Maybe it was ingrained, maybe it would come later if the degeneracy progressed; even his physique was being neglected, since they could see in some ways that his physical condition was ten to fifteen percent worse now than when he had arrived in the summer.

How did they know that? Oh well, that's what they claimed.

Had Hamilton really been so unwelcome in Sweden, as he was now proclaiming to the whores? What was this about politics, about someone high up in the government who didn't like him?

Chivartshev sighed. There was no getting around it. The case had to be checked. It was important, if true. So he'd have to ask his colleague, the KGB man. Better to tackle the matter immediately, like pulling out an aching tooth.

He locked the Hamilton report in his safe and called his colleague on the other side of the building. Yes, of course, he could come at once. With heavy steps Chivartshev walked to the offices of the KGB, where the view of Stockholm and the open water would have suited him better than the dreary brick façade of the crazy anti-Soviet newspaper.

It *was* like pulling out a tooth. It was quick and unpleasant, and it produced results.

The KGB knew all about it. It was true that Hamilton was in political disfavor. The person who didn't like him was Cabinet Secretary Peter Sorman, and the reason was the operation in the Middle East that had obtained the release of the two kidnapped Swedish doctors in Lebanon. While Sweden's official version was that Swedish diplomats, with phenomenal adroitness, had freed the hostages by diplomacy, the truth was that Hamilton had freed them and killed the bandits. Sorman didn't want it to get out, and that's why they had sent Hamilton to hell—well, that's the way they put it—that is, to Moscow.

Chivartshev was pleased when he returned to the relative security of his own section of the embassy. It had been worth the unpleasantness; this was important information.

Still, a lot of things seemed *too* good. In more than one respect, Hamilton was living a double life in Moscow. He was deceiving his own people when he behaved like a parody of a security risk. But what was the intention behind pretending to be an alcoholic? His specialty was without a doubt wetwork, meaning murder and sabotage. What or who could be the target of such actions in Moscow?

It was always good to follow the rule never to draw hasty conclusions, and never to believe that the obvious was obvious.

So. Reject any suggestion of young-boy provocations. Wait for the presumably more intimate reports they would get from the pianist. Wait at least six months. Then try the direct approach. If Hamilton said no, it would just mean no for the time being, and if he later changed his mind, it was his own business to make the next contact; he knew the game.

A very peculiar man, this Hamilton. Thirty-four years old, with more accumulated experience in tactical activities than others acquired in a lifetime. And though Chivartshev had never seen him except in pictures, not to mention met him, he was one of the Russians who knew him best. When the time came, he might go home and carry out the approach himself. He smiled at the idea. It would be sensible for someone to handle it who knew a lot about Hamilton and about Sweden.

That would be an interesting moment, however it turned out.

In six months, it would be the end of his Swedish residency. What a pleasant thought: that as a conclusion to his time as Resident in Sweden, he would recruit one of their very best.

Carl sat on the floor of his office, swearing over various electrical diagrams spread out on the floor around him. The reserve power unit had finally arrived from Stockholm and the Foreign Ministry's bureaucracy for diplomatic deliveries.

Theoretically it was very simple. The batteries were charged by ordinary electricity from the wall socket, and then you simply attached the computers to the unit instead of to the wall socket. But various security systems made it impossible to forget about the wall socket, the connection to the outside world. When the whole thing was hooked up, it wasn't just a matter of punching a button; you had to get several circuits functioning simultaneously, and they could be attached correctly or incorrectly; so far, with unfailing precision, he had managed to do it wrong. Hardware was not his strong point.

At last it worked, and he heaved a sigh of relief at the same moment that a pipe-smoking Colonel Nordlander knocked on his partially open door.

"How's it going? Are the machines from hell going to work?" shouted the colonel, as if it were a matter of drowning out the totally silent computers.

"Sure," muttered Carl, gathering up his diagrams as he got to his feet. "As luck would have it, we only need to take care of this once, and then it'll work. We can start practicing soon with, well, you know what."

Carl pointed meaningfully toward the probable bug that was always presumed to be in the ceiling, as in the old days.

"Yes, I know," said his superior quickly, "but we have a small problem. There are complaints about you."

Carl sat down uneasily, at the same time offering his guest the visitor's chair in front of his desk: Carl had one visitor's chair; his superiors had two. Everything according to regulations, presumably from the Housing Authority.

"Nothing serious, I hope?" said Carl with a neutral expression.

"Yes, extremely serious," said the colonel with an overly worried expression. Then he grinned. "The Directorate for Foreign Affairs has made what's known as a comment, and that comment has to do with your car."

"My car?"

"Yes, it's bad enough that you drive a Russian car, but you're driving a rental car from Intourist—a civilian car without diplomatic plates. That's considered unsuitable."

"It's the fault of their bureaucracy. My own car was supposed to have gotten here from Helsinki, and the last message I received was that it had left Helsinki and was already in Moscow. Tell them I'll get rid of the rental car as soon as my own car makes it through the red tape. Maybe that will speed it up."

"Sounds reasonable. What kind of a car is it, by the way? A 740?"

"Oh no, no Volvo for me. It's the same kind I have, a Lada 1600."

"Well, I'll be damned!"

"Why do you say that? A Russian car in Russia—you can't go wrong with that. You're supposed to stick to the local wine, why not the local cars?"

"It makes a rather eccentric impression. In the best of cases."

"And in the worst case?"

"A dubious impression. Unnecessary, I should think."

"What do you mean dubious? Do Russians consider their own cars so worthless?"

"Well . . . it's not a common car among Western colleagues. It might seem that you want to be a little too discreet in Moscow traffic."

"Then let them think that. I'm not doing anything fishy."

"No, of course not. But you don't have to make them think so, either. Oh well, what's done is done. So we'll soon have a little Lada in the diplomatic parking lot?"

"I hope so, yes."

"But you'll take our car tomorrow night. I heard that you were invited to the French embassy. You're certainly popular, I must say. Isn't it difficult going without a wife?"

"Yes, I'll take the car and chauffeur. Already ordered it. No, it's not too hard to be without a wife. It just means that they have to round up an interesting dinner partner who isn't married to a military attaché, and I don't have to be in on the wife swapping."

"Well, well. Take care. We have a meeting tomorrow morning at nine, remember."

Carl tried to keep his expression neutral as his superior stood up, nodded, and left. Both the colonel and Commodore Hessulf probably thought it unfair and possibly odd that Carl was receiving so many personal invitations. And Carl had no desire to explain why.

But the invitations had rained down on Carl ever since the first little introductory party that Nordlander had arranged in his bungalow. This was not because of his extraordinary social graces or his interesting opinions. It was simply that the West German military representative could never pass up a young, green Western colleague who was a commander of the Bundesverdienstkreuz. And the medal of the Legion of Honor had an almost religious significance for the French. And when the American naval attaché was introduced, his eyes had immediately fastened on the slender gold wings, with the claw holding the trident, discreetly decorating Carl's right breast. One thing led to another, and Carl had now reached a level of two or three invitations a week.

That suited him fine. Every evening on duty was an evening excused from his more dubious duties at the bars at the National or Intourist.

Tonight was a night when he could get out of behaving like a pig, because he was going to visit Irina and have dinner with her parents. They were moderate with alcohol.

By Russian standards, they lived in grand style, in a three-room apartment on Bolshoya Akademicheskaya Street with a view of a park and a large artificial lake. It wasn't centrally located or near the subways, but it was nice and big, and they had gotten it because of their combined scientific merits. The biggest room was dominated by Irina's piano, and the family always gathered for a music hour before dinner—it was the family's gathering place, a combination music room, living room, library, and dining room.

Conversation at the home of the Dzerzhinsky family touched on the obvious topics of the day: Gorbachev, glasnost, the reduced risk of war in the world, the end of the unfortunate war in Afghanistan, President Bush's visit—everything that breathed of optimism when you talked to ordinary Russians, everything that his military colleagues also constantly talked about, although still with the nightmare scenario. If it all went to hell with perestroika and traditional forces returned to power, the world would be plunged back into the cold war again. It was the Russians' third chance for a thaw, after all, and in the view of the Western diplomats, including the Swedes, their last.

Things should have been good for the Dzerzhinsky family. The girls had received an education, and the parents had good jobs, even a little dacha they went to on holidays in their own car. The mother, not the father, was a party member who had even been nominated to the party congress that had ratified Gorbachev's policies. But Irina's personal decision to apply for an exit visa, which had now transformed her into a refusenik, hung like a black cloud over the whole family.

Her friendship with Carl would harm the family, too, and he knew it. Afterward they would be suspected of participating in a Western conspiracy, and if it were during Stalin's time or even Brezhnev's, they would be imprisoned or liquidated. Now there was no way of knowing what would happen to them.

He took the subway straight to Rizhskaya, and then the trolley bus to her street, punching his five-kopek ticket on the wall of the bus like a law-abiding Soviet citizen.

He had never arrived alone at her house before. He took the chance of fiddling with the combination lock to see if it worked as he thought it did. And it did. He forced the combination in less than a minute.

That could be a horribly long and indiscreet amount of time when it was crucial. He locked the door again and rang the bell.

She opened the door herself, and to his surprise he found her alone.

The family had gone to the dacha but they sent their greetings, she explained briefly.

He awkwardly handed her two bottles of the embassy's Beaujolais Royal—the surplus of that wine at Swedish embassies had something to do with the royal family, apparently.

He sat down in her father's big, worn leather armchair at her request, and then she played for half an hour without pause or hesitation, as if it were a real concert. A Beethoven sonata.

Far off in the twilight through the big windows he could see the lights on the radio and television towers. In that direction, at just about the same distance on the other side of the towers, was where the suburb of Bibirevo-Medvedkovo-Babushkin lay, at the end of the Medvedkovo subway line.

It was not a nice suburb, he was told. It was considered better to live on the south side of Moscow.

When she had finished the sonata and he had applauded—slowly and with emphasis, the way you do when you're alone—she turned and looked at him for a long time in silence.

"Do you think I'll ever play for a Finnish audience?" she asked at last. She looked as if she didn't believe it.

"*Konechno*, yes, of course." He smiled quickly and freely. He knew she would never get any kind of exit visa.

She got up from the piano bench and quietly came over to him, kneeling on the Kazakh carpet with her arms across his thighs.

"You're a very beautiful woman, and you have so much beauty within you," he said softly, carefully weaving the fingers of his right hand through her thick black hair and pulling her toward him. He put his other hand on the back of her neck and kissed her. This was the first time they had ever been alone with each other indoors.

He expected her to respond cautiously, but she was surprisingly eager and passionate, and continued to kiss him as she raised herself up and pulled off his tie and then his jacket. They were entangled in each other's clothes for a while, and then he stood up . . . pulling her along with him, and lifted her up and carried her into the room she shared with her sister.

There was something almost desperate about her way of making love, and he felt as if she were the one leading and he merely following, as in some feverish Latin dance. And he noticed he had no difficulty making love while on duty.

Afterward she lay quietly on her stomach with her face buried in the pillow. Was she ashamed? It didn't fit with the way she had succumbed to passion. He stroked her gently on her long, bare back. She was so slender, almost skinny, and his fingers slid palpably up and down her vertebrae.

Finally she turned over and kissed him almost shyly or modestly in the hollow of his throat, and then burrowed her mouth near his neck.

He lay there for a while, looking up at the ceiling. It was almost dark outside, and there were plenty of cracks in the ceiling. He was waiting for something.

"Who are you really, Count Hamilton, and what are you really doing here in Moscow? I know you so little," she whispered at last.

He understood the situation. "I'm a diplomat, but not just a diplomat," he replied calmly and quite loudly. "I'm the military attaché, and that means I gather information about the Soviet Union's defenses, exactly as Soviet diplomats do in Sweden. That way we'll all know more about each other. That's not so strange."

She turned her face into the pillow again; almost at once he could feel her slim back shaking with sobs.

Suddenly and impulsively she turned to him again, her face swollen with tears and streaked with eye makeup, and she pulled him toward her, whispering into his ear so only he might hear her say that she wanted to take a walk. They had to go outside so they could talk.

He shook his head. If there was one thing he absolutely did not want to do right now, it was to go out for a walk. "No," he said, "that would be wrong."

And then he bent down and whispered quickly to her a time and a place; he looked at her and tenderly wiped away her tears. He kissed her face, at first cautiously, then, when he reached her mouth, with growing ardor, so that they would start over instead of going out. She met his unspoken suggestion almost in desperation.

He left her after midnight, telling her that he had to return to the embassy residence every night because both the Swedish and the Soviet guards took note if he didn't.

When he emerged into the silent, dark street, he knew it would be hard to get home. It was a quiet neighborhood, and far from the big streets heading into town where he might be able to find a taxi.

When a taxi, as if by chance, appeared out of nowhere, and the driver rolled down the window and asked him if wanted a ride, he had a hard time not showing his amusement when he said no thanks. The taxi driver asked again, and he said no again.

He walked for half an hour toward the center of Moscow on an unpleasantly wide boulevard with sparse traffic, and the sidewalks were deserted. It was the first time he was certain of being watched.

He wouldn't know until the next day whether the situation was as good as he hoped. He let his thoughts drift off in another direction.

The second taxi that now wanted to pick him up idled along beside him. Laughing, he walked toward the car. If they were so insistent, they could just as well drive him home. The yellow Volga drove straight to the Swedish embassy.

Without his mentioning the address.

Inside his apartment, he looked with curiosity for signs that it had been searched; only the embassy's locally hired personnel had access to the area, but everybody assumed that at least half of them were KGB.

Yes, someone had discreetly and professionally searched his few belongings. So they hadn't found anything fishy, and if they thought the way Swedish security people did, they might have concluded that this fact itself was fishy. Maybe he ought to leave some semi-innocent papers around so that they'd have something to report. He hoped they couldn't get into the closed department in the embassy.

He stood at the window for a while, looking out into the darkness. Even in daylight he had a dreary view across the construction site where the new West German embassy was being built, on a little street which the Russians had kindly christened Olof Palme Street, with a little black-iron memorial.

It was the first night in a long time that he was totally sober, and he enjoyed this condition as an alcoholic enjoys his first drink, feeling restored.

He showered off his and her combined odors and sat down resolutely at his desk. For the first time in many years he wrote a long love letter. In his own language, to one of his own kind, to a police officer.

Her eyes were as frightened as a deer's when he discovered her by the boat rental in Gorky Park. It was drizzling and it was hardly a time to go rowing. He felt like an English gentleman as he switched his umbrella over to his left hand, kissed her gently on both cheeks, and offered her his right arm.

It would be a long walk, and she was the one who would make the first move. She walked tensely before she was able to begin, and she kept looking around, as if she knew or feared they were being observed. She was a Soviet citizen, and had grown up that way.

"Carl, my love, I will be completely honest with you," she began in her fine, tentative English. "Something horrible has happened, and if they knew I told you, I would be in a lot of trouble." Then she lost her nerve and fell silent.

"Who are 'they' you're talking about: the KGB or the GRU?" he asked finally, soothing and direct.

"Not the KGB. Military people of some kind."

"So, the GRU. Well, that's not so dangerous, dear Irina, not so dangerous as you think. They're just doing their job. Every country has something like it—we do too. They're always suspicious, both here and back in Sweden. They poke around a little and write up reports that end up in archives, and it doesn't necessarily lead to anything."

"They say you're a spy," she snapped.

"Well," said Carl with a smile, looking straight at her to reassure her, "in actual fact they're right. There are overt spies and covert illegal spies, both here and in Sweden. I've worked for many years as an illegal spy, and they know that. But after you've done it long enough, you get burned—you're so well known by all the other spies that the job has to end. Then you can become a military attaché, for instance, as I have now. But it's a legal diplomatic job. There is absolutely nothing to get upset about."

"They say—it's so terrible!—that I have to cooperate with them or else."

"Because otherwise you'll never get an exit visa and all that. Well, those are the rules of their game. It was worse before, when they would have threatened to send you and your whole family to the gulag. In the best case."

"How can you take it so calmly? Don't you see I've landed in a terrible situation for your sake?"

"Yes, Irina, I know. And if I *were* an illegal spy, you and I would both be in trouble. But that's not the case."

"How can you say that? You're not one of us, you don't understand. It's a dark shadow you know is there, which you grow up with all your life and hear stories about. And then one day the bad dreams come true, and your life is destroyed."

She was right, of course. She was trapped; she had a case officer somewhere, maybe at Zentral near the old airport; she was a number on the list, with her own file folder with her name and birthplace stamped on it. It was irrevocable.

And now she was on her way to acquiring yet another case officer from the other side. Possibly they would understand that later, and, given the choice between blaming her and blaming her Russian case officer, they would choose her.

And she was absolutely not stupid. Her own worst enemy now was not her lack of intelligence but her terror, which he would make use of. He was her enemy.

He had been walking in silence at her side long enough to seem as though he spoke with calm consideration. "It's true, Irina, that I'm not one of you. I'm not a Russian, and I haven't lived in a country with Dzerzhinsky on the square—"

"You pretended you didn't even know who it was!"

"Yes, you're right. I didn't want to upset you. But let me continue. You, on the other hand, are not one of us. You're not a spy and never have been. I know your Russian spies and spy chasers just as they know me; we're colleagues in the same business. We're officers serving our countries, Russia or Sweden. I know how they think, and that's why I'm not worried. No, don't interrupt me, let me explain. This is the way it is. They obviously have some idea what I worked on in my old job; they can even read it on my uniform."

"Do you have a uniform too? You're a soldier, not a diplomat!"

"No, no. All military attachés have uniforms; it's so that you act completely openly in this job—that's the arrangement. They just want to be sure it's true that I've switched over to open, legal activity; it's purely routine. I've behaved a little strangely here. That's what makes them want to check up on me. And we would have done the same in Sweden with any Russian who behaved as I did, and that's still not so strange."

"But what have you done? What have you gotten into?"

"The problem is you, Irina. I shouldn't have gotten to know you, I shouldn't have fallen in love with you, I shouldn't associate with you. It's considered rash behavior; people like me are supposed to be suspicious and careful. But I'm tired of that life; I don't want to live like a spy anymore, I'm a normal person and a normal man with normal feelings. When I heard you play for the first time, I gave in to my feelings at once, and that's what they think is strange."

"You're an idiot."

"Yes, I'm an idiot."

She walked in silence at his side and seemed soothed. They reached a little food cart where heavy smoke was rising from a charcoal grill.

"Perestroika," she said suddenly with a laugh. "Come on, I'm hungry, haven't eaten for nearly two days."

"What do you mean, perestroika?" he asked as he let her pull him along.

"These people are from a cooperative somewhere out in the country; they make their own sausages and sell them for capitalistic profit."

"Not capitalistic profit, Irina. They are participating in the modernization of the Soviet economy with the help of a permitted form of individual economic initiative."

It was a great relief when they both laughed.

The sausages lay in rings on the grill, looking like something Fido had made, and there was no beer, so it would have to be Pepsi-Cola. It was with only moderate enthusiasm that Carl ate the sour, hard, smoked sausage and drank his Pepsi, but she ate voraciously.

"You don't have anything against perestroika pigs?" he teased her.

"No, not at all, we are secular, and the Russian who doesn't eat pork won't eat much meat. This is a pork-eating country; surely this has not escaped your attention?"

"I thought you were beer drinkers too. Why can't you get beer with the pork?"

"Gorbachev again. For two years it has been forbidden to drink alcohol in Moscow's parks; it's part of the sobriety campaign."

"Which means that all the sugar and yeast disappears from the shops."

"That's right. Then the Russian housewives get angry and don't like perestroika, and their husbands get angry too because it's so hard to get any vodka. Perestroika has its problems."

"Yes, but you can solve them."

"Is that what you want, you in the West?"

"Yes, it's extremely important that things go well for perestroika, not because we feel any sentimental love for Mother Russia but because a well-functioning Soviet Union will be less inclined to start a war."

"You view us as enemies, as if we were the ones who would start a war and not you?"

"Yes, that's about right. We can destroy you a little better than you can destroy us, but no one can win."

"The Soviet Union would never start a nuclear war."

"No, you love peace and you suffered during the Great Patriotic War and it will never happen in Russia again and all that. Nevertheless it's good for all of us if things go well for Gorbachev and perestroika; that's the important thing, more important than glasnost."

"Why?"

"A new Brezhnev would mean greater suspicion, greater armaments, greater suspicion about arms, and more arms—it would be the cold war all over again."

"But isn't glasnost important?"

"It belongs to the outer framework, the superstructure, you might say. It's good to have freedom of speech, and punk bands on Arbatsky Street, and a more liberal emigration policy, but if things go to hell with perestroika, then glasnost will disappear, both here and out in the world."

"Do you think I can get an exit visa, now that—"

"Are you done eating?"

"Yes."

"Come on, let's walk some more."

She stood up quickly; she wanted to get back to the real subject. They walked in silence toward the lake with the fountains, as if they wanted to distance themselves from anyone who might listen, as if that would make any difference.

Just when he thought that she would go back to their serious conversation, she seemed to get an idea and, giggling (it was hopeful that she could giggle), pulled him toward several booths with shooting galleries. "If you're a soldier, show me how a Swedish soldier shoots," she commanded.

You bought bullets for the air rifle at three kopeks apiece, and then you loaded with a repeating action. The targets were little moving animals made of black and red tin and grotesque masks with a bull's-eye as big as a five-kopek coin hanging from a string under the neck; when you hit it, the mask made faces and emitted sounds and red lights lit up inside the eyes.

Carl took aim at a spot on the wall and fired two rounds.

"You missed!" She laughed.

"No," said Carl. "Now I know I have to aim two centimeters below seven o'clock. Which mask would you like to kill?"

"That one, second from the left."

It was the first time in several months that Carl had held a weapon—the longest absence from guns in twelve or thirteen years. It felt pleasant, as if he were back in real life again. He fired ten rounds in quick succession. Each time the mask grimaced as if it were whimpering at the shots.

"Look at the mask, look closely," she said as he handed the air rifle on to the next woman in the line.

"So? A monster of some kind. So?"

"Don't you see?"

"No. It's a mask made of cardboard and tin."

"It's a Jew, an anti-Semitic caricature."

He gazed at the grotesque mask. A crooked nose, malicious, with a beard and something that *could* be earlocks. "Come, come, Irina, you're imagining things. It's a nice ordinary monster."

"You don't know Russia. That's a Jew, the most popular target at the shooting gallery and other places."

They continued toward the lake with the fountains.

"The exit visa—what do you think? Is it all ruined now?" she asked at last.

He waited before answering, looking up at the huge, high trees, beginning to turn fall colors at the top. It had stopped raining and a hesitant sun was brightening the incipient gold and crimson. "You should just do what they tell you to do and answer all their questions about me—everything, without lying. Except on one point, one single point that's easy to remember. It was a mistake for you to tell me they had forced you to become an informer; naturally they must have given you strict instructions not to, didn't they?"

"Yes, of course."

"Don't tell them you told me. When you have to lie, it's important to remember what you're lying about, and you should have as few things to remember as possible."

"Spoken like an expert."

"Yes, I lied a lot in my old job. But not now. Answer all their questions about me, everything, with complete honesty. They will check your information as best they can, and they will realize that you always tell the truth. Eventually the operation will be over, and it will just become a file they could have done without."

"The operation?"

"Yes, they're in the middle of an operation, as it's called. An officer has an assignment, and he has been given certain resources and certain assistants by a higher officer. Now he has to solve the problem and present answers to certain questions, and you are one of his helpers."

"What questions?"

"Why have the Swedes sent Hamilton to the Soviet Union? What is his formal assignment at the embassy? How is he handling the job? What does he think about life in Moscow? Why is he ignoring security regulations so nonchalantly? How much is he telling his female companion? Can we conclude that he has switched over to open activity? Questions like that—routine."

"How can I be used for something like that? Why did they pick me?"

"They think I might have told you more than I have. Throughout history, spies have been caught because they talked too much to women."

"But not you, evidently."

"Dear Irina, dear, dear Irina. I left that life behind me. Why should I ever bring up old memories with you when I don't even want to with myself? You would have fled. I would have scared you off. It had been a bad time, and I thought it was over, buried in files marked Classified. Now it hasn't turned out that way; now I'll have to tell you some of it so they'll get a little of what they're looking for. That's the only way that we can get rid of them—that you can get rid of them, I mean. They can't hurt me; I'm a diplomat and I'm not doing anything illegal."

"If you're lying to me, as you obviously can since you're a spy, they'll come after me. You'll manage all right because you're a diplomat, but what will happen to me?"

"That's not the way things work, Irina. If I were a spy, then I'd go straight back to Stockholm and report; I'd say thanks for the tip and go home. And you'd be left in the lurch, and it would be your fault that I left. You would have saved me out of what they would regard as ignorance."

"It's not just me—there's my family."

"I know that, Irina. Don't you think I know that? But I'm not a spy, so I don't need to flee, and we don't have to behave as if we had guilty consciences. I'll tell you about myself, which I had never planned to do, and you will tell them what you want, and in the end we'll be rid of the problem."

"If what you tell me is true."

"Exactly. If I lie to you, then they'll come after you, but also after me. So I won't lie to you, and we'll take up, as I said, a lot of topics that I hadn't planned on."

"What you did as a spy?"

"Yes, some of it, but not everything. It would seem strange if I told you everything. I'll tell you things that may make you understand me better, understand why it's a world that I had to leave."

"Because you couldn't take it anymore?"

"Yes, partly, but some politicians wanted to get rid of me too. I knew too much about their lies. Our world is not so different from your Soviet world as you might think."

"If they give up in the end, if I help them without lying, then can I get my exit visa?" She bit her lip and looked down at the ground.

They had reached the end of the park and were near the Lenin Stadium. He had forgotten the name of the bridge, but if you walked over the bridge past the Frunze Embankment, then the next subway station, Sportivnaya, was about twenty minutes away on the orange line called Kirovsko-Frunzenskaya, which you had to take to the Kirovskaya station, where you walked through the corridor to Turgenevskaya to get to the yellow line with the end station called Medvedkovo. The end of the line.

"I would wish for two things," he said, to end the silence.

"That you had never met me and that right now you were in a totally different place in a totally different country," Irina replied sadly. It was not a means of appropriating solace and reassurances.

"No, not at all. First, I would wish to go to the theater with you more often. You can explain the plays to me when I don't understand, and I'm very fond of theater when it's real theater, on a stage. Second, I would wish to go to your house and make love all night long."

She looked astonished, and then she smiled. "So that they can listen to us, you mean?" Suddenly she was serious.

"I don't think they're doing that. They'd probably rather get their information from you. It's not as great as people think, couples making love on tape; you never hear what they're really saying, you just hear the irrelevant things. No, I want to make love to you again. I don't want them to destroy what there is between us, and your parents are away, and we'll be careful."

"You've got a lot of nerve."

"It's left over from my days as a spy. I'll confess afterward."

"Without lying?"

"Yes, of course without lying. That would ruin everything. I mean literally everything, Irina. Trust me. I'll never lie to you; I'd leave before I'd do that."

She smiled at him for the first time since the grilled perestroika sausages with no beer. He surprised himself. He almost always had told the truth, and almost without lying he had recruited an agent in the middle of one of Moscow's parks. He had even succeeded in avoiding answering her last question. The answer, the real answer, was that whoever participated in an operation against a Western intelligence officer, whether voluntarily or under pressure, would never get to leave the Soviet Union.

"I'm already longing for home," she said, smiling at him again.

"Good, then we'll take a taxi as soon as we get out of the park and over to that street, whatever it's called."

"It may be hard to find one at this time of day," she said, as if it were both obvious and irrelevant. They still had a whole day and a whole night, after all.

"I have a feeling that we'll get a taxi as soon as we reach the street," laughed Carl. He bent forward and kissed her on the cheek. The most natural thing in the world.

It was September. Sandström would be dead before fall had turned to winter.

And she would truly get a large part of the blame.

They found a taxi at once.

September was a busy month in Kivik.

The apples ripen at different times, depending on how early or late a type they are. September is one of the big harvest months.

The immigration board and the accursed police had now put a stop to the influx of unbelievably industrious Polish students who had once made up most of the moonlighting apple pickers.

But the Old Man had two new arrivals who acted as if they had never had any other ambition in life than to pick apples. It seemed to be natural for both of them to work hard, evenly, and talkatively. If you could disregard their exceptional vigor and overall fitness and strength, they looked like ordinary students recently returned home from the United States. They were already full-fledged liars, so persuasive that O.M. was almost moved by them.

Both of them had signed up without hesitation. A week ago they were Lieutenant Lundwall and Lieutenant Steelglove, employed in the covert special-missions department. They were forever bound together, not just to each other, but also to Carl, who O.M. hoped would be their boss.

There was nothing strange about his having a couple of apple pickers living in his house; during the harvest season, there weren't many empty beds to be found anywhere in Kivik. So he could devote the evenings to finding out about their training and their expectations. They sat by the fire and dutifully drank cider, noting not only the considerable difference in military rank between them and Carl, but also the distance that O.M. wanted to maintain from them. They were, in a sense, his own creation, but he was going to retire soon, and someone else in the service would have the honor of breaking them in.

At any rate, his last years had produced a number of successes: Captain Hamilton and Lieutenants Lundwall and Steelglove were odd but valuable reinforcements in precisely that area of operations where Swedish intelligence had previously shown weakness. In addition, the boys were talented and pleasant. It was hard to imagine that they had the same capabilities that Carl did, but they might.

And two new commandos had just left for San Diego to do their military service, extended by five years. It had certainly been a hard sell, but the Chief had given in, partly as a gesture to O.M. and partly with specific references to certain practical results associated with such training.

A better advertisement than Carl was hard to imagine in that regard. So the Old Man could, with some peace of mind, adapt to the idea that before long he would be gone from the service and forever— well, for the rest of his life—be associated with apples instead of with intelligence.

"When is Hamilton coming home?" asked Joar Lundwall, invariably polite. It was the third time in two days he had asked the question.

"If you pump the bellows a little from underneath, under the grating, I think it would be more effective," said O.M.

But then he relented. "Unfortunately we have an election this year," he began, but quickly realized that the wording could be misunderstood. He continued with a quick modification. "Well, not unfortunately. But the thing is that the government controls appointments, and three appointments are in the pipeline—the government decides on two of them. I myself will have a successor, and who it is depends directly on which party controls the government. Some people don't like the Social Democrats, some do. So there are two options for the service. Then it will be Lallerstedt's turn to retire, and before long Sam himself. All this depends on politics, unfortunately."

"Yes, but does Carl depend on politics too? He doesn't have anything to do with the Social Democrats or the Conservatives, does he?" asked Steelglove in his lilting Finnish-Swedish.

"Well, no, you can't say that he does. But the idea is for Carl to take Lallerstedt's job so Lallerstedt can go out on the seven seas again. But it's the chief of OP5 who selects the head of our special-missions department, and the question is whether Carl will make it home before we have a new chief of OP5."

"In that case, wouldn't it be a good idea to bring him home from Moscow in good time?" asked Lundwall, gentle and polite as ever.

"Yes, of course," grumbled the Old Man, "but he has to finish installing that computer so that we get a little consistency in our Moscow reports; a little order, at any rate."

"Well, that ought to be finished in a couple of months," objected Lundwall.

It was hell trying to lie to intelligent people, thought O.M. "Are you a computer expert too?" he changed the subject ostentatiously.

"Yes, I have the same training as Hamilton."

"And you think the programming will be finished in two months?"

"Yes, without a doubt. It depends a little on how much basic material they have and what condition it's in, but two months ought to be enough."

"Hm," said O.M. "And what about you, Steelglove, did you give up this computer stuff?"

"Well, sort of. We already had two of those damned wizards in the company, and it doesn't suit me much. I went into a different field of technology, so to speak."

"I see, and if I remember correctly from a rather ironic report from our esteemed captain, your new technology had something to do with American literature. Well, well, who knows, that might come in handy, too," smiled O.M., raising his eyebrows in his ironic owl look.

"Well, that literature *was* a little confusing." Åke Steelglove was embarrassed.

O.M. regarded him with amusement. The man was a physical giant that everyone would notice in the field, at least in daylight. That restricted him a great deal, but now there were other unknown, new limitations. "Well? Perhaps the lieutenant will be kind enough to spit out the awful truth and nothing but the awful truth?"

"I've worked on audio surveillance technology for the last two and a half years," the giant managed to say, in a voice that was almost falsetto in his nervousness.

"On what?" asked O.M. in a loud voice. His dismay was genuine.

"Bugging, you know . . ." said the blond giant hesitantly.

"And?" O.M. asked sternly. "What have you learned?"

"You might say that I know everything about eavesdropping and the little gadgets you need for it and how to protect yourself against them," replied Steelglove softly and cautiously.

"But that's splendid!" exclaimed O.M. "That's an area we've been lagging in. Yes, I know, it's strictly forbidden and unconstitutional and all that, but it's damned practical. The question is how we're going to order the equipment before there's a change of guard in my job and some moderate comes along who believes that only Social Democrats can differentiate between God's law and human regulations."

Lundwall had found it harder and harder not to laugh, and now he exploded. "You might as well tell him and get it out in the open pronto," he said to his friend.

"Well, the thing is," muttered Steelglove shyly, "I brought practice equipment home with me."

O.M. looked back and forth at the two young men. They looked so damned innocent in their running shoes and California T-shirts. He was still having a hard time picturing them as two new Carls. "You did *what?*" he asked at last, with as much stern authority as he could muster.

"Well, I brought home two suitcases full of audio material and went through the green line at Arlanda. And they stopped me for having too much whiskey, but everything turned out all right even though it was touch-and-go at first. They never looked in the suitcases. The equipment is in our new offices." Steelglove looked down at the floor. Lundwall made an effort to appear neutral.

O.M. sat motionless and completely silent for several seconds. Then he burst out in a resounding roar of laughter. "That's just splendid—stupid but splendid. Brilliantly stupid, but God protects idiots. Besides, the items may come in handy. At least for . . . shall we say, realistic exercises." And then he laughed so long and so hard that the two new operatives joined him.

"Damn it all, I think I should offer you a little homemade Calvados, and has anyone seen my cigars forbidden by the doctor?" asked O.M., standing up. Chuckling to himself, he went out to the kitchen in search of the forbidden goods.

The two lieutenants exchanged a relieved look. Now the issue was in the open.

. . .

Yuri Chivartshev didn't like the whole operation. It wasn't the GRU's business to deal with KGB conspiracies; the GRU was a serious intelligence service and not a collection of political schemers.

On the whole, it was absurd to spend hours of thought and human resources filling the Swedish tabloids with disinformation. But it was still necessary.

Because, of course, the people at the madhouse had begun to leak information to their favorite evening paper via their usual channels: about the Peacock story and his political immunity; about the government protecting Russian spies for tactical party reasons. At the moment a complicated and quite disgusting scandal was in progress about Social Democratic elites devoting themselves to drugs while guarded by policemen on private duty. It was only a matter of time before the rumors about homosexual aspects of this came up.

But in the other evening paper, journalists who were regarded as "spy experts"—the word was incomprehensible when translated into Russian—could now explain that the hunt for the Peacock had begun several years ago within a secret research group in Säpo, and the question of immunity for captured spies was in reality not so controversial; it was an established and effective technique among the world's large spy-catching organizations, no stranger than the technique of exchanging condemned spies. The personal punishment was not so important as national security. So it was from Säpo itself that the clever idea of immunity had originated, and with some difficulty it had convinced the government of the wisdom in acting like the other big boys in the West.

So far so good. But who would play the card about the suspected military men and the Tristan report? That was the sensitive issue.

It was better to anticipate than to be caught off guard. That's why Chivartshev had already made his decision.

Säpo journalists on the Social Democratic paper would spread the news that the Peacock had been Sandström's safety net the whole time, and that this was how, by means of their own extremely clever work, they had been able to track him down.

Chivartshev made a note of what orders he had to give at the afternoon meeting, cleared away the newspaper mess, and switched, with greater appetite, to the new Hamilton report from Moscow.

The investigation there had brought pleasantly swift results. The

Lark—a fitting code name, by the way, considering her musical background—was able to report that Hamilton had, in certain weak masculine moments, told her about various episodes in his earlier life.

Before he was sent off to Moscow he had been deployed on what was to be his last wet job, and his most unpleasant because one of the victims was a Palestinian boy no more than sixteen years old. But since a leading politician wanted to take credit for the outcome, Hamilton had been neutralized by sending him as far away as possible. (A footnote explained that in a telephone call several months old, buried deep in an archive somewhere, they had found a conversation between the Swedish ambassador in Moscow and the then Swedish foreign minister, in which the latter rather cryptically regretted that it wasn't possible to send Hamilton to Ulan Bator.)

Hamilton had given the Lark other information that could be checked. He had hated an operation that had taken place several years ago in West Germany—he even talked about Nazi behavior—when the special police there had slaughtered a dozen terrorists in Hamburg; Hamilton had been an infiltrator among the terrorists and had been the one who had called them in. He had some kind of regret about all this.

Why? He was an officer, after all. But the pieces fit with other parts of the puzzle. They knew that Hamilton had been in West Germany, that for a brief period he was treated at a military hospital in Syria and was interrogated by air force intelligence there; copies from Damascus had been requisitioned but hadn't arrived yet. Chivartshev had always supposed that Hamilton was somehow involved, and here was confirmation.

The picture was getting clearer. Hamilton had gotten the boot from his highly classified job; he had been sacrificed for political reasons; and they had sent him to Moscow, almost ironically, to fool around with trivial processing problems, a job which he rightfully had to regard as demeaning.

He was thirty-four years old and unmarried, and surprisingly sentimental as well. He thumbed his nose at every imaginable security regulation and openly went behind the backs of his superiors. He was already a frequent guest at Western embassy functions. He drank too much and was preoccupied with brooding thoughts. A classic pattern.

But perhaps it looked *too* good. Hamilton was young, but he was no greenhorn. Why should a few setbacks make him start falling apart and start talking to women in bed?

It was definitely too early to make any operative decisions. Chivartshev firmly rejected all such plans, which enthusiasts at Zentral were already preparing.

Nine

Carl's new Lada 1600 moved like a spear, almost as if the GRU had taken it in for a special tune-up when they attached the radio beacon under the left fender; something, anyway, was discreetly welded on there. What would they do when they had to change batteries? Make him take his car in for repairs? Well, it didn't make any difference—he wasn't going to use it when he went to the end of the line.

He tried to concentrate on the time ahead, a week from now, when there would be only two things of any importance.

Leningradskoye Chaussée would soon turn into Leningradsky Prospekt, where one of the possible theaters was located, Teatr Romen, the Gypsy theater. But Irina had already taken him there, and the same play was running all autumn, a twelve-year-old success called *We Gypsies*. It was probably the best, most intense acting he had ever seen—Nikolai Slichenko would be an incredible hit if it ever toured in the West—but they had only just seen the play and it had only one intermission. Best would be a play or a ballet with two intermissions.

Otherwise he was familiar enough with the route from Leningradsky Prospekt. He would almost pass by her home if he went the difficult way. The easy way went on the outer ring, but that was well patrolled by both uniformed and plainclothes police.

The Bolshoi Theater was in the best location. It would probably have to be a three-act play at the Bolshoi.

When he turned onto Leningradsky Prospekt at Sheremetyevo II, halfway in to the city from the airport, he lost his concentration. Personal concerns took over.

What had Eva-Britt thought or felt about during that weekend? It had been a mistake to invite a police officer to Moscow officially, even if she was a woman. It would distract the GRU. But he had needed her. And he had needed two short days without pretense, as if to test whether there was anything left of himself.

And for the military attachés' grand ball, female company had definitely been needed. This year the Chinese embassy was host, and the locale made the whole party seem like something out of Tolstoy: five hundred dress uniforms, waltzes among marble pillars, beneath enormous chandeliers, glittering jewelry and medals, gold sashes and braiding. Like a fairy tale or operetta. Perhaps slightly ludicrous.

She probably thought it was ludicrous, and she had laughed at him for an annoyingly long time at his apartment while he desperately struggled with his stiff white collar and the difficulty of getting two medals on ribbons to hang at an equal slant on each side. She had solved the problem at last with two tiny safety pins.

She *had* come to Moscow, though. She had liked his letter and she had come, and he had promised her to come home to Stockholm soon, a pledge that went against all common sense—almost as if he was trying to be the security risk that he had been impersonating for more than three months.

He didn't want to think anymore. He slid over into the officials' lane and increased his speed in order to make himself pay more attention to the driving.

Memories of their night together seeped mercilessly through his effort to concentrate on driving. His hands began to sweat, and the steering wheel was slippery. It was incredible that he could be so frightened when it was serious, when it was someone he cared for. With Irina, in contrast, he had given a number of brilliant performances for the eavesdropping opposition.

Leningradsky Prospekt turned into Gorky Street, and out of old habit he parked the car outside the Intourist Hotel, as if he were on his way up to one of the disgusting bars to drink disgusting white wine or disgusting gold champagne.

But instead he strolled over toward the neighborhood around the Bolshoi Theater in order to go over everything one more time. It was Sunday, and the main department store, Zentralny Univermag, was closed. But in the pillared arcade around it, on the way to the parking lot that she would most likely choose, merchants were selling knick-knacks and fruit along a row of little stalls. The lines were longest for green bananas and apples.

At one stand little tool sets were on display, and he found a small plastic box with a Phillips-head screwdriver, an ordinary screwdriver, and an awl, each about fifteen centimeters long.

He gazed at the little plastic boxes. A ruble apiece. It was like a sign from the gods—the last link in his preparations. He bought a set, shoved it into his pocket, and continued on through the passageway to the little cross street at the other end where there were stalls selling ice cream. They apparently never stopped eating ice cream and drinking kvass.

He got a cup of kvass and kept on strolling, gazing at the parking lot with the various street connections to it as he rehearsed it in his mind.

Their next theater visit would be to the Bolshoi; they had already decided on that. If the performance had more than two acts, it would be on.

He realized that he had asked her to come over from Sweden so that he could say goodbye without actually saying so.

In his breast pocket he carried a little blue identity card, a *diplomaticheskaya kartochka*. It would certainly persuade the perpetually grumpy Intourist guards at the luxury hotels, but if he and the opposition met up out there in Medvedkovo, it wasn't worth the paper it was printed on.

It was sensible to have seen her in order to say goodbye. It was less sensible suddenly to invite, via the official bureaucracy and through the controls, a Swedish police officer as a private guest.

When he returned to the embassy, he put on his sweatsuit; he was now down to one round of the track every other day according to the plan for his deterioration. But in the next few days there would be no alcohol at all; he was free of that now.

He ran as far as his turning point on the quiet, wide, autumn-colored street, and he went slower than ever. It was more like jogging than running. At the signpost he glanced at his watch. Yes, he had estimated correctly.

Then he returned at full speed, at his absolute maximum—and it was as if he suddenly felt liberated, as if he were a fighter plane that abruptly shot straight up and out, switching on the afterburners right after the landing gear was pulled up. At last he was *airborne*.

His body had taken a real beating, and she had noticed that he had put on weight. But now the first act was over.

He held two days of intensive, final, and general exercises with his colonel and his commodore. As might be expected, they had both developed a joyful, boyish enthusiasm for the computer's magic tricks.

He used all the data about the SU-24 fighter plane, "the Fencer" in NATO parlance, as a sample exercise. The information was classified within both the orange and the red systems, and what they pulled up using power from the normal electrical system showed pretty much all the known data on the plane, as well as a series that could be traced to reports at home on the SU-24—the Soviet Union's attempt at a counterpart to the American F-111.

When he switched to the reserve power unit, so that all physical and theoretical connections with the outside world were broken, it was possible to pull up even more information, classified red—for example, earlier reports about how an SU-24 had been observed in Riga without any markings; conclusions they had reached about the reassignment to the Baltic republics of the heaviest and best-armed fighters; and what consequences this might have for Sweden, considering their capability and range.

The information about prototypes B and C, among the few genuine Swedish tidbits, was also found in the red classification. Type B was the strategic plane, equipped with tactical nuclear weapons. Type C had robots exclusively and was intended for naval targets in the Baltic region.

Among the recent reports entered partially under red and partially under orange was information about a pullback of the weapons— threatening to Sweden as long as they were at Leningrad's military base or at the base in Riga—and speculation as to whether this had as much to do with glasnost as with cutbacks.

If one punched in "cutbacks," a series of numbers appeared about reports on all kinds of wide-ranging topics, and suddenly one could see a pattern that could not have been noticed as clearly before: the Russians were cutting back defense resources focused on the Swedish field of interest. Military glasnost, in a way.

The system cross-referenced through naval, air force, and army data, and it was easy to look up anything under the different classifications. The two older men, who never in their lives thought they would be able to handle those damned machines, were now practically competing in inventiveness and dexterity.

The new system was now *airborne* too. And with that, Carl's official assignment was over.

They had an impromptu final exam celebration afterward, in a beautiful nineteenth-century Moscow *hôtel de ville* where the commodore lived alone, although the ambassador had plans to take this magnificent residence away from him and turn it into some sort of Swedish cultural institute.

Carl once again had the feeling that he was about to say goodbye, and he drank very cautiously.

Directly across the street from the gray department store, Zentralny Univermag, on Petrovka Street is a row of side doors from the Bolshoi beneath a roof supported by slender pillars. It takes exactly fifteen seconds for someone coming out of one of the side doors to disappear into the passageway to the department store across the street, and then less than forty seconds to reach the other side on Neglinnaya Street, where it's widest, near the kiosks and the improvised parking lot.

From there it's only fifteen minutes down to the big main street of Prospekt Marksa.

Carl stood on the corner of Neglinnaya and Prospekt Marksa studying the traffic. She would certainly come from the other direction.

No car turned left across the continuous line in the middle of the street—it must be a traffic offense, and then it would be a very short trip and a month of making new plans.

So he would have to turn right in the beginning.

Glazunov's *Raymonda* was one of the Bolshoi's perpetual favorites in the repertoire; the original stage production from 1898 was still performed.

It had taken a great deal of extra effort to get tickets for that evening's performance because the title role was going to be danced by Nina Ananshvili and the other principal role of Jean de Brienne by the great star Andres Leipa.

The performance was several hours long. And in three acts.

It had started to rain, and he walked up the street to the crosswalk opposite the back of the department store, and with growing unease he watched as one parking lot after another filled up.

He moved in under the roof of the passageway and watched as she arrived and took the next to last parking spot on the same side of the street where he was now standing. Perfect, couldn't be better. And the ballet had three acts.

He waited for her, and she gave a start when she noticed him. He quickly explained that he hadn't wanted to wait in the crowded theater lobby, because it would be harder for them to find each other there.

He thought that tonight she seemed more fearful than before, but perhaps that was just his imagination. She certainly looked more beautiful than usual, even though she was still wearing low-heeled shoes. Maybe she owned only low-heeled shoes. He wouldn't have minded if she had been taller than he was, but maybe she had a complex about it.

It smelled of mothballs inside the theater, and they sat high up in the third balcony on the side, looking practically straight down at the enormous stage with the awful sets.

The first act was inexpressibly tedious, a heavy Russian version of chivalrous eighteenth-century French dancing. Now and then a little blue flash from a camera would flicker in the orchestra—a Soviet citizen who wanted to take home a souvenir for life. But they wouldn't get much on film except the backs of people's heads and a blurry stage. To his surprise, Carl felt that he was falling asleep.

In the first intermission they made their way down one level and enjoyed a soft drink.

When the bells rang and they were on their way back up the stairs, he said that he had suddenly remembered a telegram that he would have to go back to the embassy to answer; he borrowed her car keys, kissed her on the cheek, and watched as she joined the crowd on the third balcony. Everything was happening very quickly, and he noticed no surprise or uneasiness on her part. He promised to meet her for the third act. He had an hour and ten minutes.

The Dzerzhinsky family's car was sluggish shifting into reverse, and the gears ground alarmingly when he shifted into second. He drove calmly down to the corner of Neglinnaya and Prospekt Marksa. There was little traffic, and for a moment he considered making the forbidden left turn. But there wasn't a single car in his rearview mirror, so no one would be suddenly forced to commit the same traffic offense and thus give themselves away.

He turned right and sped up as soon as he came out onto Prospekt

Marksa. This is going to be sightseeing to start with, he thought, smiling, as he saw the rose-colored façade of the Bolshoi Theater out his side window.

In majestic solitude he drove around the awkwardly named Square in Memory of the Fiftieth Anniversary of the Revolution, glancing up at the big red Soviet flag, illuminated as usual, and as usual in perfect folds despite the rain. He managed to catch two swift glimpses of St. Basil's Cathedral, then a left, then a red light, which of course seemed to last forever. A Volga with curtains in the back and a yellow taxi stopped in back of him. He decided they couldn't be that stupid.

When the light changed he drove quickly up Prospekt Marksa, passing his starting point and driving through just as the traffic light changed at KGB Square; the other cars stopped calmly at the red light behind him.

It was dark and drizzling. The façade of the KGB's big yellow building with the gray stone foundation was not lit up, and most of the windows were dark, except on the top floor.

He picked up speed on Dzerzhinskaya Street, which changed to Sretenka Street as soon as he passed the inner ring; he had practiced this part of the route ahead of time.

He continued straight on, looking out at the grand Prospekt Mira, "Peace Boulevard." He laughed suddenly—what an ironic name!

It was a weekday evening. There was very little risk that Sandström would still be working this late. The risk that he might be out on a binge as in the good old days was nonexistent. The risk that he had some woman with him to abuse or practice strangling on was the greatest. There couldn't be any witnesses.

When Prospekt Mira ended at the Park for Soviet Sciences and Culture—or was it the Park of the Soviet Republics?—he drove for the first time into unfamiliar territory. Now the boulevard's name changed to Yaroslavskoye Chaussée, and then came the five difficult route choices to make. This was a suburb where on the one hand he risked getting lost, and on the other hand he had to discover any pursuers.

It took twenty minutes from the start to the goal; he didn't get lost and he was not being followed.

Across from the subway station a great deal of construction was going on, and below that an entirely new area was being built. He turned down the street at the subway station without signaling, but neither of the two cars behind turned after him, and behind them the street was empty. He was alone on the road, and not expected.

He drove cautiously past the subway station and parked the car fifty yards away, near where some other cars were parked; there weren't any parking problems in Moscow suburbs, apparently.

Then he walked back to the subway station. A train had evidently just pulled in, and a few passengers were coming out, going in different directions, almost all of them with bags in their hands. People always carried them so that they could join any unexpected queues for unexpected wares.

The subway entrance was built of dreary gray cement blocks, and next to it was a closed tobacco kiosk, some mineral-water vending machines, and several rows of kvass automats—all of them locked up.

On the sidewalk, he looked first at the three public telephones on his left and then, finally, his eyes sought out the eighth-floor window in the corner of the white building opposite.

The lights were on.

He paused. He felt a kind of peace, as if it were all over. He wanted to stay there; it was completely peaceful.

But it would be best if he were back for the second intermission. He took a deep breath and walked slowly across the asphalt and around to the back of the building.

Next to a rather decrepit ice-hockey rink were several swings of the sturdy Russian design with steel arms instead of chains. He turned toward the door, outside which stood a leaky green wooden bench on which parts of the back had collapsed. The door was blue and unlocked. He went in without even looking around; it was too late now, anyway. Either they were here, and if they really were the best in the world he wouldn't see them. Or else they weren't.

The elevator came almost immediately. It had the usual Russian system: double doors and a button that you punched after the inner doors were closed. He pressed the button for the floor below Sandström's. The elevator was, as usual, free of graffiti.

The doorway was cramped and dark. The stairs up to the next floor were very narrow; it would be difficult to move quickly down the stairs, and above all, there was a big risk of noise. He almost stumbled over a tricycle. He moved the trike aside and decided not to close the elevator doors, and then he made his way over to the light switch. He had to be able to see the lock.

The stairway was completely empty, and the sounds that could be heard seemed to be mostly TVs and music. He had soft rubber soles with small perforations on his apparently dress shoes. He checked that his shoelaces were properly tied and that nothing in his clothing was sticking out or in the way. He pulled on a pair of soft gloves of light-colored calfskin and looked at the lock for a moment. He judged it would take a maximum of ten seconds if it was the only lock. If there was a security chain on he would have to close the door and knock and say something in Russian.

The lock opened a little faster than he had calculated, and it was the only one. He could hear talking and sounds from a television set inside. He held the door open a few centimeters and listened. There was no light on in the entryway. He opened the door swiftly and firmly to avoid creaking and closed it almost all the way behind him. Then he stood in silence and listened for a moment.

The language was English. One of them was a man, the other a woman. He took out his tool box, hid the awl in his right hand, and shoved the rest into his jacket pocket.

There was no real reason for this, but he paused again for an instant, amazed at his own lack of nervousness. It was as if the whole thing were already over.

Then he walked quite quickly down the corridor, past the empty, dark kitchen, and into the bright living room and burst out in joyous laughter.

"How nice that I got hold of you, Mr. Sandström. My name is Hamilton, and I work at the Swedish Embassy," he said in Swedish.

And before the astonished traitor—who looked much as he had in the most recent pictures—had time to set his glass down, Hamilton explained to the young woman that she wasn't to worry, he was only from the Swedish embassy. He continued talking rapidly in Swedish, telling Mr. Sandström that he was welcome to come down for a chat. He put out his hand with a smile, and when the astonished man stood up, almost as if to take his hand and say hello, Carl struck him unconscious.

He went past the table with the glasses on it and over to the young woman on the sofa and grabbed her purse. It did not contain a heavy weapon. She sat completely still in the middle of the sofa, without moving. Carl went back to the unconscious traitor and turned him over with his foot so that he was lying flat on his stomach. Then he looked over the scene.

It looked like a totally normal Russian living room belonging to someone fairly well off; there was a Western stereo and a Finnish television set, and the bulky furniture looked new. It was very neat.

He looked at the young woman. Thirty or maybe younger—

Russian women tended to age quickly—quite elegantly dressed. Blond, like a Finn.

"Who are you?" he asked curtly in Russian.

She shook her head but didn't answer, terrified.

"I have to know who you are," said Carl in a businesslike voice, but he still got no reply.

Then he bent down, put his left arm under the traitor's arm, and placed his hand on the back of the man's head, pushing his neck forward. With his right hand Carl drove the awl straight into the hollow above the large vertebra, then moved the awl back and forth several times. There wasn't any reaction at first, but then one of the traitor's legs kicked.

Carl stood up and looked at the woman again. She hadn't budged, and it was hard to tell whether she understood that the man she had been talking to was now dead. During a normal autopsy the cause of death would be routinely missed—the fact that the main power switch itself had been cut off by a sharp external instrument—but as the situation now stood, under no circumstances would there be a normal autopsy. Two "ordinary heart attacks" couldn't very well happen at the same time.

"I'm in a hurry and I have to know," said Carl, stepping forward and sitting down on the arm of the sofa. She was now within his reach. She sat with her knees pressed together less than a yard away. She did not answer.

"So here's how it is," said Carl hastily because he could feel how the time was ticking away. "I'm an officer in the Swedish intelligence service. This man was a traitor who was sentenced to death in Sweden. If you're a neighbor or a close friend I will have to kill you too. But if you're one of us, a colleague, that would be out of the question. So?"

She seemed to be thinking intently. Only if she were an intelligence officer would she understand his logic, and if she wasn't, she would never be able to pretend she was.

"*Glavnoye razvedyvatelnoye upravlenie*," she whispered hoarsely and had to clear her throat. She stared hard at the floor. Few Soviet citizens knew the GRU's full name.

"Title and rank?" asked Carl quickly, looking at his watch.

"I can't tell you."

"You have to tell me, otherwise I won't know if it's true. I don't care about your name, only your rank and department."

"Sublieutenant, First Directorate, Second Section, Department of Scandinavian Studies," she said softly, blushing as if ashamed.

Carl took a deep breath. The situation was clear. "We are colleagues," he concluded. "This is not a hostile action against the Soviet Union. We regard this as our national right. But I need to get out of here without being pursued for the next half hour. Do you understand?"

She smiled ironically. She had regained hope and a little color in her face.

"Yes, that's clear, but how can I guarantee that?" she murmured.

"I extend my sincerest apologies for the discomfort I will have to cause you, and I send my respectful greetings and my apologies to your immediate superiors," said Carl hurriedly, hitting her hard on the back of the neck as he spoke.

She fell soundlessly over onto her side; he bent down and lifted an eyelid. Everything okay: she was unconscious, he hadn't killed her. And the back of her neck felt intact and unscathed.

He lifted her onto the floor, placing her in a semiprone position, and loosened some of her clothing to make it easier for her to breathe. She was breathing evenly and her pulse didn't seem irregular.

He stood up, took a little camera out of his jacket pocket, and went over to Sandström. First he took several close-ups of the head and neck with the awl visibly sticking out. Then he pulled the awl out halfway and took some more pictures. Finally he pulled the awl out all the way, wiped off a drop of blood on the millimeter-wide wound, which looked as if it might close up completely, and turned the body over.

He took more pictures: portraits at close range with open eyes and full figure. Then he wiped off the awl, put it back into the plastic box with the screwdriver, and placed it on the table in front of the sofa. He went out into the hallway, pulling the door softly shut behind him.

The more virtuoso passages came in the third act, when for the first time Leipa thawed out the audience.

It seemed more convincing this way. Truly Russian ballet on the world's most famous stage. And Carl was really sitting where he was sitting.

He was totally calm, but in some way schizophrenic. Half of his brain devoted itself serenely to the performance, while the other half tried systematically to separate right from wrong.

The Finnish-looking sublieutenant had probably been some sort of babysitter for Sandström. No, if she worked in the first directorate, she was an analyst. If she had said *fifth* directorate she would have been an agent and dangerous, with some kind of bodyguard function. No, she was just some kind of colleague.

There was no doubt she was a GRU officer. No ordinary Soviet citizen could have given a perfect answer about a credible position in military intelligence. Was it right to leave her as a witness?

He hadn't prepared enough; he hadn't worked out beforehand how to solve the problem if Sandström had company.

So. First strangle the woman, as Sandström would have done? A sudden attack according to his familiar pattern of behavior, and then have him commit suicide by jumping out the window?

No, a fall wouldn't ensure death. He would have had to be killed before he jumped, and forensic examination would have discovered that easily, and besides, it would have been harder to get away unnoticed.

As the situation now stood, at most they could claim only that *the acting naval attaché from the Swedish Embassy participated in activities that are incompatible with his position as a diplomat*—which could mean drunk driving as well as something more substantial.

The Russians would know exactly what had happened. But they would have been able to figure it out anyway, with decent forensics and an interrogation of Irina. The extent of their knowledge was not changed by what had happened. But there was a significant difference: the Swedish intelligence service had acted totally correctly vis-à-vis its Soviet counterpart.

This would exclude acts of revenge. The Russians were known for acting sensibly in such situations, as opposed to certain others: in France they would not have let the agent escape.

Presumably Carl could stroll home to the embassy without any risk, even if somewhere in Zentral's nine-story building near Chodinka Airport people were frantically evaluating the situation.

Irina might have informed them in advance of her plan to go to see *Raymonda*. They might be waiting outside the theater.

It was all over, the operation was concluded, the objective was destroyed. All planes should return safely to base, but that was not the most important thing.

What remained was the payment, the human price.

No one was waiting for them outside the theater.

It was almost eleven o'clock, but he didn't want to part from her, and she didn't want to go home right away.

They drove a short distance and parked behind St. Basil's Cathedral, and then discreetly bribed their way in to one of the so-called nightclubs in the Hotel Rossiya. A dance band with too many saxophones was playing under violet spotlights. The chairs were plastic and wobbly, and it was smoky and noisy in the half-full room, primarily a Russian crowd. The tourist season was long since over in Moscow.

They tried to order a bottle of Moldavian white wine, but it was too cheap; it had to be gold champagne again. And for the last time *sovietskoye shampanskoye zolotoye*, no matter what happened next. Carl held her hand on top of the table. She looked sad, almost as if she understood that this was the end.

But she couldn't know that. They might be waiting for her outside her door—but she had good reason to feel sad already, before she found out what had happened during the second act. Maybe she would never find out.

Her slender hand looked exactly as you would imagine a pianist's hand should: the veins were noticeable on her wrist, and the strong fingers ended with short, perfectly filed nails and discreet pink polish. Should he warn her about what was going to happen?

In the car they had already talked about the ballet, and he couldn't come up with any new topic.

Finally she broke their silence in the midst of the saxophones. "You look worried, Carlinko. A ruble for your thoughts." Her words sounded harsh because she had to talk so loudly.

"Irina," he said, looking around as if to answer first with his eyes. The room smelled strongly of Russian tobacco, perfume, and sweat, and the women at the next table looked like prostitutes. "My dear. A place like this isn't as romantic as I'd like."

"No. But still, a ruble for your thoughts."

"Never lie to them. Not about anything, no matter what they ask you."

"Yes, you've told me that before."

"But it's important, Irina. Don't ever lie."

It was the worst possible topic of conversation, and she didn't reply. But that was the last thing he said to her. They would ask her

about that, and it might very well function as a kind of greeting to
them:

*Irina never knew anything. You were not the only ones who used her.
Analyze the situation, comrades.*

He bade her goodbye at the car and told her he had a headache and
wanted to walk. He kissed her on both cheeks, quickly and lightly,
and closed the door after her, carefully so as not to damage the loose
lock; and then he stood completely still and watched her red taillights
disappear in the light traffic.

He walked home by way of Red Square, strolling right across the
middle of the whole vast, empty cobblestone area, a perfect target in
the rainy, windy solitude. It was as if he didn't care about anything
anymore, as if he were empty.

At the Square in Memory of the Fiftieth Anniversary of the Revolution, he was expecting the yellow Volga taxi to turn up as usual, as
if by chance. But there weren't any taxis, and he kept on walking
toward the embassy, pulling his overcoat tighter around him.

So they hadn't bothered to gather information about his movements
that evening in advance; they had decided the situation was under
control.

In about five minutes she would park outside her house, and they
would be waiting there in one or two black Volgas. She had five
minutes of freedom left. Their interrogators were probably about the
same as the gorillas from the DIA and the FBI who had worked Tessie
over in Santa Barbara. Sandström had been the cause of Tessie's
interrogation, and now he had brought about exactly the same misery
for Irina.

He finally found a taxi, and the driver didn't even know where the
Swedish embassy was. The rain had picked up, and the streets were
completely deserted. The guards didn't react when the car slipped
through the gates and into Swedish territory.

No reason to send the message now; it would be the first thing he
did in the morning.

Ten

Chivartshev was taking a long walk alone. It was the first fine weather in two weeks. Along Djurgårds Canal under the yellow chestnut trees, he walked with his hands clasped behind his back and his eyes on the ground. He had an unusually great need to brood by himself.

The election had disrupted all the issues. There was much unease in Säpo, and people were plotting in every corner, whispering about what the new Conservative government was or was not going to do. One common opinion was that it would shut down one of the big antiterrorist divisions so as to enlarge the anti–Warsaw Pact departments; with a Social Democratic government still in power, the reform would probably have gone the other way.

And now there were indications that a group of conspirators were preparing some sort of offensive against Sweden's own defense leadership. Within "the Säpo Ring," a secret society, there was apparently an inner circle of some kind, like a freemasonic organization, which included men who were not in the "company." No GRU informer had succeeded in penetrating this inner circle, and consequently they were now about to lose large sections of their information control over Swedish intelligence. It was impossible to tell how strong this new, secret decision-making center was going to be, and impossible to tell what they would cook up. You could guess at something in the line of a PR campaign against the defense brass, so that the new political decision makers would take an interest in reforming the military instead of Säpo.

How it would all end was impossible to tell. Based on past experience, a new government in Sweden would soon rush to stir up the Säpo pot—there was certainly no lack of willing cooks—and when personnel were tossed around as if in a lottery drum, you couldn't even guess where your own people might end up. It *was* like a lottery; you could just as easily lose as win.

The problem in Moscow was more concrete. First, Hamilton and his superiors had roundly deceived them, that was a fact. Hamilton's ruse—that's what it had been—was over. He hadn't gone outside the embassy compound for three days.

The interrogation with the Lark had yielded nothing of value. Either she was resistant in a way that confounded all understanding and all medical experience, or else she had never known what Hamilton was up to. He had simply used her as a direct means of communication. He had been very clever, no doubt.

Chivartshev cursed himself for not heeding his own hunch that the whole thing looked *too* good. They had been defeated by their own methods; Hamilton had gone to Moscow and carried out a *Russian* operation right under their noses. One could have laughed at its boldness if it wasn't so serious. Not the demise of Sandström—Sandström was never a significant force, given his mental weakness—but the possibility of treason. Someone had given information about Sandström's address to the Swedes. Hamilton hadn't found Medvedkovo on his own.

Chivartshev himself would not come under suspicion, since neither he nor anyone else at the Swedish *residentura* had known where Sandström lived in Moscow, though they knew where he worked.

Sublieutenant Tatyana Alexeyevna Lyublimova had also been interrogated without results. The idea had been discussed as to why a professional like Hamilton left a witness behind at the scene. It was elementary never to leave witnesses to a wet job, and some people found it downright scandalous, so they thought Tatyana Alexeyevna might have been involved in the conspiracy.

Chivartshev doubted it. It would have been strangely unfortunate timing if she had been a collaborator of Hamilton's, and she herself would have realized that.

Moreover, to act alone and to leave a witness seemed in some way to fit with Hamilton's psychology. There was something Swedish about it all, but also Russian: you don't go after colleagues.

Chivartshev swore again as he walked under the trees. In Moscow they had been so certain that they were preparing nothing more than a recruiting operation aimed at an extremely careless young diplomat, and they had pulled in the round-the-clock surveillance teams the week before. It almost seemed as though Hamilton was aware of that too, and had waited to do Sandström in until it was risk-free.

But there was no connection between the people in the fifth directorate who handled the operation against Hamilton and the personnel in the first directorate who knew where Sandström lived. *Two* traitors working simultaneously with Hamilton was inconceivable.

He might have refrained from removing the witness because his instructions forbade that sort of action. That would be very Swedish. Or Russian. Or he might have assumed that, since the facts would of course become known, there was no point in hiding them. Leaving Tatyana Alexeyevna unharmed might have been exactly what Hamilton himself had said it was: a gesture between colleagues. He must have counted on being believed—since she was not, after all, working with him and had never seen him before—and this would improve his own security in Moscow.

Anyway, acts of revenge against Hamilton had to be ruled out. No one would be impressed if the GRU assassinated a diplomat in Moscow, and if the news leaked out, besides the terrible publicity, it would arouse widespread revulsion in the diplomatic corps and disrupt relations with Sweden.

So there was only one big problem: who had supplied Hamilton with the address of Sweden's traitor?

The telegram lay around for three days at the Foreign Ministry before anyone took the trouble to send it up, and Samuel Ulfsson swore twice—first when the message arrived and then when it was deciphered. The text was brief and apparently routine, but the contents seemed unbelievably dramatic:

> *Call me home at once. BPA requires no further action. New computer system under control.*
>
> Hamilton

This surely meant that the man who had once been photographed by a man from BPA had now been photographed again. That was splendid. Ulfsson picked up the telephone and, whistling, dialed the Old

Man's number. He had to wait for six rings before it was answered.

"Hello, you old apple farmer, isn't the harvest supposed to be over by now?" he greeted him.

"Yes, but why?" O.M. was guarded.

"Thought you were out in the orchard—it took you so long to answer."

"No, not that. You caught me with my pants down."

"Literally?"

"Yes, literally. Just a minute." O.M. put down the receiver for a moment, and then resumed. "Strange that we always answer the telephone because we think it's something important, and then it's just the boss."

"Yes, but it is important, nevertheless. Can you come up to the city the day after tomorrow?"

"Yes, if it's important. Remember, I'm retired."

"Not before the Conservatives have come up with some suitable blue-suit successor, and the broom hasn't reached our little department yet. Yes, it's important enough. Carl is coming back."

"Is he?"

"Yes, I'm calling him home today, so he ought to arrive on the SAS plane the day after tomorrow."

"Why is that?"

"We always fly SAS. We don't need to give money to Aeroflot."

"No, I mean, why is he coming home?"

"The matter has been taken care of, and that's what I call good timing. Now we can appoint him ourselves before the Conservatives get mixed up in it."

O.M. did not reply.

"Hello, are you there?" asked Ulfsson at last.

"Yes, I'm here. Yes."

"There's lots to discuss. I've heard that Borgström is interested in the job, and well, you realize what the consequences would be."

"He's hardly qualified, is he?"

"No, but he's certainly moderate enough for our new defense minister."

"God help us."

"Well, forgive me for being a heathen, but I think it would be better if we handled this ourselves. So you'll come?"

"Yes, I'll come. There's lots to discuss, as you say."

Ulfsson put down the receiver, immediately wrote out in longhand his order calling Carl home, and asked his secretary to see that it went with the diplomatic mail immediately.

Then he threw himself into preparations for a report to the Chief, which seemed very easy to plan. The appointment of the head of the special-missions unit lay within the boundaries of the Chief's decision-making powers, and now they were going to take care of it before new politicians came tramping in and stirred things up. It was best to strike while the iron was hot.

In the worst case, Borgström would apply to be head of the entire OP5, but then they could argue against him, asserting that the personal chemistry between Borgström and the head of the special-missions department wasn't good, and since the latter had already been appointed . . . well . . .

Hamilton couldn't have played his card with Sandström at a more opportune time. And the Old Man could go into retirement with peace of mind.

After three days of uneasy waiting, which Carl was largely successful in enduring by training his two older colleagues in the new computer system, everything suddenly happened very quickly.

As soon as the ambassador routinely notified Carl that he was to return home for consultations, a summons arrived from the Directorate for Foreign Affairs of the Armed Forces. They wanted to carry out their second meeting with Carl promptly. That was routine: after three months, every new military attaché was summoned for renewed discussion, and at the second meeting, which so to speak finalized the accreditation, the chief of staff was usually present in person. But since the chief was a busy man, it was peculiar that he suddenly had time for this just as he received word of Carl's routine temporary return to Sweden.

Carl thought of trying to get out of it, but that was futile; the decision would have to be made by the ambassador, and there would have to be very strong reasons for such remarkable rudeness. He was caught in a trap. He couldn't explain his hesitations to the ambassador, since the ambassador was Sweden and Sweden wasn't supposed to know.

He decided that it didn't matter. They couldn't very well liquidate him right in front of a Swedish colleague. Well yes, they could. He could receive a discreet little pinprick on his way in or out, and the illness could break out later and turn out to be as hard to trace as it was incurable.

But it still didn't matter, Carl told himself. If they wanted to use that solution, they could just as well do it in the streets of Stockholm or in Drakens Lane. That was their problem. If they wanted revenge, they would do it somehow. The question was whether they knew how few people in Sweden would understand the reason for killing him. The smaller the circle who knew, the greater the danger for him. Right now the circle consisted of a single person, the Old Man. O.M. would know and understand. But he could hardly pass on his knowledge, no matter how grief-stricken he might be.

In the embassy Volvo on the way to the pretty pistachio-green building, Carl tried to come to terms with his life. But he was disturbed by his colleague's jocular recollections of the first, unconventional meeting with the Russians only a short time before. "Don't talk back to the defense chief of the Soviet Union, whatever you do!" Commodore Hessulf joked.

Carl imagined the end at the age of thirty-four. Was it just the end of something that should naturally cease now? As a human being he was a failure, as a murderer a success; continuing as a personal fiasco or a murderous success, the only alternatives, was not much to look forward to. The same remarkable peace he had felt on the street for a moment outside Sandström's apartment now engulfed him. Was there anything he could do for Irina? No, recommendations from him would hardly improve her situation.

But the meeting turned out to be very different from what the optimistic commodore and the pessimistic captain anticipated, and just as incomprehensible as the first time.

First, neither the defense chief nor the chief of staff was present. The Swedes were received by the head of the Soviet Navy; the same commodore as before once again acted as interpreter.

Around the polished table in the conference room, everything happened very quickly.

"Now that you are leaving us," began the Soviet fleet admiral, getting right to the point, "you ought to know, young Captain Second Class, that we regard your competence with great respect as, I believe, my colleague the commodore here in particular, or rather *your* colleague, will agree. We desire the best of relations between our two countries, regardless of professional technicalities, and we do not want to see those relations destroyed. This is the attitude of the Politburo as well as of the defense authorities. We regret that your stay here in Moscow has been so brief. We do not regret anything else."

Both Swedes understood the gist of these brusque words as soon as they were spat out in Russian, but they waited for the translation to be certain they could believe their ears.

Carl recovered first. "It is with great respect," he began without really knowing what he would say, "that I have listened to your words, sir. It is, of course, also Sweden's wish that relations between our two nations should improve in the very near future. Regardless of professional technicalities."

The fleet admiral stood up. Was the meeting already over? The other three stood too. He said goodbye brusquely and departed, leaving his commodore to escort the guests to the door. Hessulf looked as if he were about to fall over from astonishment.

On the way to the door, the interpreter commodore muttered pleasantly to Carl, "Tatyana Alexeyevna sends her warm regards and her respectful gratitude." He maintained a stony face, and Carl paused at the door as he let his Swedish boss pass.

"I don't seem to remember meeting any Tatyana Alexeyevna," he said doubtfully.

"Oh yes," said the Russian, his stone face unaltered. "Perhaps she only introduced herself by title and rank."

"You mean first directorate, sublieutenant?"

"Correct."

"In that case, I am glad to hear that Tatyana Alexeyevna is in good health and good humor."

"Correct. We are, too."

"May I make a brief comment?"

"Go ahead."

Carl looked around as his superior was already busy being helped into his cape by a cadet a few feet away.

"Irina knew nothing," Carl whispered swiftly.

"That has already been determined," replied the Soviet commodore in the same low voice and with an unchanging stony expression. He motioned Carl over toward the cadet holding Carl's coat.

"What the hell was that all about?" shouted Commodore Hessulf as soon as they were under way in the embassy Volvo.

Carl did not reply at first. He noticed they had repaired Carl's air-conditioning.

"What the hell did they mean about you leaving us? It seemed as if they wanted to send you home, didn't it?"

"I don't understand it. I'll have to discuss it when I get back home. It's not likely that I'll be returning, but I don't know how the hell they'd realize that."

"Why aren't you coming back?"

"I think they have a new job for me at home. It might have to do with the change in regime, but I won't know until I see Sam."

"How would the Russians know about that?"

"Mm, that is definitely disturbing."

"And what did they mean by 'technicalities'?"

"I'm asking myself the same question."

"Who was that girl you were whispering about?"

"A private matter."

"So, you've been dipping your wick?"

"I'll make a report to Sam when I get home."

"That's probably best."

"Yes. It probably is."

It was overcast all the way across Russia, but as the Latvian coast approached, the clouds began to break up.

He saw the sea. The Gulf of Riga. A little while later, long sandy beaches, miles long, and two large islands. They had to be Hiiumaa and Saaremaa in Estonia. The plane was still in Soviet territory and would soon be in the position where the Russians had shot down a Swedish spy plane before Carl was even born. The Swedes had been busy with radar and signal surveillance, and finally the Russians had grown tired of it, probably because they suspected or knew that it was a question of getting information for the American strategic bombers, the B-49s, which took off from Norway and had their flight path right about here if they were on target for the major cities in Russia, Byelorussia, and the Ukraine. That was as far as they could reach in those days. The Swedish people had never been told anything that even resembled the truth, and the Soviet people hadn't been either.

He tried to calculate in his head. The Soviets kept the twelve-mile limit. A few minutes left before international airspace.

But they would never go after an SAS plane that was already on radar screens at Arlanda.

They weren't easy to understand. "Good relations between our two countries, in spite of technicalities"?

He considered for a moment how Commodore Hessulf must have strained to find an explanation. But he didn't smile.

He had been through it all before. He gazed out across the sea and the clouds and far beyond—and over everything, like a double-exposed image—there was a woman's face. Her name was Irina. Melancholy, dark Russian eyes and thick eyelashes.

Innocent. Sacrificed as a technicality.

No, it was pointless to be sentimental. She was a victim of war; she happened to be in the wrong building at the wrong time, and the only difference was that this time the bomber pilot knew the victim. The Soviet Union lost between twenty and thirty million people during the Great Patriotic War.

He declined the airplane food and waved away the offer of a free drink; if you pay a thousand kronor more for your ticket, you are entitled, for instance, to a quarter bottle of champagne that would otherwise cost twenty kronor. He had had nothing to eat or drink since he left the embassy, but he couldn't be sure whether this was because of fear of being poisoned or whether he was feeling nauseated and without appetite.

He used to sleep in planes, but now he could tell that it wasn't even worth trying.

Swedish coast, islands in the sunshine, then the gold and brown of late autumn across Uppland, and when he saw the runway, his eyes failed him. It was like a black shutter constricting on the screen, the way newsreels used to end in the old days. He had a strong taste of iron in his mouth and he could feel his hands shaking convulsively.

He was unconscious for a moment, or maybe not. Instinctively he took his pulse as the plane taxied in toward the gate, but it seemed normal. A terrible headache came welling up behind his brow.

With difficulty Samuel Ulfsson tolerated O.M.'s repeated furtive smoking as they waited, using the time to run through his proposed personnel changes and the maneuvers or possible intrigues that might be necessary.

In front of him on his otherwise empty desk Ulfsson had a roll of undeveloped film, according to the label one of Kodak's most common types of color film. But that was very far from the truth.

When Carl entered, they both studied him intently. He looked tired, at the same time haggard and puffy. Something about his attitude put a damper on their heartiness as they greeted each other and sat down.

"So things went well in Moscow?" began Sam in a tone intended to strike a cheerful note.

"The assignment is completed, yes," replied Carl curtly with his eyes on the crease of his pants.

"We have some good news here at home too. You'll be taking over from Lallerstedt, and he'll be going out on the briny deep again," continued Sam in the same tone.

Carl took a deep breath. "Sandström died on Tuesday at 2103. I took care of that on orders from O.M. The orders included not reporting to the head of OP5 until afterward, which I have now done." It seemed to come out in one breath.

Sam slowly leaned back in his chair. He looked inquiringly at O.M.

"That is correct. If necessary, I am prepared to put my position at your disposal," said O.M. with a smile, which he kept to a minimum only with the greatest effort. As a moonlighting retiree he wasn't much of a scapegoat.

"Give me one of those cigarillos!" commanded Ulfsson, and O.M. swiftly shoved the red-checked tin box and his disposable lighter over toward his boss, who hadn't smoked in months.

Ulfsson lit one of the slim cigarillos and inhaled deeply. His hand shook slightly. "There's going to be hell to pay if this gets out," he said, exhaling his second deep lungful of smoke.

"The risk doesn't seem large," O.M. pointed out dryly.

"Who knows about this?" continued Ulfsson, turning toward Carl.

"We three, and the Russians."

"Do they know it was you?"

"Without a doubt. They even passed on a greeting to us with the implication, as far as I can make out, that they don't intend to make a fuss about the matter."

"Fine. This roll of film? We haven't developed it since you didn't supply the number of the method."

"No," said Carl without the slightest intention of being funny, "it might be inappropriate, considering the subject matter."

"Which is?" Ulfsson was now smoking in earnest.

"There are six or seven exposures. The first one shows the back of Sandström's neck with a ten-centimeter-long awl driven into the medulla oblongata at the base of his skull. The next exposures show Sandström at close range with eyes open since he is dead. There is another picture of his outer door, and the last picture is of his building, but in the dark, so you probably will only be able to see a silhouette and his window. I had planned to do the developing myself."

"Why the hell did you take pictures like that? And did you walk around with them in your pocket in Moscow?" asked Ulfsson, glancing furtively at the roll of film in front of him.

"They could have taken the film away from me, but they could never have developed it. Since I'm a suspected Russian spy, I didn't want to come home and report that Sandström was dead without having a picture to prove it."

"It's possible to counterfeit pictures like this," the Old Man pointed out as he lit a cigarillo himself.

"Yes, but the risk of the forgery being discovered is not insignificant. Besides, it's undoubtedly Sandström in the pictures, and it seems to me a rather un-Russian method to give you snapshots like this, considering the never-ending risk of Swedish publication. That just doesn't work."

"I understand your concern, or whatever we should call it. But I wonder whether we should have documents of this type in the building," said Ulfsson, pulling the film out of the cassette and tossing the cassette into the wastebasket.

"It can still be developed. Burn it if you want to destroy it," said Carl with the hint of a smile.

"It's not still possible, is it?" objected Ulfsson. "I've exposed it."

"If you take my word for it that Sandström is dead," replied Carl, "then you can also trust me on such a simple technicality." He stopped short.

"Yes, of course," said Ulfsson as he picked up the film, placed it in his ashtray, and held the cigarette lighter under it; crackling and hissing, it curled up in little bright-green flames.

O.M. looked as if he were watching a million kronor burn.

"Well," continued Ulfsson when the film had finished burning and lay a sticky black mass in the crystal ashtray, "then it's the three of us who know—and the Russians, you said. Can you give us your complete report here and now?"

Later the same afternoon, after O.M. had taken Carl off for a soul-soothing conversation and a welcome-home dinner in a safe apartment with the two newly appointed lieutenants, Ulfsson went to the Chief's office for one of his programmatic reports. Most of it concerned the periodic signal surveillance results, and the proposal regarding personnel changes had been well prepared.

But it was probably going to be impossible to avoid reporting the death of Sandström. The Chief had ordered an operation to ascertain that Sandström was truly in Moscow, so that they could then request extra appropriations in order to protect themselves efficiently against him. What would he think of this news?

When all the other business was taken care of and both men were finishing up, Ulfsson gathered the last of his papers and said it: "Oh yes, there's one more thing. Sandström. In Moscow."

"Yes, of course," said the Chief with curiosity, "how did that go?"

"Unexpectedly well. Sandström was killed on Tuesday at 2103," said Ulfsson, as if he were merely reporting the time. He started toward the door as if he were already thinking of other things, and the Chief naturally stopped him.

"Is that reliable information? Do we know that for sure?" he asked, walking in front of Ulfsson as if he suddenly wanted to prevent him from leaving.

"Yes, we have completely reliable information. There is no doubt."

"Yes, but how the hell did it—?"

"Are you totally sure you want to know?" Ulfsson looked the top boss of the Defense Ministry straight in the eye.

The Chief stood still for about five seconds, glaring back. Sam thought it was five minutes. "That's all for today. Thank you, Sam. See you the day after tomorrow," said the Chief, returning to his desk as if he were already thinking about something else.

Ulfsson closed the door quietly behind him. He had an intense craving for a cigarette.

Eleven

It wasn't only that they were grisly murders—"carried out with significant force, difficult to explain," as the medical examiners formulated it—but so far they were incomprehensible. First of all there was no obvious connection between the two victims, except that both of them were fighter pilots in the same wing, off duty at the same time and at home.

Judging by appearances, they met up with the same murderer or murderers in the course of a few hours. They had literally been beaten to a pulp. The medical examiner's report spoke laconically of an estimated fifteen to twenty wounds each, any one of which could have been fatal. The color photos were appalling.

The wife and children of one were away visiting her mother. The wife and children of the other were at a children's party. The two families did not know each other well, didn't spend time together. How had the perpetrator or perpetrators known that the coasts were clear? Both murders had been committed in the living rooms of the respective row houses. So each air force captain had let the murderer in.

Detective superintendent Rune Jansson, newly appointed head of homicide in the city of Norrköping, was almost desperate. Nothing had yielded any clues. Even the smallest scrap of information would be of great value, but he had nothing.

Expressen had, in a sense, given him an idea, though he didn't think much of it. In giant headlines and countless articles, the evening paper was insisting it was a pure and simple act of war by a foreign power, hinting at the Soviet Union, perhaps a military act of revenge because, "according to anonymous sources in the Security Police," a virtual state of war existed between the Swedish and Soviet armed forces.

But when Jansson tried to get this confirmed by Bureau Chief Henrik P. Näslund in Stockholm, Näslund had been dismissive. "*Expressen* is trying to increase sales, that's all. Those 'highly placed' sources probably don't even exist," he had said.

In any case, Jansson was now reminded that there were certain military personnel who were experts in extreme violence; he had had a lot to do with one of them over an unsolved murder case in which the violence had been extraordinary.

So he took a roundabout, official route through the air force wing's head of security, who went to someone higher up in Stockholm, who said that they'd be happy to send over a couple of men, but only on condition that there be no publicity during the preliminary investigation.

Jansson already knew Hamilton, in a sense. The other man in the back seat didn't give the impression of being a dangerous assailant, but then, maybe Hamilton didn't either, if you didn't know who he was and what he was capable of—slitting a hijacker's throat, for example.

As agreed, Rune Jansson met them alone at the train station and drove them straight to the medical examiner's office in the county seat of Linköping. He gave them a report as he drove, and the two men sat in silence, listening.

He had a feeling Hamilton had changed in some way. His eyes had grown harder, almost unpleasant. A big scar on his cheek underscored the new impression of cold brutality.

The other man was completely different; he seemed more like a combination of teacher and rock musician—a gentle fellow who introduced himself by first name only and was dressed in jeans and an American sweatshirt with four big letters across the chest—UCSD. Some American university, no doubt.

There was snow mixed with rain for the first time in November, and road conditions were slushy and nasty. By the time Jansson had finished telling them about the case, they were in Linköping. At the medical examiner's office, they looked around as if checking to see if they were being followed before they got out of the car. But that was probably due to the danger of reporters, not killers. If there are any officers in the Defense Ministry the murderer had best stay away from, it was these two, thought Jansson.

After the medical examiner had shown them the color photos and listed the various injuries, Hamilton and his colleague began asking questions. They were both immediately interested in one of the few injuries that both victims had suffered identically: a crushed larynx. They seemed completely familiar with the results of the damage.

Then they asked to see the bodies, and after some hesitation the medical examiner took them to the morgue and pulled out two stainless-steel drawers with the remains of the two Swedish fighter pilots.

They asked to be left alone so they could discuss things more freely—that is how Hamilton put it—but the medical examiner refused. They accepted his refusal without demur and began systematically to study the two black and blue corpses from the top down, pointing and muttering, nodding and shaking their heads. After a while they said that they had seen enough. The bodies were shoved back into the cooler, the group went to a neighboring office where there was coffee in a glass pot and a stack of the usual Swedish white plastic mugs, and the younger of the two officers served the others.

When everybody had sat down, Hamilton began the discussion. "I think we can most likely rule out military violence—but Joar, why don't you sum up?"

"Well," began Lundwall without a trace of nervousness or uncertainty, "to begin with, we have to assume that military violence looks pretty much the same—anyway, has the same objectives in mind regardless of which nationality uses it. What we have seen goes against all known military experience, except possibly on one point. This concerns the blow to the larynx, done with precision in both cases, perfect hits. With such a blow, the victim immediately suffers breathing difficulties, a great deal of pain, shock, and unconsciousness. That was probably in each case the first blow. After that the perpetrators kicked their victims to death."

"Perpetrators?" interrupted Jansson. "How can you be sure there was more than one?"

"We can't. It's a qualified guess. A single person would have to keep at it for a long time; two seems more credible. There are kicks on both sides of each victim, whom we assume was prostrate. The kicks were placed with a certain calculation and knowledge of the functions of the human body—for instance, they destroyed the liver and spleen in both victims. And remember, we are also dealing with at least one perpetrator who can knock a person cold with a single blow, and that requires a great deal of training and, shall we say, a certain interest in the technique."

"How is such a blow done?" asked Jansson, who was starting to feel a macabre fascination.

"Well, if you'll permit me to demonstrate," continued Lundwall with a glance at Hamilton, who put down his coffee cup and stood up, "it's a blow struck by surprise against a defenseless and unsuspecting victim who has his hands at waist level as Captain Hamilton does now, and if we imagine a situation in the middle of a conversation, then . . ."

Lundwall struck lightning-fast and very hard up toward Hamilton's throat; Carl blocked the blow just as quickly.

"Well, something like that," Lundwall went on, as he sat down. "Naturally, an amateur doesn't have a chance of protecting himself as Captain Hamilton did, and the results are as we stated."

Hamilton reached for his coffee cup, waiting for his colleague to continue.

Dear God, what a blow that would have been, thought Jansson.

"The impact point in both cases is about two centimeters across, and both victims were struck perfectly. So far we are dealing with a person, or persons, who use violence that might even be characterized as military. But the rest, in our opinion, is incomprehensible and absolutely not military."

"Why exactly? How would you have handled this?" asked Jansson, and then regretted it at once when he saw the medical examiner raise his eyebrows.

But Lundwall seemed to have no objections to the question. "If we assume that Captain Hamilton and I had a mission in which we were supposed to kill two people, we would inflict only the injury I have said was the primary one. But it's possible to miss that larynx blow, and then trouble starts; there are more reliable methods for rendering the objective defenseless. After which you'd be dealing with a corpse from which one couldn't determine the cause of death. We'd have taken additional very rapid measures, and we certainly would not have stayed on the scene for five to ten minutes in order to kill and maim over and over again. Military violence is intended to be swift and silent; what we have seen is the effect of something quite the opposite. It's also possible that we would have used weapons of some kind."

"What type of weapons?" asked Jansson.

"That would depend on whether it was essential or not to hide the external cause of death. If it didn't matter, small firearms of some kind would be most likely—they're the quickest and most effective."

"And if you wanted to hide the cause of death?" asked the medical examiner skeptically.

"The most common method is simply to puncture the medulla oblongata with a thin, sharp instrument. The little penetration hole can close up so tightly that no outer wound is visible. To discover the cause of death you'd have to be sufficiently suspicious to cut open the medulla oblongata, and even then it's not certain that you'd find the puncture."

The medical examiner nodded and groaned.

"There are chemical solutions, too. Compounds you can inject that are difficult to trace and that produce an effect that has the look of a heart attack. That's mostly an East European technique," continued Lundwall. "Under any circumstances, what you would not do is stay and do all that kicking and mayhem. It's not only, shall we say, unethical but involves needless risk-taking, and above all it's totally unnecessary."

"Are the Russians trained in the same way as we are in the West? I'm thinking of what it said in *Expressen* about the Spetsnaz boys and all that," wondered Jansson.

"Military techniques are similar," said Carl. "Something like fighter planes. They have about the same performance level and the same functions whether there are three gold crowns or a red star on them. But there is no military logic in this."

"Do you have any notion why the perpetrators behaved as they did?" asked Jansson.

Carl shrugged. "We can make as good or as bad a guess as you. Intense hatred is what it looks like, but that doesn't fit with the two different and unconnected victims. Well, anyway, one should be looking for two or more people who have devoted themselves to karate— that much is clear. As Joar said, nobody can strike that kind of a blow to the larynx without having trained for a long time. I have a funny feeling that the murderers wanted to tell us something."

Jansson tensed up. "Tell us what?"

"It's just a feeling, but these killings were in some way a kind of *show*. It's as if they wanted to create a sensation, a lot of publicity, and wild speculations of perhaps a totally different sort from what we've seen."

"You don't believe the stuff about the Russians?"

Both men shook their heads emphatically. "Not for a moment," said Carl. "Partly because there are terrible risks, political risks, in a case like this. We can't imagine anything that would be worth such great risks. Partly because the victims are politically and militarily insignificant. And, as I said, military men would never, for numerous reasons, behave in this fashion—neither us nor the enemy. Never."

Samuel Ulfsson took two deep puffs in succession on his Ultima Blend and gave a look of disapproval to the man seated directly across from him at his conference table. You should never let Näslund get any closer than three arm's lengths, he thought.

Ulfsson was furious, which was extremely unusual for him. Half an hour before Näslund arrived, a particularly impudent television reporter had peppered him with questions and wouldn't take no for an answer. On the evening news they were evidently going to run *Expressen*'s lies as if they were true, and naturally they would make his own denials look like indirect confirmations. No matter what you did, it came out wrong; if you said "No comment," they interpreted it as a confirmation, and if you made a comment, they twisted your tapes until you sounded as if you were confirming what in fact you were denying. And Näslund was now frowning as if he already had his suspicions. Ulfsson spoke harshly, through clenched teeth. "If the intelligence service of a foreign power wanted to stir up trouble for us—and you know very well which foreign power I'm talking about, who are experts in this sort of maneuver—they could hardly have been more successful than you and your *Expressen* people."

Näslund had decided absolutely not to get into a fight, and he replied with unctuous calm. "I agree that the situation is annoying, but I don't agree with your interpretation of what is going on."

"Then why the hell do you keep publishing this kind of story?"

"We aren't the ones who are publishing them; it's *Expressen*."

"Crap. Since when has *Expressen* dug up information without your willing collaboration? What are you trying to prove?"

"I'm as much in the dark as you, and so is everyone in the company. None of it makes sense."

"So *Expressen* made it all up? It's all their own imagination? That you're convinced the Russians are murdering our pilots, and you know that that's what *we* think? That's what it says, in great big headlines, too. Yet you *know* that here at headquarters we don't believe that idiotic Russian theory for a minute."

Näslund dug into his briefcase and took out four or five pages stapled together. At first he seemed about to slide them across the polished table like a beer glass in a cowboy movie, but then he changed his mind and rose, placed them in front of Ulfsson, and returned to his seat. "The defense minister asked for a report from me by lunchtime, when he learned what was going to be in *Expressen*. That's what I gave him. Read it yourself."

Ulfsson read through it quickly. The contents were in no way vague: in the opinion of the security department of the Swedish National Police Board, there was no basis for believing that the murder of the fighter pilots in Norrköping had been carried out by a foreign power. The Defense Ministry shared this opinion, and no one in Säpo had any doubt on that point. There was no basis whatsoever for the information in *Expressen*, and Näslund found it all but impossible to believe that any employee in his department might have spread intentional disinformation.

"Well," said Ulfsson dryly, "I see I have no reason to believe that you would misinform the defense minister. But the fact still remains that that fellow Per Wennström, the reporter on *Expressen*, whom you usually use when you want to leak classified information, is at work on this story. Why should he suddenly start making things up when you've always given him material in the past?"

"I don't understand it. Maybe it has something to do with this: you know we worked for a long time to find sufficient grounds to expel at least one Russian agent. Finally we succeeded, and then the Foreign Ministry wanted it kept secret at all costs—you might ask yourself why. It's not surprising if a Säpo employee or employees decide that the Swedish people have the right to know that we aren't just idiots at Säpo, you know?"

"A decision made with your sanction."

"Well, sanction isn't exactly the right word. But I don't see any great need to track down or punish the leaker."

"One ought to feel the need now, certainly."

"It's not that simple. There are constitutional laws protecting newspaper sources, you know. You're assuming that someone has leaked classified material, which isn't proven. Second, we would have to bring in the attorney general; and third, that kind of investigation never leads to anything. None of this fits; that's the problem. The information is false."

"Spreading disinformation must be illegal in some way, no?"

"Well, maybe breach of duty or something like that. But that doesn't eliminate the press law about informant protection."

"So you have one or more small-time saboteurs down at the company who are organizing a vast amount of damage for us and you, but there's no legal . . . that's outrageous."

"The whole situation is outrageous."

"Do you know Wennström?"

"Yes, quite well."

"Call him up and tell him it's all false."

Näslund ran the steel comb twice through his hair. "He'll just take it as confirmation that the source is right."

Ulfsson lit another cigarette. "How's it going with the police? Are they getting anywhere?" he asked after a moment. His antagonism had abated; he believed Näslund.

"They're working like beavers down there in Norrköping, but they haven't found any connection between the victims, so it's hard to make any progress. There's no conceivable motive. Anyway it isn't the Russians."

"No, the crime isn't a security matter, but this propaganda is making it our business. Who's trying to do what?"

"I have no idea. At least *Expressen* isn't after the government."

"And I assume you aren't either. This time?"

Ulfsson's insinuating question was a slap in the face, but Näslund took it calmly. "Whoever is giving stuff to *Expressen*," he said smoothly, "must have an objective that involves harming Sweden or the Defense Ministry in some way."

"In that case, it's a security matter."

"Yes, in my opinion."

"Then it's a matter for you. Bring in the devil and strangle him, or at least kick him. As long as the union doesn't object."

"Well, yes, I think you've come up with a legal possibility; we can start investigating it."

"Can't you interrogate Wennström?"

"Impossible. That would make it worse. Constitutional rights, unbelievable commotion, and no information. We can't very well torture him. But I agree with you it's serious, and I'll make every effort to find a solution."

Ulfsson nodded. As far as he could recall, this was the first time that he and Näslund had ever agreed about anything.

MEURSAULT, it said in capital letters right on the discreet label, *mise en bouteilles au domaine*. Whoever has a lot to offer doesn't need to boast. The vintage was 1984—the same wine they had had the first time. And it was the first time in over a month that he was drinking. His days in Moscow had come back to him at the very thought of alcohol.

Eva-Britt Jönsson, now a permanent police inspector, had reached the stage where she asked herself how much in love she really was. She had disappointments behind her, and she didn't want to make an impulsive mistake. But she found herself wanting to be with him as often as she could, and she thought he was changing, as if he were somehow thawing out from the frozen time he had had in Moscow. Yet he still feared not being able to perform; he would fling himself away from her at the last minute, and he never talked about it.

Carl was stroking her hand gently with his forefinger, gazing out at the nasty weather. The warm light from the colored glass lamps and the mirrors and the brass fittings in the Restaurant Reisen made for coziness, and he was enjoying himself.

It was as if he had begun a new life. He dressed more simply, and he had started doing his apartment over with simpler, more modern furniture. It felt exploratory—he was searching for himself behind the discarded personae, behind the old habits, trying to become a real person. The other life was over now, he told himself. He was head of an office where no one wore a uniform and they did important work that was exclusively mechanical and intellectual.

"Is there anything to the story that the murders in Norrköping have something to do with defense?" she asked.

"Does Police Inspector Jönsson have anything to do with that investigation?" he asked, teasing.

"No, I was just wondering. You can't tell what to believe; one day it's one story and the next it's something else. It seems to be complicated: no motive, no connection between the victims except that they were both fighter pilots in the same wing. And that peculiar, revolting way they were killed. Can military officers do a job like that?"

"I don't know. I work with computers. But no one at the defense ministry believes in the Russian theory."

"Still, it might have been a military man."

"Why do you say that?"

"Simple police logic. In both cases the victim let the murderer in, and that might have been because he was in the military."

"Hardly, dressed in a Soviet uniform. Here's another idea: he might have shown a police ID."

She stopped short. "You're perfectly right," she whispered. "That would be logical, unpleasant but at least logical. I wonder whether they've thought of that."

"Well, there have to be limits even to what your most brutal abusers of drunk drivers might do. Do police officers train in karate and martial arts, by the way?"

"Did the MO indicate something like that?"

"I was just wondering."

"Well yes, they do, but not in my group."

"How am I supposed to interpret that?"

"I'm the interrogator here," Eva-Britt said, smiling prettily. "You didn't get along very well in Moscow, did you?"

"No."

"Why was that?"

"Lonely, very lonely, and technically a very tedious job. I was supposed to modernize the reporting system and train a couple of old men in data processing. I can think of more amusing things to do. The best part was when you came."

"Yes, but that was a bit silly, like a comic opera. Though it was wonderful to see Red Square."

"Yes, and the stuffed Lenin."

"Let's go to your place afterward."

"I don't know . . . have to start work early tomorrow." Carl shifted, and poured more wine.

Now was the time to broach the subject. And Eva-Britt did. Understandably he resisted, embarrassed. He told her that when he was engaged—yes, when he was studying in America—it had never been a problem, or later, with casual affairs. But when he genuinely cared for a woman, when it wasn't pretense or a game, then the unease would come over him and he would go around in circles: *I won't start thinking about it now because then it will be like last time*, and then he would start thinking about it anyway, and then it *was* like last time.

She was very gentle. "You have to stop thinking I have contempt for you or won't see you if you don't sleep with me," she said, logical and patient like a good officer. "That just isn't true. We have all the time in the world. I *want* you to have all the time in the world.

"And look, we're not in Moscow now; we actually live here, in Stockholm! Now it's still autumn, soon it will be winter, then comes spring and then summer and fall again. We'll be here the whole time, working too hard and drinking wine that's too expensive."

"I'm doing some remodeling in my flat," said Carl with relief. "Come back with me and see what you think of it."

3

Enemy's Enemy

Twelve

It was a murder that made you think of American gangster movies, and it was done with a high degree of professionalism.

One Thursday afternoon in Stockholm two men were sitting in the little coffee and pastry shop in an office building of Näsby Park Centrum. It was the time of day when the staff has the least to do. Since the coffee shop has large glass windows, anyone outside can easily wait for just the right moment to enter without drawing attention. It was brightly lit inside the shop and dark outside.

The owner of the coffee shop and her assistant had very little to report. Two men had come in and walked up to the counter. The man who ordered spoke ordinary Swedish. They had gotten their coffee and pastry and sat down at a table in the outer retail area where the pastry cases were. Since there were no other customers, the staff had left them alone and gone into the back to take a look at a drain that was giving them trouble.

That was when they heard the two shots.

At first they had not looked out because they were afraid. When they did peer through the little glass window in the kitchen door, they saw the two guests lying on the floor—no, one of them was lying on the floor and the other had fallen forward across the table.

Witnesses on the street had seen two other men come out wearing black leather jackets, but no one had seen any weapons.

The getaway car had evidently been parked on the far side of the office building, near the railroad station, where there were plenty of parking places. Vague reports from witnesses mentioned a Volvo, either a 740 or a 760.

Two shots had been fired from a shotgun at a distance of less than a yard. The buckshot was of the ordinary Swedish type, number 5, used to kill rabbits and game at a distance of twenty-five yards. At close range, that kind of shot is instantly fatal, practically anywhere in the chest area. Judging from the impact pattern in relation to the estimated distance, the shotgun or shotguns must have been sawed off.

It was rainy and slushy and muddy with dozens of indistinct footprints inside the coffee shop. No clues there.

The manner in which this double murder was committed was enough to create a sensation, with the usual big headlines in the evening papers. That would have been the case even if the victims had been ordinary Swedes.

But one of the men was Igor Terasimov, third secretary at the Soviet embassy and long ago identified as a member of the KGB's *residentura* in Stockholm. The other victim was foreign trade secretary Erland Winblad, who had worked closely with the minister of foreign trade in the previous government.

Before the complicated diplomatic procedures started, the police managed to carry out a number of routine tasks that, technically speaking, might have been regarded as impermissible once a diplomatic ID had been discovered in the breast pocket of one of the victims. After that they called in Säpo personnel and passed the buck all the way up to Näslund.

They sorted out and made a record of the victims' clothing, pocket contents, and, in one instance, briefcase. On the Russian they found folded inside his jacket a twenty-page document from the Swedish Foreign Ministry, stamped Classified, blood-spattered and partially destroyed. On the Swede they found an envelope with eighteen thousand-kronor bills in numerical sequence.

Näslund ordered them to take the fingerprints of the dead Russian, which, of course, was diplomatically inappropriate. But, as they expected, the same fingerprints were soon found on the envelope with the money and on both the top and bottom bills in the stack.

In one respect the case was crystal clear. A Soviet intelligence officer and his Swedish agent had met for a conspiratorial meeting, and they had managed to do a switch, exchanging money for materials, before they were killed.

The Foreign Ministry, swiftly apprised, conveyed the government's instruction for immediate secrecy. But it was difficult to explain how the Soviet diplomat might have been shot in such pure gangster fashion. By one or more people who must have had prior knowledge of the conspiratorial meeting. How could the impression be avoided that Swedish authorities were in some way implicated?

The attempt to make the case classified naturally failed. *Expressen*, under the overall heading AGENT WAR, devoted an entire section to the Foreign Ministry's obvious distress at the possibility that Swedish authorities might be under suspicion. And it could once again quote "outraged" and "well-informed" sources in Säpo who were convinced that this was a revenge murder for the Russian murder of two Swedish pilots. The other mass media promptly followed suit; that well-known "investigative reporter" Per Wennström had been publishing reliable leaks from Säpo for years.

Denials—in one instance a furious denial—from defense headquarters were brushed aside because denials were, of course, part of the "game," and spy organizations—Swedish or foreign—never confirmed liquidations unless they were caught red-handed, as the French intelligence service had been when they blew up the environmentalists' boat, *Rainbow Warrior*, in New Zealand. Among the follow-up reports, naturally, were stories of known or allegedly known "agent assassinations" in recent decades.

Things looked terrible even on the first day. But on the second day, *Expressen*'s man was able to uncover something more. "Well-informed sources" at Säpo could now report the full extent of the vendetta between the Swedish and Soviet intelligence services. The Russians were taking revenge because Swedish intelligence had executed a Russian agent somewhere abroad, and they wanted to show their little neighbor country that it shouldn't pretend it was a world power. And now Sweden had replied by sending out special assassination units to take counterrevenge, the message being: "In Sweden we make our own decisions."

And on the subject of assassination squads, a background article headlined RIGHT TO KILL? explained that in the ultra-secret part of Swedish intelligence there were one or more people who, like James Bond, in extreme situations were "licensed to kill."

As an example, the article mentioned the well-known hijacking story of a few years back, when the world press had hunted in vain for the mysterious American who averted the hijacking of an Air France plane going from Cairo to Marseilles. In the end, Peter Sorman himself at the Foreign Ministry confirmed that the person who had prevented the hijacking and under spectacular circumstances had killed three of the hijackers was "a Swedish officer in the secret service whose identity naturally cannot be divulged out of consideration for the safety of military personnel."

Sorman, newly appointed as ambassador to Cuba, declined to comment.

The article ended by asking whether it might have been the same covert intelligence officer they had recently seen in action.

There were more emergency meetings at headquarters, in the Defense Chief's conference room.

The Chief himself was not present, since if he were, any decision taken would be regarded as his and the entire staff's. This way, if the future should demonstrate that the decision was wrong, he and all the defense authorities collectively could deny responsibility. There was also a significant risk that, in a meeting of such an illustrious, excitable, and unconventionally composed group, the Chief might learn something he shouldn't know and thus in crucial respects lose his deniability. Whatever the chief of intelligence might say later in private did not affect his ability to make disclaimers or—to be frank—to play dumb.

The civilians were represented by Näslund and the head of Säpo, whom no one ever called anything but the Mailman, a reference to his former occupation in a post office or perhaps to his relationship to the government. Aside from the obvious military participants—Samuel Ulfsson, head of OP5; the Old Man, about to retire as chief of special missions; Lieutenant Colonel Lennart Borgström, head of the security department; and Hamilton, newly appointed chief of SM's operations division—there was one person whom they all regarded as an interloper: the Old Man's successor, newly appointed, a civilian of some kind who had gotten the job because he was a close friend of the new defense minister. He had always been interested in spy novels, it was said. He had spent several days working with the Old Man in order to learn about "normal routines" firsthand. But this unstructured meeting could hardly be called normal.

Ulfsson attempted to act as a moderator, but it wasn't easy to keep order, since minor quarrels flared up over and over.

The worst was when Borgström suddenly asked Carl whether he had an alibi for the time of the murder.

Carl tried to push the question aside. "Which murder?" But it wasn't a good joke under the circumstances.

"The latest," Borgström insisted, and repeated his question.

The Old Man exploded. In official language it might be said that he strongly questioned his colleague's judgment and intelligence, at the same time as he gave a brief lecture on the virtually unheard-of use of sawed-off shotguns in the armed forces, and the military's access to methods and weapons that were significantly tidier.

Ulfsson managed to bring the meeting to order. "For the sake of clarity, since the question was asked," Carl said patiently, "I was in my office with six or seven Defense Ministry people at the time of the coffee-shop murder." The men all fiddled with their pencils and muttered banalities.

Not unexpectedly, they descended to chaotic speculation, which in turn gave rise to more minor quarrels.

The first question to arise concerned who or what group might have known about the meeting between the Russian officer and the Swede.

Borgström suggested the GRU, and took off like a rocket with ideas about the GRU's being behind both the murders in Norrköping and the murders in Näsby Park in order to create the illusion of this vendetta, so vividly described in *Expressen*; it might be one of their famous destabilization operations.

The Old Man remarked dryly that even the slightest familiarity with Soviet intelligence routines ought to make it clear that the GRU could not and would not have any knowledge of the KGB's operations, and vice versa. That was elementary. In addition, it would be scandalously out of order to murder a KGB officer for purely dramatic reasons; and besides, you had to ask yourself whether the GRU, in the midst of glasnost, would want to risk political disaster for itself and for the Soviet Union.

When O.M. didn't get his, as he put it, "very simple" ideas accepted—partly because the Mailman and the civilian tended to side with Borgström—he sourly pointed out that the only place where anyone might have prior knowledge of meetings of this nature, aside from in the KGB, was in Säpo.

Then it was Näslund's turn to explode.

What kind of an insinuation was that, he wanted to know. And then, unintentionally hilarious, he pointed out that since Säpo had never succeeded in capturing a Swedish KGB agent red-handed, they would surely have been content with ordinary intervention in this instance.

The men could agree on only one thing. There were no indications whatsoever, either in defense or in civil service intelligence, to support *Expressen*'s speculations.

On their way out of the conference room, the group was met by the Chief's adjutant on his way in with the evening papers.

On the front page of *Expressen* was an enormous picture of the spy Sandström. The accompanying headline asked a single three-word question: MURDERED IN MOSCOW?

The lead paragraph explained that, according to highly placed Säpo sources, the prelude to the current agent war could be that Sandström had been murdered by Swedish agents.

"For once Säpo has overestimated the capabilities of the defense department," Ulfsson joked nervously.

But he took the Old Man and Carl along with him into his office, closing the door right in the face of the newly appointed SSI chief.

"This defies comprehension," he said, tossing his copy of the evening paper onto the conference table. Then he lit a cigarette.

"How could information have slipped to the monkey house?" O.M. sounded mournful.

"It's impossible," said Carl heatedly, "it's totally impossible. I haven't told a thing to anyone except you two."

"I don't want to ask the next question," said Ulfsson gloomily as he puffed while the others stood there in tense silence. "But I guess I have to. So here it is. The Chief has information that Sandström is dead. I haven't touched on the matter with anyone, and Carl has stated his position. So I have to ask you, O.M."

"This is nothing to joke about," said O.M.

"Am I to take it that you haven't even hinted about the incident to anyone?"

"Of course."

"Then we know that much. We can conclude that in fact the information is not to be found in the monkey house and they couldn't have leaked it. Sandström's death is known to the GRU, but it's difficult to—"

He broke off when he noticed an envelope on top of his in-tray. He snatched it up almost hostilely and tore it as he opened it and began to read.

It was a short message, but he read it three times, slower each time.

Then he stubbed out his cigarette and immediately lit another one. The other two waited.

"Read it," he said at last, pushing the little handwritten card across the table. "Read it out loud, Carl."

Carl picked up the card with the seal of the Soviet Union embossed on the upper left-hand corner. He cleared his throat nervously and then read:

Mr. Commodore of the First Degree!

In my capacity as chief of the military section of the Embassy of the Union of Soviet Socialist Republics, I would like to make official contact with you so that no misunderstanding will arise. The subject is of the utmost importance and concerns the mutual security of both our countries and the good relations between them. For specific reasons I would like to meet with your representative Captain Carl Hamilton as soon as possible in order to explain in more detail a matter that should not be put in writing. I look forward to your prompt reply.

> *Yuri Chivartshev*
> *Chief, Military Section*

"The Resident himself, I assume," said Carl. "Amazing."

"That's right, in person. He wants to have you all to himself." Ulfsson was exhaling like a chimney.

"If this is a *maskirovka*, then it's one of the worst I've ever heard of," said O.M., shaking his head.

"*Why* does he want to meet with Carl?" Ulfsson was insistent.

"There's only one way to handle this," said Carl.

"It sounds dangerous," said Ulfsson.

"I don't know," sighed O.M., "that's not certain, despite everything. I mean, they wouldn't very well write formal invitations to wet operations. We should take into consideration that the GRU is *writing* to us, via the chief too, on what he calls an *official* matter. That means it's really official; it's tied to Moscow."

"He says he wants to explain and will supply information," said Ulfsson. "We should attach a certain importance to that. It's reasonable to believe he knows something we don't know."

"Which he wants to talk about, in the best interests of both our countries," added O.M. "I think we should set up the meeting, if Carl has no objections."

Both of the bosses looked hard at Carl. He was feeling uncomfortable, not because of any possible risks but because of something quite different.

"It's a little odd," he said slowly, "for the Resident to think I'm his best contact. It's disquieting, but I can't see any risk. If they want to carry out an operation against me, they hardly needed to send a written invitation to my own funeral. The GRU isn't known for delivering that sort of document."

"Could it be a fake or a joke? Or *Expressen*?" pondered Ulfsson.

"We'll find out once we set up the meeting," O.M. pointed out dryly.

"Well, there's nothing to stop us from accepting information, even if it comes from the East. But be careful when you arrange the meeting," said Ulfsson. His voice made it clear that the discussion was over for the time being.

They met first at the St. Eriksplan subway station at the precise time arranged, identified each other, said goodbye to their respective escorts, and then carried out the usual routine under such circumstances; they took turns deciding when they should change trains.

It took them half an hour to get to Brommaplan, where they strolled through a residential area. They still hadn't uttered a single word of any significance.

Carl felt the dreamlike solemnity. The man beside him was thin and gray-haired, in his sixties, probably. Head of Russian military espionage in Sweden. What peculiar company. They walked along, looking cautiously around from time to time. It was unlikely that they had been followed, and they seemed to be alone in the gray twilight of the leafy suburb.

"Well, I think we can start," said Yuri Chivartshev as he stopped and pulled the glove off his right hand. "Let me begin, as an officer and a colleague, by congratulating you on your brilliant work in Moscow." He extended his hand.

Carl was caught off guard.

"Yes, I can understand your surprise, Captain Hamilton," beamed Chivartshev as they shook hands and continued walking. "From our point of view, we regret that you succeeded in the elimination of a Swedish informer. That has caused problems for us. But as an officer and a colleague I still must congratulate you on an operation well done. Now the whole thing is over."

"It doesn't seem to be. I can hardly discuss my assignments with you, Colonel Chivartshev," said Carl, trying to sound authoritative.

"No, obviously. But when we're alone, you and I, we can be honest about even this sensitive area."

"Was that why you wanted to meet me?"

"Yes, partly. But you also have a central position within Swedish intelligence, as we understand it. Anyway, you know what happened in Moscow, and clearly we don't know how many other Swedes do. I couldn't speak so freely with anyone but you, and the operation against Sandström seems to have a certain significance for those who are working against us."

"Who is it? Do you know?"

"Not so fast, my young colleague. One thing at a time. And besides, you're already burned; we know your identity, if from nothing else, then from your assignment in Moscow. So by having you as the contact for our organization, no Swedish personnel relationships will be exposed."

"Very diplomatic."

"Oh yes. We are also diplomats. Didn't they tell you that in Moscow when you played the diplomat yourself? Just imagine your fooling us like that."

"Get to the point."

"Take it easy, young man. We have to be cool in this difficult situation. First of all, I wanted officially to report the Soviet Union's position in the matter of Sandström. The matter is closed as far as Swedish-Soviet relations are concerned. We know, just as you know, that you were the one who did the job. But it is a strict policy not to muddy the waters in situations like this."

"Yes, that was my impression. Next, Colonel?"

"Next I want to say that we don't believe for a moment, not for a moment, and I want to emphasize this, that it was you or any other officer who murdered our KGB colleague, if you can call him that. That was the second item. And now we come to the third, and here you will have to decide for yourself whether you want to respond. We can't imagine for an instant that you believe that we or any other Soviet institution would carry out terrorist actions in . . . what's the name of the town?"

"Norrköping. Correct. We don't believe it for a minute. It doesn't fit with our information on Soviet operations behavior, and it's ill suited to the political climate. I can respond without any hesitation; it's virtually self-evident."

"So you think in political terms too. That's good. And now we come to the main issue. Someone else is undeniably trying to make it look as if we're murdering each other's officers."

"Yes, at least *Expressen* is trying."

"Do you think they're making it up?"

"No, someone is supplying them with false information, and the latest batch is such that it could only come from you in the GRU or us at defense headquarters. And it's not us."

"It's not us either. It would be contrary to our interests. Surely you see that."

"It's difficult to understand what interests are in play. No, we don't believe it's in your interest, but the part about Sandström could come only from you or from us. And it didn't come from us."

"There's an error in your logic, young man. The information could also come from Säpo, precisely as the paper claims."

"They'd have to know Sandström is dead."

"Unfortunately they do."

"How, if I may ask?"

"Naturally I can't tell you. But I can tell you something else. After the election, routines in your Foreign Ministry were altered, and they started sending out information that the previous government would have kept secret from Säpo—yes, we know how things were."

"Maybe, but the Foreign Ministry couldn't have sent any message to Säpo about Sandström's death."

"No, they didn't. They sent a routine message that Captain Hamilton had been suddenly and unexpectedly called home from Moscow and would take on a new assignment in Sweden."

"That doesn't automatically lead to the conclusion that Sandström is dead."

"No, but at the same time another message was received from defense security. It stated that the spy Sandström, presumed resident in Moscow, was no longer an issue since it could be reported that he was dead."

"Is that really true?"

"Yes, unfortunately. This is information I know you could verify."

"It's unbelievably sloppy."

"Things like this happen in all bureaucracies; I wouldn't have been as surprised if it had happened in ours. So with a minimum of intelligence, which is occasionally found at the . . . do you call it the madhouse on Kungsholmen?"

"The monkey house on Kungsholmen."

"Fine. I've always wondered which. Well, you've worked there in the past, at the time of that Israeli terrorist action, for example, and when you went to Germany."

"You're well informed."

"Flattery, flattery. I've followed you with interest over the years. It's my job, and you no doubt know a few things about us too. Well, it couldn't have been difficult to put two and two together, even at . . . uh, the monkey house. Hamilton, expert in wet jobs, returns hurriedly and unexpectedly from Moscow. Sandström, the spy who escaped while on leave—it wasn't easy to believe that at first, by the way, but you finally did sweep away our doubts—has just as suddenly and unexpectedly died."

"That's not definite information."

"Yes, that's what we or you would have thought, but not our enemies. They think, This is the way things are. And then they create a reality on the basis of a premise that cannot be disproved unless Sandström walks back on stage. We know he won't be doing that."

"So you conclude that whoever is acting against you, and us, is inside Säpo. Is that it?"

"Correct. They are your enemy, for reasons I am still unsure of, and of course they are our enemy, just as you are. So we have a common interest in protecting ourselves against the enemy's enemy."

"What are your suggestions?"

"Here we come to the unconventional part I didn't want to put on paper. I want formally to present to your chief the proposal that, through our combined efforts and combined resources, we track down the enemy's enemy and render him harmless."

Carl was very calm, and kept on walking. "Surely those must be the most extraordinary words anyone in your position has ever spoken to someone in my position."

"Correct. But we're in an unusual and dangerous situation, so we have to go beyond traditions and . . . conventions."

"Do you mean a direct operational collaboration?"

"We should investigate what the possibilities are for working together."

"Do you have any order of priorities in operations work?"

"Yes. First, track down the Säpo disinformer. Second, investigate Expressen's strategic intentions. Third, track down the terrorists who killed both your officer and ours."

"Search and destroy?"

"Correct."

"I can't answer you now, Colonel Chivartshev, but I doubt we can agree to allow you to carry out operations work here. And it would be rather tricky for us to attack a Swedish institution, obviously. But I imagine that we can accept information from you."

"Can you supply it as well?"

For the first time Carl laughed, and it was a sudden liberation. "Are you thinking of recruiting me, Colonel? If so, this has been the most roundabout agent recruitment I've ever heard of."

"If we don't exchange information it will complicate both your and our information gathering, as well as our analysis," objected Chivartshev, annoyed.

"All right, all right. I didn't mean to answer your questions negatively; it just struck me as funny. The correct answer, Colonel, is, I should think, that you will receive such information as we might be able to contribute in exchange for your own. Precisely as spies usually do."

Now they both laughed.

"One thing more, which may be obvious," said Chivartshev after a moment. "Whatever may be claimed later on, the official Soviet position will be a blanket denial. As far as we're concerned, Sandström was never in Moscow, much less eliminated there. We will deny everything on that score as propaganda from circles that want to damage Swedish-Soviet relations."

"Understood. And now, Colonel, I must return to report on this. If we can meet tomorrow, I will give you our official reply."

"Can't we meet later tonight?"

"I don't know how long the decision will take, but we can set a time for tonight, and tomorrow afternoon the same time as we met today as an alternative."

They quickly took care of the details.

Two hours later Samuel Ulfsson, grumbling, got into his car outside his house down by Tyre Lake and drove in to Stockholm. He met O.M. and Carl in a safe flat on Grevgatan, and they very quickly reached some decisions. Less than half an hour later he went back home.

Just a little before eleven o'clock that evening Carl was again walking beside the highest chief of Soviet intelligence in Stockholm and reporting the brief message:

The Joint Chiefs could under no circumstances sanction any Soviet operation on Swedish territory. Any operational work, in accordance with the law, would have to be carried out by Swedish personnel. Any information that Soviet intelligence wanted to supply would be accepted gratefully and studied with interest. Any information going in the opposite direction would first be presented to the head of OP5 before being passed on.

Chivartshev walked in silence with his hands behind his back and his brow furrowed.

"Tell me, Captain, do you always obey the law?" he asked at last.

"In every way possible, yes," replied Carl with no hint of a smile.

But Chivartshev smiled. "That's good, young captain, very good. Actually, quite funny, too—I mean, that I will have to ask permission for certain operations. That's out of the ordinary. All right, the Soviet Union will reserve the right to decide independently how it will set up its operations program. Now tell me, which would be harder for you to go against—I mean, as regards your laws and bureaucracy—the newspaper or Säpo?"

"The paper, without a doubt. It's a breach of the constitution, and we can't get involved in anything like that."

"Interesting. So you can't wire the reporter and find out his source at Säpo?"

"No, impossible."

"Fine. It's a topsy-turvy world, isn't it, but that's fine, since as for us, we'd rather not operate against Säpo except in a friendly way."

"Through your informers?"

"We must have proper cooperation, Captain. You're not thinking of trying to recruit me, are you?"

"I beg your pardon, it was just an impulse. But we know you can get information there; you knew more than we did about those reports from the Foreign Ministry and JSC/MS."

"I'm afraid we'll both have to pay a price for this collaboration —though it's necessary and in both of our interests. We'll have to think about the disadvantages later. Our first priority is to get at the connection between the reporter and whoever is giving him his assignments. That's not against *our* constitution."

"If Säpo catches sight of us, let us presume we're acting as agent and case officer."

"All right!" Chivartshev had thought of this, too. "That's amusing! But I have a hard time imagining that they will; we're not amateurs."

"If your theory is right, they saw your KGB colleague and *his* agent."

"Yes, and we'll find out how. Chekists can be so sloppy."

"Do you say 'Chekists' too? I thought we were the only ones who used the term."

"You see, now we've exchanged a little information. The proper derogatory term for Säpo is 'the monkey house on Kungsholmen,' and what we use for the KGB is 'Cheka' and 'Chekists.' Was my information correct about the reports between the foreign ministry, JCS/MS, and the monkey house?"

"It hasn't been checked out yet."

"For the time being then, the captain owes me one; let's hope it evens out eventually."

"Let's hope that our collective knowledge will be sufficient to knock out this provocation, as you would say."

"Not bad. And I agree."

Thirteen

It was the very last chanterelle expedition that autumn. Samuel
Ulfsson had been putting it off, but time after time he had promised
his wife, and besides, she had an irrefutable argument: as commodore
his salary was a good bit lower than hers as a university instructor
(and probably lower than the wages of a newspaper reporter), but
they were expected to entertain, so the chanterelles fulfilled an important social and economic function as well as a culinary one. There
was a dinner party to arrange.

For years they went to certain special places, and when they found
the right spot, the work went quickly, almost mechanically. It didn't
do any good for him to complain about cold fingers after a few hours:
she'd start in on him for smoking again and talk about heart attacks
and vascular spasms and how unloyal he was, preparing for his death.

They went from place to place, picking in silence. The woodlands
smelled powerfully of wet grass and early winter. They startled a doe
and her two fawns hiding in the brush, unwilling to abandon the
warmth of a sunny resting spot.

He tried to think logically, both for and against.

First, there was no "agent war." He had already tested his most
paranoid and terrifying idea: that the two new operatives might have
decided on some kind of American "action," that they thought something should be done against the KGB, and so on. But they weren't
crazy, and besides, as Borgström reminded him, they had an alibi for
the murder of the Soviet diplomat and the Swede, along with Carl and

four other defense employees. At least one of the sides in the agent war was not participating.

As for the murder of the pilots in Norrköping, the GRU would hardly be likely to condone it without a political reason, and considering the present world situation, this was unlikely. Besides, the MO spoke strongly against the idea that military personnel were involved.

So the absurd dilemma was whether really to trust Soviet intelligence. Chivartshev's information was correct in one important and verifiable aspect: Borgström had received a memo from the Defense Chief in which Sandström's presumed demise in Moscow was mentioned; and since the matter concerned military intelligence *and* Säpo, he had "routinely" transmitted the information in one of his weekly reports, a report that coincided with the Foreign Ministry's memo reporting the abrupt end to Hamilton's career in Moscow. With a minimum of intelligence and imagination, anyone with knowledge of Hamilton's previous activities could have put two and two together.

So Chivartshev was telling them something valuable. The GRU had a certain insight into Säpo, and Chivartshev paid a price when he passed on the information: it would later lead to a mole hunt inside Säpo. They were trying to start the same kind of civil war between Säpo and defense that they had so successfully done in England between MI5 and MI6.

But Soviet diplomats and spies were cautious, and they liked absolutely to control every aspect of whatever they planned. Events now had every likelihood of galloping off in an entirely different direction. The person or persons responsible for the campaign in *Expressen* might be able to control the paper's reporters, but how could they be able to influence the rest of the mass media and the political events they had triggered?

Russians surely did not work within such uncontrolled formats.

It might be possible to solve part of the problem using political pressure. Ulfsson had been called in for a special session with the new minister of defense that very afternoon. The Chief would also be there.

They walked home, swaying with the mushroom baskets filled with heavy, wet chanterelles. His wife didn't say much. She knew about his meeting, she had read the papers, and he had joked that in the future he might have more time for mushroom hunting. They would be alone at dinner: he would tell her everything then.

He took a hot shower and rubbed his numb fingers. Then he put on his gray flannel suit and climbed into the Mercedes the Defense Ministry had sent.

In a kiosk on his way into town, he noticed a placard with Carl's picture under a banner headline: SANDSTRÖM'S MURDERER? Ulfsson ordered the chauffeur to stop, and he got out and bought a paper.

He stared at Carl's picture on the front page—it looked like an old passport photo and wasn't much like him. Read calmly and systematically, he told himself, and he turned to page five, where the awful mess began.

The main article claimed that Count Hamilton had been sent to Moscow undercover in order to liquidate Sandström and that this was well known at Säpo because, at the same time that he was abruptly and unexpectedly called home from Moscow, they had learned from defense headquarters that the Sandström problem no longer existed.

A second article concerned a terrorist action that had occurred several years before, and not surprisingly, Count Hamilton was pointed out as the Säpo man who had killed the Israeli commandos in Täby.

A third article, based largely on guesswork and misinterpretations, claimed that Count Hamilton had been sent to Cairo as a military attaché in order to establish contact with certain PLO factions, and that in this way Sweden had learned of a planned plane hijacking, and that Count Hamilton, on the orders of the Foreign Ministry, had thwarted it. Articles from the world press of the time were quoted, including extensive accounts from passengers on Air France flight 129 about how the man they thought was an American had intervened against the hijackers and killed all but one of them.

A last article claimed that several years ago, when Count Hamilton was still with Säpo, he had been loaned to the West German Verfassungsschutz and had led the operation that ended in a total military massacre of the remnants of the Baader-Meinhof gang.

Under a headline asking DID THE SOCIAL DEMOCRATIC GOVERNMENT KNOW? the paper ran speculative statements that were clearly intended to make the previous government entirely accountable for all these actions. It was mentioned that Count Hamilton, on at least one occasion and possibly two, had been awarded the Royal Medal for bravery, which supposedly proved that he had been acting with the government's approval. The requisite number of denials and "no comments" followed, along with outraged political remarks from Conservative politicians.

Samuel Ulfsson's hands were shaking as he lit a cigarette and turned to the editorial. Surely this was the biggest catastrophe ever to strike the intelligence service during his tenure as chief. The paper revealed nothing that couldn't have been known inside Säpo. On the other hand, there was nothing that Säpo couldn't have known about, and that made the catastrophe, if possible, worse. The main editorial theme was that Social Democrats had never learned that the security of Sweden was a serious matter; that they always acted with their own private scouts; that they had regarded the secret service and intelligence organizations as either unreliable or as instruments of their own party politics. No matter how grave the consequences of this attitude, they stubbornly hung on to it. But now the dirty laundry had to be washed. Whether or not this irresponsibility had precipitated the present agent war, order had to be restored to Sweden at all costs, and as a first step, the previous government's responsibility for the chaos had to be investigated. "Off to the constitutional committee!" the editorial ended.

Ulfsson's car stopped at the rear of the ministry, and Ulfsson went in through the chauffeurs' entrance.

The Defense Chief was already sitting in the minister's waiting room. "Have you read *Expressen?*" he asked curtly.

"Yes, on the way in from Tyre Lake."

"Well, what do you conclude?"

"It's all coming from Säpo, but I don't understand the intent. No matter how I look at it, I don't get it."

Like a teacher ushering in schoolboys to be reprimanded by the principal, a female secretary showed them into the big, bright room with its view of the palace and Strömmen. The office was in disarray; open file folders and documents were strewn everywhere, as if the new minister was exploring all the options and getting all the information about everything the Social Democrats might have withheld from him.

Two chairs placed in front of the desk indicated that the meeting was intended to be more like an interrogation than an informal get-together in easy chairs over coffee. The atmosphere was heavy with uneasiness. The men greeted each other very briefly and formally before sitting down.

"We might as well start with Sandström," began the minister in a tone that signified extraordinary resolve, "and for the sake of good order, I want to tell you that I will be giving the prime minister a report on this conversation later this afternoon. The government wishes to have absolutely relevant and absolutely truthful information on all relevant issues. Is that understood?"

The two officers nodded gloomily.

"All right. Sandström. What *is* true?" the man barked, his glasses flashing.

The Chief replied slowly, never losing eye contact with the minister. "We have, ahem, indications that Sandström was in Moscow from the time of his departure from the Swedish prison system until recently, when he was supposedly killed."

"Supposedly killed?"

"Yes, that's the information I have."

"From Sam here?"

"Affirmative."

"Would you clarify the message, Sam?"

"Right. I gave this information to the Chief."

"Were you the one who sent Hamilton to Moscow?"

"That is correct."

"And what was the objective behind your order?"

"There were two objectives. The first was to modernize our report procedures from Moscow, to create a new computer program to facilitate this, and to secure the computer program against intrusion."

"Does Hamilton know how to do that?"

"Yes, that's his basic training."

"And the second assignment, the other objective?"

Ulfsson took a deep breath and considered asking for permission to smoke, but changed his mind. "The second objective was to photograph Sandström so that we would have definite proof that he was working in Moscow, having indications to that effect. Definite proof would have facilitated a request for extra appropriations that the Chief was going to make in order to counteract certain harmful effects of Sandström's presence there."

"That was the explicit assignment you gave him?"

"Affirmative."

"Nothing else?"

"Negative."

"Well, did he carry out the assignment?"

"Yes, he brought back film, and I had it destroyed."

"Why?"

"Because . . . according to Hamilton's information, the photographs supposedly showed Sandström in a deceased state . . . and . . . I thought it especially inadvisable for such documents to be found at headquarters or for any employees there to see them."

"You never actually saw the pictures?"

"No."

"You assume that Sandström is dead?"

"Yes."

The minister stopped abruptly. He knew he was suddenly entering a minefield. He hesitated before formulating his unavoidable follow-up question.

"Would Hamilton have acted on his own initiative?"

"No."

"Then a very interesting question arises. Might Hamilton have taken orders from someone other than you two gentlemen? From the previous government, for example?" The question was directed to the Chief.

"Theoretically, yes. But there's no reason to assume that the previous government had anything whatsoever to do with the matter," he replied carefully.

"They must have been in on Hamilton's being sent to Moscow, and they can't exactly have been ignorant of his, shall we say, special qualifications."

"Yes, but Sorman wanted to get rid of Hamilton for entirely different reasons, and they happened to coincide with our interests." Ulfsson came swiftly to his superior's aid.

"Why did Sorman want to get rid of Hamilton?"

"It's a complicated story that really has nothing to do with this matter," replied Ulfsson in a hopeless attempt to evade the question.

"The present government is very interested in the answer, and you gentlemen can lie as much as you want in the newspapers, but not here. Why did Sorman want to get rid of Hamilton?"

"Because . . . well, it had to do with the rescue of the Swedish doctors in Lebanon."

"Weren't they freed through diplomatic negotiations?"

"No, not entirely. Sorman sent Hamilton there on reconnaissance with very vague instructions. It ended when Hamilton, together with units from the PLO, raided the kidnappers, killed them, and sent the hostages to the waiting diplomats, who . . . well, came to believe that their work had brought it off."

For the second time during the conversation the defense minister seemed to lose his composure for several moments.

"To summarize," he began again slowly, still thinking it through, "Hamilton was sent at Sorman's, that is, the government's, request to assist in the work of freeing the Swedish citizens. Hamilton accomplished the task by force. Sorman then presented the matter as brilliant proof of clever Swedish diplomacy and needed to get rid of Hamilton for political reasons, since in some ways he knew too much."

"I can't be the judge of that," replied Ulfsson cautiously. "We don't get into political judgments. But the risk of Hamilton going to *Expressen* must be regarded, under any circumstances, as nonexistent."

"Even in this situation?"

"Yes, especially in this situation."

"Let's continue with the chronology. Hamilton is sent to Moscow with your assignment to photograph Sandström. And the Foreign Ministry has no objections even though they know what kind of man Hamilton is?"

"Yes, that's how you might summarize it."

"Here's the crucial question. Did Hamilton receive other orders from some other military authority than Sam? What do you think, Chief?"

"Well, the instructions that he received through me were as Sam has described. But the head of SSI called me this afternoon and orally presented his resignation. After he saw *Expressen*, that is."

There was total silence in the room. Ulfsson forced himself not to smile. The Old Man not only had retired, but now had also handed in his resignation. Nice. But would the sacrifice be sufficient, or would more heads have to roll?

"I think I understand," said the minister at last. "But if we botanize further in today's paper, we come to that hijacking story. Sorman has confirmed that Swedish military personnel were involved. Hamilton that time too, Chief?"

"Affirmative."

"What was his actual assignment?"

The Chief fidgeted. "It involved one of this country's most sensitive and best-kept secrets, at least until now," he replied carefully.

"Meaning what?" asked the minister, unblinking. He stared at the Chief, stony-faced and steadfast.

"Hamilton's assignment was to escort a Soviet defector, an admiral, to Sweden, a certain Koskov, who, among other things, was head of diversionary activity in the Baltic Sea area. We regard the hijacking effort that occurred during that trip as part of the Soviet Union's efforts, by proxy of course, to prevent Koskov from getting safely to Sweden."

"But he did?"

"Affirmative."

"And what did that lead to?"

"First, to one of the most comprehensive collections of data ever transmitted to the West by a Soviet defector."

"Has the information been compiled?"

"Yes, in the so-called Koskov file, of which only one copy exists."

"I will have to requisition that file as soon as possible. What was the second thing the action led to?"

"Only four people in defense and four people in the previous government have full knowledge of this."

"Are you among the four defense representatives?"

"Affirmative."

"Please describe the mission in detail, in that case."

"It would take a while."

"Go ahead, Chief."

Ulfsson leaned back in his chair and clasped his hands over his belt. He looked almost peaceful.

One's initial response, he thought, was that this was all but indecent. Until a moment ago this rather young man with glasses had been a politician on the outside who under no circumstances would have gotten so much as a hint of Operation Big Red. Now he was defense minister, and those were the rules of the game, democracy's rules. One couldn't object, didn't want to. It was for this system, among other things, that intelligence was supposed to act, as an antenna in Sweden's external defense of democracy.

The Chief gave a succinct account of Operation Big Red, but still it took half an hour, and when he finished speaking, the minister took a long time to think. No doubt, Ulfsson guessed—and he didn't know why—he was struggling between, on the one hand, the temptation to file suit against the previous government for its total incompetence in dealing with a crisis situation of crucial importance and in considering selling the Soviet defector for a sub rosa agreement; and, on the other hand, the quick realization that these relationships must be kept secret forever, no matter who was in power.

"Could it be that the point of *Expressen's* information campaign, or whatever we call it, is to expose Operation Big Red and thus create a crisis in our relations with the Soviet Union?" the minister finally asked.

"Until now, there have been no indications of that," replied Ulfsson. "*Expressen* has been able to report only information that was known or could have been known in Säpo. They haven't said anything about operations or events known only in military circles or by the previous government."

"Could foreign powers have some plan for getting us into trouble?"

"That can't be ruled out. But it's difficult to see any kind of Soviet interest in this publicity."

"And the so-called agent war?"

"We don't believe it for an instant," said the Chief.

"A motive of revenge—for what happened in Moscow?"

"No, their first concern was to hush it up. They don't want publicity that might lead to Operation Big Red. Quite the opposite."

"Some *other* foreign power acting via Swedes in Säpo?"

The question was left hanging in the air. It was impossible to answer since they didn't know who or what was giving the classified information to the *Expressen* reporter—or with what motive. And of course, the government couldn't intervene against a Swedish newspaper. And the armed forces even less so.

Carl was in a good mood, almost cheerful. After his morning workout and shooting program, he had devoted himself to cleaning up his apartment while he listened to music. He had thrown out much of his furniture, a parody of the furniture in an English gentlemen's club, and switched to brighter colors. In the library there was now a warmly inviting Italian sectional sofa upholstered in soft green leather, and between its two sections was a low polished table of pink granite. The primary lighting in the room came from a lamp shaded in white alabaster-like material hanging from a long steel arc above the table. The white light created a handsome interplay with the shiny red stone and the matte green.

Was all this more genuinely himself? Less an executive stage set? (He had sent the old furniture over to his office.) Would she like it or think it looked too expensive? Of course it *was* expensive, but not ostentatiously, he thought. It had been hard to set up the lamp and get it attached properly, but he wanted to have everything ready in anticipation of her praise.

He had had the phone unplugged all day long. Whatever problems there might be at work could wait till tomorrow. He wanted to devote himself to just the two of them and nothing else. He reserved a table at Ulriksdal's Inn in a few hours, and he felt as if he were on his way to liberating himself from something.

Now it was nearing dinnertime. He decanted a bottle of Corton and put it on a silver tray with two glasses, which he placed first in the middle and then to one side of the stone table. In the refrigerator he had some "liverwurst" canapés, as she would predictably call the pâté de foie gras.

He sat leaning back with his eyes closed in the green armchair that matched the sofa, listening to the Brahms violin concerto at such a high volume that it was a wonder people didn't call the superintendent to complain. But still, he had the phone unplugged, and an unlisted number too—double protection.

She rang the doorbell during the quiet beginning of the second movement, and he jumped up, noticing that he was smiling radiantly even before he opened the door.

The first thing he saw was himself.

She was brandishing *Expressen*, holding it between her thumb and forefinger as if it were filth. But she said nothing as he helped her off with her coat, took the newspaper, and followed her into the library. She nodded briefly at the room—"Nice," she said—then sat in the armchair, where she would be inaccessible.

He went over to the stereo and turned off the music. Brahms was too expressive and emotional for now. He made a gesture at the newspaper indicating that he would read it, and she nodded again. What did her expression mean?

He read through all the articles and the editorial—quickly and methodically, just as Sam had done—and put the paper down on the stone table, carefully poured the wine and went over to her with a glass, and then returned to the sofa. They toasted each other without a word. Then she set her glass down so hard it almost cracked; it was one of the antique goblets he had inherited, and he had time to think that stone was probably not very practical.

"Is all that true?" she asked with a nod toward *Expressen*.

He lowered his eyes. "Parts of what it says are true," he said, "parts are totally false."

"So that's what you were doing in Moscow. While we were dancing at that hoity-toity ball you were quietly planning a murder?"

"I can't tell you, or anyone else, what's true and what's a lie in that paper," he said gently, not daring to look up.

"But there is a great deal of truth in these stories?"

"Yes."

"So you travel around the world killing people?"

"Eva-Britt, you can't interrogate me. This is all classified. National security. It's a criminal offense for me to talk about it, and you as a police officer should respect that."

"Nice fellow I've gone and fallen in love with. Really nice. I once split up with a colleague because I thought he was too violent—black and blue marks on the crooks, things like that."

"This is not the same thing."

"No, obviously. How the hell—excuse my language—could you deceive me like this? I should have realized it. Dumb as I am, it was easy to fool me."

"I wasn't fooling you."

"No? Well, I'll be damned!"

"You don't usually swear."

"No, but I'm so damn mad!"

"I haven't been fooling you, and I haven't lied to you. What I've done is refrained from discussing top-secret information. Otherwise we would have been committing a crime, and that's not good for a police officer, and it's not good for an officer holding a classified job. It's not any stranger than if I had been a radar operator."

"So that's what you say, that you—how'd you put it?—'refrained from discussing top-secret information'? There are other ways of saying it. Don't you understand how this makes me feel? Here I've gone and fallen for a man I thought I was getting to know better and better, and whom I've been naked with and slept with and made love with—well, that wasn't so great, but anyway—and then I find out the whole thing was just an act, that you're someone else entirely and scary as hell. You know?"

Carl stared at the floor, his face twitching, and she thought suddenly that he was going to cry.

"I'm sorry," she said in a gentler tone, "that was stupid. I didn't mean it like that. But don't you see, I feel duped and betrayed? How would you feel if it were the other way around?"

"If it was about your job, it wouldn't bother me. But if it concerned you and me privately, I'd be hurt." Carl was trying hard to stay under control. "Besides, I assume you *have* fooled me."

"I have?"

"The first time we met at Reisen, you came armed. I didn't like it, but I never asked you about it."

"How do you know that?"

"You see, now we reverse the roles. Because I noticed when you put your pocketbook down. Shall we say the weight corresponded to a Sig Sauer, nine millimeter, with fifteen rounds in the magazine, and a pair of handcuffs?"

"Yes, you might say that. Yes, that's quite correct. But they're the tools of my trade."

"Still, I had a hard time understanding why you need tools of your trade when you're having dinner with me."

"It had to do with my job. We were on the lookout at that time for certain dangerous persons, and I wasn't alone in staying on the alert even during my free time."

"You see?"

"See what?"

"You go around with a nine-millimeter pistol in your pocketbook, and as a matter of principle are prepared to use it in the performance of your job. The difference is only that I've actually done it, and so far you haven't had to."

"You can't compare the two! I'm a real cop. We have the right to use force on the job, but we don't go around killing people."

"We also have the right to use force on the job."

"Who's 'we'?"

"A covert section of the Swedish . . . uh . . . it's about right, the way they put it in *Expressen*. We are by definition a standing, mobilized part of Swedish defense. In short, we are always at war."

"So Russians might suddenly storm in here, you mean? Please."

"No, not like that. That 'agent war' doesn't exist."

"You can say that with complete confidence, and I'm supposed to believe you?"

"Yes. If anything like it had existed, there'd probably be some classified info on it, and then I couldn't have said anything. But there's no agent war; it's that simple."

"How many people have you killed?"

"I don't know."

"Lost count? Please."

"No, but I don't know, and I can't answer that kind of question."

"Who are you, really? Have I actually met you or was it just your nice twin brother, the civilian version?"

"You have met me, the way I want to be or the way I'm trying to be."

"A simple bureaucrat in a military office somewhere, slaving away over peculiar computer printouts?"

"That's right. That's what I've been doing, and now it will be even more true. The operations *Expressen* was trying to describe are a closed chapter for me. From now on I work in an office, if I'll be allowed to stay in defense at all."

"Is that true? And are you sorry about it?"

"You keep asking questions like an interrogating officer."

"Maybe that's because I *am* a cop, as a matter of fact. Let's take it one more time. Was the last thing you said really true, and are you sorry about it?"

"Yes, it's true, for operational reasons if nothing else. I've been burned, more burned than any Swedish officer has ever been."

"What do you mean 'burned'?"

"Professional jargon. That's what it's called. The trick in covert work is to stay incognito. Anyone who ends up with his name and picture on *Expressen* posters has to go into some other profession. It's happened before to other agents, and now it's happened to me. It's rather a relief—you can look at it that way, too."

"So from now on you're out of the business?"

"I don't know how long it will take to wind things up, or how it will be done. We're being subjected to a hostile campaign in that newspaper, and I'm not the target. I'm just a means of creating bigger posters and more chaos. I don't know what will happen now, and I don't intend to figure it out so long as you're here."

"Do you want me to leave?"

"No, that's not what I meant at all. I mean that I plan to leave the phone unplugged and devote myself to nothing but us until tomorrow morning when I go to work. I've been looking forward to this evening. I thought it'd be a new beginning in some way. I reserved a table at a romantic inn."

"That's probably impossible now, isn't it? You'll be recognized."

"You're right. I have some open-face sandwiches in the fridge, that's all. Shall I get them?"

"I want you to tell me about yourself, with or without the sandwiches."

Carl paused. "It was about ten years ago when I left the one woman I'd been closer to than anyone else, and it was because I didn't tell her anything. I didn't tell her a single military secret either, and that's why I left her. Her interpretation was that I was having an affair and that I didn't trust her. Now I'm in the same situation."

"Don't make the same mistake again, in that case." She smiled a little, and suddenly he couldn't help smiling himself.

He hunted for Paganini's first violin sonata to put on instead of the Brahms, and after he'd changed the disc he went into the kitchen. Opening the refrigerator door he almost felt like crying when he saw the sandwiches sitting there, looking so lonely in the glare of the refrigerator light. They seemed like a pathetic idea now. But he took the plastic wrap off carefully so he wouldn't mess up the pâté and went back to the library. He served her in silence, turning down the dimmer on the lamp above the table and turning down the volume of the music a little, and then he sat down in his old place on the sofa, strangely far away from her, and tried to tell her about himself.

As soon as he started he realized that he was probably trying to tell *himself* too. Who was Carl Gustaf Gilbert Hamilton?

Born wealthy, of course. To a very conservative family, of course. Childhood in Skåne, first pheasant hunt at the age of twelve.

Then Stockholm and high school and conflicts in the family because of his newfound political ideas. For a while he was ashamed to be named Hamilton and he wore work clothes with suspenders, but that passed. In the radical student organization called Clarté you learned the precise difference between "class affiliation" and "class point of view," and it was the latter that mattered. Especially considering the affiliations in Clarté.

He and his father became enemies and his father, as the saying goes, "took his hand from his son." He lived alone in a studio apartment on Östermalm during his school years and never saw his father again.

Then came the question of military service. This was during the Vietnam war. Clarté was far from being pacifist—on the contrary— and took the position that the comrades should infiltrate the defense instead of evading their military obligations as other left-wing organizations proposed, being of the firm conservative conviction that defense was an instrument of the bourgeoisie to oppress the working class and so forth.

Infiltration meant that the comrades should apply for the elite groups if possessed of physical prowess or classified positions if intellectual prowess were the case—the interpreters' school in Uppsala or a commando unit. The intent was not to spy or commit sabotage but

rather to "strengthen" Swedish defense. For him, it had been the navy
and training as an underwater demolitions expert—yes, that's why he
was good at diving—and during that training Swedish intelligence
had recruited him.

Yes, precisely because they knew he was a "leftist extremist"; it was
a typical intelligence paradox.

During five years in the United States, he learned computer technology on the University of California at San Diego's supercomputer.
Well, let's skip the technical details; it is what it is.

But his training wasn't merely civilian. And the other part of his
training is classified.

Then there was Tessie—part Irish, part Mexican, a liberal Catholic
who wanted to study law in order to be able to defend the rights of
Mexican farmworkers and illegal aliens. It all ended with her when he
was gone a lot and couldn't explain why. Maybe it wouldn't have
worked out anyway. She hadn't intended to move to Sweden, and he
didn't want to live permanently in America. Anyway, she was married and had a child.

When he came back to Sweden, he was an officer, promoted rapidly due to various exceptions to the rules. Then he had to make up
his mind—and honestly he didn't know how or why he did it. It was
hard to say no, anyway, for reasons of some sort of decency—after all,
the armed forces had invested a lot of money in his dual training.

So he began at Säpo; well, that would probably be extensively
reported within the next few days in *Expressen*.

Yes, *Expressen* was right about that too. When he was working for
Säpo, officially in the computer division, he was part of a group of
officers who investigated the murder of the Säpo superintendent—
Axel Folkesson—and in the end that led to a confrontation with Israeli
terrorists. Yes, yes, all of that was true, but he couldn't go into the
details.

So during a certain period they had been colleagues. It's true he had
killed people. But first as a police officer.

He had been living in a kind of play; he was acting the role of some
kind of aristocratic, rich caretaker. Yes, it was more than a "cover,"
because he really was a rich count, but everything—the way he
dressed and talked, the way he furnished his home—had been theater,
a game, a cover.

But nothing that had anything to do with his feelings for her was
theater. There had been no plan and no trick that first time when she

had stopped him for speeding. He was obeying some kind of instinct and nothing else. In a way, she had been the center of his life ever since—something real, a real person—yes, that's how he used to think in private—who had no connection to all the rest of it.

When he came back from Moscow, he got a new job as head of a department where the work had more to do with machines and computers than weapons. He had felt hopeful, as if he could return to something, as if his work as a "field operative"—hateful euphemism—was a part of his life that was over with, and now it was a matter of just finding his way back.

Eva-Britt listened carefully, letting him talk and talk. She sipped her wine and ate the pâté. Then, startling Carl, she got up and went over to the television set and turned it on. He protested, but she said, "No, we must, for the news. It's important to find out what they're saying."

It started off as might be expected, with the passport photo and all the rest. Then they interviewed a defense spokesman whom Carl had never even seen before, which was odd. The mystery spokesman said that *Expressen*'s allegations would be neither confirmed nor denied, "no matter how preposterous they may seem," because it was a vital policy never to confirm or deny reports about secret intelligence activities. In this case this might seem regrettable, particularly for the officer in question, but unfortunately, that was the policy.

After that, the defense minister appeared, very sharp-tongued and very worried. "Let me begin by saying that the reports in *Expressen* and elsewhere about an 'agent war' and the like are sheer nonsense, with no basis in fact whatsoever," he said fiercely. "But these reports are indirectly harming Sweden's defense and national security; they constitute some of the most irresponsible reporting I've seen a Swedish newspaper come up with in fifteen years. There is no reason to convene a constitutional committee to go into any of this, since, as I have said, there is simply no basis for suspecting that the previous government ordered murders abroad or anything else. As far as I know, and I believe I am well informed, no such orders were ever given or even came to the attention of the government after the fact."

As to whether the spy Sandström was dead or not, he could not comment.

"What did he mean that he couldn't comment?" Eva-Britt wondered quietly as she turned the television off.

"Either he didn't know or else he couldn't say anything for security reasons," replied Carl resolutely.

He anticipated her next question.

"And what are your comments?"

"As you know, I'll have to refer to the defense spokesman."

There was silence between them. Carl smiled gently. He got up and put on the most serene and most beautiful music he could think of: Mozart's clarinet concerto. From 1791, the last year of Mozart's life.

In the homicide division in Norrköping, they finally had a breakthrough. That was clear on Monday morning when they found the car.

Rune Jansson felt optimistic for the first time. Not because he thought he could catch the murderer or murderers, but at least they weren't fumbling around in the dark anymore.

It had been his own idea, and at first, in spite of his official position as chief, he had had trouble getting support. The Stockholmers in the National Criminal Police, as might be expected, regarded him as a simple village constable, and made fun of his Norrköping accent. But finally they had to give in, and now, rather furtively, they were even apologizing.

The hypothesis was simple. His idea was to explore the only connection between the victims, that they were pilots in the same wing and had both been off for the day. Operation Door-Knock was then instigated at all the pilots' residences in Norrköping and Linköping. It had been difficult to get the addresses from the wing's security section, since information like that was supposed to be classified. But they had results in less than twenty-four hours. A dark blue Volvo 240 was reported as having been in the vicinity of several pilots' homes that day. A time-specific sighting in Norrköping was less than forty minutes from the estimated time of the first murder. Another sighting by a disabled neighbor in Linköping occurred almost two hours before the critical time.

So someone had been on reconnaissance in a car, going from one pilot's residence to another in the two towns.

Until they found auspicious victims.

One witness had also seen men who might be the perpetrators. The wife of a pilot in Linköping had found a strange man in her garden when she came around from the back yard, but he had shown her a police ID and explained that many break-ins had occurred in the neighborhood lately. Then he had walked back to the police car, she said, although later she acknowledged that of course it had been an unmarked car, but wasn't it natural for detectives to have unmarked cars?

She seemed to remember the digit 8 on the license plate. She claimed that the man had been a giant, a typical dark-blond Swedish police officer, although he didn't speak with a local East Götland dialect. She was from Mjölby herself, so she ought to be able to tell the difference.

Now the car had been found. Using extraordinary resources they located a Volvo 240 in the Norrköping-Linköping region that had been stolen on the same day as the murders; now it was parked down by the river and had two parking tickets on it. The homicide lab was working on it, hoping to find fibers or anything else that matched up with what had been found in the murder victims' homes.

Jansson called in the wing's security chief—it was always best to deal with the military on your own turf; otherwise they would just start ordering you around—and practically under duress, the air force officer told him who and what groups might have access to the pilots' addresses. There were not many choices:

1. Foreign powers—Polish Gypsies selling pictures door to door had been all over the district, and could have mapped out the fighter pilots' whereabouts.

2. Staff personnel of the wing, the security chief, mobilization officer, duty officer, and possibly certain office personnel.

3. Säpo.

4. Organizations with higher-ranking positions, such as air force HQ.

Jansson cautiously questioned the order of the list, but was content to have the options. A certain number of military officers, among others, could now be interrogated, regardless of what the wing commander thought.

So the victims had been chosen by chance, simply because they had been home alone at a given time. And they had voluntarily let their killers in.

Perhaps because they showed police ID—someone had earlier in the day—though no police investigation had been going on in the area.

The choice of the car, a Volvo 240, certainly had a police smell to it.

It was concrete, logical, and most unpleasant. Not only because of the obvious anguish that would now strike at the detectives, as it always did when colleagues became the target of police investigations.

Worse, this was a matter of police authorities with special privileges and a special relationship to the political higher-ups and the law: Säpo.

Jansson had unpleasant memories of a murder investigation that had also led to secret higher-ups, individuals who couldn't even be interrogated under their real names. The file was down in the basement somewhere in a cardboard box labeled "no investigative results." But that wasn't precisely the truth. There hadn't been anything wrong with the results: the probable perpetrator had been identified— Jansson had recently run into him again, an expert in extreme methods of violence who had even been promoted and was now a captain.

It was hard to imagine what possible national interest there might have been hindering the case of Maria Zepelinska-Adamsson, and it was even harder in this case. It could hardly be in the national interest to have Swedish policemen murdering two air force officers, especially with such extreme and despicable methods.

This time Rune Jansson decided that he was not going to give in.

Carl's work went smoothly all day on Monday, though he had to spend a good four hours on logistics maneuvers by subway and other means in order to make sure he was unobserved on his conspiratorial way to a meeting with Yuri Chivartshev, then on to his own office. Perhaps someone in the big industrial building where the operations department had its quarters, camouflaged as a computer company, might recognize him in the elevator. He changed his style of dress and got out a pair of smoke-colored glasses, and now he looked like an overage American university student with running shoes, jeans, and a baggy sweatshirt with an American inscription on it under a fluffy down jacket.

Chivartshev raised his eyebrows when Carl himself arrived for the meeting instead of a substitute. But this was partly because they hadn't decided on a routine for that eventuality—which they now did; the passwords were *Tatyana* to the other's *Alexeyevna*—rather unprofessional but, according to Chivartshev, funny enough to be accepted—and partly because Carl thought that for security reasons it would be a mistake to resort to country mailboxes. It was unpleasant to stick your hand into something you weren't familiar with. They didn't want to cause anxiety or suspicion, and besides, the best relationship was an already established personal contact.

Chivartshev handed over a briefcase, which he first opened to show

Carl the contents—numbered and dated cassette tapes. Carl gasped: it was easy to imagine the worst had already happened. Chivartshev was calm: "There's no reason to discuss this material until we meet again, after our Swedish comrades have had a chance to evaluate and analyze it." But it was easy to see that it would be wiser for Carl to accept the cassettes without knowing for sure what they were, in case it all had to be explained or justified after the fact.

Carl then made his way via convoluted detours to Gärdet and down to the underground garage beneath the electronics company, taking the elevator straight to the operations department—all without complication or incident. He went straight into the innermost, closed sections and called in Lundwall and Steelglove. He had a bad conscience about devoting so little time to them lately, but now things would change. Here there would be plenty of both technical and operations work to do.

He kept all references to the weekend publicity to a minimum, mostly mumbling and nodding, and then they got to work.

The cassettes contained, as expected, wiretapped and recorded phone conversations from the past twenty-four hours arranged in chronological order. And the very first words on the first tape, after a telephone operator answered "*Expressen*" (apparently the entire switchboard had been bugged and not one particular phone), made them gasp:

"Yes, hello, Wennström, *Expressen* . . ."

They divided up the material in three stacks and systematized it; Steelglove quickly transferred the conversations they provisionally judged to be uninteresting and unimportant onto a separate tape with time codes programmed in—conversations with people who sounded like or could be identified as journalist buddies; chat about whether anyone else might possibly threaten Wennström's obvious right to the year's big journalism prize; a few exchanges that appeared to concern an affair he was having.

On another tape, also with the time codes, they transcribed all of Wennström's discussions with his source in Säpo. The source never identified himself, but the two seemed to know each other well.

The next step, so obvious that Carl didn't even have to discuss it or request it, was to make yet more tapes on which certain segments of the conversations between the reporter and the source in Säpo were separated out—first with everything that the reporter said erased, and second with the source saying only ordinary remarks that could not identify him as a Säpo officer or journalistic source. So they ended up with several series of selected sound bites.

The next phase required some brief deliberation. Carl was not suitable for it, for obvious reasons—it might be discovered later on and cause a lot of trouble. Steelglove was not suitable because he spoke a recognizable Finnish-Swedish. So it was Lundwall who called Wennström at *Expressen* while the others taped the conversation.

Lundwall pretended to be a worried, anonymous source in the intelligence service, complaining about *Expressen*'s irresponsibility, methods, lies, speculations, and so forth. He elicited from Wennström a fairly long, rather arrogant defense, wordy enough to give them plenty of material for the next, purely mechanical stage of their work.

Steelglove analyzed the sound of the original tape from Chivartshev to search for erasures or cuts, while Carl and Lundwall made exact measurements of the frequencies of the two voices; to the average human ear, they both sounded like Wennström, but the computer technology would reveal a clever impersonator.

The result was as they had expected. The first tape seemed to be genuine and unedited. They were one hundred percent positive that it recorded the reporter Wennström talking to an unidentified source.

Thereafter they turned, finally, to the actual contents of the tapes. They started by listening to the interesting sections in a circular, repetitive pattern while technical personnel in a neighboring room were busy transcribing them. Then the transcriptions were copied into a report document and a working document on which they could make corrections and remarks.

The actual transmittal of information was not surprising. There was talk of that man Hamilton and what he was up to and about how the government must have been involved, how they thought they could send madmen and James Bonds anywhere in the world, and how all this had now led to this catastrophic agent war.

One item really interested Carl. They played the section three or four times:

I'll be damned if the Social Democrats aren't behind all this. You know they don't trust Säpo, and it's Säpo this and Säpo that, and that's why they're operating now with their special-mission people, just the way they did before, as if they had their own damned Säpo. I mean, why else would they have given that bastard those medals for bravery? It had to be a government decision, and there wasn't one; I've tried to check it out. So, first of all, they must be keeping it secret, don't you think? And second,

I don't give a damn that they gave him the medal twice. We tried to check it out, but I don't really trust our sources in this case.

"There *is* a way to find that source and identify him," said Carl thoughtfully after they had listened to the segment for the third time. "But we'd have to tread in police territory."

"I can think of worse things," said Steelglove coldly. "We can't very well go to Säpo with this and ask them to circulate the tape in order to tell us which damned little shit it is."

"No," said Carl, "but maybe we can arrange it so that it's not even illegal except for one point that doesn't ever have to come out, and maybe even that isn't illegal. Can you take care of a technical matter for me at home?"

"Yes, of course."

"Here, take my keys. You know where I live. Rig up my library so that we can record conversations in there, with the tape recorder and backup in the dining room."

Steelglove dug out the appropriate equipment and took off. Carl and Lundwall got the report folder and sound test material ready.

Then Carl made a call and invited someone over for later in the evening. The invitation was formulated in such a way that there was no doubt that the guest would show up.

In spite of the inevitable long-winded meetings, the Old Man surprised himself by having an easy time seeing the various ludicrous aspects and black humor.

Partly retired and partly resigned he might be, but he was still participating in all this feverish activity at the center of the machinery, and, to top it all off, he was doing it with a civilian nobody who was suddenly defense minister and who complained that he felt left out and now was forcing his presence on everything.

Disregarding the purely physical threat—the risk of a new assassination—the Old Man thought things were under much better control than could have been expected on Sunday afternoon.

The new defense minister obviously understood that the scandal shouldn't be aggravated by politics, for now the shadow of Operation Big Red hung over him, as well.

Carl's future in the field was obviously ruined, but on the other hand, he had already been transferred to staff as the new head of operations, which from a psychological point of view was the best solution—for Carl and for the new boys. And people in general probably wouldn't be as upset as *Expressen* was about Sandström's demise. They had been through it all before. Besides, nothing had leaked out that only the Defense Ministry could have known; everything that had been published could be found in one form or another at Säpo, and there weren't any tidbits that might lead to a world crisis, as the Old Man had first feared when he saw Sunday's newspaper.

He didn't have much faith in that so-called journalist at *Expressen* who ran errands for a fanatic in Säpo or whoever it was. But he didn't have to worry as far as the most dangerous scenarios were concerned—comprehensive international publicity, a domestic political crisis in the Soviet Union in which the Stalinists took their last chance to destroy Gorbachev, succeeded, and threw the world back into the cold war.

Against this background, the last meeting of the evening, with all its agitated ups and downs, seemed almost like a parody.

Before Carl arrived to report on his dealings with Chivartshev, they hadn't expected much, since he'd only advised them he'd be late. The first thing that bothered both the Old Man and Ulfsson was Carl's informal attire, and they even spent some time on this issue, only delaying the moment of detonation.

As Carl finally made his report—stacking up the cassettes and folders of transcriptions and analyses both contextual and technical—O.M. began to chuckle while Ulfsson grew pale and the civilian looked as if his ears would fall off.

When Carl was done, Ulfsson lit up a cigarette, of course. He seemed to be trying to decide on the degree of severity and outrage he would now have to show. "If I understand this correctly, Soviet intelligence has tapped *Expressen*'s telephone and passed the material to us," he began unnecessarily.

"Yes, that's correct," replied Carl politely. He looked boyish and surprisingly innocent in his unusual clothes.

"The Soviet Union has, in full view and with what might be regarded as some sort of sanction on our part, committed a serious crime, a breach of the Swedish constitution. And they have, technically speaking, practiced espionage."

"Oh, the last probably isn't true," objected O.M. cheerfully. "They've turned over illegal material to us and haven't kept it themselves, and we have merely received it. So we are free to report the

Soviet Union to the police. But I don't think that would be wise, aside from being, under the circumstances, rather impolite."

"Explain yourself, or resign one more time," snarled Ulfsson. Carl had never heard that tone from his top superior.

"Gladly," said O.M. courteously, clearly amused. "The case isn't so complicated. Carl, as we naturally have to assume, has correctly conveyed your restrictions, noted by us, to Soviet diplomatic personnel, including the part about no operations and so forth. So *we* haven't instigated any crime—quite the opposite. They, on the other hand, have committed a crime that they can't be punished for. In our field of activity, we have the right to receive information procured illegally, as you know. And we can also look the other way if it's deemed justifiable. As in this case it is."

The others in the room looked with amazement at the Old Man, and O.M. couldn't resist the temptation to fill the vacuum with yet another irony—or was it meant seriously? It was impossible to tell from his expression. "If nothing else, you can call it constitutional self-defense," he said.

Ulfsson was rattled. Swiftly he decided to conclude the meeting; he didn't want too many people involved in the sensitive decisions that would now have to be made. And there was no getting around them: illegal material was lying in the middle of his desk in neat black folders and a little plastic box of meticulously numbered cassettes. It couldn't be more concrete than that. So he asked the Old Man and the minister of defense to leave, not rudely but firmly.

When they were alone, he turned to Carl with a harsh, direct question. "Does the operations department have any plans for action in the near future, and if so, what are they?"

"Yes," said Carl, "we would like to concentrate on determining the identity of the Säpo source, so far unknown."

"Until further notice, you will not be allowed to use this recorded material. Is that understood?"

"Yes. The order is understood and will be obeyed."

Carl waited, and Ulfsson thought for a moment. Carl's acquiescence had come quickly and without objection, as if he were almost intimating the other options. There were now two alternatives: to establish some sort of completely unequivocal travel ban on the operations department, and not to say too much.

"When is your next meeting with the GRU?" Ulfsson asked curtly, managing to sound stern, but almost chuckling at the absurdity of the question, put by the chief of Swedish intelligence to his subordinate.

"Tomorrow at 2100 or at midnight or at 2100 the following night," replied Carl in the same curt voice. The absurdity did not strike him in the same way.

"Under no circumstance must the operations department violate Swedish law. Is that also understood?"

"Yes, that is perfectly understood."

"Fine. Then moving on to another matter—and I'm afraid it involves certain future unpleasantness for you—we have reason to believe that Parliament's committee, despite the defense minister's expressed understanding of our situation, will call for a public hearing into this whole *Expressen* mess." Ulfsson paused to search for a new pack of Ultima Blends.

"Oh yes?" Carl was intrigued. Surely he would have little to do with the matter. Whatever the politicians and press were busy with would hardly concern the operations department.

"And according to our information, they're going to force their way into this and . . . well, you're going to be the first one to testify."

Carl felt as if he had received a hard blow to the head, and a strong, mixed feeling of humiliation and surprise welled up within him. He took a deep breath but didn't say a word.

"We've discussed it," continued Ulfsson, "well, that is, the Chief has reviewed the problems that might come up and has given instructions. Time is short and it's still just the two of us here, so I can probably take this opportunity to pass them on, all right?"

"Yes, of course," replied Carl feebly.

"They are as follows. You have the Chief's support and that of the department, naturally. In the event you are called before the committee, you *must* present yourself in uniform, and if you don't understand why, I will explain it at once."

"Please."

"In uniform you are representing not only yourself but the armed forces. You are not Ebbe Someone or some so-and-so; you are Captain Hamilton from OP5."

"That's nice to hear."

"Spare me the sarcasm. You will not lie. Don't lie under any circumstance, but with reference to national security, you will refrain from answering certain questions."

"How can we predict the questions and put together a plan for what is approved and what is not approved?"

"More easily than you might think. Everything that has to do with operations activities connected to the Soviet Union or the Warsaw Pact Nations is classified; it cannot even be discussed behind closed doors, and in all such instances you are to refer them to the Chief. He will also be called."

"And anything else?"

"Honest, truthful answers. Those are your instructions."

"About anything at all? About the hijackers and the Red Army Faction terrorists, and so on?"

"Affirmative. Take the hijacking incident, for example. All the details about what happened on the plane are okay. But everything relating to Koskov's identity and nationality is top secret. This is quite an ingenious way for us to keep clean. You won't have any difficulty remembering the difference between the two. As soon as the hammer and sickle is on any information, it's classified; otherwise it's public, starting with your testimony."

"When will this take place?"

"Probably next week. Anything unclear?"

"The uniform. With or without service ribbons?"

"With, of course. I don't need to explain why. *Expressen* wants to show a scoundrel to the nation; we want to show them something else."

"Unconventional for an intelligence officer to be a walking public advertisement."

"Yes, Sweden is the land of unconventional methods. But this is our only way out. We plan to win this one, and I hope you share this attitude."

"The orders are understood and will be carried out," said Carl with a completely unsuccessful attempt to sound sarcastic. Ulfsson looked pleased.

Less than an hour later Carl began his interrogation. Everything had been well prepared; he had even managed to change into more appropriate clothes. The man across from him on the green sofa was noticeably nervous and just as noticeably conscious of the media description of Carl Gustav Gilbert Hamilton as the ruthless murderer, Sweden's James Bond.

"As you know, Lelle, this is going to be a very serious conversation," Carl began deliberately.

"Yes, you said that we were going to discuss my position," replied the building custodian in a low voice, his eyes lowered. "Technically speaking, I am permanently employed."

"Yes, that may be, but I'm afraid this is about something much more important than what has to do with my responsibilities as an employer. In that regard, I have a serious complaint, but this has to do with certain special assignments I want to discuss with you." He paused briefly and held up a report so that his victim could see the first page. It was stamped with a big red Classified seal and entitled:

Break-in with the Apparent Intention of Committing Espionage
640117-1279 Kenneth Henrik Carlsson
510606-1377 Lars-Erik Sundberg

Carl put the report down on the stone table as soon as he could see that Lelle had grasped the essentials. Then he continued. "So you hired a certain Kenta to commit a crime here with the help of your key. Kenta's price was fifteen hundred kronor in advance and fifteen hundred kronor after the crime was completed. Is that right?"

"I can't answer that. I've taken one of those pledges of silence," replied Lars-Erik Sundberg.

"To whom?"

"I can't answer that either."

"Then I'll answer it. As you see, you are suspected of espionage. And as you've probably read in the papers, a mole was discovered inside Säpo this summer, a Russian spy. Whatever you may think, you have been working not for a Swedish authority with some kind of legal purpose but for something quite different."

He paused. He reminded himself to make no threats, since that would look less than favorable in transcription. But the allegedly involuntary spy didn't seem to have digested the terrible news, and he didn't look as if he were planning to say anything. On the other hand, he was starting to look scared—which was probably more *Expressen's* fault than Carl's.

"The question of whether the Swedish government has given me one or more medals of a certain kind is of significance to a certain foreign power. If you were fooled into working for a foreign power in the belief that you were working for Säpo, there is a good chance you'll get out of this unscathed. But then you'd better start explaining things right now," he continued rather more aggressively.

"I thought it was Säpo," Lelle said suddenly.

"So you thought it was Säpo. We can understand that. You knew your employer worked at Säpo?"

"Yes, he showed me his ID, and he had another guy with him who was a policeman too. They said that you were under suspicion of something."

"What are the names of these men?"

"The one who was the boss was named Glücher, Hans Glücher."

"And the other one?"

"He never told me his name."

"But he showed you police ID too?"

"Yes, but I never caught his name."

"You're sure about Hans Glücher?"

"Yes, it's a kind of unusual name."

"Can you describe the other man?"

"Yes, that's easy."

"Why?"

"He was at least 195 centimeters tall and looked like the Hulk, except he was blond and had a crewcut."

"Fine. You'll have to expand on that description in a while. Let me first say one thing. We are taping this conversation. I hope you understand that."

"Taping. But you don't have any . . ."

"This is the intelligence service, not Säpo. Our equipment is more discreet. But we can get started on that description now; you'll have someone to compare it with. Åke, you can come in now!"

The door to the dining room opened at once, and the giant Steelglove entered the room, dramatically menacing.

The exonerated spy gasped at what he saw.

"About this size?" asked Carl nonchalantly.

Ulfsson had long been dreading his next meeting with Näslund. But he couldn't see any way out of it, and there was no reason to question the man's loyalty when it came to matters of national security. Especially in this case, with a common enemy.

Since Ulfsson had already made up his mind in advance, he skipped all the introductory courtesies and small talk and turned on his tape recorder as soon as Näslund sat down. It played the tape that contained only *Expressen*'s source in an edited selection.

Näslund listened attentively, frowning. After several minutes, Ulfsson turned off the cassette player.

"Which of your employees was that? Do you know?" he asked with as little melodrama as he could manage.

"Yes, without a doubt. Is that bowdlerized information?"

Ulfsson raised his eyebrows. He never thought Näslund could have mastered such a term. "Yes, obviously. Well, who is it?"

"You ought to answer my question first and explain this funny business."

"I'll tell you this is the man behind *Expressen*'s campaign, the one who's supplying them not only with information but with suggestions for political interpretations."

"I'll be damned."

"Yes, it's a hell of a mess. Well, what's his name?"

"I don't think I can tell you."

"You're joking."

"No. There's a preliminary investigation going on in the department about breach of security and dissemination of false information. It would be a dereliction of duty for me to give out information while that's going on."

Ulfsson sighed deeply. It was not very refreshing to be duped like this. "It's serious, Näslund," he said. "Here is someone leaking information that's damaging the nation and its defense, and you know who he is. We should know that too."

"No, you shouldn't. This is a matter for the police, not the defense forces. How sure are you, anyway?"

"One hundred percent. Not ninety-nine. One hundred percent."

"That means you have the source on tape together with that reporter."

"That's your conclusion."

"It's a criminal offense to make tapes like that."

"Don't tell me you're thinking of starting an investigation against me, too."

"No, I'm not. It was just a remark. Can I get part of the other tapes?"

"That's inadvisable—I mean, if such tapes did exist and had been acquired illegally. You will have to settle for my assurances that we are one hundred percent certain. And I'm not planning to discuss how we arrived at that conclusion. But we did not commit any crime and did not make the tapes ourselves."

"If we need proof at some later stage, if he denies it, can we count on your help?"

"Listen, Näslund, there are still certain limits. I would advise you to proceed very calmly and cautiously—do you want to hear my opinions?"

"Yes, gladly."

"The greatest damage, publicity-wise, that this fellow in your department can do has already been done. As far as we're concerned. We don't expect more from him about Hamilton or other matters involving us. Are you with me so far?"

"That could be."

"We know who he is, but we don't know why or in whose interests he's doing what he's doing. That ought to be important, don't you agree?"

Näslund took a moment to think, without his steel comb for once. Ulfsson lit another cigarette. The two men regarded each other, not with hostility, but thoughtfully.

"Here's the situation," began Näslund. "We have on the one hand some extremely strange murders, and none of us believes they're caused by this agent war the 'source' wants us to believe in. Either he has latched on to the events and is exploiting them for his own purposes, whatever they might be, or else there's a connection between his campaign and the murders themselves. Is that what you're thinking?"

"Exactly. Have you had any contact with the Norrköping police? Well, excuse me for intruding, but are there any prospects for progress in their work?"

"I called the superintendent down there who's in charge. But he wasn't very helpful, not very polite, either. I'd almost say suspicious."

"He may have his reasons."

"What do you mean by that?"

"I mean . . . imagine if he started suspecting a Säpo connection. That would explain his brusqueness when you called."

"That's a thought."

"I'd like to suggest that you proceed cautiously with that preliminary investigation regarding a security breach, and wait for other opportunities and more explanations. Is that possible?"

"Perhaps—there's no danger in delaying things."

"What does *that* mean?"

"The breach of security has already happened, and it's possible to keep the lid on it while we concentrate on an even larger picture, exactly as you suggest."

"Good to hear. Anything we can help with?"

"No, thanks! As I said, this is a police matter. If you'll take care of foreign powers outside the country, then we'll take care of crimes within Sweden's borders."

"But you're having trouble protecting yourself against leaks. We could make available both personnel and resources—"

"No, thanks! If there isn't an agent war, then we don't want to start one either. I'll have to take a realistic look at how this should be handled operationally, but this is totally our concern. May I take the tape?"

"Go ahead."

Henrik Näslund stood up energetically and straightened his jacket; his shoulder pads gave him an almost rectangular appearance. Then he sauntered over to Ulfsson, took the tape that Ulfsson had removed from the machine, shook Ulfsson's hand firmly, and left.

Ulfsson sat quietly in his chair and finished his cigarette. Then he smoked another one. When he looked at his watch, he realized he was one minute late for a meeting in the Chief's office.

The Chief glanced discreetly at his watch as Ulfsson arrived, but said nothing about punctuality. The head of intelligence was actually one of the few officers who were entitled to arrive late.

"Well," he said instead, getting straight to the point, "how did Hamilton take it all?"

"Hard to say, but he's had more complicated orders than those."

The Chief forced himself not to laugh at the understatement. A number of the "more complicated" orders Hamilton had been given had caused problems.

"I've spent a large part of the day trying to educate myself in the art of Swedish propaganda," continued the Chief, walking over to the sofa to indicate the informality of the conversation. "And I cannot claim, with all the best intentions in the world, that we in the defense leadership are good at this. But we've gotten some expert advice from several fellows in the psych division who are helpful about this kind of thing."

"Journalists, you mean?"

"Yes, journalists. First, from what I've been told, we'll have to use intermediaries. You'll be the intermediary between Hamilton and me."

"Why is that?"

"If he's asked a question during the hearing such as, uh, when did you last meet with the Chief, then he can say it was a long time ago, so that it doesn't look as if we were close. You're the buffer between us. I'm going to be taking the second wave of the attack after Hamilton."

The Chief gave him an enthusiastic coaching on the well-tested strategy: offense is the best defense.

First. Hamilton was burned—that was already irrevocable. But he was valuable in internal service, wasn't he?

Second. Plenty of rumors were already circulating regarding Hamilton's part in various activities, so retracting, denying, disclaiming, or evading would only make things worse, and would prolong the agony.

Third. A counteroffensive in the form of confirming and explaining what had already been said, or other matters that might come up, would give a much more positive impression of the Defense Ministry than retreating behind information stamped Classified, as politicians did.

The aim was to win the game against the politicians. But they lacked tactical polish; for instance, Hamilton should do what so many politicians and criminals in government departments and the police had done over the years: play the media off against each other. The Chief had learned, for example, that if you agreed to appear in one evening paper but not in another, you could make the favored newspaper play totally by your own rules as gratitude for your commercial assistance. The same thing with the broadcast media: you could choose one of them and just stick with them while you steered the whole game. The Chief was enthusiastic as he explained his new expertise. Ulfsson was bewildered. As head of Sweden's intelligence service, a highly serious organization, he was sitting in the office of the supreme commander, getting lectures and instructions in the art of conspiring with the mass media. They might do things like that at the monkey house on Kungsholmen, but it wasn't right in the armed forces.

Late in the evening Carl finished his long recital of admonitory instructions to Joar Lundwall and Åke Steelglove.

Glücher had to be watched by legal means. The most important thing was to record his movements and his contacts. That could be done with the usual legal methods. No wiretapping, unfortunately. Steelglove had brought almost fifty kilos of equipment with him to Carl's apartment. Even the very possession of some of that equipment might be regarded as illegal, but in many cases, it was difficult to see where the line was.

Before testing the equipment, Steelglove had swept Carl's whole apartment for listening devices. The result was negative, and that made their ensuing conversation more relaxed.

Work over, they gave themselves up to memories of America until the wee hours.

Fourteen

The People's Party and the Center Party kept up their pressure to have a constitutional committee investigate the Hamilton affair. The official reason they gave—that scrutiny was warranted for the claims published in *Expressen* about the previous government using military intelligence as a spy service for party ends—was one thing; the real reason was different, and more human. None of the scoundrels, politicians, economists, bureaucrats, paranoids, mythomaniacs, police officers, and security men who had been interrogated by constitutional committees and in front of television cameras had the same mythic power as "Sweden's James Bond." People simply wanted to see him in real life. And this overwhelming force quickly broke down the resistance of the moderates and Social Democrats. They tried to argue that the risks to classified activities, relations with foreign powers, and defense secrets were too great. But the Social Democrats' credibility was limited, of course, since it was their mishandling of events that might possibly be revealed, and the moderates couldn't go it alone against their Conservative coalition partners, especially if they ended up looking as if, absurdly, they were defending some Social Democratic villainy. And efforts to hold the hearing behind closed doors collapsed, given the general thirst for sensation.

Carl was not nervous. On the contrary, he was filled with a kind of calm fighting spirit, and felt almost joyous about the impending moment. Eva-Britt had spent the night with him, a wonderful night, a glorious night, and he felt closer to her than ever before.

As soon as he learned of the committee hearing and his instructions, he told her about it, beaming. Now she would learn all the secrets he had once denied her out of regard for order, discipline, security, and the law. After all, he was under orders to tell the truth within extremely wide parameters, and it was easy to imagine the television cameras as Eva-Britt. She promised to take the afternoon off and come back to his apartment to watch, so she would be sitting on the green sofa there, and he would answer all her questions right there in the room with her, on the television screen.

He dressed almost ceremoniously in his naval uniform, and they kissed for a long time before he went down to the waiting black car.

For security reasons he entered the Parliament building through the back entrance. The spectator gallery was packed full, and the atmosphere was crackling with anticipation when Carl, precisely on the hour and surrounded by three security police officers, entered through a side door. With his uniform hat under his arm, he strode forward to his place and stood at attention in front of the committee members, who stared at him as if he were some peculiar animal; then he took his seat. He sat straight-backed and rather tense, one leg crossed over the other, his hands clasped in front of him on the table.

According to new regulations, the minority opposition was entitled to chair such a hearing, and thus it was the parliamentarian who had been committee chairman during the previous government, well known for his unwillingness to censure Social Democrats.

Now he pounded the gavel lightly on the table and began to speak, clearing his throat while the buzzing in the hall died down.

"Yes, well . . . ahem . . . uh, that is . . . So, we can begin the committee's hearing for today, and we welcome you, Captain Hamilton. Welcome to the hearing. By way of introduction, let me say, as we say to everyone here, that . . . uh . . . if Captain Hamilton would like to make some introductory remarks, that would be fine."

Carl found the chairman's perpetual smile perturbing, and it took him a moment to realize he had stopped talking.

"No, thank you, Mr. Chairman," he replied somewhat hesitantly. "First of all I am not here on trial, so I feel no need to make any sort of introductory remark, and second, I don't know exactly what the honored members of the committee would like to know. I respectfully await your questions, which I will try to answer as accurately as I can."

Now it was the chairman's turn to pause. He was used to politicians who made long speeches and proclamations before the questioning started.

"All right . . . yes, well then, well, then I will start the questions. Captain Hamilton, you are employed by the special-missions section of military intelligence, are you not?"

"Yes, that's correct."

"And you were previously at Säpo?"

"Yes, that's correct, I was employed there."

"What were your duties there?"

"I was responsible for data processing and analysis of certain records."

"I see, so it was, so to speak, a purely intellectual job, is that right?"

"I hope so."

"And your present position, can you tell us something about that?"

"Yes, I'm responsible for both data processing and operations."

"I see, and your job is classified?"

"It was until recently. Now, with all the best intentions in the world, you couldn't claim that my work is as secret as it probably ought to be."

There was unexpected snickering in the hall, and Carl felt disappointed by it.

The chairman looked through his papers. "May I ask you whether, in the intelligence service, you have in any way what is apparently called on the international scene 'the right to kill' and whether the government has any responsibility for this?" He was still smiling, a smile that contrasted sharply with the rapidly changing mood in the hall.

"Both the government and Parliament are responsible for instructions given to the armed forces. All branches of the armed forces have, as far as I know, the right to kill; that's what the basic training of draftees is all about. That's obvious."

"Yes, but in peacetime."

"The operations division of the intelligence service, in which I have been active, find themselves in roughly the same situation as members of the coast guard air force interceptors."

"Can you explain further what you mean?"

"Yes. A naval officer of my rank, if he is the captain of a vessel, might, for instance, fire warning shots at foreign submarines in Swedish territory. A pilot has not only the right but also the obligation to fire on foreign military aircraft that pass over Swedish territory and refuse radioed instructions to turn back."

"Yes, but this can't apply to the intelligence service, can it?"

"No, of course not. I just wanted to demonstrate that the issue might not be as strange as it sounds when one speaks of some special right to kill. It's not a right; in certain situations, it's an obligation for Swedish officers. Within the operations division of the intelligence service, we are considered permanently mobilized. We don't live in the same apparent state of peace as other sections of the armed forces. Our obligation to fire warning shots or take comparable measures is determined by the situations as they arise. Sometimes the obligation, not the right, to resort to force arises."

"You have no specific orders from the government in that regard?"

"No, nothing beyond what applies to the defense forces as a whole."

"I see. May I ask you if there is any truth to the statement . . . if you have ever received direct orders from the government?"

"You mean from any cabinet minister?"

"Yes."

"No, I've never even spoken to a cabinet minister, and I've received no direct instructions from any member of the government, neither the present one nor the previous one."

"I'm asking because we're here to investigate the government's responsibility, you see. But I still have to ask you: Is it true that you, with or without orders, supposedly killed the condemned Swedish spy . . . Sandström . . . during your time as military attaché in Moscow?"

"Unfortunately, I can't answer that question."

"Can we interpret that as a denial?"

"No, neither confirmation nor denial. I have specific instructions from the Joint Chiefs about what I may discuss here; certain questions, such as this one, I will have to refer to the hearing you will hold later with the Defense Chief himself."

The murmuring grew louder in the hall, almost drowning out the chairman as he continued. "You have never, in any way, received any instructions from the government?"

"No, I've already said, I never received any instructions from any cabinet member."

"All right, thank you. Then I give the floor to the vice chairman."

This gentleman was now struggling with sharply contradictory feelings. As a moderate conservative, he didn't want to make trouble for a sensitive section of the defense establishment, but he had picked up on a certain nuance in Carl's answer, which even the Social Dem-

ocratic chairman ought to have heard. And the temptation of this
nuance came to guide his questioning, which very quickly veered off
from the direction he had intended.

"Thank you, Mr. Chairman. I seemed to detect a certain shift in
your answer, Captain Hamilton. Have you received instructions from
any direct representative of the government?"

"Affirmative."

"I see. Who was it, and what did it concern?"

"It was Cabinet Secretary Peter Sorman. The matter concerned an
assignment to travel to Lebanon and assist there in the work of win-
ning the release of the Swedish doctors who were kidnapped this
summer."

"I see, and did you?"

"Affirmative."

"What exactly did you do?"

"I led an action together with military forces from the PLO's intelligence service. We freed the hostages by force and sent them to our
diplomats waiting in Beirut."

Suddenly the fidgeting and whispering and paper rustling stopped
among the whole row of committee members. They all sat stock-still,
staring straight at the witness in Swedish naval uniform. Even the committee's usually unflappably self-confident vice chairman seemed to
lose his self-control. "Do I understand you correctly, Captain Hamilton," he went on, not knowing what direction his question was going
to take. "You went to Lebanon at Mr. Sorman's request, initiated operational collaboration with PLO guerrillas, and then freed the Swedish hostages by force?"

"Yes, that's correct."

"How does it happen that we haven't heard mention of this before?"

"The hostages themselves were unaware of the action, there were
no surviving witnesses, and there was no interest in spreading the
story, from either the Palestinian or the Swedish side. That's my
explanation, at any rate."

"Do you mean that the kidnappers were killed?"

"That is correct, yes."

"Did you participate in that?"

"Affirmative."

"You personally killed the kidnappers?"

"No, only three of them. The others were executed later by the

PLO, having been condemned to death because of their grave treason."

"Is this . . . are things like this . . . part of your job activities?"

"Excuse me?"

"I mean . . . is this in accordance with . . . did these events take place in your capacity as an officer of Swedish intelligence?"

"Yes."

"So you have the right to kill other people? You thought it was necessary in this situation to save Swedish lives?"

"Yes, without a doubt. The kidnappers had made impossible demands: they had said they would kill the doctors unless they were allowed to fly out of Lebanon to an undisclosed location, with Swedish diplomats as protection, and with a substantial sum of money—I recall it was about two million dollars. Our negotiators understandably rejected these demands. The kidnappers had set a deadline, after which they said they would kill one of the doctors and then the second one. I observed them make preparations for phase one of their plans. There was a great risk that instead of continuing to negotiate they would kill both doctors and try to escape. Under those circumstances, we found it necessary to resort to force."

"Did you receive instructions from Mr. Sorman in this regard?"

"My instructions from Mr. Sorman were, first, to obtain information about the situation and then, via radio, to inform our negotiators. What I was to do after that was left up to my own judgment, with the vague type of wording that is standard in intelligence work."

"Would you give us an example of this type of wording?"

"Yes. For instance, I was not supposed to take any *unnecessary* risks and I was supposed to act *at first* as an adviser. And if things went wrong, I would bear the responsibility and the Swedish government would not recognize any association with me. And so forth. Finally, Mr. Sorman wished me *happy hunting*. These are phrases that cannot be misinterpreted."

"I see. And when you came home, did you then report the events to Mr. Sorman?"

"Affirmative."

"And what did he say?"

"His first words were literally: 'Why the hell are you reporting this to me?' After that he said that this information should absolutely not be public, and that it had to be kept between the two of us."

"I see. And was it?"

"No, it couldn't be. I don't regard myself as under the authority of the Foreign Ministry; I am, as I said, an officer of Swedish intelligence, so I reported the whole thing to my immediate superior when I returned."

"I see, and unlike the Social Democratic official, he didn't yell at you for reporting what you had done?"

"No. His comment was that it was a brilliant operation splendidly carried out. He congratulated me. He shared my opinion that the Swedish doctors would have been dead if we hadn't intervened."

"Do the doctors themselves know of this?"

"If they're watching television right now, they do now. Not before."

"Have you, on any other occasion, ever received instructions from any other government, past or present?"

"No. I have received all my instructions from Swedish military officials."

"Have you ever received explicit orders to kill another person?"

"Unfortunately, I can't answer that question. I must refer you to the upcoming hearing with the Defense Chief."

"But at least you must be able to say no if that's the correct answer."

"I regret I cannot answer at all. I must obey instructions."

"From the Defense Chief?"

"Yes."

"He has personally given you these instructions?"

"No, I have received instructions via the chief of Swedish intelligence, Commodore Samuel Ulfsson."

"When did you last see the Chief?"

"I seem to recall it was some time right after Midsummer."

"Thank you, Mr. Chairman. Naturally, there are quite a few more questions I would like to ask . . . Here's one more: What are your instructions for this hearing, Commodore Hamilton? Can you tell us that?"

"Captain, not commodore. Yes, I can at least explain my instructions. First, I obviously am forbidden to lie. Second, on certain matters regarding foreign powers that are considered classified, I am not permitted to answer at all, and must refer you to the Chief, as I have done."

"Thank you, Mr. Chairman. Considering the things we've seen here in this committee over the years, we should be very grateful when one of our witnesses has actually been given orders not to lie. Perhaps a resolution to that effect might be introduced to advantage among the Social Democrats—given our previous dubious pleasures of trying to get the truth out of them here. Thank you, I have no further questions."

The floor was turned over to the member from the Center Party, the agrarian group; he was an attorney specializing in public law. He looked up from his notes, which he had been careful to bury himself in while his predecessor was wasting time on the usual political agitation. "Captain Hamilton, it's extraordinarily interesting to hear you sit there and tell us that a military official somewhere above you should somehow decide what the nation's constitutional committee has the right to know. Don't you find that strange?"

"Negative."

"And why not?"

"The Defense Chief decides what is classified and what can be released to the public; a captain cannot make those decisions on his own."

"The captain doesn't seem a stranger to making his own decisions otherwise, but then it involves less serious matters such as taking other people's lives in foreign countries. Have you done this in Sweden, too, by the way?"

"That is a question I cannot answer, with the same explanation as stated previously. You will have to ask the Chief that question."

"Tell me, Captain Hamilton, when you acquire this right to murder, and we assume that you apparently do have this right, what is it based on, aside from the right of might, of course?"

"The right of self-defense."

"Captain Hamilton has that down pat?"

"No, I can't say that. I'm an officer and not a lawyer."

"A little information about the captain's legal rights might still be of interest. Do you have any small examples of the right of self-defense?"

That was the one question Carl had prepared for—had been warned about. He looked straight into the television camera behind the chairman's back, where Eva-Britt was sitting, and then he answered. "Those who, in order to avert a danger to their life and well-being, act out of necessity shall be found innocent of blame, if—given the nature of the danger, the harm incurred by others, and the general circumstances—their act can be considered justifiable."

"Well, I have to say, you've done your homework . . . but if we apply this to the situation you described a moment ago, then your necessity involved your killing other people in order that those Swedish doctors might go free—is that how I should understand it?"

"Yes, that's correct."

"Wouldn't it have been sufficient to knock them over the head, say?"

"No."

"Why not?"

"With the first one—a guard outside the building where the hostages were being held—it's not easy to, as you say, 'knock someone over the head' in the dark. It had to take place without the slightest commotion, and the risk involved was great."

"You consider yourself competent to judge that?"

"That is exactly the kind of thing I am competent to judge."

"And the other two—how was that done?"

"After I entered the building. The other two were armed, and I fired first."

"Did you shoot to kill?"

"I shot so that I would be certain to strike; with most modern weapons, it's the same thing, since you aim for the middle of the target."

"This is done *routinely?*"

"No, only when time is short and in very tight situations. This was one of them."

"Thank you, Mr. Chairman. I find this too despicable to continue for the time being. I presume this is more a matter for the public prosecutor than for this committee, and it might perhaps be said that it is wrong to investigate any possible crimes on the part of the captain here and now. I have no more questions for the moment."

Next came an MP from the Liberal Party, one of the most adamantly opposed to the committee hearing in the first place. Carl had been warned to be on his guard against her and not to be swayed by the fact that she was a woman—rather meddlesome advice, Carl thought, coming from men of an entirely different generation.

"Thank you, Mr. Chairman. We are here primarily to investigate any possible responsibility on the part of the government, and not to be distracted by operational details, however exciting or peculiar they might be. So I will start by asking you, Captain Hamilton, whether I understood correctly when you said that you do not come under the authority of the Foreign Ministry?"

Carl suspected a trap. "I am presumably under the authority of my superiors in the defense ministry," he answered carefully.

"But you said that you could not take orders from Mr. Sorman—at least that's how I interpreted it. You reported to your boss about the events in Lebanon, didn't you?"

"Yes, that's correct."

"But how could Sorman send you to Lebanon in the first place?"

"I asked him about that. He said that the directive came from the government. The other part—I mean, about not reporting to anyone, and so forth—I interpreted as his personal request."

"There is a difference, in your opinion?"

"Yes, of course."

"You wouldn't have ventured out on this expedition if you hadn't believed you were acting on orders of the government?"

"Yes, that's correct."

"Did Mr. Sorman expressly state that he was giving you orders from the government?"

"Yes, he did, because I asked him. Later he also told the Joint Chiefs that I had been loaned out, so to speak."

"How was the message formulated?"

"I don't know. It's possible that the Defense Chief can answer that."

"I see. But you never doubted you were being sent on a government assignment?"

"No, not for a moment. Mr. Sorman was adamant, he was in charge of Sweden's foreign policy, and he supplied me with a diplomatic passport. There was no reason to doubt his authority."

"Well, Mr. Chairman, as far as I can see, we will now be forced to call in Ambassador Sorman in order to hear the other side of this story. But allow me to continue, Captain—and I want to emphasize that my questions are intended to clarify the government's responsibility. Have you ever been given any commendations by the Swedish government?"

"Yes, on two occasions."

"Are they those colored bars you have? I'm sorry, but I don't know what they're called."

"Service ribbons."

"I see, and those . . . ribbons . . . do they indicate which commendations you have received?"

"Yes, that's correct."

"Can you tell us what they mean, in case we are not familiar with them?"

"Yes, the blue-and-yellow represents the King's medal for bravery in the field; the red, black, and yellow one represents the commander's medal of the West German Bundesverdienstkreuz; the red one is the comparable rank of the Legion of Honor; and the gold wings are an American badge, a service medal, I think you can say."

"And you have acquired these, so to speak, in your military work?"

"Affirmative."

"Who exactly decided to award you all of these?"

"The president of France, the West German president, the Swedish government, and, I believe, the chief of the American navy."

"You have obviously been out traveling in the world on more than one occasion, but if we could now confine ourselves strictly to Sweden and the Swedish government. You have been commended in this way twice by the Swedish government?"

"That's correct, yes."

"Which government?"

"The second award was decided, so far as I know, by the previous prime minister, and the first by his predecessor."

"Was the decision made by government committee or the prime minister personally?"

"I don't know."

"All right, but as far as you know, two different prime ministers made the decisions?"

"As far as I know, yes. The medals were not awarded to me in person."

"I see. And for what activities has the government or the prime minister decided to sanction your actions and even commend you?"

"I can answer you regarding the first instance. When I was working in the security department of Säpo, I was assigned to the murder investigation regarding police superintendent Axel Folkesson. In the final stage of that work I confronted four terrorists sent out by the Israeli state, in a villa in Täby. Unfortunately, I arrived too late to prevent the massacre they had already instigated."

"Yes, that is a well-known incident. But what it said in the press, that it was Captain Hamilton who shot the Israeli group—is that correct?"

"That is correct, yes."

"And that is why the government or the prime minister at the time commended you?"

"That is also true."

"And the second occasion, what is the background behind that?"

"I may not answer that question."

"The operation is covered by the pledge of secrecy you have already reported to us here, Captain Hamilton?"

"Yes, that's correct."

"But the decision to commend you for this secret operation or effort came from either the government or the prime minister?"

"Yes."

"Then we have to assume the government expressed its approval and approbation, whatever may have been involved?"

"Yes, that is naturally a reasonable interpretation."

"It did not concern the murder of Sandström in Moscow?"

"I may not answer that question. I can neither confirm nor deny anything regarding this matter."

"Do you know whether Sandström is still alive or not?"

"That question I may not answer."

"Thank you, Mr. Chairman. I have no further questions."

Then followed a round with one of the committee's junior members, an elderly conservative MP who thought he had heard Carl admit that he regarded it as a natural function of his job as a Swedish officer to collaborate with Palestinian terrorists. Carl answered—for the first time somewhat provoked—that first, he did not share this opinion as to the meaning of his choice of words; second, that he had received explicit instructions from Mr. Sorman to initiate just such an operational collaboration with the PLO's intelligence service, which, moreover, had occurred on several previous occasions and had proven to be a good working arrangement; and third, that Swedish intelligence had no restrictions or prejudices limiting its choice of working partners.

To the question whether, in that case, there had even been collaboration with the Eastern bloc, Carl replied with his formula, which everyone now regarded as a confirmation, that he could not answer the question.

The old man stepped up the level of aggression and asked whether Captain Hamilton, in his toy soldier activities, had also been loaned out to foreign institutions. Carl quelled his impulse to reply to the insolent remark about the toy soldier, and said that as he understood the question, it asked to what extent he had been obligated, while on duty, to cooperate with foreign security and intelligence services. And the answer was yes, it had happened once when he was a police officer, a quite routine occurrence in the framework of West European police cooperation and not unusual.

Carl's opponent fumbled around for a moment for new points of attack and finally came up with a question about whether the West German commendation was a result of this last-named action, and whether it was true that he had participated in a West German extermination assault against terrorists. Carl confirmed that such was the case, that he had lived with West German terrorists for a while, and had then called in special police for a final confrontation. The information in *Expressen* had been largely correct in that regard, although they had exaggerated his role.

The moderate Parliament member now took a chance on a rather obvious question about what was behind the Legion of Honor, and Carl explained that the news reports on that point were also correct, that he had prevented the hijacking of an Air France plane in approximately the manner described in the mass media.

"If I understand you correctly, Captain Hamilton, you do not discriminate between Arabs and Israelis in your assassination work, since we've heard here how you apparently found it necessary to kill four Israeli officers several years ago, but you also kill Arabs, if I've understood the matter correctly." He looked quite pleased at finally flattening his opponent.

Carl said nothing.

"Could I possibly get an answer to my question?" continued the moderate.

"I didn't perceive what you said to be a question, but rather a statement of your personal reflections and almost a personal insult," replied Carl without raising his voice.

After that it was finally the turn of the Communist Party. Its representative—a former journalist—was no knucklebrain, but as a firm opponent of the armed forces and the police, especially the secret police, he experienced the hearing as a torment, for the spellbound audience in the spectators' gallery (like the millions of viewers no doubt glued to their television sets) was determined to have a hero, and that inhibited any political effort on his part to harness this activity or any prosecution of a crime. He felt it his political duty to bring this inane activity back to earth.

"Mr. Chairman, I have to say this is one of the strangest, if not *the* strangest, thing I've ever experienced on this committee. Here we sit listening to reports of deeds that in my opinion can only be described in criminal terms such as murder and assault, and it seems to me that the committee has not fully realized what a terrible morass of law-lessness is involved. The committee hearing that we saw broadcast several years ago from the United States comes to mind, in which Colonel Oliver North presented himself as some sort of hero reporting a type of Rambo activity. I think it's scandalous that we are being seduced into the same kind of situation here."

"Excuse me, what was the question?" wondered Carl coldly when the man seemed to have concluded. Even the television audience could see a growing fury in his face for the first time.

"Yes, well, *do* you think you're some kind of Oliver North?"

Carl waited a moment before replying, as he did when concentrat-ing on shooting. Stay calm, he thought. Squeeze the trigger gently.

"Do you really think I should answer that question?" He assumed there could be only one reply to this riposte, and now he had a little more time to polish his statement.

"Yes, please, answer the question."

"I want to say first that it is rather impudent not only toward me as a person but primarily toward Sweden as a nation. The question contains an implied comparison between Sweden and the United States. I find it incomprehensible—I don't know quite how to put this—that even a Communist member of Parliament should have the preposterous idea of comparing our country with an imperialistic su-perpower. As if Swedish defense directed its forces and resources to fighting against the liberation of the third world, when on the con-trary, our activities are aimed at defending Sweden, Swedish inter-ests, and Swedish lives in a world dominated by superpowers that send out gangsters as well as armadas of fighter planes wherever they please. As for myself, let me just say that the only political affiliation I've had, aside from a good deal of anti-imperialistic solidarity work, was with the student association Clarté. Consequently, I have never voted for the Swedish Communist party, not only because it is out of date and conservative, but, above all, Mr. Committee Member, be-cause your party has such strong ties to the *other* imperialistic super-power."

The committee sat very quietly, as if turned to stone with aston-ishment. The chairman finally leaned forward, still smiling broadly, and asked the Communist MP if he was done with his questioning.

"No, Mr. Chairman, not yet. I have to say, you never cease to surprise me, Captain Hamilton. Shall I interpret this to mean that within one of the Defense Ministry's top-secret departments we find an officer with a political attitude that has traditionally been considered to create security risks? I mean, it's not exactly the common image of the Swedish officer corps, is it?"

"I can't take responsibility for your image of the Swedish officer corps," Carl replied. He retained his composure. "I can only say that within the intelligence service we do not look at party politics or overall political background. What is important for us is solidarity with Sweden, professional competence, and discretion. I don't think my view of the world situation is particularly unusual or unique within the company."

"The company?"

"Yes, the intelligence service. Excuse the expression, but that's what we call it."

A concise and dramatic exchange, Carl realized. Clips would appear not only in the Swedish news coverage, but overseas as well.

After that came more rounds of questions with the committee's junior members, a session with the chairman, who answered his own questions with long harangues of his own. The vice chairman refrained from further questions, saying that he did not find it proper to present in an open hearing any further details of the kind he himself regarded as classified; he would follow up on a number of juicy lines with people in higher positions of responsibility, with all due respect.

Then it was once again the turn of the attorney from the Center Party.

"Mr. Hamilton, these are undeniably terrifying insights we've received into your thought processes. I hope you are not representative of the Swedish officer corps. You clearly do not hesitate to murder people in any situation or by any method. Did I understand correctly, in your recounting the hijacking incident, that you killed someone with a knife while you were sitting in an airplane seat like any other peaceful passenger?"

"Yes, that is correct."

"And if I understand your way of thinking, you contend that even on that occasion it was a question of self-defense?"

"That is also correct."

"It wasn't enough to knock this person out, but you had to stab him to death with a knife, if I understand correctly. Given your very special training, don't you have the capability of knocking people out?"

"Yes, of course. But not when I'm sitting in an airplane seat with a seat belt on. As I tried to explain before, I was quite far back in the plane; the other hijackers were up front. The hijacker next to me had to be put out of commission so I could advance on the others farther forward in the plane, and this had to take place without any noise or other disturbance."

"It doesn't disturb you to cut the throat of a fellow human being, since that's evidently what you did?"

"Yes, of course, it disturbs me greatly."

"But still no hesitation?"

"Not in that particular situation. If one feels too much hesitation while an operation is under way, one ought to ask for transfer to another department in the intelligence service."

"You have not done so?"

"I have been employed as a military attaché briefly, and now I have an office job working with computers. After this hearing I won't be able to work in the field again."

"Do you believe an officer should obey orders at all costs?"

"No, not at all costs; the Nuremberg trials demonstrated that. But on the other hand, it's difficult to imagine that kind of a situation in our country."

"If you were given the order to murder a Swedish spy in Moscow, you wouldn't refuse to obey the order?"

"That's a hypothetical question."

"Yes, of course, but that's how our honorable colleagues in politics usually proceed, and if I understand you correctly, you were given orders to answer all questions truthfully which did not concern a specific security matter, isn't that right?"

"Yes, that's right, and I am attempting to do so."

"Well, then I will repeat my question, hypothetical or not. It might have a certain interest for those who are leading this country to gain some insight into what is possible or impossible. So will you answer the question?"

Did his pledge of silence also extend to hypothetical questions? Carl felt that the longer he hesitated, the closer the television cameras would come, and Eva-Britt was watching him.

"If I received such an order, I wouldn't give a thought either to refusing orders or to the Nuremberg trials," he replied at last.

"But you still are not answering the question whether you received such an order and, if so, from whom. As a diplomat weren't you still . . . I mean, didn't you come under the Foreign Ministry?"

"No, military attachés are directed from the Defense Ministry, from a department concerned with overt activities of Swedish intelligence."

"You still aren't answering my question about whether you did receive such an order, regardless of who might have given it."

"I'm sorry. I must again refer you to the Chief."

"Do you think it was a laudable action to cut the throat of that person?"

Carl looked very patiently and calmly at his questioner. "I refuse to answer that for personal reasons, since I find the question offensive. This much I can tell you: the president of France considered that having more than two hundred people escape unscathed from a plane hijacking was worthy of the Legion of Honor."

The Center Party veteran wasn't used to being put in his place by witnesses.

"If Captain Hamilton wants to drag in international aspects, I have nothing against it. I might wonder, for example, if the current so-called agent war is a consequence of your various self-defense actions, whether they took place in the seat of an airplane or in Moscow or in places that you, according to your orders, cannot name."

Now Carl couldn't help smiling. "There is absolutely no agent war going on."

"Can you say that with complete confidence?"

"Yes, without hesitation. Whatever this rather exaggerated term might mean, I'd either be involved myself or at least know about it. There is absolutely no agent war going on between us and the Soviet Union or any other foreign power."

"Quite a few incidents have undeniably occurred, Captain Hamilton, which lend a certain credibility to such reports."

"I can't agree with that. Some reporter of the useful idiot variety has, against his better judgment or in ignorance, dreamed it up; or else, as is the habit of certain journalists, he's reporting only what others dictate to him. Either way, it's not true."

"So you think the journalist is an idiot, Captain?"

"No, I said a *useful* idiot. That's quite different."

"Pardon an ignorant Parliament member, but I fail to see the difference."

"I'll explain. 'Useful idiot' is a Russian spy term. It means a person who runs errands, for instance for local authorities, without knowing that he's doing so."

"And you don't think reports like that should be in the papers?"

"No, I don't think so, and I regret that they have been."

"Perhaps you think, Captain, that we should abolish freedom of speech and freedom of the press, so that you could carry out your activities with fewer restrictions?"

Carl had seemed rather uninterested for a while, but now his look became steely, and he answered slowly, his voice deeper and unmistakably intense. "On several occasions in my work, which you describe with such contempt and derision, Mr. Committee Member, I could as easily have been killed myself. That knowledge has always been easy to bear, because the purpose has always been to make a contribution so that in my country—*our* country, Mr. Committee Member—useful idiots would be entitled to write whatever they please, and politicians in *our* Parliament have the right to be as insolent as they like. Everything has a price. And the price of my life is not too high for your right, and our right, to practice democracy."

Good. One more segment that would be broadcast over and over again all over the West.

Last of all came a middle-aged woman from the Social Democrats who had just discovered that the question she wanted to ask had already been asked. Instead she burst out with something totally apolitical, and straight from the heart.

"There has certainly been a great deal of drama in this hearing, but I can't help wondering, Captain Hamilton, how a person can be like you and sit here apparently so unmoved and talk about the most horrifying things. Isn't it difficult, and aren't you ever afraid?"

Carl pictured Eva-Britt on the sofa at home on Drakens Lane, and instinctively he turned his glance to the camera behind the chairman's back, looking more directly into the eyes of three million viewers.

"It's difficult to answer your question concisely. I've tried to be neutral and correct here, and it's possible this is not only because I'm here on the orders of my superiors and as a representative of the Defense Ministry, but because everything you've asked about and I've been ordered to answer touches on my innermost self. But I'll try to answer your question. Yes, it is unbelievably difficult. There are very painful questions you have to ask yourself every day, when you're working in the operations section of Swedish intelligence. Most of all, you're afraid of losing the person you love, afraid not of dying but of what the consequences of dying will be. And if you've also caused people as much harm as I have, then in every lonely hour you ask yourself whether it's worth it, whether you've been doing the right thing. I've asked myself all these questions every day for years, and I've had long conversations with one of my superiors, whom I'm personally close to. But I became an officer because I wanted to use my skills to defend Sweden's independence. I've had this conviction ever since my days in Clarté. I don't run away from anything, but neither do I strive for anything—except to do a job that's so difficult that many people don't want to handle it. It has to be done, it's part of our defense, and I am part of our defense. When I follow my conscience, which I always try to do, I have only one thing to fear: losing my freedom and the person I love. I'm not afraid of anything else."

When Carl finished, something happened that had never happened before. Wild applause broke out up in the spectator gallery and even in the tightly packed reporters' section, as if a storm of feelings that had been long and painfully suppressed was finally released. Chaos and confusion followed as the chairman, steadfastly smiling, thanked Captain Hamilton and a horde of newspaper photographers rushed forward to take pictures. Carl looked around in bewilderment for his bodyguards. But before they could reach him, a chubby man wearing glasses popped up among the photographers and stuck out his hand. "Wennström, from *Expressen*. I too am just doing my job. May I have an interview?"

Carl froze, looking first with disgust at the outstretched hand before raising his glance. All the courtesy he had displayed during the hearing vanished. He gave Wennström a glare that should have induced nightmares. "I don't talk to traitors," he said through clenched teeth, pushing his way toward his bodyguards and out the door.

Via underground tunnels he reached the other side of the Parliament building, where a JCS car waited for him with open doors. To his disappointment there was no car telephone, or he would have called Eva-Britt. He was taken directly to Lidingövägen, with the message that the Chief was expecting him.

Not only the Chief. Almost the entire defense leadership was in the room, with a dozen chairs scattered around in a semicircle in front of the television set, now turned off. Here and there uniform jackets with gold braid hung on the chairs. The room smelled of smoke and sweat and beer, and except for Samuel Ulfsson and the staff who were removing ashtrays and empty glasses and bringing in new ones, Carl was the only man in the room with a rank lower than brigadier general. He didn't know anyone except the Chief and Ulfsson.

The Chief—in shirtsleeves—shook Carl's hand for a long time, and then introduced him to the back-slapping officers. They seemed unused to being in the company of other officers with as many or more stars on their shoulder boards than on their own.

Champagne was brought in. Carl couldn't believe his eyes, and wondered for a brief, terrifying moment whether there were journalists present. The Chief proposed a toast to the day's efforts. "We won the day, or rather Hamilton won the day for us," he said as he raised his glass.

The mood was almost euphoric, and everyone suddenly wanted to talk to Carl alone. The Chief escaped with Carl to a corner.

"A brilliant performance, Hamilton," he chuckled, raising his glass once more.

"I must admit that I'm surprised by your enthusiasm," said Carl in a low voice, as he reciprocated the toast.

"You don't realize the impact of this?" The Chief seemed truly astonished.

"No, to tell the truth, I don't," said Carl. Champagne sloshed over the rim of his glass as the navy chief slapped him on the back.

"Well, those of us who have been sitting here in front of the television have a very clear-cut impression," continued the Chief, "and it's hard to imagine a more candid performance in an extremely difficult situation. As far as all of us can see, the Swedish people have for once gotten a true officer as a true hero. Your expression when you looked into the camera as you said that last bit, and when you told off that Communist, was remarkably strong, I must say."

"Yes, but there are still some hard questions I didn't have to answer, and you'll have to bear the brunt of that yourself. I can't imagine how you're planning to do it—forgive me, it's obviously none of my business."

"It won't be all that hard. You rolled up the whole front, and the only thing left for me is to mop up the last pockets of resistance, so to speak."

"They're going to ask some tough questions."

"Of course. But now the politics in an open hearing are over. I'll appear behind closed doors out of consideration for national security; and I won't answer their questions out of regard for the same thing; I'll even have the support of the defense minister."

"That sounds simple."

"Yes, but it can be. The Social Democrats don't want to drag us into this, because it just implicates them. The moderates understand the delicacy of the foreign-policy aspects, and they hold the majority, no matter how much the Communists and Farmer Unionists and Libertarians shout for your blood. They want your head, but they'll hang themselves in the opinion polls."

"I think we've been amazingly open, in any case."

"Maybe it seems amazing, but actually we've just confirmed what was known already. If we'd squirmed around as the politicians do, it would have prolonged the agony, and it wouldn't have ended in victory."

"Are you so sure that this is a victory, Chief?"

"Yes, absolutely."

"Do you know what happened in Moscow?"

"No. How did that cabinet secretary put it? Damn it all, don't tell me anything? Something like that?"

The head of the information department very respectfully interrupted their conversation. There had been requests for interviews from the media, he reported. Most important were ABC, NBC, CBS, and CNN, *The New York Times*, *Time* magazine, *Newsweek*, and the *Washington Post* from the United States; *Le Monde* and *Le Figaro* from France; *Die Zeit*, *Neue Zürcher Zeitung*, and *Der Spiegel* from Germany and Switzerland; *The Times*, the BBC, and ITV in Great Britain. New requests kept streaming in; they had never experienced anything like it.

Carl felt a momentary panic, but when he asked the Chief for permission to refuse all interviews, his request was granted at once. And when he was finally able to escape from the Chief's celebration, he went to a telephone and called home.

She told him that Drakens Lane was besieged by reporters and in the streets all around were cars with cameras mounted on their roofs and antennas sticking up and that the security phone at the front door had been ringing incessantly until she disconnected it.

They made plans to meet at her place; she would have to make sure that no one followed her home. She seemed to be in a splendid mood, giggling, as she promised him to do her best to evade the *Swedish Ladies' Journal* and the gossip columnists.

For several days the Hamilton affair gave Sweden more international press attention than all other Swedish events combined for years.

Within a day at least a billion people saw the "real-life Swedish James Bond" speaking before his country's constitutional committee; Swedish television made a fortune selling its footage. And the slant was quite simple: everyone ran the stories as if they were confirmed. A Western agent, as it said in journalist prose, had crept into the Bear's own lair and right under their noses had liquidated a traitor, and this man was the same mysterious Swedish officer who had averted a hijacking several years ago.

A picture of Carl on the cover of *Time* was headlined THE SPY WHO DID THE IMPOSSIBLE.

It continued like this for several weeks. The reactions of the Swedish press were somewhat more mixed. *Expressen*, which had already committed itself to the indignation angle, had a hard time following the shifting wind and switching to enthusiasm. The editorial pages of *Expressen* and the Moscow-leaning *Northern Flame* and a few other small papers ended up, a minority among the Swedish papers, calling for reason and pointing out the inherent dangers. That opinion was drowned out in the flood of reader and viewer enthusiasm. The afternoon dailies ran huge articles about the rescued Swedish doctors, pictured surrounded by their wives and children, and quoted them thanking Carl Hamilton and defense intelligence for their lives. Interviews with the family members reported their reactions as they sat in front of the television like everybody else and suddenly heard Hamilton reveal the truth about their loved ones' rescue from the kidnappers in Lebanon.

This irresistible kind of journalism is self-perpetuating, what with a flood of favorable letters to the editors, little articles about the thirty-six thousand telegrams and the twenty-two thousand bouquets of flowers that poured into defense headquarters, broadcasts of footage showing trucks loaded with flowers driving up to the door. And it is easy to see why very few politicians could raise objections, no matter how much they may have wanted to. And since they were politicians, they no longer wanted to.

The Attorney General commented dryly that no allegations of any crime had been raised that would give occasion to investigate further. The minister of defense stated that Commander Hamilton had clearly performed an invaluable service for the country, and that if he had been in the government at that time he would not have hesitated to award Carl the commendations he received. This also applied to the operation that must forever remain a secret—yes, he was familiar with the background—where the medal for bravery was the best they could do, given that the Social Democrats, in their zeal for equality, had abolished the old Order of the Sword.

The office of the Marshal of the Realm let it be known in a press communiqué that His Majesty the King had personally decided to award Captain Hamilton the King's medal of the eighth degree, and that the award ceremony would take place on Carl's name day, January 28, of the following year. The medal is worn on the Order of the Seraphim's light-blue ribbon, or is indicated with the same color service ribbon.

Sweden had acquired the world's most famous spy. And the most celebrated.

Fifteen

Joar Lundwall was not freezing or impatient. During an exercise in Alaska he had once sat for thirty-six hours on a similar stakeout in severe cold. This time it was only several degrees below freezing, with a layer of light, powdery snow on the ground and more snow in the air. The risk was that there might be enough snow to show tracks. But that would not influence his own freedom of movement, although it might affect Steelglove.

They were less than a kilometer apart, and theoretically had radio contact. But the short distance and need for other equipment and great freedom of movement meant that they had chosen a very simple radio, transmitting and receiving on an FM band that was easy to pick up and eavesdrop on; even an incomprehensible code would prompt attention. So they were observing radio silence until something happened, if anything ever did happen.

His mother had become suspicious. Like everyone else, she had been glued to the television set when Hamilton was questioned. She was not a suspicious person, but she wasn't stupid, and what she knew about her son was that he had an M.S. in computer science and that now, on his return from America, he had gotten a not very well paid job in defense. When she had tried to telephone him on several occasions, the switchboard had had no knowledge of any Lieutenant Lundwall. He and Steelglove had become lieutenants in the coast artillery. She had been understandably puzzled. She had also noticed that that man Hamilton was in some kind of computer division, and when she asked her son whether he knew Hamilton, he had reacted edgily, and it had nearly ended in a quarrel. Well, it wasn't hard to imagine a mother being uneasy when she suspected that her son had landed in a very dangerous job. He would have to reassure her somehow.

Steelglove apparently did not have this kind of problem.

Lundwall had in some senses modified his view of Steelglove. People had observed that he was the worst sort, and this was still true: strongest in the world, biggest and toughest, a boaster who wouldn't mind being attacked by thugs in some pub just for the pleasure of putting his skills to use. But in some way he had pulled himself together. Before Operation Big Red, Lundwall had thought Steelglove would never be able to handle the civilian studies in San Diego. But after Big Red, he had pulled himself together. Wiretapping techniques were no easier to master than computers, but he had done it. As far as Lundwall could see, and he ought to know, Steelglove had gotten very good at it.

Hamilton probably did not fully realize Steelglove's expertise, but there had been many disruptive events lately. Ironically enough, they had been forbidden to use Steelglove's techniques. Hamilton had spoken in a tone of voice and with a choice of words that left no room for doubt, and Hamilton was probably the only man whom Steelglove recognized as in some ways being stronger than himself—not physically stronger, of course, because no one was. During practice exercises Hamilton had almost as hard a time standing up to Steelglove as Lundwall did. But in real life, when it wasn't an exercise? Then even Steelglove might lose confidence.

It was as if they had an alliance now, the three of them. Even though the operations department was bug free, they never talked about the issue, but now and then they'd glance at each other—just a quick glance that would be meaningless to anyone else around, but for them explained everything. They were the three who had carried out Operation Big Red, the three of them and no one else. And the one who had changed the most, matured the most afterward, was Steelglove. So one thing was clear. There was no problem in carrying out an operation with Steelglove. You could trust him in every sense of the word.

Åke Steelglove was enjoying the situation. He enjoyed hardships, and he enjoyed his own control and lack of impatience. It was already the next day, it was getting dark, and soon parts of the equipment would be unusable, and probably nobody was going to come.

But it was still real work, with everything under control, from his body temperature—all the way down to his feet in the thick, round-toed American Arctic boots that could make your feet sweat even when it was ten degrees below freezing and you were sitting still—to the band of wolfskin around his head and the magnum revolver's secure weight against his body.

In the glade near the house there was apparently something edible, because two deer had appeared several minutes ago. Now they were browsing less than ten yards away; he could have shot both of them with his revolver. The fact that even they weren't aware of him meant that he was well hidden, though of course he was also benefiting from being downwind from them.

Steelglove relished his situation. Now and then the deer would raise their heads and listen and look around; he could see their ears moving. Then they would nervously return to their eating for a while.

He tried to figure out Joar Lundwall. From the start, he thought he was a little shit. A queer, too, and he'd always had trouble with queers. But whoever had been part of Operation Big Red was no shit, and Joar had done very well, no getting around it. Besides, there was no reason to wish himself away from the fundamental relationship. And it was fundamental. Queer or not, Joar was the right stuff. *He wouldn't crack*, he thought in English, as he did now and then.

It hadn't been possible to avoid telling his father, but he was also the only person to whom he had so much as hinted. His father was an old officer, had fought in two wars against the Russians; he wasn't stupid, and he could handle military secrets.

His father had easily put two and two together: the way the JCS had financed Åke's university scholarship in America, his rank as an officer even though he hadn't gone to cadet school, and finally his classified service. Steelglove admitted that he was working directly with Hamilton. And his father had had tears in his eyes, and he hugged his son for the first time since he was a child.

Steelglove had almost told him about Operation Big Red then. But he hadn't, and that was probably lucky. Because it hadn't come out, and those politicians in Parliament obviously hadn't a clue about the matter. Still, their hearing had allowed Steelglove to learn a lot about Hamilton that *he* hadn't had a clue about. Damn, that was a hell of a boss, actually. You could never lose faith in a boss like that. Damn, what he had managed to do!

Big Red had been the biggest. He'd never leak anything about Big Red, but it was a shame that Sweden and Swedish-speaking Finland would never know how the Russians had once been punched in the nose. Only three people in the world knew exactly what had happened. One of them was sitting a few kilometers away, and one thing was clear: It was no problem carrying out an operation together with Joar. You could trust him in every sense of the word.

He heard a signal in his headset.

The warning signal. A message followed about two cars, three or four people, and, after a moment, the distance signals.

Only that. You could always rely on him, queer or not. Steelglove inspected his equipment. Everything was under control, from his own breathing and his body temperature to the apparatus.

Police Inspector Eva-Britt Jönsson—she still refused to use her title —snickered as she pulled on her uniform. She had intended just to drop in for a short visit and talk a little, but there hadn't been much talking. And soon she was supposed to be on duty downtown tonight (they were short on officers).

She looked at Carl as he lay there on the mattress on the floor, pretending to be exhausted, proud of himself and her and both of them. His arms were stretched behind his head, his chest was heaving hard, perhaps with some exaggeration, and the five long scars gleamed in the light from the floor lamp. The room had only a mattress, a floor lamp, and a black military-type radio.

She thought he looked happy.

He had changed after that hearing and was much more like the man she had sailed with at the beginning of the summer. He told her he was freed of everything from the past, that it was all over, that he was turning into an ordinary person—no, a real person, he called it—with an ordinary job like the one he had described to her in the beginning; real life was catching up with the truth, or vice versa.

She decided to think of him as a fighter pilot who had gotten too old to fly missions and was working at headquarters. That's what he had suggested. And though her common sense protested in some ways, the changes had persuaded her emotional sense. He joked and teased her, and he made love as if he had never had any problems; they even played at it, childish games, pretending to be furry animals, rabbits, things like that. All of this was stronger than the dark and dangerous side of him that she imagined behind his terse comments on television. And at work there had hardly been any other topic of conversation for weeks. Most of her colleagues loved Captain Hamilton in their own way, and would have given their lives to be in his uniform instead of their own. If they only knew.

Some of them did, but she had asked them to keep quiet, and they did; among the sailing bunch, they had had no difficulty remembering the naval officer who dived like a seal.

She wasn't using contraception, and he said that he wouldn't mind if she got pregnant. No, that's not what he said; he said he would like her to get pregnant, since real people had children.

"So, finished and ready and I'm late and the thugs will be calling if I don't run," she said happily as she buttoned the last buttons on her shirt with the insignia of her rank on the upper left sleeve and the word POLICE above her left breast pocket.

"Do you have time to look at a few photographs?" he asked as he opened his eyes and blinked at the light. He reached his hand under the mattress and pulled out a stack of enlargements, which he quickly spread out under the floor lamp. She wasn't the least bit suspicious as she walked over and looked at the pictures. They looked like pictures from a stakeout, taken with a telephoto lens in unfavorable lighting conditions; men getting in and out of cars. The usual.

"Cops," he said curtly. "But the question is, which cops?"

She glanced through the pictures, nodding now and then with growing recognition.

"The Leather Gang," she said shortly with a sudden growing uneasiness. "Why are you photographing them?"

"Possibly because they're murdering Swedish military officers," he said bluntly, pushing himself into a sitting position with his legs crossed.

"How do you know?" she asked cautiously.

"I don't, but I think so. What does the Leather Gang mean in your circles?"

"Are you asking me as a cop or as a potential mother?"

"As a cop. First as a cop."

"You can't get involved in criminal investigations, can you?"

"No, that's just it. So let's take the formal route. As a cop, to whom do you report suspicions of a crime?"

"To my superiors, I assume."

She knelt down and quickly glanced through the pictures again.

"Isn't it possible that you might, according to regulations, report it to the superior cop who's in charge of the criminal investigation?"

"Yes, even better. Carl, dear, I'm in a hurry."

"On the back of the top picture there is the name and telephone number of the superintendent in Norrköping. See that he gets the pictures and give him my regards; I owe him a few favors. But see that it's some kind of official business from 'anonymous sources' or whatever you call it. Identify the ones you can."

"Will this be a breakthrough?"

"I don't know. Maybe. We think these guys have something to do with the case. The one in the middle is named Glücher and is *Expressen*'s source. We don't know who the others are, unless you do. We'll talk more about all of this later."

"Not a very romantic way to say goodbye."

"Oh yes, it is. It would have been less romantic to take this up in the beginning when you got here, if nothing else because we would have been cops instead of rabbits, and this way, amazingly, we got to be both." His laughter was infectious. "You can find your way out? First around the block and then down to Strandvägen?"

"Don't worry, this area is part of VD1; it's our district."

"Take care of yourself."

"You too."

She glanced at her watch and quickly picked up the pictures and left. On her way out she stopped in the doorway and winked at him. "Rabbit, rabbit," she said, shutting the door.

Carl got up at once and went out to take a shower. In the empty bathroom there was a bar of soap, a tube of toothpaste, and a plastic bottle of shampoo, but no towel.

In the other quite empty room of the apartment a knapsack stood in the middle of an otherwise completely bare, newly polished oak parquet floor. It was one of the Old Man's apartments that was not yet in use. Carl couldn't live at home anymore, partly because of the unremitting journalists' siege, and partly for security reasons. The *police*, as the Old Man said in his special, ironic tone of voice whenever he talked about Säpo, had come up with the reasonable idea that Carl's life was now in danger. Not because any foreign service might want to go after him, but because about a thousand crackpots in Sweden might want to go down in history as "the man who shot Liberty Valance." In Näslund's estimation, Carl Hamilton had become some kind of thirty-point buck for the crackpots. So Säpo had recommended that for the time being they keep Carl company, which he as well as defense headquarters had rejected with a mixture of disgust and terror, politely but firmly turning down the offer, referring to operational reasons and to the fact that the intelligence service was not lacking in resources to protect its own personnel.

There was reason to be very cautious. Not only because they actually had an operation under way against their own security service, but with the best of intentions.

Näslund was worried. Ever since all the harping about its being Säpo's fault that a prime minister had been murdered years before, they didn't really want to be dragged into another political murder. And he said so, even though it was probably a slip of the tongue.

Carl punched in the prearranged signal on his radio when he was ready to leave. This meant that within minutes Lundwall and Steelglove would take off in separate cars and in separate directions from the operations department garage, each on his way to a different subway station.

And so it didn't really matter whether Säpo attempted any kind of discreet observation of their own.

Carl drove for half an hour before he found a suitable parking place near the suitable subway station. He relied on smoke-colored glasses and loose-fitting clothing to disguise him among the crowds of people in the subway. People wouldn't believe that the man who reminded them of someone they had seen somewhere was really Carl Gustaf Gilbert Hamilton, at the moment the world's most famous spy.

Then up to a new train and then the usual routine until he quite calmly could approach the meeting place in Hässelby.

Yuri Chivartshev turned up on the dot at exactly the right street corner, and Carl didn't even have to stop his car entirely before the Soviet spy chief was sitting comfortably with his seat belt fastened, precisely as if he were a Swede.

"It's nice dealing with a pro. The common opinion among us here in the West is that you are still the best in the world," Carl greeted him as he headed the car in the darkest possible direction.

"You're much too kind, Captain," chuckled Chivartshev. "How far have you gotten with the enemy's enemy?" he continued, more businesslike.

"The situation is complicated," said Carl, genuinely worried. "And by that I don't mean in technical or surveillance or operational terms, but in a bureaucratic or legal sense. I have very strict instructions. Our enemy is to be found inside the Swedish police, right?"

"Yes, we already know that," said Chivartshev dryly.

"But for Swedish intelligence to act against Swedish authorities is practically the same thing as if you went up against the Chekists; there would be problems."

"In a situation like this, can't you get the backing of the party—the government?"

"Yes, maybe after the fact. But my freedom of movement is rather restricted by recent events."

Chivartshev burst out in loud laughter. "Young captain! Not only do you adopt the rather eccentric method, in our profession, of appearing on television all over the world, but you have a sense of humor too."

"What did you think about the performance?" Carl smiled uncertainly in the darkness.

"From the Soviet Union's point of view, I can't report any objections at all. Those people in the Security Police at—what was it you called it—the monkey house, don't know anything about your diving activities, do they? And parliament doesn't either?"

"But by implication, you do, Colonel?" Carl looked in his rearview mirror. A car that had been behind them for a while had just turned off and disappeared.

"Well, Captain. Most often secrets don't get out. Sometimes they do get out, but most often they don't, and that's lucky for us. Do you have any suggestions?"

"Yes, but I'm going to end up on the verge of technically being regarded as a Soviet spy, and that's not exactly what I had in mind in life."

Chivartshev laughed again, but this time there seemed to be no reason for it. "You know what, young captain? I had planned to end my long career by recruiting you. I was actually having thoughts like that as I followed your extraordinary pretense of deterioration in Moscow: the unhappy young attaché, bitter at his superiors, forever excluded from important assignments, and all that. That was about what you intended, I assume?"

"Yes, that's what I intended. Sometimes I thought it was too transparent."

"It was, but it was so *Russian*, and we couldn't believe you'd be bold enough to play it in the Russian style in Moscow. Well, that's all over. Can we do business?"

"Yes, that's what I'm brooding over. The question is whether we can go any further without me recruiting you or vice versa."

"You're either being impudent or you don't know what you're saying."

"There's an envelope on the back seat. In it is all the information on Glücher—that's his name, your *Expressen* source—and pictures of what we assume are his collaborators. We haven't identified them yet."

"What's the problem?"

"We can't wiretap them; it's strictly against the law. And, of course, I can't ask you for that favor or even hint at it, since it would breach my orders and the law as well."

"Of course." Chivartshev looked very serious. "I understand what you're saying."

"I need a trade."

"To even things up, in case the auditors demand an accounting?"

"Something like that. Do you have a trade to offer, Colonel?"

There was a pause, and Carl devoted his attention to his driving. For the second time he was playing it like a Russian with the Russians themselves. It was foolhardy. But Säpo—in his eyes the worst security police in the West—would otherwise have sole responsibility for tracking down and annihilating the enemy's enemy. A choice between the GRU and Säpo wasn't really a choice at all. As long as they were looking for the enemy's enemy.

"Young captain," said Chivartshev after a very long silence. "How nice it would be if you were one of us—no, I just mean it as a general observation. I have the following suggestion. Give me the material. Withdraw your own operatives. If I can deliver results you can use, then we'll make a deal. This would be the proper way to propose a trade."

"No matter what the circumstances or conditions, you will have to leave the final phase to us, if there ever is such a thing."

"Yes, that's clear. God save me from any other alternative; it's a matter of your own police, after all, your own Chekists."

"Fine. If I'm going to prepare my own half of the deal, can you give me a hint what the price is?"

"Yes. We have a problem, a big problem. It's really bothering us."

"And what's that?"

"How did you find that informer, what's his name, in Moscow?"

"Sandström?"

"Exactly."

"Is that what's worrying you?"

"Correct."

"Who the traitor is in the GRU, or whether there's some other explanation?"

"Correct. That's our price."

"I'll have to let you off at the next station."

They continued in silence. Carl tried for a moment to systematize his own legal knowledge about the fine line between espionage and nonespionage. If Chivartshev were representing the United States and he had been some other captain, he thought to himself, it would hardly have been an issue, either legally or morally. But he wasn't anyone else, and Chivartshev was the GRU.

As he drew up near a safe subway station, he turned to look directly at the Resident. He could not see the expression on the other man's face; it was too dark.

"Okay," he said as he stopped the car. "We have a deal. You can have what you want. And then I want to ask for something that I know you can do and that doesn't even involve lawbreaking on your part. Can we meet according to the previous schedule?"

"Yes," said Chivartshev, putting out his hand for a firm and rather extended handshake. "We'll meet according to the agreed-upon schedule." He climbed out of the car, turned around, and glanced swiftly at Carl, smiling broadly. "So now we'll see who recruits whom; who's going to make the big break—you or me?"

And then he quickly closed the car door and stuffed the envelope inside his coat.

Surely the last remark was a joke.

It was possible Carl was committing a crime of some kind. But that wouldn't be known before the enemy's enemy had been tracked down and annihilated; "the final phase," to use the Russian's term. And who would worry about laws and the constitution then?

The Old Man had managed to get rid of his civilian companion temporarily—they were all still having a hard time thinking of the defense minister's buddy as the new SSI chief—and this meant that all three of them felt freer in both talking and making decisions.

But they had been captured by television just as the meeting was about to begin—Sam had a set in his office.

There was Peter Sorman on the screen, straight from Havana in a white linen suit—suntanned, hatchet-faced, cocksure, and just about as devious as you might expect.

He swore over and over again to the cameras that before sending Captain Hamilton to Lebanon there had never been mention of anything other than that Hamilton should try to establish radio contact if he happened to get in touch with the kidnappers. Indeed, Sorman had carefully instructed Hamilton not to take any kind of weapon in his baggage or to requisition any. An express prohibition against the use of weapons couldn't very well be misunderstood. Yes, in a sense it was true that Hamilton had been instructed to use his contacts in the Middle East, but Sorman had made no recommendations, and he said he didn't even know that the PLO had a special intelligence service.

They had met briefly when Carl turned in his passport upon his return home, but with no mention of any military operations. As far as Sorman knew, the diplomatic negotiations alone, and nothing else, had led to the release of the two Swedish doctors, and he would be surprised if Hamilton's version were correct. But there was no reason to believe it.

Yes, he realized this meant that Hamilton would have given a completely false version of the parts he himself knew about. Yes, this could be interpreted to mean that Hamilton had lied.

No, the hijacking story was true, on the other hand. Sorman was not familiar with the German project; that was a matter for the police, but that story might be true too.

No, except in the case of the two doctors, Sorman could not accuse Hamilton of lying, but that was certainly bad enough. It was also hard to explain, but possibly the armed forces were feeling pressured by the current publicity.

Since Hamilton had received no assignment other than as a radio operator, the question of the government's involvement was purely academic; Sorman himself had naturally never referred to "the government" during his brief and uneventful conversation with Hamilton.

Why hadn't it been eventful? Well, it didn't concern any armed action or anything else out of the ordinary; it was simply about establishing a certain type of radio communication. Yes, intelligence personnel were suited to this sort of assignment because they had both the equipment and the technique; besides, in a purely bureaucratic sense, it was practical, since Carl already had diplomatic status, an advantage in even a rather trivial assignment in a country like Lebanon.

That a prime minister in a previous government had decided to award Hamilton a medal could not be taken as a sign of anything other than that he had wanted personally to reward a policeman who had carried out a difficult and dramatic assignment. No, Sorman had never heard mention of a second medal of this type, and thus had no opinion as to what might have been rewarded or commended. He could not, however, imagine any kind of political "sanction" for either action, and since he had never heard mention of Hamilton in connection with such dramatic circumstances as might reasonably be expected in relation to a second medal, he personally doubted that he had one. No, he couldn't say that it was a lie, but he had his doubts; perhaps the former prime minister ought to be questioned.

Samuel Ulfsson turned off the television and thoughtfully walked over to his desk. "Does this mean problems for us, and if so, what?" he muttered as he pulled out another pack of cigarettes from his desk drawer.

"There's going to be a lot of crap in *Expressen*," said the Old Man.

"What was his reason for lying? I can understand that he didn't want to be connected to anything relating to Big Red, but why did he lie about the doctors?" wondered Carl.

"He's hurt. You took away the glory. Or else it has something to do with the government's culpability or lack thereof. Maybe he didn't have the mandate to give you instructions on behalf of the government, but he regarded himself as the government anyway. Something like that. We still have to assume that your version is the correct one and not his, don't we?" asked Ulfsson, regretting the remark at once when he saw Carl's face. "No, forget it; I take it back."

So. A certain superintendent Glücher in the Russian Bureau of Säpo had some strange hanky-panky going on with some tough Stockholm policemen known as the Leather Gang. They were right-wing extremists of some kind; they had even come under suspicion during the time when the search for the prime minister's murderer was at its most chaotic. And Glücher was leading the propaganda campaign in *Expressen*. The question now was, first, whether this hanky-panky had any connection with the murders, and second, what they ought to do about it.

It was a police matter—that's what Näslund would say. But it wasn't a pleasant thought to turn over suspicions like this to Näslund, whose men would rush to their telephones to tell the media that defense authorities were spying on the police, singling out a police officer, and so on. At the same time, the situation might be dangerous.

Sitting there with their arms crossed, waiting for new acts of terror, was so risky that the legality of such passivity might even be debatable.

Could they go to the government? No, then the government would have to go to Näslund, and things would turn out the same.

JK or R? No, it would just end up with Näslund.

"I've taken certain liberties," Carl reported reluctantly after a while. Conversation ceased at once. The others looked at him expectantly.

"I've passed on our information to the police, or rather to Superintendent Rune Jansson in Norrköping—he's the one in charge of the investigation there. I thought officially it couldn't be regarded as wrong."

"How did you do it?" asked the Old Man.

"Anonymously through an intermediary police officer, so we have transmitted the information through official channels. We won't have to explain to Näslund exactly how we know Glücher's identity. That's how I thought of it, at any rate."

"It wouldn't have hurt if you had told one of us first," grumbled Ulfsson, but he looked more thoughtful than displeased.

"Well yes," said the Old Man, "but the way things stand now, we won't have to make the decision; and going to the police with information which rightfully belongs to them can't be improper, and now we'll avoid Näslund and his publicity merry-go-round."

"The other question is, though, how are we going to deal with our own publicity merry-go-round?" Ulfsson asked this almost in passing. "The Chief is after me to get Carl to give some interviews and so on, and the pressure won't be any less now that Sorman has made us look like liars. Will Carl's honest blue eyes be enough, or is there some other way?"

"Naturally there's no other way," said Carl impulsively. "What Sorman hasn't thought of is that the PLO don't want my story contradicted; it was a joint Swedish-Palestinian operation, and the PLO received certain political promises from me which I passed on to them, on Sorman's instructions."

"You haven't reported that before," said the Old Man with a mixture of disapproval and surprise.

"No, I thought it was of minor importance. Sorman promised them a visa for a new representative at the PLO office in Stockholm and several other things. But these don't matter anymore, now that there are members of the People's Party in the government."

"Whatever are you talking about?" Ulfsson was astonished.

"Those people hate Arabs, especially the PLO, but that doesn't prevent the PLO from wanting to join in and bask in the glory of the rescue operation. They have only two alternatives now, for or against, and naturally they will choose for."

"I know a journalist I think you know," said the Old Man cautiously. Carl clenched his teeth. O.M. continued. "I think it would be a good idea for you to refute Sorman yourself, and to set up a good contact with the PLO so that they will support you."

"Why is that such a good idea?" asked Carl doggedly. He despised the very thought of reporters.

"First, because *we* can't very well have a liar as a department chief in the intelligence service—and, well, that should be enough. You have to come out of this affair white as snow."

"And which journalist are you thinking of? If you say Wennström or anyone at *Expressen* I'll commit hara-kiri on the spot."

The Old Man's big bushy eyebrows shot up to their owl position, and he smiled at Carl almost with a sneer as he paused before answering. "No," he said at last, "*Expressen* probably wouldn't be appropriate. What would you think about the radio, the 'Echo of the Day' program, for example?"

"You mean Erik Ponti?"

"Yes, you know him; he helped you with some operation, if I'm not mistaken, didn't he?"

"Yes, that's right."

"So what about Ponti?"

"Would he be enough?"

"Yes, if you go on radio with information that's interesting enough, the others will copy it, that's the way things are," concluded Ulfsson. It was something he had picked up from the Chief, who in turn had mobilized half the psych department of the Defense Ministry to teach him the art of carrying out a propaganda war in his own country.

That very day Carl received Erik Ponti at his temporary residence, still bare of furniture. Ponti was wearing a hunting jacket—perhaps the same jacket he had worn four years earlier when an overly enthusiastic Säpo man accused him of killing a policeman. That seemed a long time ago, and Ponti's hair had started turning gray, but he still looked fit.

Carl showed his guest into the completely empty living room, where he had placed the floor lamp from his bedroom, and they sat down in a corner with their backs against the walls. Ponti had a big tape recorder over one shoulder and a package of extra tapes in a briefcase that also contained notes and a notepad.

"What are you planning to ask about?" wondered Carl as Ponti began to hook up his equipment.

"First, about what Sorman said to the committee today—that's the news angle, after all. Then there are probably thousands of other interesting questions."

"Not so likely that you'll get an answer."

"No, probably not. We might as well start on what we *can* talk about. It's about time."

"What do you mean?"

"I helped you when you were at Säpo and wanted contact with Jihaz-ar-Rased, which you evidently got, and then you got on the right track, didn't you?"

"Yes. You could hardly avoid noticing when things came to a head."

"The massacre in Viggbyholm?"

"Exactly. There's one thing I've always wondered about, and maybe you could give me an answer."

"What's that?"

"The next day *Expressen* was full of information about Libyan terrorists; it seemed like a campaign prepared in advance. Was it?"

"Of course, that's probably just what they're doing now."

"The Israelis had tipped off the company that there was going to be a Libyan or Palestinian terrorist action, but how the hell could *Expressen* latch on to it so fast?"

"Because either the Israeli sources or their Säpo sources told them."

"And then you reporters just write it up; I've never understood that. They say that that man Wennström is supposed to get some big journalism prize. Is what he's doing considered admirable in your field?"

"Sure. Big headlines, big sales, and heroic deeds in investigative reporting."

"Then you might as well send that prize straight to the source at Säpo who invented the story."

"Sure, and a couple of years ago when *Expressen* ran stories about scandalous Swedish business deals with Libya, they could have sent the prize straight to Mossad. Some people write from dictation, that's the way it is."

"What if it's all wrong?"

"That can't usually be proved when it's Säpo material. How could the Kurds prove they *didn't* murder our prime minister?"

"But this agent war doesn't exist."

"No, I understand that. Give me a series of in-depth interviews and I'll get a prize too, at the same time as your friend Wennström."

"Very funny."

"That's the way things work. Right now you're a worldwide scoop because you haven't said a word since the hearing."

"Why does *Expressen* want it to look like war with the Soviet Union?"

"They don't. They just want big headlines about something that's their exclusive and they have sources for, which they have because they have Säpo. So the question is, Why does Säpo want it to look as if you, and not them, is at war with the GRU and the KGB?"

"They probably don't. The Säpo leadership doesn't believe in it any more than we do, and Näslund assures us that it's not one of their propaganda ploys."

"Do you believe him?"

"Yes, for once I believe Näslund."

"You're not especially good friends, are you?"

"No, but you're sitting there interviewing me and we haven't even discussed what we're going to talk about."

"On the one hand, you can say things on tape under your own name—the whole thing about Sorman, for example. On the other you can give me information as an anonymous source; then I'll call you a well-informed intelligence source and keep your identity to myself."

"How can I trust you on that?"

"Because you're protected by the constitution, and I would be committing a crime if I revealed your identity against your will."

Carl uttered a sound that was a cross between a laugh and a sneer. "A breach of the constitution! Some people think that's the same thing as a breach of parking regulations."

"Sure, but for me it's my bread and butter. The day that I'm compared with someone like Wennström at *Expressen* I might as well throw in the towel. So here's the important question. Is there any connection between the campaign that's in *Expressen* and those murders, which have actually taken place, and what kind of connection is it?"

"Straight to the heart of the matter."

"Yes, that's how it has to be."

"I can't answer that question, no matter how much I'd like to."

"Hey! This is serious. Why don't you create a counterattack? Why won't you defend yourself? You can imagine how it's going to look in *Expressen* tomorrow."

"No. How?"

"The slipping halo. That's how it started for Ollie North. The truth is beginning to seep out about that so-called hero who takes the truth as lightly as he does people's lives. The fascist superhuman ideal. He has to be stopped. Investigative commissions, the end of the espionage service's independence in Sweden. Et cetera. Shall I go on?"

"No, that's convincing enough."

"So what can we say in tomorrow's broadcast? How will you refute Sorman's allegations?"

"There's one other party you can check with."

"Who's that?"

"The PLO."

"I've already done that." Ponti broke into a smile when he saw Carl's surprise.

"What did they say?"

"Sources with Jihaz-ar-Rased confirm the incident and have described it in great detail for me."

"By telephone?"

"Yes. After all, it concerns matters they want to make known at all costs."

"I'll be damned. That was fast work. I thought I was going to give you a tip."

"If you shoot with firearms, I shoot with journalism—the opposite probably wouldn't be a good thing for either of us."

"Do you know how to shoot?"

"Yes, deer and rabbits and occasionally not even that, but still I assume I'm a better marksman than you are a journalist. I'm going to be in contact with Arafat some time tonight when he reaches his headquarters in Tunis. He will confirm your version. But now I want you to convince me too."

"Isn't Arafat good enough?"

"No, they have a vested interest in going with your version in order to borrow a little of your hero's halo. So, one of the kidnappers stood out from the rest in some way. How?"

"His name was Karim, and he was a bright, intelligent boy, about seventeen years old."

"Actually, he was only sixteen. What kind of weapon did you use?"

"A semi-automatic gun with a silencer, brand name Ingram, and two knives, although I only used one of them."

"How did you kill one of the guards?"

"There was only one guard."

"Right. But how did you do it?"

"I killed him."

"Yes. But how?"

"Standard military procedure."

"That's obvious, given the situation. You're not answering my question."

"Is that a serious, journalistic inquiry?"

"Yes."

"In what way? It sounds more like *Expressen* than 'Echo of the Day' to me."

"Look, I don't want to know so I can tell my listeners; I want to know if you tell the same version as my PLO sources. If not, somebody is lying."

"Would you like a glass of wine?"

"Yes, thanks. But not instead of an answer to my question."

Carl gave him a crooked smile and went out to the kitchen. He took a bottle of wine out of the refrigerator and remembered that in a cupboard he had put a six-pack of cheap wine glasses he had bought on his way home. He opened the bottle and wrestled for a moment with the plastic wrap around the wine glasses before he gave up and went into his temporary bedroom and took out a knife from under his mattress. Back in the kitchen, cutting off the plastic wrap, he realized it was the same type of knife he had used in Lebanon. He put it down slowly and stared at it lying on the stainless steel counter, lit from the side by the lamp above the sink. A black, nonreflecting blade. Camouflage-colored handle made of light metal, welded to the knife blade.

He had to pull himself together for a few moments before he was able to go back to Ponti with the wine bottle in one hand and two glasses in the other. He didn't say a word as he served the wine and then raised his glass, nodding briefly.

"I'm not planning to comment on the wine until you answer my question," said Ponti.

"I severed his spinal cord and his aorta three or four vertebrae up from his lower back, if that's of any interest," replied Carl in a neutral tone, his face turned away.

Ponti sipped his wine, letting it roll around in his mouth, and held the glass under the lamp, as if trying to ascertain the color.

"This is not exactly Bulgarian table wine," he said after a moment. "Radio Sweden's salary level isn't adequate for something like this. But then, we've had a Communist union since the 1960s. Burgundy, but I wouldn't dare guess the district."

"Meursault. Are you interested in wine?"

"Yes, so long as the money holds out."

"Then we have at least one interest in common."

"Two, if we include our politics. So, your version agrees with the PLO's. I can report it as true with comments from you and Arafat. Sorman is fried. Great—it's not often anyone can touch him."

"Just because you report it on 'Echo of the Day'?"

"Yes, this isn't *Expressen*, this is the voice of the nation."

"And if you hadn't believed me or us?"

"Then I wouldn't have done the story, notwithstanding the burgundy or anything else. Very simple. Can we start taping your version and your comments on Sorman now?"

The first interview segment was quickly done. Then Ponti dragged out of Carl some cautiously reluctant rebuttals to *Expressen*'s notions of the agent war, and they broke off. For a while they drank the wine in silence.

"I heard that *Stern* offered you five million marks for exclusive rights to your memoirs," said Ponti matter-of-factly as he held out his glass for a refill.

"Yes, but an American publisher bid higher. They're crazy."

"Interested?"

"No, not at all. It's not my job to sell military secrets—on the contrary."

"As long as you're not reporting them for free to a parliamentary committee?"

"Yes, well, I talked only about things that had already appeared, more or less correctly, in *Expressen*. It would have been ridiculous to deny them; at least so the Chief thought, and he was right. Still, it was a strange experience."

"So five million marks or whatever is a speculation on what you didn't talk about?"

"Apparently."

"Is it worth it?"

"I'm not a journalist, you know. But I could get at least as much from the Russians, tax free, in a more discreet transaction, with life imprisonment in Sweden as the only risk."

"But the Russians already know whether you killed Sandström."

"Yes, they know."

"And you don't plan to confirm it?"

"You want your worldwide scoop for free?"

"Yes, preferably. You know how much tax there is on an income of fifteen million kronor."

"Yes, if it's counted as author's royalties, it's fourteen million and something; so 'Echo of the Day' is in the running, since the difference wouldn't be so great."

"According to the latest report, your fortune is up over thirty million."

"Yes, but that's a fictitious world—it might be twice that or half that, but it's enough for the burgundy, anyway."

"And two million to the Afghanistan drive."

"Yes, for example. Thanks for your help, by the way. It was nice of you not to let on my identity or steal the money."

"Since when have Clarté people stolen from each other?"

"Are you still in Clarté?"

"A subscriber, not a member. What about you?"

"Not even a subscriber."

"Where do you stand politically?"

"I can only define it negatively. Not a Moscow Communist, not a Swedish Communist, not a Social Democrat, who the hell knows? What about you?"

"About the same. But I have a professional excuse: 'The truth is always revolutionary,' you know. I'm against all politicians, and I've paid for it. That wasn't what we had in mind back then, was it, when we were going to infiltrate the mass media, crush the bourgeois pro-imperialist dominance and all that. You belonged to the comrades who were going to infiltrate the defense establishment, didn't you?"

"Yes, and you might say that I succeeded. Many other comrades were purged because they were listed in Säpo's files as traitors, and it was a pretty close call for me."

"Were you called a traitor?"

"Well, a number of security people seemed to think that was the right label."

"They'd prefer to forget about it today, wouldn't they?"

"Well, you know how things like that go. Now I've proven that I'm a very clever traitor who's disguised myself as the opposite, just as you're an adroit imitation journalist, which proves you're a traitor."

"Is that what they think?"

"Yes, I read reports like that about you and some others."

"Could you get a copy?"

"What for?"

"To publish."

"You're crazy! We're starting to talk too much without guidelines—you keep on getting me to say too much. Let's make an agreement. What else do you want besides Sandström's murder?"

"The truth about the agent war."

"Fine. Then once we make an agreement we can see how much the constitution is worth."

Carl quickly sketched out a fairly formal agreement. If any type of verifiable truth about the agent war should be established in Carl's interview, Ponti would get an exclusive on it, including anonymously supplied background information and direct interviews. Only that and nothing more.

Ponti pondered this for a moment with his wine glass held up in front of his eyes. Then he gulped down the rest of the wine and sat in silence, his eyes closed, before speaking. He formulated his words with care, yet did not seem to expect a reply.

"There's another alternative. I could report your whole story but fudge some of the details. That would be reporting and not reporting at the same time, and many people would understand it. What you're doing has a bigger effect on more Swedish citizens than those big shots sitting in the government or the defense leadership."

"No," said Carl. But he promised to keep his side of the original bargain.

Afterward he regretted it, but real people keep their promises; it's only spies who regard promises the way some people regard the constitution.

Sixteen

Chivartshev put off all further meetings with Carl for a week. If the prearranged phone signal, with specific timed lapses and a specific number of rings, finally did come, Carl was to know that something important was about to happen. At last the phone rang, and Carl tried to persuade himself to stay calm. Chivartshev might just as well be getting into his car with clockwork precision outside Midsommarkransen subway station to report negative results.

Both Joar and Åke noticed that he was tense and that something special was going on. Carl had called another meeting with both of them for later in the evening, superseding any private plans they might have had.

It was quite unnecessary to specify this last item. They more or less knew what was going on, and why Carl had suddenly pulled back their own operative efforts, even though he hadn't explained it. They didn't know what Näslund was up to, but at worst a problem may have come up with Glücher. It would be bad enough if Säpo and the GRU ran into each other; if the SSI landed in the same fix, a swarm of misunderstandings would ensue.

Chivartshev arrived with the same clockwork precision as on previous occasions, and once again Carl's car didn't even have to make a full stop before he had climbed in and fastened his seat belt.

They drove for a while in silence as Carl concentrated on the routine pattern of checkpoints and evasive maneuvers.

"Well," he said simply after five or six minutes, decreasing his speed to indicate the maneuvering was over.

"Our situation is extraordinarily grave," began Chivartshev gloomily.

Carl did not reply.

"The fascist and anti-Soviet extremist forces behind this disinformation campaign have now also committed terrorist acts," he continued. "They are now desperate, and they'll try to strengthen their weakened position with new displays. *Expressen* is tipped off and lying in wait."

"Did the tip come by phone?" In this situation there ought to be a good chance of tapping Glücher's phone legally.

"No, they don't dare use the phone anymore. They've seen indications that somebody may be bugging them."

"You?"

"No, the people in the monkey house. They're not as discreet as they should be. Well, we've used that in the past, but right now it's not an advantage."

"But they've still got some plan?"

"Yes. You know, it's our turn to murder you, in a manner of speaking, in this so-called agent war."

"Swedish officers?"

"Correct."

"Do you know when and where?"

"Yes, with great probability. We're getting closer to our deal, young captain."

"Yes, it seems to look that way. But there are certain mutual problems to take care of first."

"Mmm. Tomorrow is St. Lucia's Day, the queen of light. The coast artillery academy in Vaxholm is having a party in one of their dining halls, a Christmas party for officers in their training course. The party will be attacked."

"Do you know when? How many people in the strike force?"

"Three or four men with automatic weapons. Presumably toward the end of the party, but before people start going home. The party starts at seven o'clock—shall we say toward nine?"

"Do you know for sure or are you guessing?"

"The target and the attack were discussed but not the specific time yet."

"What's the purpose?"

"To change the political climate, I suppose. They think that the Western world, including Sweden, has let itself be seduced by glasnost and all that, and they want to warn their own people, and of course realign the security service."

"It sounds strangely similar to ordinary European terrorism: false consciousness through provocation."

"But this is hardly any leftist deviation; this is fascist terrorism, and it's a serious threat to both the Soviet Union and Sweden, not to mention relations between them."

"The enemy's enemy."

"Yes, but the phrase isn't quite correct. Our common enemy."

"Do you have tapes with you today too?"

"No, that obviously caused too much trouble last time, so you're getting this information orally, in concentrated form."

"Then the question arises whether this is a trap or provocation on your part."

"Captain. You know we don't commit individual acts of terrorism, and we know you don't. Why should either of us start now?"

"Logical."

"Yes, logical. It doesn't really matter to me what you do with the information now, but it *is* important, isn't it?"

"Yes, if your information is correct, then it's absolutely crucial. We may see the end of this terrorism within a day, but that remains to be seen."

"I'd suggest that you name your price."

"Okay. You'll find out within twenty-four hours how this develops, and if it goes off without a hitch, then our deal is on—shall we say that?"

"Yes, that sounds fine."

"Here's my price. You know who Irina Dzerzhinskaya is?"

"Of course, your unsuspecting communications conduit with my not very esteemed colleagues."

"I understand that she can't very well be allowed to emigrate after what happened. But I want to see a debut concert in Moscow and a review, preferably positive."

"I don't know whether we have that kind of influence."

"Of course you do."

"That's your price?"

"Correct."

"A debut concert, acceptance on the concert circuit and so on, and a reasonably favorable review?"

"Correct."

"That's not so easy, in these new times."

"I can't exactly feel sorry about that."

"Well, you ought to in this case. I honestly don't know whether we can influence such cultural-political processes."

"Do it anyway."

"And we'll get a verifiable, definite indication as to how you found your way so well in Moscow?"

"Yes, precisely."

"I've noted your request, but I can't make any promises."

"No debut concert, no deal."

"Then for the present there's nothing left for me but to wish you happy hunting, my honored colleague."

Carl's nervous but systematic preparations began that very night. There could only be a few hours' sleep before the St. Lucia celebrations.

Steelglove and Lundwall took off immediately for Vaxholm for the first outdoor reconnaissance. When they were able to make some rough outline sketches of the area, they quickly drew up a preliminary strategy.

The first thing they would do in the morning would be to get themselves uniforms, the coast artillery's new blue uniforms with the onion-shaped eyelets and all the accessories. They would have to appear as perfect lieutenants, and no expense would be spared, even for Steelglove's possible fitting problems. They would have to be finished with that before noon.

Lundwall would contact the head of the academy and see to it that he and Steelglove were invited to the party. There shouldn't be any difficulties; two commandos who had become officers and worked at OP5—those were good enough qualifications.

Unfortunately, there would be no blue and yellow service ribbons of a certain type on their uniforms because that item, considering how things stood after the committee hearing and all that, would stir up speculation. Regrettable, but that's the way things were. Steelglove grumbled a little, but accepted it.

At five in the morning Carl called and woke up Samuel Ulfsson. An hour later they met in the darkened and apparently completely deserted defense headquarters.

Carl felt they were treading gingerly, but they tried to be systematic in their discussion. First, they agreed this might be a trap set by the Russians, but that was extremely unlikely. Second, it was probably a matter for the police, but they didn't know who or which police to involve, and they were dealing with an organization famous for leaks. Talking to the police was like talking to *Expressen*.

When Carl showed his sketches of the target layout, Ulfsson, relieved, noted that it lay on military territory, and that changed the situation.

Now they were approaching the part where the important thing was not to say too much. Anything could go wrong, and then whose responsibility would it be? On the other hand, if they didn't strike now and take those gangsters, who would do it? Näslund? And at what cost? After more agent wars?

"Here are your instructions," Ulfsson said at last, very thoughtfully. "Obviously you'll have to appear as uniformed military guards. Study all the orders for their conduct. You are to serve as guards this evening, and you will be responsible for the most advantageous tactical plans you can think up in that context. Clear? Understood?"

"Yes, quite clear."

"Fine, then we're done. You can reach me at home by phone tonight."

Carl had some difficulty finding the right department in the defense building to get printed instructions from, but he was soon studying the regulations for military guards. Had Ulfsson known about these surprising rules? Carl found them astonishing.

Around nine o'clock he got a phone call from the police in Norrköping, a call that had evidently been sent back and forth through the switchboard several times until it finally, quite by accident, reached Carl's extension in the hallway behind Ulfsson's office.

"It's damned difficult to get hold of you," Superintendent Rune Jansson greeted him.

"Yes," muttered Carl, "I have a supposedly secret job here. At least just for today."

"You were damned terrific on TV. The whole paddy wagon here was sitting in front of the tube that day, and as far as we can tell the crooks were doing the same. Crime was way down."

"Why, thank you. Is this why you phoned?"

"Thanks for the material."

"We thought it belonged with you. Has it been any help?"

"Yes, a breakthrough."

"Good. How?"

"An old lady in Linköping had a visit from one of the presumed murderers, a big thug who showed her police ID. We have reason to believe that the murderers were looking for pilots home alone that day, more or less haphazardly. So there's a witness."

"And she identified a certain big police officer whose picture you got from me?"

"Yes, it's a good make on the photo."

"Have you identified him?"

"Yes. Do you know anything about the Leather Gang in Stockholm?"

"Yes, sure."

"So now my question is . . . I'm not going to get any of that shit like last time about national interests and so on, am I?"

"No, no, I know what you mean. No, these guys are enemies of the nation, and the sooner you take them out the better."

"Well, I wanted to make sure before we pick them up."

"Do you have anything else besides that witness? I'm not a policeman, but one old lady seems rather thin."

"The forensics lab has come up with a whole bunch of technical stuff. Fibers from the front seat of the getaway car matching a sofa at one of the murder scenes. Nylon wool of some kind, might be a Helly-Hansen hunting type of jacket. Other things of that type."

"Police officers ought to know enough to get rid of all the clothes they were wearing during the crime, don't you think?"

"Yes, you'd think so. You did, in any event."

"No comment. That wasn't why you called, was it?"

"No, goddammit. I wanted to know if there were any obstacles this time."

"Säk, maybe."

"Exactly. When we requested a wiretap on a guy, it turned out that he was already being tapped. What does Säk know?"

"They know that Glücher is *Expressen*'s source, but I don't know whether they've connected him to the murders. It should be obvious, but you never can tell with Säk, as you've probably found out yourself."

"Mmm. This isn't any kind of trick this time, is it?"

"No, but could you do me a favor?"

"That depends."

"Wait until tomorrow to bring anyone in for questioning; we may have a clearer picture of it all by then."

"You're planning to fill me in, I hope."

"Yes, you'll undoubtedly be advised if what I have in mind produces results."

"Shall we talk tomorrow afternoon?"

"Yes, if not sooner, but in that case I'll communicate in some way."

She found him sitting on the mattress with his chin on his knees. He was in uniform, and he seemed confused at first when he looked up.

"Hi," she said hesitantly. "I just wanted to drop by and tell you that I get off my shift at midnight and we could get together. I mean, you don't have a telephone here and I . . ."

She stopped. Carl's face seemed gloomy, with clouds passing over it.

"Fine," he said. "I've got a towel, and some breakfast things, and a little wine, if you want to come here. Otherwise I can come to your place; that might be better."

"Has anything happened?"

"Yes, I had to give an interview, and I have to go to a military party tonight I don't want to go to. But it'll be over in plenty of time before midnight. I'll see you at your place. I'll bring along the wine and borrow your razor if you have fresh blades. Do you?"

"Yes, I ought to be able to find some. And Salubrin instead of aftershave."

"Good, I'll see you then."

He didn't get up, and stayed in the same position as she left. She felt an uneasiness bordering on fear.

Half an hour later—it seemed only a minute—the black radio started beeping. Carl got up and walked briskly to the hallway and then shut the door quietly behind him.

Lundwall and Steelglove were waiting in a Volvo 245 with a radio and car phone and all their equipment stuffed into the compartment behind the back seat.

Forty-five minutes later all three of them were in place in Vaxholm. Carl was sitting in the back seat wrapped up in a sheepskin coat, with night-vision binoculars, an image enhancer, a suitable precision weapon, and a radio.

Lundwall was inside the academy's hall, standing at the party near the banquet table, with what looked like a hearing aid in his left ear.

From the dark hallway leading to the back door, which was not locked, rose a half flight of stairs in a corner leading to the upper floor. There Åke Steelglove was lurking like a spider. He liked the dark, he liked the situation, and he hoped intensely that the murderers would come his way.

When dinner was over, the festive party moved from the dining room into the salon, close to the main entrance. There were about twenty officers and almost as many women; a few newly arrived guests were disrupting the social equilibrium. Lundwall moved behind a sofa with a view of the entrance, where his old chief at the academy accosted him, naturally wanting to ferret out how his student had become an officer. It was hardly party talk, but then, Lundwall had no choice. He explained that he was in OP5, and that of course led right to Hamilton. He confirmed that they worked in the same department, that Hamilton was in fact his boss, although no one knew what would happen now after all the excitement. This was the perfect evasive answer, and the coast artillery chief quickly changed the subject with a wink "just between us men with secrets to keep."

Lundwall was surprised at his own calmness and self-confidence, but perhaps it was because the other two had been in on Big Red with him.

Carl touched on the same thought out in the car. Had Chivartshev figured out that the people involved were precisely the three who had carried out Big Red? The only three witnesses with a rank lower than admiral or cabinet minister.

He tried to brush the thought aside. The Russians couldn't very well be starting a war, sending in a whole platoon, could they? No. They'd suffer casualties themselves, not to mention a huge political crisis. The Russians were logical and meticulous, and sometimes predictable for that very reason. They hated risky undertakings and uncertain projects.

Anyway it was too late to back out. Forty happy Swedish partygoers were celebrating the most luminous and cheerful holiday of the season, and according to instructions and orders, he was the guard.

He pulled the sheepskin tighter around him. His feet were freezing since he was wearing ordinary shoes; the car window had to be kept open a crack to prevent condensation on the windshield.

A car pulled up very slowly, with its headlights off. For a split second Carl thought, How stupid to drive without headlights, but then he had already aimed his image enhancer toward it and was grateful he wouldn't have to worry about glare.

He could see three men in the car, Glücher driving. The giant was sitting next to Glücher in the front, and he couldn't get a clear picture of the man in the back.

They stopped near a lane about thirty yards from the main entrance and turned off the engine. They wouldn't discover Carl, in the middle of a row of parked cars, unless they had night-vision instruments.

They opened the car doors on both sides carefully, the way you do when you go hunting, and shut them very quietly before going around to the trunk.

"Attention!" Carl muttered to the two men with earphones inside the building. "Three possible bandits, distance thirty yards, observe radio silence from now on."

Lundwall, talking to an officer's wife, lost the thread of the conversation and had to repeat his last remark. He realized he didn't have a clear line of fire to the front door and somehow would have to move to the right.

Out in the dark by the back door, Steelglove pulled out his weapon, slipped off the safety, and placed it alongside him on the step as he did a few hasty knee bends to get rid of the stiffness and raise his temperature. "Dear God," he said silently to himself, "please let those damned devils come to me."

Carl watched as the men came cautiously around their car from the trunk. They were all carrying automatic weapons in the crooks of their arms—AK-4s, he thought. That wasn't good; he had been hoping for the sawed-off shotguns again.

Glücher was clearly going to stay with the car. They all looked at their watches before separating, and the other two headed toward different doors. They had done reconnaissance, obviously.

"Attention!" said Carl again, straining to make his voice sound completely normal. He thought the pounding of his heart might be heard through the radio transmission. "Attention! Two bandits on their way to the building, distance fifteen yards. Armed with automatic weapons. Heading for opposite doors. Orders as follows: Steelglove, disarm enemy number one and put him in cuffs. Lundwall, open fire at once if enemy number two shows up armed. Confirm your orders by coughing. First, Steelglove."

Two brief coughs followed.

Carl watched as the men from the car kept checking their watches. He had a further thought.

"Attention! Expect a synchronized action from the front and back. Obey previous orders and confirm!"

Two more coughs followed.

Inside the festive drawing room Lundwall suddenly turned away from the officer's wife. Almost sotto voce he said to her, "Excuse me, but I have very good reason to want to be alone. Would you be so kind as to move at least fifteen feet away for a moment?"

The woman stared at him boldly. Her amazement at such an incomprehensible remark was mixed with outrage at the rudeness. She tossed her head angrily and went to the chief's wife, and whispered something to her as they both glared in his direction. Lundwall could feel himself blushing, and then blushing more at the thought that he was letting himself be bothered by an irrelevant distraction in such a critical situation. Now he had a clear line of fire, and he moved a little closer to a group of four or five men smoking and drinking cognac by one of the sofas. He put down his own untouched glass on a side table and unbuttoned his uniform jacket.

He estimated that he would have two seconds from confirmed sighting until firing. In an exercise that was no problem, but in an exercise his racing pulse would not pound so violently. This is not an exercise, repeat, this is not an exercise.

Meanwhile, outside, the situation was changing drastically. A solitary van, whose tinted windows Carl's sights could not penetrate in the glare from the headlights, drove up and stopped right near the parking place by the lane where Glücher was standing. Carl swore, and he stiffly changed position to pull out an automatic carbine. He placed the weapon, icy cold, next to his rifle, as the side door of the van opened with a hiss. Carl moved his cross-hairs from Glücher to the van. He held his thumb over the safety catch, which strictly speaking was incorrect procedure under the circumstances but ingrained from his childhood hunting lessons in Skåne: never take off the catch before you can see clearly what you're going to shoot.

At the very next moment a pretty young girl stepped into his cross-hairs, dressed in a long white dress, with a crown of lighted candles on her head. It was St. Lucia together with her retinue of giggling boys with starboy hats and girls with glitter and long white gowns. Someone—their teacher?—also dressed in white fussed about, lining them up beside the van.

Carl moved his sight back to Glücher, who appeared completely unaffected by the appearance of the children. He had lit a cigarette and stood, leaning against his car, with the automatic weapon hidden at his side, pointed at the ground.

The first bullet in Carl's rifle was a dumdum, meant for hunting animals but forbidden by the Geneva Convention for hunting humans. The other five bullets in the rifle's magazine were regulation full-jacketed ammunition, forbidden for hunting animals.

Carl moved the cross-hairs to Glücher's right lung and considered quickly taking out the dumdum bullet and then firing a full-jacketed one with no warning. But that would be against guard regulations and thus illegal. And meanwhile the Lucia procession was advancing toward the door. The children had not yet begun to sing; he could hear their happy chatter. They were heading right into his line of fire toward Glücher.

He turned his head to check on the other two. They were standing near their separate entrances with their eyes on Glücher and the approaching Lucia procession. All three seemed unsurprised by it, as if it were actually part of their plans. So they had planned the break to coincide with the Lucia procession. Automatic weapons firing from two directions in semidarkness at a festive crowd of children—that's what they were planning.

Glücher made a sign and the other two suddenly moved. The giant disappeared around back; the other headed toward the main entrance.

Lundwall was still next to the sofa, like a statue; only a moment or two had passed, but the pounding pulse through the middle of his chest and down the insides of his thighs assured him of his supreme readiness.

He heard a slight scratching in his earphone and then Carl's voice: "Attention. Two men advancing on separate doors. Lucia procession of children approaching the front entrance. Steelglove—same orders as before. Confirm when carried out. Lundwall—same orders as before, but be prepared to hold your fire."

An instant later Lundwall could hear the sound of children's voices singing a carol faintly outside, and the commander's wife was rushing about turning off the lights and ushering the guests into the ballroom—all except the men by the sofa in front of Lundwall, who seemed to have decided that they were comfortable where they were. Fine for an assassin coming on the scene, since they were sitting facing the front door.

Lundwall shifted closer to the back of the sofa. Everyone was focusing on the ballroom, where more St. Lucia's candles were being lit. Lundwall pulled out his pistol slowly, released the safety and cocked it, and then held it down along his side, hidden behind the sofa. He now had less than a second from preparation to firing. A thin border of light around the hinges of the hallway door indicated that the target would appear in silhouette against background light. The children could now be heard clearly, singing "Staffan Who Was a Stable Boy."

Steelglove watched intently as the back door handle carefully moved down. He had heard footsteps in the snow outside and had already shifted position. The door opened, and a man every bit as huge as he took a quick step into the darkness and firmly pulled the door shut behind him. The moment was at hand.

Carl was shaking from cold and nerves. The column of singing children was between him and the man by the front door who seemed to be waiting for them. Carl shifted around, trying to get a clear line on Glücher; the children were only a few yards away from him. He cocked his rifle to switch to full-jacketed ammunition, looked for the target again, had to change his position again, and accidentally breathed on the lens, which immediately fogged up. Swearing, he pulled out his shirtsleeve at the same moment he heard Steelglove's cough in his ear.

Action accomplished in the back hall, then. So now the attack could come only from the front. At just that moment the man at the main entrance went quickly into the building.

"Attention!" Carl barked. "Enemy number two on his way through the main entrance, distance from the children less than ten yards. Dressed in black, children in white. Lundwall's orders still stand, but only if the line of fire is clear. Confirm!"

Carl was sweating, despite the cold, and as he once again changed position to look for Glücher, he heard Lundwall's discreet cough. The children, singing loudly now, were on their way through the door.

Lundwall felt that he was in a vacuum where only one thing existed: the door, seven yards away, which would be opened either by someone dressed in white or by someone dressed in black.

I must aim high, he thought. The enemy is taller than any child. Not the middle of the target, but high up.

He had a brief nightmare that he was paralyzed and wouldn't be able to move when the door opened. And it would open quickly.

And it did.

The door opened out—a crucial detail, and the man in the black leather jacket behind the children had to pull it aside before gripping his weapon with both hands in order to take aim and open fire—and in that moment he died.

Lundwall stood holding his double-barreled pistol out in front of him; he thought briefly he had fired exactly as in practice, at a doll that was suddenly falling forward. He had fired two shots, he realized, high up at the center of the target. The mark of the shot was evident; he had hit the man in the head.

The silence following Lundwall's shots was total.

Then a second later bewildered screams came from the doorway, hysterical piercing screams. Inside, the men on the sofa didn't move, and the people in the ballroom looked back at the figure now stretched out in the doorway.

"Stay where you are, it's over!" Lundwall was calling out in a voice that threatened to crack into a falsetto. And his command—for that's what it was—had an immediate effect. The impulse to panic had been cut off before it could begin.

"We are personnel from OP5. Police and ambulances are on the way. I must ask you to stay where you are!" he continued in a more controlled voice, releasing the hammer of his pistol, pointing the muzzle upward, and advancing toward the door.

Two children stood just behind the door, screaming hysterically. One wore a starboy hat now splattered with blood, and the girl who was wailing so was drenched in blood that had splattered across her face, neck, and chest. When he reached her he slapped her lightly across the face and hugged her at the same time; relief washed over him.

"Enemy number two hit, probably dead. Children not hit but soaked."

"Good." Carl's voice was controlled and focused. He had not released the third man from his gaze though howling children were now jumping into his line of fire. "Lundwall, tell them your chief will be there to explain everything. Steelglove, return to base."

He had Glücher in his cross-hairs with one eye, trusting he could perceive Steelglove's movements with the other. Too late, he realized he had made a mistake. Glücher was suddenly raising his weapon and taking aim at some unseen moving target.

"Steelglove, take cover!" he screamed, and an instant later Glücher fired three quick shots. The children, screaming still more, scattered in all directions.

Carl searched desperately for a clear line of fire among the starboy hats and glitter, as Glücher once again fired three times. There was a moment when the line of fire was clear. Carl pressed the trigger and saw the hit.

"Steelglove, report!"

"Okay, slight graze but no hit," came Steelglove's voice. "Graze" might mean something serious.

"Are you hit?" he shouted.

"No, not hit. The damn idiot missed by inches in all six tries." Steelglove lumbered toward him.

"Return to the car at once. Lundwall, tell them it's all over," commanded Carl. But *was* it really all over?

He dialed a number on the car phone and called in the police and ambulances. Be calm, he said to himself, think clearly. "Steelglove, round up the children first and account for all of them. Make sure none of them is hurt. Then give Glücher first aid, but not until the Lucia procession is okay. How's the situation in back, by the way?" He climbed rather stiffly out of the car.

"Reporting one tied-up and handcuffed package, right next to the radiator in the back hallway," said Steelglove triumphantly.

"That's fine, Steelglove, fine. Round up the kids, contact whoever's in charge of them—I saw someone who's probably their teacher."

Carl started toward the building. How had he actually shot Glücher? Normally and calmly, with good support and without jerking the trigger. But first he had aimed to the left of center—so Glücher would be shot on the right side, nowhere near his weapon, spine, or heart, and at the moment of firing, he had lowered his arm and pulled the trigger when the sight was somewhere in the abdominal area.

Lundwall had put his pistol away and buttoned up his uniform.

"My boss will be here in thirty seconds to report on the situation! We can turn on the lights!" Lundwall tried to sound reassuring and decisive. Rising murmurs subsided once more.

Then, only a moment later, an officer whom they all recognized at once stepped through the door.

"We must offer our apologies to you for all this confusion, but the men who were attacking you are the ones behind the so-called agent war. And this evening, we three from OP5, on orders from defense headquarters, were on guard duty here," said Carl.

From somewhere in the far reaches of the ballroom came the sound of muffled sobbing; the people stood like statues.

"What happened outside?" asked the chief hoarsely. He had to clear his throat. "What happened to the children?"

"One of the three terrorists opened fire and we neutralized him; none of the children, as far as we know, has been hurt, and we're checking that further," replied Carl with a calm that required great effort.

Then he looked inquiringly at Lundwall and pointed at the blood-soaked corridor.

"It's okay," said Lundwall. "They were spattered from the penetration wound; shock but no injuries from fragments or anything like that."

Carl nodded and pointed toward the back door. "Check that the third one is under control," he said, and as Lundwall moved toward the back, he turned once again to the ballroom.

"Ambulances and police are on the way. On behalf of defense headquarters, we would like to make the following requests. That you tell no one—not the police and not anyone else—who we were. Defense headquarters will handle this issue in an appropriate manner; just say that we were personnel from OP5, in secret service with secret identities, and remember that revealing our identities is a punishable offense. Any questions?"

"Yes, one quick question. Who were the men who were attacking us?" asked the host and chief of the coast artillery academy.

"Personnel from the Swedish Security Police and the Stockholm Police Department," replied Carl tersely, "but not"—and he smiled—"on official assignment." He saw that Lundwall had returned with an all's-well signal.

"You have one more, alive and handcuffed out near the back door. Turn him over to the police when they get here," said Carl, as he gave a sign to Lundwall. And then they left, with no particular haste, stepping over the dead policeman in the black leather jacket, his black hood, bloody and torn, pulled down over his head.

The cold was a relief as it struck their faces. They could hear the far-off sound of approaching sirens.

Steelglove signaled an all-clear.

"All the kids accounted for?" asked Carl as he got into the front seat. Steelglove was going to drive, and he was fumbling with the heat regulator on the dashboard.

"Yes. All the children accounted for and unharmed. Two had to have their faces washed; they had some blood and some police brains on them. Damn good shot, Lundwall," said Steelglove as he turned on the ignition and shifted into gear.

As the car rolled out of the parking lot, they could see the flashing blue lights off in the darkness, and the sound of the sirens was growing loud and clear.

"Glücher's state of health?" asked Carl. Suddenly he was very tired.

"Well, he'll survive for the trial. But after several years in prison he'll probably get chubby and have a hell of a high-pitched voice."

Steelglove slowed down and pulled over to the side to let the first ambulance pass.

"What do you mean by that?"

"Well. You aimed a little low. There's not much man left there. You were aiming at his hip or thigh, weren't you?"

Carl stared out the window. "Yes, probably the hip. He must have turned just then." The second ambulance passed, followed by a police car.

"Get Sam for me, would you," Carl said to Lundwall. "By the way, I have to agree with Åke. You're a great shot; you aimed high, didn't you?"

"Yes, I was worried about the children right behind. We had fully jacketed express loads to take care of bulletproof vests. But I don't think I had time to think about it much."

Carl took the telephone receiver and briefly reported what had happened and asked his chief in turn to contact the homicide division in Norrköping.

They drove on toward Stockholm in silence. It was three minutes past ten o'clock on the festival day of St. Lucia. Bureaucratic procedures at defense headquarters would probably take several hours, Carl calculated. He could go home to change, get the wine, and be out at her place by midnight as planned.

Epilogue

Swedish military guards in regulation uniforms in military areas—even off duty—have the right to open fire without advance warning if it is deemed unavoidably necessary, given the seriousness of the situation. Defense authorities have a general license to bear arms, so there are no limits as to when it's a matter of arming the guards.

This was approximately how the communiqué from defense headquarters began when it was sent out at five o'clock the following morning, in plenty of time for the first broadcast of "Echo of the Day."

Further, defense headquarters confirmed that personnel from OP5—whose identity remained secret, for national security reasons and generally because of military regulations—acted on special instructions from defense headquarters as guards at the Lucia party given at the coast artillery academy.

There had been indications that a terrorist attack might be carried out by police personnel, so defense headquarters had not found it feasible to inform police authorities in advance about what might possibly take place. Besides, it was normally responsible for its own guards and security service.

By afternoon the prosecuting authorities in Vaxholm were able to advise that there would be no investigation of any criminal offense or breach of duty. Everything had taken place in accordance with applicable laws and military regulations concerning military areas.

. . .

At first *Expressen* had a hard time, but it adapted adroitly to the line purveyed by all the other news media in covering the trial of Police Superintendent Glücher and his surviving colleague, a police assistant employed part-time by the Stockholm police and part-time on special assignments, difficult to explain, as a bodyguard for certain highly placed politicians.

In a purely legal sense, the trial was simple. The evidence in the murder investigation in Vaxholm was accepted as satisfactory without calling the defense personnel on guard duty as witnesses. (Defense headquarters protested in vain on that point.) Technical evidence and eyewitness reports linked one of the surviving assassins to the murders of the two Swedish fighter pilots in Linköping.

No real evidence linked the suspects to the murders in Näsby Park. But the prosecutor provided a general argument about Glücher's access to information about the suspected foreign-trade secretary; considering the nature of the crime, it could be regarded as proven that the defendants were guilty on that count as well.

The defendants themselves admitted nothing except that they had been at Vaxholm. The police assistant remained silent, and his boss— since that was naturally the way he regarded Glücher—admitted nothing, though when he was allowed to speak he made confused political statements about the threats that were continuing to undermine Sweden, about how the whole thing had started with Prime Minister Olof Palme and his conciliatory policy toward Russia, about how the Swedish people had to open their eyes to what was happening, otherwise Sweden would become a Soviet republic, and so on. He seemed to believe that in some way he had acted in the nation's interest, and that laws should not stand in the way of such an all-embracing goal as Sweden's independence as a nation, an attitude, by the way, shared by many highly placed persons.

Wennström, the *Expressen* reporter, won Bonnier's big journalism prize for his investigative journalism leading to one of the most harrowing revelations in modern Swedish history. In the radio category, Ponti got the same prize for his penetrating interviews and reports on the new tactics and personnel attitudes of Swedish intelligence, a series that included an interview with Carl Hamilton, who confirmed what everyone in Sweden already thought they knew—that he had been in command of the final confrontation with the Leather Gang.

To everyone's surprise the Soviet press gave extensive coverage to the trial, and to that exceedingly competent officer Carl Hamilton and his background in a Communist student organization. An editorial in *Izvestia* commented almost gleefully on rumors spread by friends of the fascist police gang in Stockholm: that Hamilton had supposedly committed hostile actions in Moscow. And they hinted broadly of a collaboration between Soviet and Swedish intelligence in the days preceding the neutralization of the anti-Soviet fascist clique within the Swedish police.

At first, Swedish defense headquarters refused to comment on these sensational reports. But in Ponti's interviews, Hamilton himself confirmed that there was a basis for the Soviet point of view, though he was forbidden to say more.

Consequently, it did not seem surprising when the Soviet minister of defense conveyed, via the Swedish embassy in Moscow, a personal invitation to Commander Count Carl Hamilton to receive the Order of the Red Star in Moscow—which had not been awarded to a Westerner since the Great Patriotic War. According to the commentary which the Soviet news agency then distributed to the Swedish press, this commendation would once and for all put an end to speculations about hostility between Sweden and the USSR and to the rumor that Captain Hamilton, while Swedish military attaché in Moscow, had somehow behaved improperly in a way that was incompatible with his position as a diplomat. In that case he would have been declared undesirable, but obviously just the opposite was true. Therefore any alleged elimination of any alleged Swedish spy in Moscow had never taken place, and this would be proven.

One unusually cold February day two elegant men were strolling in Gorky Park. One of them was wearing a cap made of raccoon fur, the other one of sable, a gift from the peace-loving Soviet people.

In *Musikalnaya Zhizn* and *Sovyetskaya Musika*, the Soviet Union's two most influential music journals, a new female pianist making her debut received rave reviews. *Sovyetskaya Musika* also ran a big feature piece about Irina Dzerzhinskaya and her extensive training—a victory in itself for the Soviet system—starting with

a special music school at the age of six, continuing at a music pre-
paratory school, and finally at the Tchaikovsky Conservatory, where
she had been in the "school for talented children and youth," and
where she had made her debut in the Great Hall before an en-
chanted audience.

Both papers predicted a brilliant future for her. And considering
their great influence on Soviet cultural life, her brilliant future had
already begun.

Both papers were folded up in the left pocket of Carl's coat. With
some difficulty he had spelled his way through the text, which, as far
as he could make out, was completely unequivocal.

A star is born—however you say that in Russian. *Zvezda rodilas?*

"How was it to meet your ambassador?" asked Chivartshev.

"He was rather reserved. Not to mention suspicious, not to mention furious."

"Why is that?"

"*Izvestia* assured him I hadn't acted in any way incompatible with
my position as a diplomat, and he's convinced that's exactly what I
did."

"The world is never a sure thing. Have you thought of that, young
captain?"

"Yes, especially in this city, and in this park. Over there where the
children are skating I rowed a boat with a young unknown musician
who thought we were being bugged."

"You weren't, not then anyway. Not by us, anyway."

"Have you studied the material?"

"Yes, meticulously."

"You believe it?"

"Yes, it's very convincing. The Chekists had some material on that
BPA delegation, even a picture of our man as he was taking snapshots
in a suburb."

"It could have ended right there."

"No, not likely. They didn't know who we had; we can't talk about
things like that with the Chekists."

"We might have been enemies for life."

"Don't ask me to add up the pluses and minuses—imagine if the
Chekists are listening to us," muttered Chivartshev dryly.

Carl wasn't sure whether he was joking or not.

They walked on, side by side. Their breaths puffed out of their
mouths like smoke and the snow squeaked beneath their feet.

"Those provocateurs," said Chivartshev thoughtfully, "what kind of sentence will they get?"

"Life, I assume. That's what it's called, although it'll be more like eight years, with parole. As long as no psychiatrist gets it into his head to find them insane—then they'll get only a few years. Considering the political situation, I don't think a psychiatrist will do that, though."

"You mean your psychiatrists take the strategic and political situation into account?"

"Yes, at least so a police officer I know claims."

"That's funny, really quite funny."

"Why funny?"

"Well, we're in the process of abolishing any political input to forensic psychiatric evaluations—glasnost, you know. Funny that the roles are reversed in this instance. What do you think about glasnost, by the way?"

"We hope things will go well for you. We're afraid it might all go to hell in a few years, as it did with your previous attempts, because then the cold war will be back in the worst way. And Sweden is too close to you for us to . . . well, we'd be enemies again, more than ever, I assume."

"Well, let's be optimistic. I'm going to Siberia, no matter what happens."

Carl stared at his Russian colleague with astonishment, uncomprehending. Chivartshev burst out laughing.

"That's where I come from," he explained. "That's my home. You should come out there sometime and we could go hunting for saiga antelopes together. Do you like to hunt? Animals, I mean?"

"Yes indeed, but alas it's been a different kind of hunting in recent years."

"What are your own plans for the future, young captain?"

"I'm going to be a father. I'll probably stay at headquarters for the near future."

"Congratulations. Truly. I'd like to congratulate certain of your colleagues who will be out in the field. You've caused us problems over the years. Too bad that I can't introduce you to my successor in Stockholm. You'd have a lot to discuss; he has a similar background."

"That's probably going too far, don't you think?"

"True. But we've already gone rather far; we've even interfered in the Soviet Union's entirely free cultural life for your sake, and that wasn't easy, I can tell you. Glasnost also creates problems. But just imagine: if I could only end my career by recruiting the world's most indiscreet spy."

"It's not too late." Carl smiled.

They both laughed, a laughter that would not stop, and they embraced each other, tears running down their faces, to the general disapproval of the fur-wrapped Russian public.

A NOTE ON THE TYPE

This book was set in a digitized version of Janson. The hot-metal version of Janson was a recutting made direct from type cast from matrices long thought to have been made by the Dutchman Anton Janson, who was a practicing type founder in Leipzig during the years 1668–1687. However, it has been conclusively demonstrated that these types are actually the work of Nicholas Kis (1650–1702), a Hungarian, who most probably learned his trade from the master Dutch type founder Dirk Voskens. The type is an excellent example of the influential and sturdy Dutch types that prevailed in England up to the time William Caslon (1692–1766) developed his own incomparable designs from them.

Composed by American–Stratford Graphic Composition,
Brattleboro, Vermont
Printed and bound by Arcata Graphics,
Martinsburg, West Virginia
Designed by Margaret Wagner